Show Me a Hero

'I was born in Peckham over the Falcon Billiard Saloon on a wet Monday morning, which may account for a lot of things,' says Patrick Alexander. It does not, however, account for his insight into the workings of the Secret Service, or his knowledge and expertise on the use and misuse of firearms. What he doesn't know about those subjects could be written on the nose of a boat-tailed bullet. Perhaps his subsequent career as reporter and television writer and his travels in Russia and Europe writing special features explains his lately revealed talent as a master story-teller.

Show Me a Hero

Patrick Alexander

Pan Books
in association with
Macmillan London

First published 1979 by Macmillan London Ltd
This edition published 1980 by Pan Books Ltd,
Cavaye Place, London SW10 9PG
in association with Macmillan London Ltd
© Falcon Plays 1979
ISBN 0 330 26121 5
Set, printed and bound in Great Britain by
Cox & Wyman Ltd, Reading

Man, to borrow an image from a somewhat dubious source, is everywhere in chains. In South America, in Africa, in Asia and Europe, men and women are deprived of their freedom, tormented and humiliated for no better reasons than that they disagree openly with the actions or attitudes of those who hold power over them.

It is important to recognize that these dreadful and often violent manifestations of tyranny are not the monopoly or the prerogative of any single political persuasion. The burning cigarette, the electrode and the prison camp are the tools of fascist and communist alike.

Lord Chalfont in THE TIMES

What has always made the State a hell on earth has been precisely that man has tried to make it his heaven.

Friedrich Hölderlin

PART I

The Falcon

1

IT'S FUNNY how you start out to do one thing, Ashman thought, and end up doing another. Of course, if something's coming your way, well, it's coming your way.

Like he's walking up this street in the City one sunny morning thinking how nice it is for a change – bit on the warm side maybe, but enough breeze to lift a girl's skirt now and then – when all of a sudden it's not so nice any more and the street's full of camouflage denims and blue-barrelled guns. Tac Force.

They were everywhere, setting up road blocks and checkpoints and generally making a bloody nuisance of themselves. Not that he had anything special to worry about, he was clean – no hardware and an identity card that would fool even the central computer. But it was a good rule to keep clear of them bastards, especially if you happened to be number three or four on their Most Wanted list. Or even maybe number two after the bank job. His position went up and down like a pop tune in the charts, but it never went out of the Top Ten. Some consolation.

So, trying to avoid aggro, he ducked down a side-street – practically into the arms of another bloody patrol. Well, if you can't beat 'em, join a queue – which some of the more nervous citizens were already doing. The English form queues like birds build nests – automatically. Then he spotted this load of cameras and gaberdine suits, even one or two hats with shaving-brushes stuck in the side. Americans doing Europe. Americans were always a good bet.

He fell in beside a little old lady with a blue rinse and beady eyes, and tried to look like he belonged. He belonged like Southend pier belongs to Staten Island. But what the hell.

The guide, an old boy with white hair, was saying something in a high-pitched voice to a Tac Force sergeant, who was nodding politely. They'd had orders to take it easy with tourists – Britain needed the money. The sergeant, a great respecter of orders, smiled and started waving them through.

Beady Eyes looked at him sideways. 'You better take my arm, son. And try to play it American with a big A. Yeah, and hang this thing round your neck.'

Some people did it right by instinct. They didn't have to think about it or turn it upside'down and shake it to see if it rattled. They just did it. Some people. The rare ones.

'I'm a fool,' she said, 'and you're some kind of crook.'

'Whatever this lot are looking for, ma'am, it isn't a crook. Of any kind.'

'I'm still a fool.'

'We have a saying that one walks over Westminster Bridge every minute.'

'An old fool, what's more.'

'A man might wait a hundred years for one like you to walk across, ma'am.'

She gave him that sideways look again.

'Don't bullshit me,' she said.

By this time they were through the checkpoint and the sergeant hadn't even looked at him. But Tac Force troopers were still crawling out of the woodwork and he thought he'd better sit tight till the bastards pulled out.

The guide led them to the end of the street where a lot of rebuilding was going on and pointed to some big new high-rise egg-box, which he claimed was a very special bank, the safest in the country, maybe in the whole wide world. Ashman pricked up his ears. He was interested in banks.

The big difference between this and your common or garden bank, the guide said, was that the strong-room, instead of being in the basement, was at the top. Eighteen storeys up, ladies and gentlemen, right up among the pigeons. The whole top floor was just one big steel and concrete box, with no windows and no stairs – in fact, no point of entry at all except by a special lift from the seventeenth floor. And the whole caboodle was protected by every electronic alarm you've ever heard of and several you haven't – plus a twenty-four-hour guard of armed security men. Or so the old geezer said.

He said a lot more too but it was difficult to hear, what with the traffic and the racket from the building work across the street, where they were shoving up another high-rise job which looked like it was going to be as high as that burglar-proof old bank. They were already up to about the sixteenth floor and they'd got the steel framework up for the rest – and poking right through the lot was a bloody great tower crane with a boom as long as the arm of God. From where Ashman was standing, though, it looked more like something out of a number six Meccano set. He'd had a thing about cranes ever since he was a nipper. Always wanted to be a crane driver rolling

11

round the sky like God, swinging that boom about and dropping a load of old iron on anyone who got funny.

The old geezer went rabbiting on about the strong-room and the millions of quid they'd got stored there in gold bars and how bank architects came from all over to study the building and so on and so forth. But Ashman was no longer listening. He was dreaming about that beautiful crane. He lifted up Beady Eyes' camera and took a shot of it. Through the view-finder it looked like a piece of black lace spread out against the morning sky.

All major operations had to be approved by OPSCOM, the operations committee of the resistance movement. The committee took all major policy decisions as well. Its directives went out through the executive council to regional councils, which covered the whole country. The fifteen-man executive council was supposed to be the governing body, but in fact its most important function was to rubber-stamp OPSCOM's decisions and report back any difficulties facing the regional councils. It was executive in the true sense of the word: it executed other people's orders. It did, however, with OPSCOM, form the official leadership – known as the Top Twenty.

The five permanent members of OPSCOM were General Sir Henry Hudson, former Chief of the General Staff, now leader of the resistance; Joshua Murdoch, right-wing politician (Ashman didn't trust politicians of any wing); Jack Hartley (known as Bluff Jack), ex-union boss from the north, who still had a big pull with the workers; and Wally Le Gras, lieutenant-colonel of the Special Air Service (retired), a real hard nut and worth all the rest put together in Ashman's view. And, of course, Ashman himself.

He put it to OPSCOM straight: 'Give me the men and the gear and I'll get you a skipful of gold.'

Nobody believed him.

He explained about the high-rise bank with its strong-room stuck on top like a square hat, eighteen storeys up. A bit higher and you'd see God on a clear day. Explained how all the guards and electronic alarms were on the floor below. 'But the roof's clean – no alarms, nothing. And no way up, except by a special lift that's guarded like an Ulster nick on St Patrick's night.'

He paused. Committees like you to pause; it gives the dummies a chance to catch up.

12

'But if there's no way up—' Bluff Jack started to say.

'Ah, but there is, Jack, there is. This way.'

He produced the picture of the tower crane. 'It's in a high-rise block going up on the other side of the street. All we have to do is put some men in a skip one dark night, swing 'em over on to the bank, cut a hole in the roof, fill the skip up with gold and swing it back again. Simple as that.'

Nothing was as simple as that, as Ashman knew. But sometimes it pays to make it sound that way, especially when dealing with committees.

He tapped the picture. 'But this little old crane isn't going to stay up there for ever. Maybe a couple of months if we're lucky. So there's no time to frig about, gentlemen.'

Silence. They still didn't believe him. Then Bluff Jack, who always had to have everything explained, said: 'How did they get the bloody thing up there?'

'Built it in the lift-shaft,' Ashman said.

'These electronic devices,' said Wally Le Gras. 'Do we know what they are – and where they are?'

Ashman nodded, and said gravely, 'The first thing I did was a feasibility study.' Bullshit of course, but it goes down well with committees, makes them think you're serious. Didn't fool Wally though, who started grinning. 'The only device we need worry about is the closed-circuit television. They've got a camera scanning the strong-room twenty-four hours a day.'

Another silence, a big one.

'How you going to get round that?' said Bluff Jack.

'Here, gentlemen,' said Ashman, 'we had the bit of luck that makes the whole thing possible.' He paused again, looked around. They were lending him their ears all right. 'A couple of weeks back they took on a new security man. Chap called Ronnie Adams.'

'Don't tell me', Wally said in a dry kind of voice, 'that he's one of ours.'

'No,' Ashman said. 'But his big brother is. I had a word with him. And he had a word with little brother, who's just married and having trouble with the mortgage.'

'So you made him an offer he couldn't refuse.' Wally again.

'Twenty thousand if he can put that camera out of action for half an hour and make it look like a maintenance fault.'

'What did he say?' said Bluff Jack.

'Nothing easier.'

13

This wasn't the whole truth, only part of it, but Ashman thought it was enough for the committee; he didn't want the project turned down at this stage on what he considered a technicality. Wally was staring at him though, and frowning, as if he had doubts. But he didn't say anything. Good old Wally.

'How much down?' Hudson said in his cold practical voice.

'Five grand.'

'That sounds reasonable,' said Wally. 'After all, he's a key man.'

'Him and the crane driver.'

Another of those silences – they were getting bigger all the time.

'What's to stop him double-crossing us though?' said Bluff Jack.

'A full-plate blow-up of an informer with his throat cut. I showed it to him. Next point?'

'How thick is the roof?' said Wally.

'Thick as a Paddy's head. Fourteen inches of reinforced concrete.'

'What can you cut through that with?' Bluff Jack again.

'The latest thermic lance burners.'

'What about the glare?' Wally said. 'It'd light up half the sky.'

'Not from under a tarpaulin.'

'How do you know the crane will reach? Have you measured it?' Bluff Jack of course.

'Sure,' Ashman said. 'With my pocket ruler.' Ask a silly question. 'Listen, some of them cranes have a boom four hundred feet long.'

'I don't know,' said Bluff Jack. 'It seems an awful lot of trouble. Wouldn't it be simpler to use a helicopter?'

Bluff Jack wasn't really thick – in fact he was very sharp about the things he understood – but he had to show you he was just as sharp about all the things he didn't understand.

'Noise, Jack,' Wally said. 'Bloody noise. Enough to wake the dead, never mind all those guards.'

Jack opened his mouth to argue but old man Hudson cut in like a knife. 'A helicopter is not feasible.'

He had a flat neutral way of saying things that usually stopped argument, though whether he was in fact neutral, Ashman thought, was hard to tell. He never gave anything away and had a stand-offish quality that marks out a certain kind of leader. He also had a calculating quality, but that was to be expected –

you don't get to be a general without being a politician as well. In fact, Ashman thought him very similar to Murdoch in outlook, if not temperament. Hudson always played it cool, but Murdoch had a touch of the fanatic. There were even times when he had that mad gleam in his eye.

Resistance movements always attracted extremists of course – and every other kind of nut – because they took some pretty extreme actions. Ashman sometimes wondered if all men weren't extremists under the skin. The truth was that he didn't much like Hudson and Murdoch and wouldn't have worked with them from choice. But if you had to wait for people you liked you might wait a bloody long time. Like for ever.

There were a few more questions about the operation. but Ashman felt he was beginning to convince them. Then Murdoch, who had kept quiet till then, cleared his throat and gave a quick double cough, like the judge rapping the bench with his gavel. It meant he was about to make a speech. He had a pedantic, almost finicky way of speaking, as if he'd thought it all out, which he had, and couldn't possibly be wrong, which he frequently was.

'It seems a reasonable plan,' he said, 'with a good chance of success.' Then he paused, made a steeple of his fingers and looked solemn. 'It is not, however, without risks. As I'm sure Thomas himself would agree.'

He always called Ashman Thomas, just as he called Tac Force the Tactical Militia. He didn't believe in shortening anything, including his speeches. He looked at Ashman and waited for him to say something. Ashman said nothing.

He took a sheet of paper out of his briefcase. 'Now I've been doing some – shall we say? – actuarial calculations about the risks involved in these operations. And, clearly, the more operations you undertake the greater the risk of being killed or captured. I have worked out some figures—'

'I don't go much on figures,' Ashman said. 'It's like the joke about the airline passengers being told they're not due for a crash, according to the figures, till they've flown a million miles or more. And one of them says: "Yeah, but how many miles has the bloody *pilot* flown?"'

Wally and Bluff Jack laughed, Hudson and Murdoch managed a two-inch smile between them.

'The point is,' Murdoch said, 'you've already had a number of narrow escapes. Indeed, after the raid on the ammunition

15

depot in Surrey you would certainly have been captured by a patrol of the Tactical Militia but for the fortuitous intervention of a young girl.'

Beth, Ashman thought, my beautiful Beth. 'That's history,' he said. 'What are you getting at?'

'We feel, General Hudson and I, that you should play more of a supervisory than an active role in these operations. You are, after all, part of the leadership, and as such too valuable to be put at risk.'

'Listen,' Ashman said, 'if the chiefs won't put themselves at risk you can't expect the poor bloody Indians to.'

'The whole leadership will be at risk when Operation Volcano starts.'

'Operation Volcano'll never start at all without that shipment of hardware from Holland. And that'll cost you two million pounds sterling, which is known as a lot of money, even in dirty pound notes. Though I expect they'd sooner have gold bars – who wouldn't?'

'We're not against the operation itself—'

'Terrific.'

'Only against your leading it.'

'Well, I can't delegate it. It's too important and too tricky.'

'He's right,' Wally said. 'He's the expert. Be crazy to put somebody else in.'

'Hear, hear,' from Bluff Jack, who was only thick some of the time.

'We were only thinking of your safety,' Murdoch said to Ashman with a smile that did its best to be pleasant. 'You are on the Most Wanted list, remember. And probably number one on Colonel Cunningham's personal list. Didn't he offer a reward for the Falcon – dead or alive?'

Mention of the Falcon always irritated Ashman. It was a nickname given him by the newspapers.

'I couldn't care less about Cunningham and his Tac Force hoodlums.'

'Well,' Hudson said in his flat voice, 'let's not argue. The meeting is obviously in favour of Tommy leading the operation. So be it.' Then he tried to smile sincerely too. 'After all, that's what we're fighting for, isn't it – democracy?'

'You could have fooled me,' Ashman said.

It was an uncomfortable remark and caused an uncomfortable silence. Only Wally Le Gras thought it funny, and grinned.

The committee then went on to discuss the threatened

miners' strike and what the Government were likely to do about it. Strikes had been threatened before – they are one of those old British customs that die hard – but had never yet happened under the new regime. They were always settled by a labour tribunal as the Law required, or by Tac Force as Tac Force required. The sight of their camouflage denims and blue-barrelled guns had a dispiriting effect on strike pickets.

But the miners were a different proposition. They were among the toughest and most awkward of the country's workers – as well as the most traditional. Theirs was one of the few unions to make trouble over the Harmonization of Industry Act, which replaced the unions and employers' federations by syndicates. They wanted to stick to their old National Union of Mineworkers. The situation looked bad, even dangerous, till one of their fire-eating left-wing leaders suddenly sided with the Government and said syndicates would be better for the worker in the long run – and what's in a name anyway? He became the leader of the new Miners' Syndicate – after joining the ruling National Democratic Party.* The Harmonization of Industry Act laid down that all syndicate officials had to be members of a recognized political party. In effect this meant the National Democratic Party since opposition to the Party was merely token. The Government had seen to that, though it liked to maintain the fiction and appearance of a two-party system.

The latest trouble had arisen because a labour tribunal had rejected the miners' wage claim. These tribunals consisted of a chairman and a panel of assessors – all party members, of course. So the miners got exactly what the Government intended they should get – a flat no.

The Yorkshire miners, however, refused to accept it. First they elected a shop steward who wasn't a party member, then they handed in strike notices.

'Are they really going to strike though?' Hudson asked Bluff Jack, who had just come back from a tour of the northern coalfields. Strikes and industrial sabotage were his department.

'Depends what support they get from the other coalfields. And from us.'

Murdoch was in favour of encouraging the strike – anything to embarrass the Government.

Ashman was against it. 'The Government haven't had to face

* See Appendix, page 270.

a strike yet. We don't know how they'll react. Supposing they get rough?'

'That will only antagonize the miners even more.'

'We could be leading them into trouble.'

Murdoch thought Ashman was exaggerating. So did Hudson and Bluff Jack. Only Wally Le Gras agreed with him.

'Leave it to me,' Bluff Jack said. 'I'll be up there again next week. I'll see what the situation's like then.'

Ashman opened his mouth to say something, then changed his mind and just shrugged. Bluff Jack was supposed to be the expert after all.

The meeting wound up with a brief discussion about Operation Volcano. This was the operation that all the others were leading up to.

After Volcano, Ashman thought, they'd either be in power or in little wooden boxes. Of course, they had so-called contingency plans if things went wrong, but Ashman didn't think they were worth a light – just window-dressing for the nervous. They also had a whole lot of plans if things went right. They didn't often discuss them, though, because it led to too many arguments. But it was clear to Ashman that Hudson and Murdoch wanted the Prime Minister and his cabinet knocked off. Of course, they didn't say knocked off. Effectively silenced, they said. Summarily dealt with. Rendered harmless. But everyone knew what they meant. They meant knocked off.

Ashman thought differently. He thought the killing ought to stop after Volcano. He thought they should get back to free elections and all the other things they were supposed to be fighting for. He not only thought these things, he said them, loud and clear.

After the meeting, which was held in a safe house near the Angel at Islington, he took Wally Le Gras to an Edwardian pub in the area – a gloomy place full of ornate mirrors, heavy mahogany furniture and huge windows of figured glass that turned daylight into twilight. Ashman thought it restful. And so it is, thought Wally, like the grave is restful.

It was usually empty in the early evening except for a depressed-looking barmaid and a down-and-out pianist who had nowhere else to go. He was an old boy with a bent back and two fingers missing from one hand but, incredibly, he could still play. He used to play that tinkling wartime music that always sounded sad even when it was meant to be gay, or so it seemed to Ashman. But wartime music always sounds sad to the next generation, and even sadder to the survivors of the same generation.

It wasn't much of a pub as pubs go but Ashman liked it. It was quiet and broody, as if nostalgic for some ripe Edwardian past.

'I wonder what it was like at the turn of the century,' Ashman said as they settled at a table with their drinks.

'Full of whores and comic singers,' said Wally. 'You know, you'd better watch it.'

'What?'

'Getting stroppy with your elders and betters. The bastards have long memories.'

'What have they got against me?'

'The Falcon gets all the publicity.'

'Don't tell me they're jealous.'

'Maybe they're taking the long view – and thinking about the ifs.'

'The what?'

'If Volcano succeeds . . . If we come to power . . .'

'I don't follow you.'

'Who'd be the most popular figure among the leaders? Whose name – or nickname – has already caught the public imagination? Who might be looked to as the natural leader of the interim government?'

'Me? Are you suggesting me?' Ashman looked and sounded incredulous. He shook his head and laughed softly. 'You're crazy. All I can lead is the troops. I'm no politician, I'm Action Man.'

'Murdoch's a politician – and he doesn't like you.'

'Wally, in my book a politician rates less than a ponce. And I don't give a shit what Murdoch thinks.'

'If he and Hudson are looking to the future, perhaps you should, too, Tommy.'

'The only future I'm interested in is like how soon can you find me the men for this job – and the gear.'

Wally Le Gras, who was responsible for personnel and equipment, shook his head sadly. 'Sometimes, Tommy,' he said, 'you're a bit naïve, you really are.' Then he sighed. 'How many men do you want, and what kind?'

'Three pros and a couple of amateurs.'

'What sort of pros?'

'A driver for the tower crane, an operator for the thermic lance and a driver for a Leyland Clydesdale.'

'What's that, a horse?'

'A sixteen-ton skip-loader with fast lift-off facility.'

'I'll talk to Jennings about it.' Jennings was Transport Officer. 'And the amateurs?'

'A couple of handymen to help rig up a block and tackle and haul up the gold. Almost anyone'll do, but no intellectuals.'

'What's wrong with intellectuals?'

'Their own imagination spooks 'em.'

Wally smiled. 'Are you saying you've got to be dumb to be brave?'

'No,' said Ashman, 'but it does help.' He handed Wally a sheet of paper. 'Here's the equipment I'll want.'

Wally looked at the list of pencilled items, then whistled under his breath. 'Christ, man, what do you want with a Dragon? That's an anti-tank gun, isn't it?'

'Anti-tank missile.'

'Missile?'

'Only a small one. The kind that can be fired from the shoulder.'

'Only a small one, he says. You're supposed to be doing a robbery, not starting a war.'

'It's insurance, Wally. In case we run into anything big and nasty. I won't have any back-up, remember.'

'Well, I'll ask the armoury — though what makes you think they'll have any . . .?' He shook his head.

'They should have,' Ashman said. 'I stole six from the army camp at Bulford on Good Friday.'

Wally stared at him. 'You're a bloody boy,' he said. 'Anything else?'

'I'd like to take a butcher's at any prospects you get lined up.'

Wally nodded, made some notes on the list he'd been given, then sipped his vodka and tonic and contemplated Ashman over the rim of his glass.

'Tell me, Tommy, how do you put a TV camera out of action for half an hour — and make it look like a maintenance fault?'

'Well, it's a closed-circuit set-up, remember, so the fuses and most of the wiring are behind a panel in the control room. Now there's a whole mass of wires and all you have to do is loosen one of them so it no longer makes contact — and down goes the camera . . . Well, that's what the man says.'

'And to put it right they have to find the loose wire?'

'Yeah – and you can't tell by looking. You have to test each bloody wire separately.'

'And that could take half an hour?'

'Maybe more, the man says.'

'And maybe less – eh, Tommy? Maybe ten minutes, maybe even five.'

'Chance in a thousand – that's what the man says, Wally. And he should know.'

'But still a chance – which you didn't tell the committee.'

'Didn't want them old ladies putting the kibosh on it, did I?'

'If that camera suddenly comes alive while you're working in the strong-room you'll be caught like a bloody rat in a trap.'

'Listen, he's putting another camera out of action as well. It'd look too bloody suspicious if the strong-room camera was the only one to go down.'

'Well, that improves your chances, of course.' He still sounded doubtful.

'You've got to take some kind of chance on a job like this, Wally. And a chance in a thousand is bloody good odds.'

'Well, here's luck.' Wally raised his glass.

'I'll drink to that.'

A newsvendor came in with a bunch of evening papers under his arm. 'Late extry,' he said in the croaky voice that goes with the job. 'All the racing.'

Wally bought a paper, glanced at it, handed it to Ashman. On the front page was a two-column picture of a man in a stocking mask. Little could be seen of his features because he was in profile and the picture definition poor – it had been taken by a hidden camera during a bank robbery. A strapline over the picture simply said: THE FALCON. It wasn't hard to see where the newspapers had got the name: the flattened curve of the profile and the top knot of the mask gave the suggestion of a hooded bird of prey. The caption reminded the reader that the price on the Falcon's head was £50,000.

'They print that picture every week,' Wally said. 'Maybe you should take Murdoch's advice after all – and quit while you're ahead.'

'Maybe I will. After this next job.'

'What are we going to call it?'

Ashman shrugged.

'What about Dragon – since you'll be carrying one?'

So they code-named it Dragon.

21

2

HE STOOD by the window staring down into a quiet street in Brook Green full of parked cars and tired-looking plane-trees. But all he could see were images of tower cranes and thermic lances and sixteen-ton skip-loaders.

He heard Beth turn over and murmur in her sleep. At least he thought it was in her sleep – till she said, 'Can't it wait till tomorrow?'

He hadn't told her anything but of course they all picked up signals you didn't even know you were sending out. Besides, why else would he be standing there stark naked in the middle of the night staring out of the window? He always found it difficult to sleep when he had a job on his mind.

He got back into bed, put his hands behind his head and stared up at the ceiling. He thought she'd gone back to sleep but after a moment he felt her arms going round him.

'Is it a big job?'

'In money terms the biggest.'

'Can I come along?'

He didn't answer.

'Just this once?'

'You know what we agreed.'

She went on about being stuck at home like a middle-class housewife (why did the middle-class hate being middle-class? He wished he was middle-class) and how she was in the movement too, remember . . .

'You're supposed to be dead,' he said. 'And if you don't shut up you will be.'

There was a time when he used to take her on jobs if they seemed safe and simple. Well, some were simple enough, but you couldn't exactly call them safe – as he found out when he and a friend known as Fingers McCall were walking out of a country bank early one morning, very early – about 3 a.m. – each carrying a well-filled Revelation suitcase.

They were crossing the pavement to their car – Beth already had the rear passenger door open – when a couple of Tac Force jeeps and a police car came roaring round the corner, headlights blazing, sirens starting to wail.

'The US cavalry,' said Ashman, pushing Fingers into the back of the car and piling in after him. Maybe they'd tripped some bloody alarm wired up to the local nick.

Beth, who had the engine running, let the clutch in with a jerk and trod on the loud pedal. They took off like a stage-one rocket, which Ashman thought was just as well since troopers in the leading jeep were opening up with Sterling submachine-guns.

Fingers, a lately retired safe-cracker known for his delicate touch and dislike of violence, was almost blubbering with fear.

'Stop,' he said. 'Stop. They'll kill us!'

'Shut up,' Ashman said, knocking a hole in the back window with the metal butt of a nine-millimetre Uzi and giving the leading jeep a two-second burst. You need luck to hit anything in those conditions. Ashman had luck. The leading jeep swerved across the road and into a traffic island. The following jeep went into the back of it. The police car avoided the crash and pulled up on the grass verge. Not that they were likely to catch up anyway, Ashman thought. Beth was driving a fuel-injected BMW with a top speed of 130 miles per hour and she was as good as any man driver Ashman had known. Better. She didn't keep having to *show* you she was good. You know men.

Next morning the papers said two Tac Force troopers had been killed, one by bullets, the other in the crash. There was also a picture taken with an infra-red camera from the police car. It wasn't much of a picture, of course, but it showed Ashman, McCall and Beth getting into the BMW. The two men were in stocking masks and Beth had her back to the camera. All you could see was a girl in a woolly ski-cap and a black tracksuit. However, there was a big white arrow pointing to her with the words: THE FALCON'S GIRL?

It wasn't much to go on but it would be enough to alert Tac Force Intelligence – and all their informers and undercover men. It would at least give them another target to aim at. Catching her might lead them to the Falcon. That's what they'd think. It was the way they always thought.

So Ashman had her taken off the active service list. To save arguments he said it was only for a time.

'How long is a time?'

'When they've forgotten about you. Or when I'm captured.'

'What do you mean, *when* you're captured?'

'Just a manner of speaking.'

'It's not a manner I like. It's unlucky.'

23

'Don't be so superstitious.'

'I *am* superstitious.'

'You and your spooky sister. She always thinks I'll come to a bad end.'

'She's a natural pessimist.'

'She's a natural pain.'

They always argued but the arguments never amounted to anything. And the real things between them couldn't be put into words anyway, though he sometimes had the feeling there was another conversation going on underneath the conversation they were supposed to be having.

Some weeks after Beth had been taken off the active service list another girl was killed in a night raid on a Tac Force barracks. She was about Beth's size and general build, and she was wearing a black tracksuit – but that was practically the uniform for night operations.

So they let it leak out through selected informers that she was the Falcon's girl and that he was in mourning. This was followed by a two-column obituary in the underground paper, *Combat*, which, though it made no mention of their relationship, was signed 'The Falcon'.

It wasn't long before the national press was splashing the story on their front pages. There were even a couple of those back-to-camera interviews with a husky-voiced informer who swore he'd had it from an underground source that the Falcon was all broken up over his girl's death.

The object of this disinformation exercise, stage-managed by Murdoch, was to deceive Cunningham into calling off any search for Beth. Murdoch was sure he had succeeded, Ashman less sure. He thought it would take a good deal more than a few stories and reports from informers to fool Cunningham.

However, now that she was officially dead Beth could see no reason why she shouldn't go back on active service. For what he realized were purely selfish reasons Ashman was against it.

'If something happened to you,' he told her bluntly, 'I think it'd finish me.'

'And what about me?' she said. 'If something happens to you?'

The cut-out said they'd find him at the working men's club in Kingston, either at the bar or at the snooker-table. How would they recognize him?

'Can't miss him. Five foot five in his gaucho boots and no more than a hundred and thirty pounds sopping wet – but it's all whipcord and barbed wire. Red hair, pale eyes, two front teeth missing if he smiles, which he doesn't. Talks mostly in grunts but they're prettier than his Glasgow accent, and easier to understand. Don't approach him from behind though; he's nervous since he was beaten up by a Tac Force trooper. That's how he lost the front teeth. The trooper lost his life.'

They found him at the bar.

'Good evening,' Wally Le Gras said, and gave the code-phrase. 'We're friends of the man from Catford.'

He looked at them, then nodded towards an empty table and went to it. They followed. They knew from his file that he was a thermic lance operator. Before that he had served ten years in the Army, including a tour of duty in Northern Ireland. So he'd know how to handle a gun too.

'We've got a job coming up that'll need a thermic lance,' Ashman said as they sat down. 'Should be easy . . . Could be dangerous. Interested?'

'Aye,' he said. But for all the interest he showed they might have been discussing the weather.

'We'll supply the gear, of course. Any questions?'

His pale eyes fixed on Ashman. 'Is it legal?'

'Not that you'd notice.'

The pale eyes turned to Wally, then back to Ashman. The hard little face split into a gap-toothed grin.

'When d'ye want me?'

'The man from Catford'll let you know.'

The Paddy was playing darts in the public bar of the Boileau, otherwise known as the Boiler, and sinking pints of Guinness as if they weren't going to brew any more.

'You married, Paddy?' Ashman tried to avoid using married men if the job was dangerous.

'Me da always says don't t'ink about marriage till ye're forty, and then don't bother.'

'What do you drive?'

'Anything from tankers to artics.'

'What about a skip-loader?'

'Where would ye be wanting me to take it?'

'From A to B.'

He looked at Ashman, then sank the rest of his pint. 'That

went down rather prettily,' he said. Ashman bought him another. 'Is it likely to get rough?'

'Would it worry you?'

He gave a soft laugh. 'I'm not the worrying kind.'

He sounded brave enough. But maybe it was the beer talking. 'You always drink like this?'

'Only on me birthday.' The soft laugh again. 'But I have a terrible lot of birthdays.'

Afterwards, as they were driving to Soho, Ashman said, 'Anything else on him?'

'You want to see his file?' Wally said.

'Just tell me the bits I want to know. First about the drink.'

'He never touches it when he's working.'

'When he's working for me he'd better not. What's he like in a tight corner?'

'Typical Paddy – sooner fight than have his breakfast.' He looked at Ashman. 'If you're doubtful, I've got some others lined up.'

But in his mind Ashman had already settled for the Paddy. He wasn't sure why. Instinct mostly. Instinct could be wrong too, of course, like female intuition, but in the end what else is there? Everyone's an unknown quantity. You might as well follow your instinct.

'A Scotchman, an Irishman,' said Ashman. 'What about an Englishman? Then we'd have a funny story.'

'I've got just the joker,' Wally said.

They parked in Soho Square near the top of Greek Street. Wally pointed to a fluorescent sign over a doorway, which said *L'heure bleue* in fancy lettering. Under that, in block capitals, it said NIGHTCLUB.

'What it really is,' Wally said, 'is a clip-joint with ideas above its station. It has a four-piece band, a six-piece chorus-line and some tired hostesses. The band's not bad, though – mostly due to the guitarist, Joseph Benedict Lamont. That's our man.'

'The one you're recommending?'

Wally hesitated, stared at the lighted sign across the street, then turned and looked at Ashman.

'Not exactly . . . recommending.'

'What do you mean?'

'I'm not sure. Maybe he's too . . . well, sensitive.'

'Then why bring me here?' Ashman wasn't angry, merely inquiring. Wally would have his reasons.

'He keeps asking, through his cut-out, to be put on active service.' Wally hesitated again. 'He's dead keen. Almost suspiciously keen.'

They were always on the watch for Tac Force agents trying to penetrate the movement. Some undoubtedly had – just as their own agents had penetrated Tac Force and every other government agency.

'He's been checked out?'

'Of course.'

'Interviewed?'

'Four times. I monitored each one myself.'

This simply meant sitting in another room watching and listening on closed-circuit television.

'And?'

'Nothing – except that somehow he doesn't strike me as the type for active service.'

'He's been told?'

Wally nodded. 'He keeps on asking just the same.'

'What did the other interviewers say?'

'They recommended him.' Another hesitation. 'I'm the only one out of step.'

'You think he's trying to prove something?'

This was an old problem. Some youngster would join the movement and ask to be put on active service so that he could play the big hero to his girl and his mates. The big hero with his mouth, of course. And before he knew what was happening he'd find himself hanging by his thumbs in a Tac Force interrogation centre – and the playing would be over.

So the resistance were wary about the people they recruited, especially the fire-eaters. On the other hand they didn't want to turn away support. They couldn't afford to. Ashman could see the problem all right.

'How old's this joker?'

'Thirty-five.'

Ashman whistled under his breath. 'He ought to know better.'

'Some never grow up,' Wally said, and went on to fill in the background. Lamont had been making his name as a classical guitarist when he signed a petition for the release of a conductor who had been arrested for anti-State activities (which covered what is known as a multitude of sins). He and the other musicians who had signed the petition were expelled from the

27

Musicians' Syndicate. And without a syndicate card he could get neither work nor unemployment benefit.

'So after a lot of one-night gigs in pubs and discos, he ends up at this dodgy bloody club where they don't ask about cards if the labour's cheap.'

'For him that's hardly one step up from being piano-player in a brothel.'

'Not even one step,' said Wally.

You could see what he meant, Ashman thought, as soon as they got inside. Everything about the place was ribby and going to seed, even the bouncer. He had a mean look, though. Or maybe it was just his big face, which looked like it had slipped when it was hot.

They sat down and Wally ordered champagne.

'I'd sooner have beer,' Ashman said.

'They don't sell beer.'

'That's what I thought.'

Two tired-looking hostesses came over, and Wally bought them drinks, then sent them away. This brought the big-faced bouncer over.

'You don't like our girls?'

Ashman felt it was time to explain. 'Piss off,' he said, and stood up. The bouncer looked at him, looked at Wally, muttered something and turned away.

'I like a man who knows when to take a hint,' Wally said.

'He only wanted to show us his muscles,' Ashman said. 'He wasn't serious.'

The band, which had stopped, started up again and Lamont played a solo on guitar with such virtuosity that even the table-chatter died down, which only happened for strippers.

Afterwards, during a band interval, Wally invited him over for a drink. He had no idea who they were, of course. He only went because he hated the bouncer, who was inclined to bully anyone weaker than himself. He was a small dark man with a thin face and big dark intelligent eyes. His long-fingered hands were as slim as a girl's and he used them when he talked. He looked younger than thirty-five, Ashman thought. But he was the kind who would always have a young look.

He nodded towards the bouncer. 'You certainly cooled Angel Face. I've never seen him put down like that before.'

Big deal, Ashman thought. A third-rate bouncer in a fifth-rate club.

Then Wally mentioned the code-name of the cut-out. Lamont's dark eyes widened, his slim hands made nervous little movements.

'Still keen on active service?' Wally said.

He swallowed and nodded.

'We might have a job coming up.'

He swallowed again and said, 'Am I allowed to ask . . . what sort of job?' He tried to keep his voice steady, but his nervous hands gave him away.

'Fund-raising,' Ashman said. 'But you won't be going round with a hat.'

He smiled. He looked like a kid when he smiled. Ashman liked him.

'We'll let you know more about the job when we know if we can use you,' Wally said.

'Please try to use me,' he said. 'I won't let you down.' He looked at Ashman, smiled again. 'I'd like to work with you.'

In the car afterwards Wally said, 'Well?'

'I like him,' Ashman said. 'Nice little guy. And some guitarist.'

'But?'

'Too jumpy. He's not ready for it. Try him on something easy.'

'We don't have anything easy. And you know it.'

He waited for Ashman to say something but there was nothing to say. They drove the rest of the way to Brook Green in silence.

'One for the road?'

'Why not?'

Ashman took him into the kitchen. 'We've only got wine.'

'I thought you were strictly a beer man.'

'Beth's educating me.'

Wally looked around. 'This is new, isn't it?'

Ashman nodded happily. 'Beth saw this kitchen all done out in Oregon pine in some posh magazine – and wanted one just like it.'

'Very nice. Must've cost a bomb though.'

Ashman shook his head. 'Did it myself. Well, it's my trade, isn't it?'

Wally smiled. 'Of course.' He knew Ashman was a carpenter. He just didn't think of him as a carpenter.

'I always think of you as a fighter.'

Now it was Ashman who smiled. 'At thirty-eight? I haven't been in the ring for ten years.'

He poured two glasses of red wine from a ship decanter.

'I remember one of your last fights – against that negro—'

'Busted my right on the bastard's head. I had a useful dig in that hand too.'

'It mended all right though?'

'Oh sure. But the doctors said it might go again. Not very likely, they said. Chance in a million. But it might. So I started favouring it. Pulling the punches a little. Not deliberately. Unconsciously – like a reflex action. And when I was working with the heavy bag sometimes I'd feel a twinge. Or imagine I did. That's when I started thinking about carpentry.'

'According to the papers you had class. Cheers.'

'What do they know? Cheers.'

The phone rang – there was an extension in the kitchen – and startled them. It was Hudson with the name and address of a suspected informer. Once a spy or an informer was uncovered he was killed. That was the rule, and it was one of Ashman's jobs to see that it was carried out. Not that it was difficult. It was never difficult to find men to do a little killing. And all the psychopaths weren't in Tac Force.

Ashman was against this blanket rule. A man should only be killed if he was a danger to the movement. But most informers were small fry who'd been bullied into it by Tac Force hoodlums, and weren't a danger to anyone but themselves – most were junkies. Why kill a junkie when he's making such a good job of it himself? All right, there was a time for killing. There was also a time for going easy, especially with the small fry. Killing wasn't only bad for the image, it could become a habit. Look at Tac Force.

He had put these arguments to OPSCOM, but the vote had gone against him. So the blanket rule stayed – spies and informers to be killed regardless.

This one was a man called Matcham. He had been reported by the London Regional Council. Ashman would pass on their suspicions to the IS (Investigation and Surveillance) Squad. On their report Matcham would live or die.

'The bastards have only been in power four years,' Ashman said, pouring more wine, 'yet I can hardly remember what it's like to lead a normal life.'

A normal life . . . It was nearly two o'clock when he got to bed, undressing quietly in the dark so as not to wake Beth. But as he slipped under the covers he felt her arms going round him and the whole length of her against him, warm and sweet-smelling. That was normal all right. He felt himself relaxing and smiling in the dark.

He fell into a deep sleep, but the lean and chilling figure of Colonel Cunningham walked in his dreams and disturbed him.

3

Colonel Julian Giles Cunningham, immaculate in dark-blue velvet jacket, ruched shirt and black barathea trousers, looked at the glittering array of society deadheads laughing and chaffing and feeling each other's wives, and wondered how long he'd have to wait before they were smashed enough not to notice his absence. Or even his presence. Not long, presumably, judging by the way they were lapping up the free champagne supplied by the State Publishing Corporation and, like almost everything else it supplied, inferior.

This party was to celebrate publication of another of those books on marxist philosophy, if you could call marxism a philosophy. In Cunningham's opinion all you could call it was a view of history, and a singularly inaccurate view at that.

However, the book was written by the Home Secretary, the Right Honourable Harold Price. And since Tac Force was nominally under the Home Office, and Harry Price therefore nominally his boss, Cunningham felt obliged to put in an appearance among all the other sycophants and murmur a few insincerities before disappearing into the night.

He started edging round the crowd in the direction of the door. He had an appointment in a murky wine-bar on the Embankment, and though he could walk it in ten minutes he wanted to be in good time. He also wanted to give his bodyguard the slip, which shouldn't be too difficult – they would be listening to the big fight on their car radios or watching the girls go by in the Haymarket. It was dangerous for him to go out alone but sometimes necessary, and always a temptation. He was one of the most heavily guarded men in the kingdom. Also one of the most hated. Even by certain people on his own side. And of course by everyone on the other side. It made life interesting though. There was that to be said for it.

He'd nearly made it to the door when he heard a throaty French voice.

'Mon colonel, you are not leaving us?'

It was Agnès, Harry Price's French wife and, much more important, the Prime Minister's sister-in-law. She was small and slim and looked even more so beside her husband, who was large and pear-shaped. She was also formidable. And attractive – big black eyes, a big red mouth that turned down at the corners and a silver bells laugh at odds with her astringent personality.

Harry Price was fortunately deep in conversation with his editor, a kindly woman whose permanent expression of sadness was said to have been brought on by reading all those books churned out by Harry Price and the other tame authors on the State Publishing Corporation's list.

'Madame, what a pleasure to see you. May I get you a drink?'

'I do not drink that peess.'

She did nothing to lower her voice, and several heads turned. He remembered a Guildhall banquet a year before when her husband was making one of his long boring speeches, and she had turned to a companion and said, 'We do not listen; 'e is a big bag of blow.' Cunningham was sitting four tables away but her voice carried like a throaty trumpet. He had liked her ever since.

'May I get you something else, madame? A canapé perhaps? Or would you like to sit down? By the window perhaps. The view—'

'Is more interesting than the company, no?'

'It is a magnificent view, madame.'

They were on the Martini Terrace of New Zealand House, sixteen floors up.

'Colonel Cunningham. Always polite, always correct. Like a duellist.'

'Madame, it pains me to leave you but—'

'Yes, yes, of course. You 'ave an assignation. Dommage. The men 'ere are like sheep. Pas de danger. You talk to me sometime.'

'With pleasure, madame.'

She gave that silver bells laugh and looked up into his eyes. 'Julius Caesar always 'ad a mistress in the enemy camp. You know that?'

The Pothole, like its name, was underground and badly lit. Stone steps led down into a big cellar full of candlelight and shadows with a bar at the far end. It took some moments before he was dark-adapted; then he saw Frank Wilson at the bar with a bottle of wine in front of him. Cunningham moved to the other end of the bar and studied the wine list chalked on the wall till he was sure Wilson had seen him. Then he ordered a glass of red wine. It was over-priced and tasted of old pennies.

Frank Wilson picked up his bottle and moved off into the shadows. Cunningham followed. Wilson led him through two interconnecting cellars to a third much bigger and even more dimly lit cellar. There were a number of discreetly placed alcoves with rough wooden tables and guttering candles stuck in bottles. Most of the alcoves were occupied by young couples – the place was designed for them with its fake dramatic lighting and piped Muzak. So were the prices.

'Strictly for the birds,' Frank Wilson said as they settled at a vacant table. 'But better than the last place.'

Their last meeting had been at a mortuary, a fine and private place, but dead cold.

Frank Wilson was the only Tac Force Intelligence agent who had managed to penetrate the upper councils of the resistance. He was already on the London regional council, and was expecting promotion to the executive council. His main objective was to find out about the operation called Volcano. Cunningham had had reports about it for six months or more from informers of varying reliability, but the reports were too vague to be of much use. And of course you never knew if they were being deliberately leaked – the well-known technique of disinformation used by both sides. Cunningham had a feeling that this was something more than disinformation because hard facts were so difficult to come by. Disinformation leaks, on the other hand, always gave some facts, however misleading. Or were the opposition just being subtle? Frank Wilson soon put him right.

'Volcano's for real. And it's intended to be linked with an uprising in the armed forces.'

'So the rumours are right. It really is the big one?'

Frank Wilson nodded. 'It certainly looks like it. The preparations are enormous. But the movement's short of money. There's an arms shipment waiting for them somewhere in Holland, but it's going to cost two million pounds or more.'

'Where will they get that from?'

'The Falcon.'

'Another robbery?'

'From what I've heard.'

'Some robbery. Any details?'

'No.'

'We must get that bastard.'

Frank Wilson's secondary objective was to discover the identity of the Falcon. Though Hudson was leader of the resistance, the Falcon was gaining influence and, according to Tac Force Intelligence, beginning to clash with the leadership. Of course, it was difficult to sort out truth from legend about a man like that.

'The papers make him sound like a cross between Che Guevara and Robin Hood,' Frank Wilson said.

'Well, he's got colour – or charisma as they like to call it. Makes a change from their staple diet of government propaganda.'

Frank Wilson felt uneasy at the implied criticism. The Establishment shouldn't criticize the Establishment. It was like a priest blaspheming. But he didn't say anything. The Colonel was said to be a law unto himself.

'I wonder if he's becoming more important than Hudson?' Cunningham went on. 'After all, remove Hudson and what would happen? They'd just replace him, presumably. Remove the Falcon and it could cripple them – especially if they're planning a robbery.'

'I did pick up one clue – for what it's worth – from a chap on the London council. We drink together after meetings, and he's inclined to get confidential when he's had a few. The other night he told me OPSCOM had asked him to supply a dozen or more thermic lance burners – presumably for safe-cutting.'

'Did he actually meet anyone from OPSCOM?'

'Only the ones everybody knows – Hudson, Murdoch and Jack Hartley.'

'That's why he was allowed to meet them, no doubt.'

'The interesting bit is that there were a couple of other men standing in the shadows – the meeting was in a big room and only part of it was lit – and he thinks one of them, a big heavy-set chap, might've been the Falcon.'

'Why?'

'Well, whenever there was a decision to be taken Hudson would have a whispered conversation with the big chap. He seemed to be the key man. And we do know the Falcon's responsible for what they call fund-raising. Anyway, at one point he lit a cigarette and my drinking chum got a glimpse of his face in the flare of the match. He said he was very dark with high cheekbones and a slightly flattened nose. He thought he had ridges of scar tissue over his eyes, but couldn't be sure at a glance.'

Cunningham absently sipped his wine. It still tasted of old

pennies. 'An ex-fighter perhaps?'

'He had the build.'

'Why was he so curious, your friend?'

'Everyone's curious about the Falcon – even people in the movement. Especially people in the movement.'

Cunningham nodded. 'Their folk-hero. Any idea of his age?'

'He thought late thirties.'

'So what do we have? A big dark man, late thirties, looks like an ex-fighter. Not much to go on, is it? Still, we'll circulate it. Who knows?'

He lit a cigarette to kill the unpleasant after-taste of the wine, dragged on it and blew a thin stream of smoke into the surrounding darkness.

'Volcano,' he said. 'Is there a date?'

'I've heard there is.'

'Who would know it? OPSCOM presumably.' Frank Wilson nodded. 'Anyone else?'

'I doubt it . . . Maybe the executive council.'

'To which you're being co-opted.'

'We hope.'

'I've got to have that date, Frank. Or we could all be dead.'

Frank Wilson nodded. He was the best agent they'd got – young, tough, cool and intelligent. Cunningham had picked him from more than 150 other agents. All previous attempts to penetrate resistance councils had failed, Cunningham suspected, through weak security. Too many other people in the know. Now he was the only one in the know. And that's how it was going to stay.

He was back at the Martini Terrace within three-quarters of an hour of leaving, and in time to hear Agnès tell a drunken minister without portfolio to peess off.

' 'E feel my bottom,' she said. 'And I object. To the man, you understand, not the deed.'

'Perfectly, madame. Très logique.'

'Vous vous moquez de moi, salaud. Where 'ave you been? The time was too short for an assignation amoureuse. At least, I 'ope it was.' The silver bells broke out again. 'Soon after you left you were wanted on the phone.'

As if on cue the public address system announced, 'Colonel Cunningham to the phone, please. Colonel Cunningham to the phone.'

It was his adjutant, Captain Kemp, ringing from Tac Force main HQ near Alton in Hampshire.

'I tried to get you earlier, sir, but no one knew where you were.'

'Trouble, Eddie?' He could hear it in his voice.

'The Yorkshire miners decided to strike – and picket the night shift. Grigson says he'll break them up.'

Lieutenant-Colonel Grigson was the local Tac Force commander.

'On whose orders?'

'The Home Secretary's. Grigson rang him when he couldn't get hold of you.'

Harry Price was at the bar surrounded by the usual sycophants.

'Excuse me, Minister,' Cunningham said and took him aside. 'What the hell are you doing, Harry, giving orders to Colonel Grigson?'

'Well, somebody had to. Strikes are illegal, remember. And I want this one crushed at source.'

'With the greatest respect, Harry, the decision to use troops isn't one you're competent to make.'

A stupid mulish look came over his face. 'And I suppose you are?'

Criticism, Cunningham realised too late, only made him obstinate. Weak men never admit they're in the wrong, especially when they know they are.

'I'm not suggesting anyone's competent to make the decision from here,' he said smoothly. 'I'd sooner go up there and assess the situation on the spot. It's a tactical decision.'

'It's also a political decision.'

'All the more reason not to rush it. Look, I'll fly up there now, report back to you by phone if necessary—'

'No. You're forgetting – the strike's *illegal*. Crush it before it gets the chance to spread.'

'All right. All I'm saying is, let me go up there and—'

'No need. You're exaggerating the importance of the whole thing. And Colonel Grigson's quite capable of dealing with it.'

Colonel Grigson wasn't capable of dealing with a storm in a teacup, Cunningham thought, but he didn't say so. Grigson was an appointment of the Home Secretary's – they'd been at school together. He was another weak man and, like the Home Secretary (who was ruled by his diminutive French wife), felt

37

a great need to assert himself. Cunningham didn't mind that so much. He just didn't want him doing it with 500 Tac Force commandos at his back.

Cunningham had been thinking of getting rid of him for some time but hadn't bothered because it meant going over the Home Secretary's head to the Prime Minister, which he only did if it was important enough. Now perhaps it *was* important enough.

'Your responsibility, Harry.'

'Of course it is – that's the name of the game,' the Home Secretary said with the air of a man coining a phrase.

Cunningham went to a phone booth and dialled the Prime Minister's home. He was out and not expected back before midnight. Cunningham had an emergency number for messages that would be taken to him immediately, wherever he was, but this was hardly a national emergency. After all, nothing had actually happened. Yet, he told himself. Yet. He tried to get through to Grigson, made a note to try again, then went back to the party to make his excuses to Harry Price before leaving.

Then he saw Amarantha and forgot about everything. She was standing by the door, eyes half closed in that sultry look that came from being short-sighted and refusing to wear glasses. She looked elegant, glossy and assured – just as she had eighteen months ago when he first met her. And he had known even then that really, under all her shining armour, she was afraid. Of what, though? He had wondered in vain. But it was there, the fear; he could feel it, like a faint vibration in the air. He was, after all, something of an expert on fear.

Their first meeting had been at a similar literary function, held by the Writers' Syndicate. Not that he'd been guilty of writing a book, but Harry Price, who was prolific as well as dull, had invited him. Harry Price was always inviting him to functions of mind-bending boredom, most of which he managed to avoid. But even a talented liar runs out of excuses at times.

Amarantha was there because she'd written a book about fashion design, and membership of the Writers' Syndicate was obligatory (if you wanted to get published, that is). Cunningham asked the chairman of the Syndicate who she was.

'Amarantha Jones, author of—'

'Introduce me.'

She looked him up and down through those half-closed eyes and said in a soft voice whose accent he couldn't quite place,

'Colonel Cunningham? The name seems familiar. What do you write?'

'I don't. I read.'

She smiled. 'And what are you colonel of?'

'Tac Force.'

For the first time her eyes opened wide. They were a cloudy grey and beautiful.

'That goddam scum.'

'You are American, I take it?'

'I was born in Springfield, Illinois, but I now have British nationality – if that's what you want to know.'

'You speak very good English, ma'am.'

Nothing like a bit of British condescension to rile our country cousins. A flush mantled her cheeks prettily.

'And bollocks to you, too,' she said.

'Amarantha,' he said, 'Amarantha, sweet and fair, Ah, braid no more that shining hair . . . Like a clew of golden thread, Most excellently ravellèd.'

She turned her back on him and walked out. End of first romantic meeting. But a lot had happened in eighteen months.

'That is your mistress, no?' The throaty voice of Agnès. 'It shows in your face.'

He went to her, took both her hands. 'Amarantha,' he said. 'What are you doing here?'

'Looking for you.'

She had a house in Hampstead overlooking the heath, a big old house with a mansard roof that had been converted into a studio. The dominating feature was a northern light stretching from floor to ceiling. The rest was a chaos of dress material, pattern books, tailor's dummies, sketching blocks and other paraphernalia scattered about like a child's toys. There was an enormous bed, a giant wardrobe and some Victorian furniture that looked as if it had come out of a junk shop.

They lay in bed staring up at the stars through the northern light as they often did after making love. He was lying on his back with his arm round her, aware of her naked warmth, her head on his shoulder, the scent of her hair in his nostrils. An idyllic moment that seemed to contain the essential sweetness of life. The jangling reality of a ringing phone shattered it.

'Let it ring,' she said and tried to pull the clothes over their heads.

He felt like ripping it out of the wall. Instead, he switched on the bedside lamp, picked up the receiver and said, 'Yes?'

It was Eddie Kemp. 'Grigson opened fire on pickets at the Rysdale pit. Six dead, fourteen injured.'

'Jesus.'

'Two thousand miners are reported to be massing at the pit-head to march on Tac Force HQ in Doncaster. That's all for the moment.'

It was enough. 'Tell Grigson to keep his troops, including himself, in barracks. Tell him we're on our way. I'll be with you in half an hour or so. Have one of the jets warmed up and ready on the runway.'

'What about the Home Secretary? Should I ring him?'

'To hell with the Home Secretary. We'll sort it out first and tell him afterwards.'

He put down the phone, picked it up again and rang Major-General McCusker, General Officer Commanding North-East District, explained the situation and asked him to disperse the miners gathering at the pithead – 'but no bullets, unless they're rubber ones'. Not that McCusker needed telling; he was a real pro, cool, hard, unflappable – the kind Cunningham liked working with. He did not share the English love of the ama-teur.

Then he tried the Prime Minister at home again and this time got him. He didn't sound too pleased though.

'You're supposed to be in charge of Tac Force. How the hell did it happen?'

Cunningham offered no explanation, simply told him the steps he had taken. There was no point in blowing the whistle on Harry Price. They both knew he was a fool, and blaming other people, however justified, always sounded like a cop-out. Anyway, the PM would find out in the end. Cunningham would see to that.

The PM, as expected, was less concerned about the killing than the political consequences.

'This man Grigson obviously lost his head. But strikes are illegal of course, and full production is essential to the success of our social revolution.'

Cunningham was used to this sort of political harangue from the PM. The sinister part was that he actually seemed to be-lieve his own clichés.

'However, we don't want it thought, either here or abroad, that we are taking repressive measures. Indeed, such measures

40

will no longer be necessary when the revolution is complete.'

And the Workers' Paradise upon us, Cunningham thought. By which time they would all have been battered into submission.

'Yes, Prime Minister,' he said. 'Of course.'

'Meanwhile, we don't want a bad press, do we?'

'No, Prime Minister.'

'In fact, we cannot afford a bad press. You do understand me, Colonel?'

'Perfectly, Prime Minister. You may leave the matter entirely in my hands.' He paused. 'Entirely in my hands.'

Cunningham suddenly felt cold, then realized that he'd been sitting on the edge of the bed naked all the time. He got up and started dressing. The stars looked serenely down through the northern light. Amarantha's face was white and drained, her eyes dark. She hated the regime and everything it stood for. He was aware that at times she hated him too. Well, love wasn't all nightingales and moonlight.

The jet-flight to Doncaster took less than an hour. They landed at an airstrip outside the town and a car drove them to Rysdale in twenty minutes.

McCusker had the situation well in hand. A ring of searchlights mounted on Saracen armoured personnel carriers lit the whole pithead area with a harsh glare that threw bizarre shadows through which troops armed with batons and riot shields moved like figures from another planet. Two Fox combat vehicles with the long-barrelled thirty-millimetre Rarden cannon stood by the entrance gates. Near them was a dumpy water cannon.

Most of the miners had already dispersed, except for a few isolated knots of three or four men, sullen and frightened, outside the gates.

Cunningham saw no dead bodies as they drove in. McCusker was waiting for him in his command-post Saracen.

'Any trouble?' asked Cunningham.

'Bit of a scuffle when I sent in a snatch squad to grab the leaders. Otherwise it was mostly shouting and bluster.' He hesitated. 'I think they were too shaken by the shootings to do much.'

'Where are the bodies?'

'In the mortuary.'

41

'And the prisoners?'

'At the police station.' He hesitated again. 'Why did Colonel Grigson open fire?'

'I don't know the full facts yet. But I understood some of the pickets had guns – and opened fire first.'

'Oh yes?' His tone was polite, his expression deadpan. He obviously didn't believe a word of it. 'And where would they have got the guns?'

'From the resistance. We've known for some time they were mixed up in this.'

'I see,' McCusker said and nodded. He had a thin brown face, lined and impassive, with small watchful eyes. It was difficult to tell what he was thinking – except that Cunningham was a liar. That much was obvious. Cunningham wondered whose side he would be on when Volcano blew up.

On the way to the local police station Cunningham said to Kemp, 'See if you can get hold of three or four Uzis – soon as possible.'

Kemp wondered what he wanted them for. But then Cunningham's orders were often surprising. The Uzi submachine-gun, which was standard issue in the Israeli Army, was also the favourite close assault weapon of the resistance.

The man who had led the strike and organised the mass meeting at the pithead was the new shop steward. Cunningham, who had taken over the station inspector's office, had him brought from the cells. He was a big man with reddish hair, pale eyes and a drinker's belly hanging over his belt. He was trying to look truculent, but Cunningham had the feeling he was frightened. And if he wasn't he soon would be.

'Your name?'

'Johnstone.'

'You have a family?'

'Yes.' He still sounded truculent.

Cunningham pushed a notepad and pencil across the desk. 'Perhaps you'd like to send them a message.'

'A message? Why?'

'You might not get another chance.'

'What do you mean?' A note of uncertainty under the truculence.

'You will appear at a special sitting of the Bradford Democratic Court in the morning, charged with organizing and leading a strike that resulted in six deaths—'

'You did that – bloody Tac Force. You murdered them.'

'And having contacts with the resistance. You may be charged under the Emergency Powers Act or the Protection of the State Act or the Prevention of Terrorism Act – or all three. That's for the lawyers. If found guilty you may be executed by firing squad within twenty-four hours. There is no appeal.'

Cunningham indicated the notepad. 'I'll see your family get the message.'

The man looked at the pad, then at Cunningham, his pale sharp eyes suddenly dull. He groped behind him for a chair and sat down.

'It's Jenny's birthday tomorrow,' he said in a dazed voice.

'Jenny?'

'My little girl. She'll be seven.'

'Include her in the message if you like.'

'You don't understand.' He shook his head as if he didn't understand either. Cunningham thought he looked even fatter sitting down, a great big lump of blubber, shaking all over.

'You can't,' he said. 'I mean – what have I done? I didn't do anything – any harm, I mean. I wasn't even there when it . . . when it happened.'

He started sniffing. He's going to cry, Cunningham thought. The final indignity. He lit a cigarette and blew a careful smoke-ring at the ceiling. The man sniffed again.

'Listen, I-I'm sorry about the trouble.' Cunningham watched the ring widening and crinkling. 'But it wasn't my fault. I was only a spokesman.' The ring was beginning to break up slowly, almost languorously. 'Can't you help me in some way?' His voice had started shaking, too. 'Can't you help me? Can't you?'

The ring was hardly visible now – a faint blue stain on the upper air.

'Help you? To lead more strikes, make more trouble?'

'Sir, I swear to you – on my life, on the lives of my children . . .'

Cunningham hesitated long enough to give the man hope.

'I'll talk to you in the morning.'

'You mean—?'

'I mean nothing.' Cunningham picked up the phone and said, 'Take him away.'

It was raining in Doncaster. It was always raining in Doncaster.

Or maybe he was just unlucky. Tac Force HQ, behind its electrified fence and rocket-nets looked like a Victorian workhouse, big, solid, bleak and sooty. The ground floor was heavily sandbagged and floodlights lit the open space around it. The entrance was approached through a double chicane of blast-walls.

He left Eddie Kemp asleep in the car and went up to the first-floor office where Lieutenant-Colonel Grigson was waiting for him. Cunningham didn't intend to spend much time there, but he listened patiently to Grigson's inadequate explanation. It was clear that he had lost his head or his temper (in effect, the same thing) and opened fire on a group of miners who went for his troops with pick handles.

'That was a bad mistake.'

'I had the Home Secretary's permission.'

'But not mine.'

'You weren't available. Anyway, he wanted the strike broken.'

'Not at that cost, I imagine. The PM certainly didn't; he was very disturbed about the political and diplomatic repercussions.'

'The scum were illegal strikers.'

'That's no excuse for over-reacting.'

'I didn't over-react, I simply—'

'Local feeling is high. Your presence could be an embarrassment. I'm transferring you to the north of Scotland.'

'The Home Secretary—'

'Won't save you this time.'

He had blond hair and the kind of fair skin that coloured easily. It coloured now, flushing almost purple.

'If you think you can dismiss me to the wilderness—'

'Be on the plane to Aberdeen in the morning. And count yourself lucky, Colonel.'

'What does that mean?'

'Work it out for yourself.'

Cunningham went out to the car and woke up Eddie Kemp. It was still raining.

'Did you get those guns?'

'Tac Force barracks at Harrogate said they've got some.'

'Harrogate,' Cunningham said to the driver.

He liked driving at night, even in rain, wrapped in the warm cocoon of the car, half watching the headlights knifing through the dark, half listening to the wet swish of the tyres.

44

'What are we going to do with them, sir?' Kemp said after a time. 'The guns, I mean.'

'Not squeamish, are you, Kemp?'

Ashman woke up soon after seven and couldn't get to sleep again – just lay there listening to the rain driving against the window. He had this uneasy feeling but didn't know why. He wasn't the sort to get presentiments – that was for Beth's spooky sister with her visions of impending doom and all the rest of it. Perhaps it was just one of those things. Mornings weren't his best time anyway.

He got up and dressed quietly so as not to wake Beth. He felt a bit cold and put on a thick sweater, then went down to the kitchen and made some tea. The rain was easing off but the wind still rattled the window-frames. April was a bastard month, cold as charity half the time and pissing with rain the rest. The tea warmed him, though, and he was beginning to feel a bit more human when he heard the morning paper come through the letter-box.

Maybe he'd been right to feel uneasy. Splashed across the front page was a banner headline: SIX TERRORISTS DIE IN SHOOT-OUT. Under that was a sub-heading: MINERS AND TAC FORCE TROOPERS INJURED. There was a five-column picture showing the six dead men sprawled on the ground near the main gates of Rysdale Colliery. Four of them were clutching Uzi submachine-guns. The story said they had terrorised the miners into striking and then opened fire on a detachment of Tac Force troops sent in, at the miners' own request, to protect them. So the story said.

Ashman got through to the resistance commander for the Doncaster area – and heard another story.

'Just as I thought,' he said. 'But who fixed up that phony picture?'

Cunningham, he was told. On his orders the six bodies were taken out of the mortuary and back to the pithead, where they were arranged in aggressive attitudes, some with guns in their hands, as if shot while actually firing, the others with fragmentation grenades. When he was satisfied that everything had been arranged to maximum effect Cunningham called out his tame pressmen for a floodlit photo session.

Ashman had hardly put the phone down when the doorbell rang. It was Wally Le Gras. Had Ashman seen the story in the paper? Ashman took him into the kitchen, gave him a cup of tea and told him the other story.

'Cold-blooded bastard.'

'But smart. If you're going to lie be bold and brassy about it, like the Russians.'

'But will it work? The truth'll come out in the end.'

'How far away is the end? Remember the Cossacks.'

'What do you mean?'

'Just after the war the good old British repatriated 50,000 Cossacks – at rifle and bayonet point. Clubbed 'em, herded 'em into cattle-trucks – women and children too. God knows how many committed suicide rather than go back to Mother Russia. Remember?'

'I remember. But what's it got to do with the present situation?'

'It took thirty bloody years for the truth to come out. We saw to that, the good old British. So what's this little problem about six bloody miners?'

Wally sighed. 'Point taken. I suppose we can make sure *Combat* gets the story. For what that's worth.'

'Not very much.'

Anyone caught reading or distributing *Combat*, the underground newspaper, could be sentenced to six months in a political re-education centre. It didn't have too many readers.

Wally tapped the paper. 'The strike's over, I see. Who says you can't dig coal with bayonets?'

'Bluff Jack should never have encouraged the poor bastards to strike in the first place.'

'Hudson and Murdoch worked on him.'

'But they must've known Grigson would blow his top.'

'They're hoping for some kind of backlash.'

'Like what?' Ashman said sourly. 'More dead miners?'

The phone rang. It was the IS squad reporting that the suspected informer, Matcham, had had at least two meetings with Special Branch. Oh well, what's a little more killing, Ashman thought as he put the phone down.

'Got any good news?' he said gloomily.

Wally told him the team for the robbery was almost complete, though he was still having difficulty finding a crane driver. Not that there was a shortage of crane drivers, even highly skilled ones or ones with the required nerve. No, it was the combination that was difficult to come by. The ones who

46

had the skill to land a loaded skip in a confined space in the dark, aided only by four small marking lights, were frightened that if things went wrong they'd be left sitting 200 feet up in the air holding the baby – while everyone else scarpered.

As for the ones who weren't frightened – three young hot-heads – they frightened Ashman.

'They're the careless type – cowboys,' he said after interviewing them. 'We need someone skilful, patient and prudent.'

'But brave,' Wally said. 'Don't forget that. And those three are as brave as a bloody bull.'

'But not quite so intelligent,' said Ashman. 'There's only one man for the job as far as I can see – and that's the chap who's already doing it. Last week I spent two days on the site watching him – and he was bloody brilliant. Touch like a midwife. So I asked IS squad for a quick background report on him.'

'And?'

Ashman held up two closely typed sheets of foolscap.

'Useless,' he said.

'The report or the chap?'

'The report's nothing – my fault, I suppose. I didn't give them enough time. And the chap – well, he sounds like nothing too. Arthur Walby, bachelor, aged forty-six, lives with his old mum off Clapham Common. No other relatives, no close friends, no contacts with the resistance, no debts, no vices, not even a parking fine. See what I mean? Nothing. A hole in the ground.'

'Nobody's that negative.'

'That's what I'm thinking.'

'Maybe he has a consuming passion for something,' Wally said. 'Like my sister has for marzipan.'

Later that morning Cunningham saw the PM in his first-floor study at 10 Downing Street. As he went up the magnificent staircase he passed the portraits of all the prime ministers who had worked and lived there, from Lord Liverpool on the ground floor, looking mad, to Percy Smith on the first floor, looking innocent. And on reflection, Cunningham thought, just as mad.

Percy Smith. You could hardly have a more working-class name if you invented it, which the PM more or less had. He was born Jeremy Percival Twistington-Smith, but when he came down from Oxford and joined the Labour Party he changed his name by deed poll to simple (forward with the workers) Percy Smith. When he became Prime Minister and founded the National Democratic Party he had all mention of his former name expunged from official records wherever possible.

Cunningham was thinking about this and the general nature of the PM's sharp but self-delusory mind as one of those faceless secretaries ushered him into the study and withdrew like a ghost.

The PM, puffing his pipe, was all boyish charm. He waved Cunningham to a chair and indicated the morning papers spread out on his desk.

'Well done. Splendid job. *And* the strike's over, I see.' He stabbed the stem of his pipe at the front-page picture. 'Where *did* they get the guns, though?'

He looked at Cunningham with eyes of perfect innocence.

'From the resistance, one must assume.'

'Ah yes, of course. Who else? They're always ready to support acts of terrorism.' He paused to relight his pipe. 'You know, I must say I feel a certain sympathy for Grigson – even if he was a trifle hasty.'

He was already starting to convince himself that the six dead miners actually were terrorists. But man's capacity for rationalisation and self-delusion had long since ceased to surprise Cunningham.

'More than hasty, Prime Minister. Dangerous. So I've transferred him to the north of Scotland. As far north as possible.'

'Bit out in the wilds, isn't it?'

'He lost his head, Prime Minister. We cannot afford that. Or overlook it.'

The PM nodded, puffed at his pipe. 'If you feel so strongly why not simply dismiss him from the service and be done with it?'

'Because he was appointed by the Home Secretary.' A delicate pause. 'I believe they were at school together.'

'Ah. I see.'

'The point is I don't want him brought back in a month or so when this business has died down – I want him *kept* out in the wilds.' Another delicate pause. 'I trust I can rely on your support, Prime Minister?'

'My dear Cunningham, that goes without saying.'

Cunningham was nevertheless relieved to hear him say it.

'North Scotland's ideal,' he said. 'Nobody much to kill up

there apart from a few Scottish Nationalists, and they don't count.'

Arthur Walby had a consuming passion all right but it wasn't for marzipan. It was for vintage cars in general and an Austin Seven Ruby saloon, *circa* 1936, in particular. He bought it as a near-wreck and spent six years of spare time and a small fortune restoring its pristine beauty. He kept it in a lock-up garage not far from his home, and every evening after work he visited it, breathed on it, polished it and quite possibly, Ashman thought, offered up a prayer to it.

Looking at him it wasn't easy to associate him with passion. He was tall, thin and pale with weak eyes and a timid manner. But though apparently friendless he was by no means unfriendly – given the chance – as Ashman found out by drinking in his local, the Butcher's Arms at Clapham Junction. It was easy enough to get into conversation with him and easier still to get on to the subject of vintage cars. In fact it was impossible to avoid it. He showed no interest in any other subject, had no ascertainable political views and seemed prepared to put up with any government that didn't actually intend to ban vintage cars.

'Yours must be worth quite a bit,' Ashman said.

'You can't put a price on a car like that. I don't suppose there's three or four like it in the country – not in that condition anyway.'

'You've got it insured, I hope.'

'I did have, but the company kept shoving the premium up each year – and what with inflation and that I couldn't afford it. Besides, who'd pinch it?'

Some nights later two specialists from the resistance pinched it.

Walby was stunned. 'It don't make sense,' he told Ashman. 'I mean, they'll never be able to get rid of it – everybody in the trade knows it. Nobody'd dare touch it.'

'Maybe some rich fanatic would. Or maybe they think you'll buy it back.'

'What with? All I'm worth is a few hundred.'

Ashman said he knew a friend of a friend who had connections with the underworld. He could ask his friend to ask around. After all, if the villains couldn't get rid of it they might be *glad* to take a few hundred.

'You think so?'

'I think there's every chance.'

'And you wouldn't mind asking this friend of yours—?'

'Leave it to me.'

'And he really has connections?'

'He really has connections. I'll bring him down, introduce you.'

'I'd give every penny I've got – plus whatever I can borrow or raise. I mean, I could flog my hi-fi gear . . .'

Walby was pathetically grateful. As if Ashman had thrown him a life-line.

'You're a real friend,' he said. 'A real friend.' Tears came into his eyes and his voice shook.

Ashman liked him, felt sorry for him. But business is business.

'Even if it's dirty business,' he said to Beth later that night as they sat in the Oregon pine kitchen over a late supper.

'He'll get his old car back, though, won't he?'

'If he plays ball.'

'What will you do next?'

'Fade from the scene. Let Wally take over.'

He poured himself a glass of wine. 'We're getting like them, aren't we? The people we're supposed to be fighting. We lie and cheat and steal and kill. Well, let's hope the end justifies the bloody means.' He raised his glass. 'Cheers.'

She reached across the table, took his hand.

'You still believe in it, don't you?'

'The movement or what we're supposed to be fighting for?'

'I thought they were indivisible.'

'So did I once.'

'And now?'

'I don't know.' He took a sip of wine. 'Wally says I have a depressed view of mankind.' He shrugged. 'I just think they're bastards.'

Beth stroked the back of his hand. 'Bugger politics,' she said gently. 'Let's go to bed.'

'You're beautiful,' he said. 'Beautiful and educated and everything . . . Whenever I think about it I wonder what you see in a slob like me.'

'You're beautiful too.'

He laughed. That was another thing he liked about her – her sense of humour. The fact that she wasn't being humorous entirely escaped him.

She got up and started to clear the dishes from the table. He pulled her on to his knee.

'Bugger the dishes,' he said. 'What about going to bed?'

'That was my idea,' she said, 'not yours.'

Two weeks later Wally Le Gras reported to a meeting of OPSCOM that Walby had agreed to operate the crane for them on condition that he got his car back.

'I also offered him the same deal as the other chap.'

'Twenty thousand?' said Murdoch.

'And five thousand down.'

'That's forty thousand we're giving away. Seems an awful lot.'

'If you pay peanuts,' said Ashman, 'you get monkeys.'

'Exactly,' said Wally. 'These are key men. And Arthur Walby took an awful lot of persuading, if that's the right word. It's that old car he loves, remember, not the resistance.'

'And love isn't enough?'

'Maybe it is. *Maybe*. But we're blackmailing the poor bastard. And I don't want him turning sour on us.' He paused. 'Money sweetens everything, gentlemen.'

There was a silence, then Murdoch sighed as if he had made a sad discovery. 'I'm afraid you're a cynic, Walter.'

'Christ,' Wally said to Ashman afterwards, 'they're like a bunch of old women moaning about the price of potatoes.'

'They *are* a bunch of old women,' Ashman said.

They were drinking in the pub near the Angel, and half-listening to the tinkling wartime music of the pianist. This time he had gone back to the First World War for 'Roses of Picardy'. Occasionally, the depressed-looking barmaid would sing a snatch, sometimes getting the words wrong. She had a voice of surprising sweetness though, Ashman thought.

'I've got all the gear – including that bloody great Leyland Clydesdale. Found a parking-place for it?'

Ashman nodded. 'There's a row of partly demolished houses within spitting distance of the crane. One of them's just a shell – no roof and no floors. All it needs is a hole in the front wall big enough to drive a truck through. We'll provide that.'

'Have you fixed a date?'

Ashman consulted a pocket diary. 'Sunday week. Should be a nice dark night – moon's in the last quarter.'

'Any problems?'

'Had a message from Ronnie Adams – our bloke on the inside. There's been a tightening-up of security precautions, and he's getting jittery.'

'Christ.'

'I had a word with him, calmed him down.'

'We can't afford that sort of thing, Tommy.'

'Doesn't mean anything. Just nerves. He's been thinking about it too much.'

'Want us to lean on him a little?'

Ashman shook his head. 'I'll do my own leaning.'

'And you're happy with the rest of the team?'

'The two handymen aren't much cop.'

'How d'you mean?'

'I think they'd panic if there was trouble.'

'Want me to find some others?'

Ashman shook his head. 'They're not important enough either way. And I can always rely on the Paddy and that spiky little Jock if it gets rough.'

'Maybe we should've given Joseph a chance after all.'

'Who?'

'Lamont. The guitarist. He was dead keen – and that counts.'

'Wally, it's not important. Forget it.'

'He took it pretty badly when we turned him down – his girl had just walked out on him, too. Everybody giving him the elbow.'

'Tough,' Ashman said indifferently, and got up to go.

'Want a lift?' Wally said.

As they drove down High Holborn Ashman said, 'That jeweller's shop, a bit farther up on the left – pull up there, will you? I want to show you something.'

It was a pendant of twisted gold wire shaped like a heart. Set into the angle at the base of the heart was a solitaire diamond. It was displayed centrally in the window on a piece of blue velvet and there was no price-tag. The shop was shut and a metal grille covered the window but allowed a good view.

'What do you think?'

'Very nice.'

'I mean, is it – well, in good taste?'

Wally glanced at Ashman curiously. 'Of course it is,' he said. 'It's simple and elegant. It's a beautiful piece, Tommy.'

Ashman continued to stare at it. 'You think she'd wear it?'

'She'd love it, Tommy.'

'It's her birthday, Saturday week.'

'It'd cost a bomb though. Well, a small bomb.'

'How much is a small bomb?'

'Six or seven hundred at a guess. Depends on the quality of the diamond.'

'I've got eight hundred in the Post Office.'

'Why do you have to spend so much?'

'I've never given her anything before. Worthwhile, I mean.'

'I bet she doesn't think so. Anyway, why now?'

Ashman shrugged. 'You never know.'

'Not getting spooked, are you?'

'You mean this job? You must be joking.'

'I mean the ruffian on the stair.'

'Who?'

'Forget it.'

'I just want her to have something decent for once.'

'She's got something decent.' He yawned. 'That's hunger, not fatigue.'

'You can eat with us,' Ashman said as they crossed to the car.

'Thank you, but I've got a nice Jewish girl cooking me chicken livers.'

Wally eased the car into the stream of traffic. 'I like Jewish girls,' he said.

'You amaze me,' Ashman said. 'I thought it was the chicken livers.'

4

TAC FORCE main headquarters occupied a ninety-acre site on high ground near the little country town of Alton, about an hour's helicopter flight from London.

It was as self-contained and self-sufficient as a walled city, which it resembled. It had its own bakery as well as barracks, its own shops as well as ammunition stores, its own newspapers, clubs and pubs. It even had its own laws. Members of Tac Force could not be prosecuted in the civil and criminal courts but only through special tribunals, which were often as biased as the spiritual courts of the Middle Ages dealing with clerks claiming benefit of clergy.

The whole area was enclosed by a chain-link fence ten feet high, a mile and a half long. Inside that was an electrified fence of the same height, hung with warning notices. Inside this were the shops and clubs and other non-military buildings, including hostels and flats for civilian staff attached to Tac Force.

Finally there was the inner area surrounded by a fifteen-foot wall with watch-towers, like the bailey of a feudal castle. This contained everything designated military – barracks, armoury, ammunition stores, gun emplacements, underground bunkers, garages for armoured fighting vehicles and, of course, HQ Staff offices, chief of which was the second-floor office of Colonel Cunningham. Directly below, on the ground floor, was the interrogation block, which included cells for important prisoners.

There were direct telephone and telex links with all Tac Force regional headquarters, the army regional commands and, of course, the Home Office in Whitehall.

There was also a direct line to the Prime Minister, which the Home Secretary wasn't supposed to know about. But of course he did know about it, and was meant to know. It was all part of the Prime Minister's system of checks and balances, designed to restrain some of his more restive and over-mighty subjects, including Cunningham, who in some ways was the most powerful man in the kingdom, after the Prime Minister.

But he was still responsible to the Home Secretary, who had the power not only to veto Tac Force military appointments but also to appoint all senior civilian staff himself, including Cunningham's personal assistant. Which was how Cunningham got landed with Peter Bishop.

Now was the Bishop, as Cunningham silently called him, a check or a balance? And did it matter a damn? Was the Home Secretary trying to limit his power at the direction of the Prime Minister or out of jealousy? Or both? And again, did it matter? More important at the moment was the Falcon – who he was and what he was up to. More important still was the timing of Operation Volcano. And perhaps most important of all, the final outcome of Volcano and its effect on one Julian Giles Cunningham.

These were some of the thoughts occupying Cunningham's mind – which was quite capable of holding several ideas in apposition – as he tilted back the swing-chair in his large and sumptuous office, put his feet on the desk and blew smoke-rings at the ceiling. Not an elegant posture but he made it appear so. No doubt the uniform helped – a dark-blue battle-dress, made of barathea and cut in Savile Row, which was never intended for battle except in the bedroom perhaps. The shoulder-flashes were reminiscent of the German SS lightning flash, and the highly polished boots of jackboots, but shorter. It was a uniform you couldn't mistake, and you weren't meant to.

Apart from an impressive bank of telephones, most of which by-passed the switchboard, the desk was a chaos of papers. The in-tray had overflowed into the out-tray which had overflowed on to the floor. The rest of the office was immaculate in its furnishings and its tidiness. On the wall opposite the desk was a larger-than-life portrait in oils of the Prime Minister smiling and puffing his pipe. It was meant to accentuate his look of wide-eyed boyish charm, but the total effect was somehow chilling.

Against another wall was an occasional table carrying a chess-board and one of the earliest Staunton sets. Above this, and in odd contrast, was a poster advertising the bullfight at Linares in 1947 in which the sad-faced Manolete was killed. Just below the poster hung a pair of crossed banderillas. Their barbed points gleamed when the light caught them.

At a desk at the other end of the office the Bishop was typing a confidential report (otherwise it would have been given to a secretary for typing). A neat unobtrusive man in a neat unobtrusive suit of charcoal grey. His pale-eyed face with its prim mouth and thinning hair was as neat and unobtrusive as the rest of him. His desk was bare apart from the portable typewriter, a blotter, a filing-tray and a telephone, which was an extension of one of the phones on Cunningham's desk.

The only other phone in the room was an alarm phone about midway between the two desks. Above it was a red light which flashed when the alarm phone rang – which it did with a note of peculiar stridency.

The Bishop, touch-typing steadily and rhythmically, took an occasional covert glance at Cunningham, still blowing smoke at the ceiling, and wondered what he was thinking about. Cunningham's thoughts and plans were of considerable moment to the Bishop. It was part of his job to report them to the Home Secretary. But Cunningham rarely confided in him – or anyone else – and when he did the Bishop had an uncomfortable feeling that it was only information he *wanted* to get back to the Home Secretary by a roundabout route. And yet Cunningham couldn't really suspect that he, Bishop, reported on him – otherwise he wouldn't be so damned indiscreet in his remarks and criticisms. Of course, he was always indiscreet in some ways ... Or was that just part of the act?

The Bishop, who was by no means unintelligent, just didn't know. Cunningham was a complete mystery to him (and not only him). Take that business of the other day. Of course it was quite trivial really ... Cunningham had been standing by the occasional table staring down at the chessboard when he turned to Bishop and said, 'The Bishop always moves sideways.'

Bishop had waited for him to go on but he didn't say another word, just went back to his chair, sat down and put his feet on the desk as usual. Bishop hated seeing him with his feet on the desk; it was so – yes, *loutish* was the word. And so unexpected in someone as fastidious as the colonel.

The Bishop's reverie was interrupted by his secretary, Lorraine. She came in with some documents for Cunningham but stood undecided before the overflowing trays on his desk. There wasn't a clear space anywhere. Even the colonel's jackbooted feet rested on a pile of papers. She tried not to look disgusted. The Bishop tried to catch her attention; the colonel ignored her.

She was a tall gawky woman in her mid-thirties, long-faced, wide-lipped and with an air of emotional restraint, as if her passions had been frozen in. She had no feminine graces but plenty of feminine feelings. She was in love with the Bishop, constantly found excuses to touch him and generally mothered him like an awkward hen.

'I'll take them,' the Bishop said and she went over to his desk, immediately unfreezing and smiling as if a secret source of warmth had been unlocked inside her.

'Anything I can do for you, Peter?' She dropped a hand on his shoulder.

'No, thanks,' he said and went on typing.

'You're sure? I'm not busy this morning.'

'Quite sure.'

She looked at Cunningham's desk. 'Some filing? Clearing-up or something?'

'Nothing, thanks. Nothing at all. Really.'

She dropped her voice almost conspiratorially. 'You still look pale.'

'I'm supposed to. I have a pale complexion.'

'You know what the doctor said – you need plenty of milk. And fresh fruit for the bowels. Roughage, that's what he said. Remember, an apple a day—'

'Really, Lorraine, I'm perfectly all right. Really.' He gave up trying to type.

She leaned forward and touched the collar of his shirt. 'You shouldn't send them to the laundry; they put too much starch in the collars. I'll always do them. I've told you I'll do them.'

'Oh, the laundry do them well enough.' He indicated the report. 'I really must finish this.'

'I like to see you looking smart,' she said, flicking at specks of dandruff on the shoulder of his jacket. 'You ought to use a medicated shampoo.'

'Lorraine,' he said quietly, trying to keep a note of desperation out of his voice, 'I've got work to do.'

She nodded, sighed. 'Oh well – if you need me, give me a buzz.'

She started to move off, then turned back.

'See you in the canteen. But I'll be a bit late. I'm going to the shops. For some fresh fruit.'

She smiled at him, her long face lighting up, and went out. Bishop breathed an exaggerated sigh and went back to his typing. Almost immediately his phone rang.

'Hello?' he said irritably. 'Speaking. You have? About time too. It's always bloody happening . . . Oh yes it is. And don't give me any back-answers.' He had a tendency to bully inferiors. 'Don't you realize how vital it is, how absolutely vital, that the system should be in working order twenty-four hours a day? Well, I hope so . . . Yes, all right . . . Yes, now.'

He got up and went to the alarm phone and stood by it.

'Testing the alarm phone,' he said to Cunningham. It was a statement that required no answer and got none. Cunningham continued to blow smoke at the ceiling.

The alarm phone rang with shattering stridency and the red light flashed on and off. Bishop picked up the receiver.

'Bell and light OK. One, two, three, four, testing. One, two, three, four, testing. Clear? Good . . . Yes, you're clear too. But in future check it every day. Yourself. Or I'll know the reason why.'

He put the receiver down and went grumbling back to his desk.

'What keeps putting them out of order? That's what I'd like to know. Last week your phone, the week before my phone – now the alarm phone. My God, supposing there was an escape or a riot or whatever – and the damned alarm didn't work?'

Colonel Cunningham blew a long delicate stream of smoke at the ceiling (he was bored with rings).

'I don't know,' Bishop muttered. 'I just don't know.'

His phone rang again. 'I suppose I should be grateful it's working,' he said and picked up the receiver.

'Hello? Er – no, I'm afraid he's not . . . I couldn't really say. He's in a meeting, you see . . . What? Oh, I'm sure he's thought of something . . . Yes, in Latin . . . Yes, I know what the date is . . . Yes, I'll ring you.'

He put the phone down and looked across at the recumbent Cunningham.

'That was the Ministry of Information, Colonel.'

Cunningham stared at the ceiling. Then he said : 'You should sleep with her.'

'Who?' Bishop said, momentarily confused.

Cunningham swung his legs off the desk and turned to face him. 'The virginal Miss Skinner, of course, who's so concerned about your health. You should show a little more concern for hers. And sleep with her.'

Bishop disliked overt references to sex. They embarrassed him. His mouth tightened with displeasure.

'My relationship with Miss Skinner, Colonel, is on a some-what less physical plane.' He tried not to sound sententious and failed. 'Besides,' he added irritably, 'she's quite inno-cent.'

'Women are never innocent, Peter. And all that elemental energy she generates is building up like static electricity. And you wonder why the phones keep going out of order. I'll tell you – it's Miss Skinner's static. Do something about it, Peter, before it blows all the light-fuses as well.'

'Very funny, Colonel.'

'No, very serious. It's beginning to disturb my peace of mind.'

To hell with your peace of mind, Bishop thought. What he said was : 'I'm sorry, but it looks like a rather disturbing day. You have four appointments—'

'Cancel them. Anything else?'

The Bishop held up some documents. 'The death warrants. You haven't initialled them.'

'Put them in my in-tray.'

'It's full. Like all the trays.'

'Then find another bloody tray.'

'Finally, there's the motto.'

The Bishop smiled as he said it. He'd been saving that till last.

'The *what*?'

'The motto for the Party. In Latin.'

'The Party? The Party wants a motto? In Latin?'

Cunningham started to laugh but was overtaken by a fit of coughing. 'Why didn't somebody tell me?'

'I put the memo from the Ministry of Information on your desk two weeks ago.'

'I don't read memos. What did it say?'

'That all cabinet ministers and certain service chiefs – including you of course – were to submit a suitable motto, preferably in Latin, by the fourteenth.' A hint of malice crept into his voice. 'That was Wednesday of last week.'

'So it was, so it was . . . And Wednesday of next week is the fourth anniversary of the founding of the Party – and they want a Latin motto already. Isn't that touching? Did you know I invented the Party's official name?'

'No, sir.'

'It was at a meeting of the Inner Cabinet Committee, or Politburo as we laughingly call it. I had suggested the National Democratic Party. Percy' – he jerked a thumb at the picture of the Prime Minister – 'our beloved Percy, felt the word "socialist" should be in the title. And that idiot of a Home Secretary said – you know what he said? He said, "What about the National Socialist Party?" And there was this horrible silence, followed by embarrassed coughing.

'Then Percy said quickly, "I think we'll adopt Colonel Cunningham's suggestion after all. Anyone against? Carried *nem. con*." '

Cunningham shook his head, smiled his slightly crooked smile. 'Comical.'

'Yes, sir,' the Bishop said, adding under his breath, 'if you say so.' But he didn't think it at all comical. The Bishop was a born conformist and devoted supporter of the party in power and all it stood for, without being quite sure what it did stand for. His total conformity and almost blind respect for authority burned in him like a small but steady flame. And it angered and embarrassed him when Colonel Cunningham showed open contempt for someone who was not only his superior but also a member of the Inner Cabinet Committee – which Colonel Cunningham attended only by invitation. He should have more respect for his superiors. He should have more respect altogether.

'If I gave them a title,' Cunningham was saying, 'I suppose I can give them a motto.'

'Yes, sir,' said the Bishop, who was feeling guilty because he disliked Cunningham. If only he could have worked for a man he liked and admired, an orthodox man like the Home Secretary. You knew where you were with an orthodox man.

'Several spring to mind of course. Latin was invented for mottoes: all that gravitas and sonority ... How's this? Oderint dum metuant.'

'It has quite a ring, Colonel,' the Bishop said, starting to write it down, 'quite a ring. Could you spell it for me, please?'

Cunningham spelt it for him. The Bishop repeated it aloud, attracted by the emphatic rhythms. 'Yes, sir, it definitely has a ring.' He saw that Cunningham was smiling at him. 'What does it mean?'

'Let them hate provided that they fear.'

'Colonel Cunningham, you can't be serious.' He sounded shocked, and he was – to the depths of his conformist soul.

'Really, Peter, when it's serious you think it's a joke, and when it's a joke you think it's serious. You confuse me.'

The Bishop gave him a sour look. 'Not as much as your jokes confuse me, Colonel.'

One of the phones on Cunningham's desk rang. He reached

for it and managed to pick it up without taking his feet off the desk. It required some effort but he was prepared to work at being lazy.

'Yes?' he said casually. 'Speaking.' Then he swung his feet off the desk, all indolence gone. 'You have? Well done, Reg.'

The Bishop stopped typing, apparently in deference to the conversation, but really so that he could listen to it. Not that he was likely to learn much – Cunningham tended to be short and oblique on the phone – but at least he had learned that the caller was probably Reg Hacker, a chief superintendent of Special Branch.

For weeks Hacker and his Special Branch team had been patiently and unobtrusively searching London's dockland after a tip-off that the underground newspaper, *Combat*, was printed on a secret press somewhere in the area. The tip-off came from the lover of a woman whose husband was a linotype operator on the press. The lover, who was also a police informer, had told Hacker he would find out the exact address but had to tread softly because, though the woman no longer cared for her husband, she wouldn't deliberately betray him – except in bed, of course.

'Just tell me the husband's name,' Hacker had said. 'I'll do the rest.'

But the informer had refused. That sort of information might be traced back to him. 'And you know what they do to informers?' Hacker had tried to pressurize him, but the man was more frightened of the resistance than he was of Hacker.

'Just give me time,' he said. 'Let me do it my way.'

Hacker gave him time, let him do it his way. That was three weeks ago.

'And now', Hacker said to Cunningham, 'he's got a result.'

'He knows the address?'

'So he says. He wants to meet me tonight – not far from here.'

'Where are you speaking from?'

Hacker was speaking from a vandalized phone box in the West India Dock Road. Most of the glass had been smashed and it stank like a public urinal, which was what it was regularly used for after the pubs shut.

Cunningham arranged to meet Hacker at a dockside pub known as the Feathers. They would then go on to meet the informer.

'Oh, and dress a bit rough if you wouldn't mind, sir,' Hacker said. 'We're trying to keep a low profile in the area.'

Cunningham smiled. He liked Reg Hacker. He was the solid type. He would never do anything brilliant but he was solid. He looked it, too, with his big solid body, heavy jaw, broad nose and small steady eyes. He was as hard as he looked but not brutal.

'Do we know his name, Reg?'

'Matcham.'

Cunningham got to the Feathers just after opening-time. Hacker, who was standing at the bar with a pint of bitter, hardly recognized him in his patched denims, sneakers and out-at-elbow battledress jacket, which looked as if it had come out of a jumble sale.

'What'll you have?'

'Same as that.'

Hacker bought another pint of bitter and they took their drinks to a table by the big figured-glass window. There were only two other customers, a couple of middle-aged dockers.

'Nice and quiet,' Cunningham said.

'It'll get busy enough later on. It can also get rough.'

'He looks as if he can handle it.' Cunningham indicated the landlord, a big fat powerful man with a broken nose, a tin ear and scar-tissue over the eyes. A face sculpted by trouble.

Hacker nodded. 'Sam Fletcher. Fifteen years in the ring. Comes from Camberwell, so they call him the Camberwell Beauty. But not to his face.'

'Does he know who you are?'

'Yes, but he's OK. Co-operative. Passes on anything interesting he hears.'

'Let's hope this Matcham has got something interesting. What's the schedule?'

'We meet him just after dark in a disused warehouse about ten minutes' walk from here.' He pulled out a street-map, spread it on the table and pointed to a pencilled cross. 'Here it is. And there'll be squad cars on call here and here – in case we need back-up.' He patted the breast pocket where he kept his personal radio.

'You're expecting trouble?'

Hacker shook his head. 'Just a precaution. I had a young officer once who was killed when he went to a meeting with a snout. The bastard had set him up for the resistance.'

'But you don't think it's likely to happen tonight?'

Cunningham tried to keep the disappointment out of his voice. Danger excited him like sex – perhaps they were connected. Hacker, who had worked with Cunningham for two years, sensed the disappointment and smiled. Brains and guts were a combination he admired – even in the wicked.

'I think he's too scared to play a double game. He's already worried that the resistance may have sussed him out.' He paused to finish his beer. 'You're carrying a gun though – just in case?'

Outside the street-lights were coming on and so was the rain. It was falling gently and steadily as if it had no intention of leaving off.

'Going to be a nice night,' said Hacker. 'Drink up and I'll get you another.'

'My shout,' said Cunningham.

The warehouse was big and gaunt and hollow-eyed – there wasn't an unsmashed window in sight. Just looking at it gave you the feeling it was no more than a shell. One side fronted a dark and deserted wharf where a couple of rotting barges creaked at their moorings and black water slapped the piles loudly when the wind gusted. Or perhaps it just sounded loud in the stillness.

Cunningham and Hacker went quickly along the wharf, past a boarded-up entrance, then turned into an unlit alley along one side of the warehouse. Hacker took out a torch and they moved slowly along till they came to a side-door. It was shut but yielded to a push, and didn't creak. Someone had oiled it. They stood just inside the door and saw by the light of the torch that they were in what had once been an office enclosed by partitions of glass and plywood, now smashed down. The wooden desk had been smashed, too. Box-files and papers were scattered on the floor. The office was part of a row of partitioned offices, also smashed.

They moved out into a storage area littered with broken crates and packing-cases, torn cardboard boxes and a sea of paper and other debris of a once flourishing commercial life. There was a smell of must and decay and the occasional scurrying of a disturbed rat.

'Where's he supposed to be?' Cunningham whispered.

'On the ground floor, he said. We have to find him.'

They moved into another storage area much like the first,

then into a corridor with rooms leading off either side. They found him in the second room on the left, sitting propped up in a corner in a pool of blood, with his throat cut. That was how the resistance always executed spies and informers.

'He wanted to do it his way,' Hacker said. 'And like a bloody fool I let him.'

Cunningham moved forward for a clear look at the body.

'Don't touch, sir,' Hacker said. 'Might be booby-trapped.'

By the light of the torch Cunningham could see that the man's head had been pulled back and stuck to the wall with strands of adhesive tape, exposing the cut throat perfectly. Blood still dripped from it.

Cunningham, ignoring Hacker's warning, reached out and took hold of the dead man's hand.

'Still warm,' he said.

'Maybe there are others about who are also warm,' Hacker said, taking out his gun. Then he called up the squad cars on his personal radio.

'Cover the back of the warehouse and the wharf frontage, and if you see two men come out of an alleyway at the side find out who they are before you shoot them because they'll probably be us. Over and out.'

Guns in hand, they moved quietly and carefully through the warehouse back to the side-door, seeing nothing but the debris, hearing nothing but the rats, smelling nothing but the damp and the decay. The oiled door swung open easily and the cold fresh rain seemed like a benediction.

5

ASHMAN read it in the paper next morning under the heading: VENGEANCE KILLING. The story was slanted to give the impression that Matcham was a daring and resourceful undercover agent who had penetrated an anti-government terrorist organization (the press were forbidden to mention the resistance) and then been killed when his true identity and mission had been accidentally discovered.

'It's a wonder they don't bury him with full military honours,' Ashman said to Beth over breakfast in the Oregon pine kitchen.

'The whole thing's nasty,' said Beth.

'But necessary.'

'You'd better believe it, hadn't you?'

He knew her hatred of violence and reached across the table and took her hand, which felt cold. His own hands were always warm. She smiled at his touch and once again it seemed to him that everything about her was beautiful – her eyes, her hands, her mouth, her hair, which she either wore piled high on her head or hanging free, as now, running down over her shoulders like a great black shining tide.

It was hard to believe he was living with something so beautiful, and there were times when he woke up with a start and put his hand out to make sure she was still there beside him, and hadn't vanished like a dream with the morning light.

'You're beautiful,' he said. He wanted to say more but he didn't have the words. Not that it mattered.

'I'm not beautiful,' she said, 'but you make me feel it.'

Suddenly they were smiling at each other and she was in his arms.

'What are you going to do today?' he said after a time.

She taught or did her best to teach English to largely illiterate twelve-year-olds at a local comprehensive school. That day was the start of the half-term holiday.

'I thought I'd go and see my father and Emily.' She hesitated, then with a hint almost of apology: 'I haven't seen them for ages.'

'I wish you'd see more of them,' he said quietly. He knew they didn't approve of her living with him and being mixed up with the resistance – and he didn't blame them after the experiences they had had. Beth's young brother was one of the first to join the resistance, and one of the first to be killed. Though her father had no connection with the resistance he was automatically arrested and questioned. One result of this was that Emily lost her fiancé, a rising young politician who wished to continue rising. He broke off the engagement as soon as he heard of the father's arrest – he was nobody's fool. He was nobody's hero either.

It was no consolation to Emily that she had known all along something like that was going to happen – she was a woman of strong presentiments – it merely strengthened her conviction that life was a dirty trick. Her relationship with her father was uneasy. She alternately bullied him and coddled him to make up for it. He knew she took it out on him because she had no husband to take it out on, and he suffered it – but not always in silence.

They lived in a big solid pre-war house standing in an acre and a half of grounds that backed on to Epsom Downs.

A pleasant house full of pleasant memories. Well, mostly pleasant, Beth thought, as her Mini crackled up the gravel drive between the almond-trees, then swung right past the clump of pampas grass (well, that's what she and David called it when they were children), and all of a sudden there it was – the house where she'd been born, where Emily had been born, where David, now dead, had been born, and where, on a stormy night full of *Donner und Blitzen* she had met the love of her life.

She got out and looked around happily. The overnight rain had given way to a warm cloudless day, and the spring flowers had opened out dazzlingly in the spring sunshine. A phrase about rain-awakened flowers – was it from Shelley? Yes, probably; he was a girl's poet if ever there was – came into her mind and she took a deep breath of clean Surrey air and started coughing. She consoled herself with the thought that it must be cleaner than London air.

She looked round again. Something was missing. Of course, Sally, her father's Alsatian bitch. If she'd been in the grounds, she would have come racing down the drive to greet Beth. And, if she'd been in the house, she would have barked excitedly till let out. She seemed to know when you were coming. She knew other things, too. The night David died she suddenly started howling at about ten o'clock. David had been under interrogation at a Tac Force barracks and, it was said, had thrown himself from a third-floor window. The time of his death had never been announced, but Beth knew what it was.

She went up to the front door and rang the bell. She still had her door-key but thought it impolite to use it since she was no longer living there.

Emily opened the door, looked straight past her and said, 'Where's Thomas?'

'Busy. Where's Sally?'

'Out on the Downs with father.'

She led the way to the drawing-room at the back of the house. It was a large airy comfortable room with chintz-covered furniture and french windows giving on to an immaculate lawn dominated by a dark majestic cedar-tree. Beth used to sit in the shade of that tree on lazy afternoons long ago, dreaming and smiling to herself in the summer heat. She smiled again at the memory.

Her favourite tea-service, the delicate Royal Worcester, was already laid on the drum table with a plate of her favourite sandwiches – paper-thin slices of cucumber from which the water had been drained – as well as home-made cake and biscuits.

Emily had gone to considerable trouble in her preparations. It was her way of showing affection. Her manner was as ungracious as ever. The sisters were fond of each other but found it difficult to be together long without quarrelling.

'Do you want tea now or shall we wait for Father?' Emily said as they sat down.

'Let's wait. It's early and I'm in no hurry.'

Beth was sitting where she could see the lawn and the cedar-tree and beyond that the flower-beds and rhododendrons and finally the small wood of beech-trees and silver birches with one or two Corsican pines sticking up above the rest, tall, gaunt and melancholy.

'You look well, Elizabeth,' Emily said dryly. 'Considering.'

Beth bit back a sharp reply and said, 'I feel well. Very well.'

'And how is' – Emily hesitated as if the name were distasteful – 'Thomas?'

'The same as ever, thank you – big and butch and loving.'

Her sister's face darkened and Beth felt sorry. But Emily always brought out the bitch in her.

'I do worry about you, Elizabeth. I know you don't think I do, but I do.'

Worry about yourself, girl, Beth wanted to say but didn't.

'You see, I know you *think* you're happy . . .'

I am happy, bloody happy, all day and all night, especially all night – even when I sleep I dream about him.

'But have you considered the future?'

'Maybe there isn't a future for us, only the present.'

'And that's what you're living for, isn't it? It's almost a wartime situation – all love and drama. But someone once defined drama as life with the dull bits left out. And what's going to happen if you ever get round to the dull bits, to everyday life, living with a man from a totally different social and cultural background?'

'We'll adjust. We've a great deal in common.'

'Oh? Have you? Tell me what. He's a carpenter from Bloxwich, you're an honours graduate of Cambridge. You like the theatre, music, ballet and medieval painting. What does he like?'

Fucking, that's what he likes. No, I mustn't say that word. He's trying to stop me swearing; he thinks it unladylike, and it'd be a shame to disillusion him.

'He doesn't come from Bloxwich, he comes from Walsall.'

'Oh, great. That makes all the difference.'

'And he's not a carpenter, he's a fighter – that's his real trade. That's what he was trained for.'

'Oh yes, you only have to look at his big ugly face.'

'A real man is never ugly,' Beth said. 'But you wouldn't know about that.'

'Oh dear, have I touched a nerve?'

Yes, you have, you bitch, but that's all you've touched. You haven't touched my love. Nothing can touch that.

Emily went on about what she called the cultural gap, but Beth was no longer listening. She had heard all the arguments before – and they were only words, and her feelings were beyond words. Besides, Tommy didn't need defending. And the cultural gap hadn't stopped him rising to the leadership of the resistance in a remarkably short time – but that was one of the things she must never speak about. Emily and her father knew he was connected with the resistance, but that was all they knew.

Her father and Sally came in from their walk and greeted her in their different ways. The dog immediately lay down by her chair and never moved from her.

Her father kissed her cheek with cold lips, asked how she was and made the usual polite inquiries after Tommy, then lapsed into silence while Emily served the tea. He was in his late fifties but looked older. He had never really recovered from the death of his son or of his wife who had given birth to the son. He had a curiously remote air, as if only the outer part of him were present to go through the motions of so-called living while the living part was occupied elsewhere with memories of the lately dead. In some ways, Beth thought, they were more alive to him than the living.

'How is work, Father?' she said.

The remote eyes turned from contemplation of some lost perspective and focused on her.

'Uninteresting, what there is of it. I don't do much these days.'

'Have a sandwich, Father,' said Emily.

'I've had one.'

'Have another.'

'No, thank you.'

'A biscuit? Have a biscuit.'

'No, thank you.'

'They're your favourite Spritzgebäck. Home-made.'

'For Christ's sake, Emily, leave the poor man alone.'

'You hardly ate a thing for lunch, Father.'

'Emily, dear, why don't you take her advice and leave the poor man alone for Christ's sake? Or even my sake.'

He said it gently, almost humorously, and turned away, his eyes searching the distance for one of those lost perspectives.

Beth felt sorry for him. All he had ever wanted to do was get through life quietly without being hurt, and without hurting anyone else – the pathetic dream of the middle-class moderate. But the condition of man, someone had said, is a condition of war, of everyone against everyone.

A loud sniff came from Emily. She took out a lace-bordered handkerchief and dabbed her eyes.

'I do my best,' she said in a trembly voice. 'I don't know what more I can do, I really don't.'

'Come on now, Emmy, none of your crocodile tears,' Beth said heartlessly.

'It's all very well for you, but I cook and clean and scrimp and save – we can only afford help two days a week, you know—'

'Shame.'

'Of course, he ought to sell the place – it's far too big and expensive – but he won't, simply won't. He doesn't think about me – nobody does – but *I'm* the one who's stuck here night and day when I could be out enjoying myself—'

'With another little pimp of a politician?'

She shouldn't have said it, shouldn't have let her irritation get the better of her. Emily coloured a little but her voice when she spoke was calm and quiet.

'I won't get angry because I know you've got nothing but sadness in front of you. And *he'll* bring it to you. I felt it two years ago when you went off with him. I feel it now – sadness. Nothing but sadness.'

Beth smiled. She'd had nothing but happiness in those two years. And it would take more than Emmy's spooky feelings to destroy it. Two years . . . yet it seemed like yesterday that she was sitting at the same drum table reading Wilfred Owen and making notes for a talk on the war poets while she half-listened to the December storm outside. Somewhere in the house a loose sash rattled as the wind got up, but it didn't bother her, any more than a fox barking or an owl calling or other night sounds bothered her.

Then something happened that did bother her – Sally whined, which she only did to greet the family or friends. But the family were at Glyndebourne for the weekend. And what friends would be calling after midnight? Sally whined again and went to the french windows. Beth looked out, saw the melancholy heads of the Corsican pines bending to the storm, heard thunder rolling round the sky like the monstrous anger of the guns ('What passing-bells for these who die as cattle? Only the monstrous anger of the guns . . .').

At first she could see very little through the ragged curtain of rain, except the outlines of trees and bushes, moving in the wind. Then the garden was suddenly lit by lightning and she saw a man staggering across the lawn. It was just before Christmas and he was probably drunk. As if to confirm it he stumbled and fell. The dog whined again. Beth held her by the collar, opened the french windows and went out. The icy rain stung her face and drove through her dress in seconds. As she reached the man he got to his feet and she could see he was hurt. The front of his light-coloured shirt was soaked in blood and he was breathing deeply and noisily, like an athlete trying to get oxygen to tired muscles.

'Tac Force are after me,' he said and pointed to the woods at the back of the grounds. 'Where does that lead to?'

'The Downs. But you'll never make it.'

He turned and started to make for the woods. She quickly caught him up.

'Come into the house, I'll hide you.'

He shook his head. 'Know what they'll do to you if they find out?'

'They won't find out. And I'm getting soaked.'

There was the sound of heavy vehicles on the road outside.

'A Saracen,' he said. 'Maybe a scout car too.'

Then the dog started barking savagely.

'They're turning into the drive,' Beth said. 'Go into the house.'

She grabbed Sally by the collar and ran round to the front of the house where a Ferret scout car and a big Saracen armoured personnel carrier were pulling up. A young lieutenant got out of the Ferret and nine Tac Force troopers and a sergeant out of the Saracen. The rain lashed everybody with equal venom.

Sally was still barking and her hair was up. Beth managed to quieten her down but she went on grumbling and growling softly to herself – and her hair stayed up.

The young lieutenant saluted from a safe distance.

'Excuse me, miss, we're looking for a man—'

'In a leather jacket and jeans? Big hefty chap?'

'You've seen him?'

'He ran across the back lawn and disappeared into the woods. I'll show you.'

She took him to the side of the house and pointed to the woods.

'That's the way he went. If you send some men after him, then take your vehicles round by the road you should cut him off.'

The lieutenant thanked her, saluted again and turned and shouted some orders to his sergeant.

She went back to the french windows. The lights were still on but the drawing-room appeared empty. It was only when she stepped inside that she saw him, half-hidden by the curtains, gun in hand. Sally went to him and sniffed him with some care, then lay down by his feet with a grunt.

71

Beth told him what had happened. Then Sally got up and started barking again. The sergeant and his men were crossing the lawn in open order towards the woods. Beth quietened the dog, opened the french windows and called out, 'Good luck.' Then she pulled the curtains and turned to the man she had saved.

'I'm Beth,' she said.

'And I'm bleeding on your expensive carpet.'

'Sod the carpet,' she said, trying to sound tough and grownup. All she sounded was young.

She saw his leather jacket had a hole in it on the left shoulder. That was where the blood seemed to be coming from, some of it running down the outside of the jacket, some inside, spreading over his shirt.

He followed her glance and said, 'I've got a bullet in the shoulder from an SLR. Only a ricochet, otherwise it would've gone right through – and taken half the shoulder with it.'

'You need a doctor.'

'I'll be all right if I can rest a bit – till them bastards have gone.'

'Follow me.'

She led him upstairs to a spare bedroom. He moved slowly and carefully, trying not to open up the wound any more, though he still bled. The shoulder was beginning to stiffen up, but he ignored it. She was frightened he was going to faint – she'd never be able to shift a big man like that – but he seemed to have endless reserves of strength.

· She went into the spare room, drew the curtains, switched on the light, pulled back the bedclothes.

He lowered himself carefully into a sitting position on the bed. He was pale from loss of blood, and the pain and effort of moving showed in his eyes and the set of his face.

'My shoes are muddy,' he said slowly, 'but I don't think I can take them off.'

He must be held together by iron rods, she thought, like reinforced concrete. She knelt down quickly and took his shoes off. Then she lifted his feet gently on to the bed. He lay back. She pulled the covers over him, then got some extra blankets from a cupboard. She knew that gunshot wounds could cause tremendous shock and that the first essential was to keep him warm. The next essential was a doctor.

'Unless that bullet's taken out it will infect the wound.'

He saw there was a telephone on the bedside table, started to reach for it, then stopped. Someone was sticking red-hot needles in his shoulder.

'Give me the number and I'll dial it for you.'

He hesitated. You didn't give resistance numbers to strangers.

'Them bastards', she said, enunciating carefully, 'killed my young brother.'

He gave her the number. She dialled it, waited for the ringing tone, then handed him the receiver.

'Wally? Tom. I need a quack. Category A. Epsom area – but tell him he might have to go through road-blocks. No, I'm OK – under cover and quite comfortable. Being looked after by a beautiful young lady in fact.' He smiled at her and she turned and saw her reflection in a mirror. She looked a perfect sight – soaking wet and hair all over the place. 'Hold on, I'll get her to give you the address.'

He handed her the phone and she gave Wally the address. 'He says is there anything else you want to tell him?' He shook his head and she hung up. 'What's Category A?'

'A doctor that can deal with gunshot wounds.'

'Oh . . .'

He smiled at her and she suddenly realized he had a battered face with a flattened nose and dark deep-set eyes under brows thickened by scar-tissue. His wide-lipped mouth showed good teeth when he smiled. He looked nice, too, when he smiled. It took some of the hardness out of his face.

'I won't be a minute,' she said and went out, almost tripping over the dog, which was lying outside the door. In her own room she stripped and dried herself, then put on slacks and a Sloppy Joe sweater. She combed her hair and started to put it up, but it was too damp. So she combed it out and let it hang loose. She inspected her young face in the mirror, wondered if it needed lipstick and decided to put some on anyway.

'You like him,' she said suddenly to her surprised reflection. 'Don't you? You and Sally – two silly bitches.'

When she got back to the spare room he was asleep – or maybe he'd fainted. His eyes were closed and he was deathly pale. Perhaps he was dying. She had a moment of panic. What would she do with a dead stranger? She knew no one to contact, no one in the resistance. She could hardly ring up the local undertaker: 'I have a dead body in the house – would you

73

please collect it?' She didn't even know his name. Was it Tom he'd said on the phone? Dear Tom, if that's your name, please don't die on me . . . Don't panic. There's still the doctor. Thank God for the doctor. He'd know what to do – he was one of them. But why wasn't he here? Supposing he couldn't get through the road-blocks? Please, Tom, don't die just yet . . . Then she felt guilty – what a beastly way to think. And only a few minutes ago she was thinking how she liked him . . . Please, Tom, don't die at all. I like you. I do, really . . .

Suddenly she realized that he was looking at her.

'Are you . . . all right?' she said, swallowing.

'Sure.' His voice sounded warm and casual, but pain still showed in his face.

'I thought – I mean, you looked so pale . . .' She stopped, made a little gesture.

'That won't kill me,' he said, indicating the wound.

She wished the doctor would hurry up, all the same. At that moment the dog started barking, and she went downstairs and opened the front door. The doctor didn't announce himself, just said, 'Where is he?' He was short, middle-aged, hard-faced and Jewish. His voice was hard, too.

'I'll take you up,' she said.

'Just tell me where. And bring some antiseptic, a bowl of warm water and a clean hand-towel or two.'

'It's the room almost opposite the top of the stairs.'

By the time she got back to the room, the doctor had already cut the jacket and shirt away from the shoulder to reveal the ugly-looking wound. He inspected it, then turned and stared at her morosely.

'He ought to be in hospital – he'll need nursing.'

'I'll nurse him.'

'Are you trained?'

'You can tell me what to do, can't you?'

'You'd better watch – unless you're the kind that faints,' he said, but the hardness had gone out of his voice.

He poured some antiseptic fluid into the bowl of warm water, dipped a swab in it and started to clean the wound. He was quick, thorough and surprisingly gentle. He dropped the used swabs on the floor, and she collected them and put them in a waste-bin. She watched him with great attention. She also watched the man she knew as Tom. His eyes were still closed and he had the same deadly pallor. The only sign of life, apart

74

from his shallow breathing, was a sign of pain – a muscle jumping in his cheek as he clenched his teeth.

The doctor gave him a local anaesthetic and, while he waited for it to take effect, got some more swabs and a pad of lint from his bag. Then he probed for the bullet. She could see he was working as delicately as possible to limit the bleeding; she could also see there are limits to delicacy when it comes to gouging a misshapen lump of metal out of a man's shoulder. The wound wept blood. She wanted to turn away, but wouldn't let herself. If he could stand it, she could stand to watch it. The muscle in his cheek was jumping again. Some pain must be getting past the local . . . Not that you'd ever know – apart from that twitching muscle . . . She felt she couldn't watch any more.

Then, suddenly, it was out – a flattened piece of lead. Death's messenger, the appointment in Samarra. The doctor handed it to her – it was sticky with blood – while he cleaned the wound with swabs dipped in the antiseptic solution. Then he held a pad of lint against the wound.

'Pressure,' he told her. 'To stop the bleeding.'

She threw the piece of lead into the waste-bin.

'He might want it for a souvenir.'

'I don't collect souvenirs.'

His eyes were open and the muscle was no longer jumping.

'How do you feel?'

'All right.'

'Any discomfort?'

'A bit.'

Discomfort. The doctors' euphemism for pain.

'Get some lint from my bag and make up another pad.'

When she had done so he put the new pad over the wound and told her to hold it in place.

'And hold it nice and firm. Don't worry about him – he's made of barbed wire.'

Then he bandaged the shoulder, working very slowly and explaining as he went.

'Think you'll be able to change the dressing in the morning and bandage him up again?'

'Yes.'

'Good. We'll put him on antibiotics right away. I'll leave you some tablets and an antipyretic in case he gets feverish. If he sweats heavily you can sponge him down – with tepid water, not cold. Have you got a thermometer?'

And so it went on – questions, instructions, more instructions. When to take his temperature, when to change his dressing, always to keep a look-out for signs of sepsis . . .

'Right, let's get his clothes off and make him a bit more comfortable.'

'I'll wait outside.'

'What are you trying to be – a nurse or a nice young lady?'

'Don't bully her.' The coldness in that warm voice surprised her. So did the coldness in his eyes. The hard-faced little doctor merely stared back.

'I'll bully everyone till the job's done properly.'

'What do you want me to do?'

He cut the jacket away in sections, which she pulled gently free. They did the same with the blood-soaked shirt and she saw the heavily muscled torso of a fighting man. There was a short furrowed scar in his side, a long jagged one on his chest.

'Bullet wound,' the doctor said of the short scar. He considered it. 'Nine-millimetre Sterling at a guess.'

The other man nodded.

'But this one's a bit of a puzzle . . . Looks like someone was trying to stab you and the knife slipped.'

'I was twisting his wrist.'

Finally they eased his trousers off and saw scars on both thighs. The doctor shook his head.

'These ones beat me,' he said.

'I fell through a skylight. Tac Force were chasing me across some roof-tops. They thought they'd shot me and I'd fallen off the roof. That's how I escaped.'

'Every scar tells a story. How's the shoulder? And don't say all right.'

'Throbbing like a bastard.'

The doctor's mouth twitched almost into a smile. He shook two tablets out of a bottle and handed them to him. Then he turned to Beth.

'I'll be back in the morning, but if anything goes wrong, or you can't cope, ring me.'

'I'll cope.'

His mouth twitched again and he nodded. She saw him out, but as soon as the front door closed she wanted to pull it open and run after him. What was it she was supposed to do about fever? About sepsis? What if he had a seizure and fell out of bed? What if . . . ?

Silly bitch, silly bitch, silly bitch, she said to herself, running upstairs smiling.

He was asleep. Exhausted and, she supposed, drugged. She switched off the light and pulled back the curtains. The storm had blown itself out and the moon shone through ragged clouds. Everything was quiet. The hoot of an owl quavered faintly in the distance. The garden was washed in moonlight, the majestic cedar blacker than the night and the Corsican pines straight and still, no longer vexed by the wind. She sighed, without knowing why, and went to her room, took her shoes off and lay on the bed.

She tried to sleep but part of her was listening all the time, listening for a sound, any sound, the smallest sound. The house creaked and she sat up with a start, holding her breath. She let it out in a long sigh and lay back. Houses were always creaking in the night. She changed her position several times but couldn't really get comfortable. Then she tried consciously relaxing her muscles and breathing deeply and evenly, part of a relaxation technique she had read about. That didn't work either.

What was that? Had she heard something – or imagined it? She listened even harder. All she heard were the little sounds that make up the silence of the night, which you can always hear if you listen hard enough.

Restlessness grew in her till she got up and tip-toed to his room. She stepped over the dog, lying across the threshold, and went in. There was enough moonlight to see his sleeping face. He was breathing evenly. There was nothing she could do for him. She was about to turn away, almost disconsolate, when she realized his eyes were open and watching her from under the scar-thickened brows.

'Did I wake you?'

'No,' he lied. He slept lightly, like an animal, and though he had heard nothing some instinct woke him.

'How do you feel?'

'Thirsty.'

She poured him a glass of water from a carafe on the bed-side table.

'Why did you come in?'

'To see how you were.'

'You should be sleeping.'

'So should you.' She managed to sound, she thought, both prissy and petulant, like a horrid little girl.

'You've been very kind,' he said, continuing to stare at her, and then, after what seemed a long time: 'I'll never forget.'

Suddenly she was embarrassed under his stare, and turned away. 'I think I'll put a bed up in here.'

From under the stairs, where it was waiting for summer with the other garden furniture, she got a folding canvas day-bed, dusted it and took it up to the room. He was already asleep – at least, his eyes were closed. She made up the bed with a mattress, pillow and blanket. As soon as she lay down and pulled the blanket over her she felt happy. If she turned on her side or simply turned her head she could see him. She could also hear the movements he made in his sleep. And if she held her breath and listened carefully she could even hear him breathing.

His physical presence seemed to fill the room and, in her imagination, enfold her. She felt relaxed and at ease, as if coming home from a journey. She fell into a dreamless sleep.

That was how she met Ashman. Thomas William Henry Ashman. Why, she wondered, did parents saddle their children with names like Justin and Warren, when there were beautiful home-grown names like Thomas William Henry?

'What are you smiling at?' Emily said, pouring tea into the thin Royal Worcester cups. 'Elizabeth, I'm talking to you.'

6

Shortly after dawn on a Saturday in early April a Leyland Clydesdale, carrying a low-sided skip with six men in it, pulled up in what had once been a cul-de-sac. A truck carrying baulks of timber pulled up just behind it. On one side of the little street was a row of partly demolished houses. The other side of the street had been torn down and replaced by a seven-foot corrugated-iron fence. Behind the fence an office block was going up – sixteen storeys had already risen massively into the sky, and more were to come. Sitting on top of it like a lopsided crucifix was a tower crane, its metal arms glittering in the early sun.

The six men, dressed as council workmen, climbed down from the skip on to the pavement. A seventh man, who had been sitting beside the driver, got out of the cab. This was Ashman. They had met half an hour earlier in a public car park and, apart from Ashman and the driver, Paddy, were strangers to one another.

Ashman and the six men unloaded the baulks of timber and shored up the front wall of one of the partly demolished houses. Then they enlarged the front door and window into an opening big enough to take the Leyland Clydesdale, which was backed through it into the interior of the house. This in fact was little more than an empty space enclosed by the front wall and two party walls. There was no back wall, no partition walls, no roof, no floors – nothing much at all except rubbish and sprouting weeds. At the back was a fenced-in yard with more rubbish and more weeds, which had long ago choked to death the one small flower-bed. The yard backed on to another row of empty houses waiting to be pulled down.

The big Leyland Clydesdale seemed to fill most of what was left of the tiny house.

'It's like trying to get a fat man into a tight suit,' Paddy said as he backed her carefully in. 'Big ould bitch, isn't she, be God?'

He pulled the lever that swung the skip out and lowered it to the ground behind the loader. In it was a pile of equipment, including oxygen cylinders, a thermic lance holder, bundles of lances, some tubular scaffolding, a block and tackle, a tarpaulin, a couple of steel-wire nets and a steel T-bar with folding arms.

Ashman climbed into the driving cab, which looked like a small armoury. There was a Dragon anti-tank missile sealed in its glass-fibre launch-tube, a 7.62 mm Self-Loading Rifle with image-intensifying night-sight, two 9 mm Uzi submachine-guns and two .44 Magnum revolvers with 8.3 inch barrels. Plus, of course, ammunition.

There were also several cans of beer and a packet of sandwiches for Paddy and Ashman, who would stay there for four hours before being relieved by two other men. These four-hour shifts would continue through to the following evening.

'Know what tomorrow is?' Paddy said. 'Passion Sunday.'

'What's that?' said Ashman.

'Bloody pagan,' said Paddy. 'What about a beer?'

The six workmen boarded up the opening and went home. They didn't even know what the job was in aid of, and they didn't ask. They were simply told to knock a hole in a wall, then board it up. They started the job as strangers and finished it as strangers.

This was typical of the resistance, which was made up of a network of thousands of separate cells, most of which had no more than three members. Each member would know the other two by sight and first name only – unless they happened to work together in firms or closed institutions like Tac Force. He would also know the first name of the cut-out and the phone number of an answering service for messages. The cut-out arranged meetings, gave instructions, received reports – either personally or through constantly changing dead drops (hiding-places where written messages or reports were left).

So if one of the members of a cell were caught the most he could give away would be the names of the other two members, the phone number of an answering service which could be found in the Yellow Pages anyway, and the position of a few disused dead drops.

It was this tight cell structure that made it so difficult to crush or even curb the resistance – and so important for Tac Force to catch one of the leadership, one of the notorious Top Twenty. And the obvious target was the Falcon since he was the one who consistently put himself at risk.

Two men climbed over the back wall, took out handkerchiefs and held them up as they crossed the weed-choked yard. The relief shift were signalling their approach.

'Not before time,' Paddy said. 'Bloody pubs'll soon be shut.'

He and Ashman left by the same route, went through an empty house and came out into the next street. As they walked towards the corner Wally's big Rover pulled up alongside.

'See you, Paddy.'

Ashman got in. 'Nice surprise.'

'Maybe not so nice – there's a hitch. One of the handymen got drunk last night, fell down some steps and broke an ankle.'

'Maybe it's just as well,' Ashman said, nodding towards Paddy's retreating figure. 'We've got one piss-artist.'

'I've already lined up three replacements, if you'd like to take a look at them.'

'What about the guitarist bloke?'

'Lamont? Thought you didn't want him. Too jumpy.'

'At least he's keen. And presumably sober. Could you fix up a meeting this afternoon? Just me and him.'

'I should think so.'

'And, Wally, remember that shop—?'

'Where we stopped before?'

'Could you drop me off there?'

The heart-shaped twist of gold gleamed yellow against the blue velvet spread out on the showcase, and the solitaire diamond at the base of the heart glittered with points of fire. Wally was right; it was bloody elegant.

'How much?'

'Seven hundred and ten pounds, sir. It is a most beautiful piece,' the jeweller said, trying to keep the nervousness out of his voice.

He looked at Ashman and had misgivings, which was understandable. Ashman was a big powerful rough-looking man. The jeweller was small, middle-aged and frail. He was also alone in the shop, having given his assistant the Saturday off in a moment of generosity he now regretted.

'I'll take it.'

The phone rang. It was on the other side of the shop, and the jeweller hesitated. Not that there was much he could do anyway if a big chap like that snatched the piece and ran off. He was still reluctant to move away though, as if he felt his presence might have an inhibiting effect. Then he realized Ashman's dark unwavering eyes were on him, which made him even more nervous.

'Your phone's ringing.'

The jeweller went to the phone, though it took some effort to turn his back on Ashman. As he answered it (to a wrong number) his heart nearly stopped. Ashman had picked the piece up. The jeweller put the phone down and went back to the showcase, trying not to hurry.

Ashman took out a wad of twenty-pound notes, removed an elastic band, and counted out thirty-six of them.

'Seven hundred and twenty.'

The little jeweller was so relieved he gave one of them back.

'Let's call it seven hundred, sir,' he said, suddenly happy that it was he who was robbing Ashman and not the other way round.

Joseph Lamont lived in a flat in the bleak urban wastes of NW10. He bought the ninety-year lease with what was left of his savings a year after he'd been kicked out of the Musicians' Syndicate. With his livelihood went his expensive Mayfair flat, his expensive mistress and most of his expensive friends. So he took a flat and a mistress more suited to his modest estate. He was a practical man in some ways. The flat he found in Willesden, the mistress in one of the clip-joints where he played the guitar. Both were shabby. But it didn't show on the mistress, who was called Yvonne, till you got to know her. Now even she had deserted him. Who would be the next? One with a wooden leg perhaps? And where would he find her? He remembered hearing there was once a famous whore with a wooden leg in the rue St Denis in Paris. Should he save up for the fare?

Of course it was all part of a pattern that followed on from success – or rather failure. Women wanted success. Not necessarily financial success (though it helped) but success of some kind. Status perhaps. Fame. Notoriety. (Are you a high-achiever?) Success was somehow connected, in a way he didn't quite understand, with manhood. Success was the great aphrodisiac. Success was the short fat bald man with the big cigar and golden balls who got the beautiful women. Failure was the seven-stone weakling who got sand kicked in his face.

The only way to beat the pattern was to stay a success – or find a nice woman. Nice women kidded you into thinking you were a success anyway. And if you thought you were, and thought hard enough and long enough, you might even end up a success – and a credit to positive thinking.

First find your nice woman.

Joseph had never found one. Or perhaps he hadn't really tried, perhaps he was fatally attracted to the ones who tried to destroy him in some way. The ball-breakers. They made him feel he had to prove something, prove that the apparent Joseph was simply a mask for a mysterious, resourceful, dashing Joseph, whose extramural activities were closer to those of a James Bond than a guitar player in a Soho clip-joint. That was why he had joined the resistance: to try to make his fantasies come true. And though he didn't actually lie about it, he *hinted* . . .

One morning over breakfast Yvonne had made some remark about a particularly daring raid on an ammunition depot, carried out, according to the papers, by terrorists.

'That was the resistance,' Joseph said with casual authority.

'How do you know?'

'They always say terrorists when they mean the resistance.'

'Yeah? What do they say when they mean terrorists?'

Of course you couldn't argue with a silly cow like that. He sighed. 'Take my word for it. It was the resistance.'

'But how do you *know*?'

He sighed again. 'I'm a member, aren't I?'

'Was you on that raid then?'

'You know I couldn't tell you that. I'm only allowed to tell you I'm in the resistance.'

'And I bet they trust you with a bloody big job too. Like making the tea.'

Well, now she'd gone. And the need to prove himself had gone with her. Just as well the resistance *hadn't* put him on active service – and found out what a bloody coward he was. It was some consolation, he supposed.

He picked up his guitar, stared at the view of Willesden Junction, which not even the spring sunshine could make beautiful, and started to play Tárrega's *Capricho Arabe*. It suited his melancholy mood.

The telephone rang with jarring suddenness and made him jump. It was Wally Le Gras asking if he were free for a meeting that afternoon. There might be a job for him . . .

He put the phone down and laughed. The joke, as usual, was on him.

They met by the entrance to the Jews' Cemetery, which is next to Willesden Cemetery and not far from a third cemetery.

'I don't know why they need all these bloody cemeteries,'

Joseph said gloomily. 'If you live in Willesden you're already buried.'

They walked to Roundwood Park and sat on a bench in the spring sunshine. It was chilly though. Joseph stared at some snowdrops at the base of a tree and felt miserable. *Schneeglöckchen*, he said to himself.

'You're still keen?'

Joseph decided to tell the truth: he had changed his mind. No longer interested. Not suited to active service anyway. His nerves, you see – no good pretending. Better to make a clean breast of it. He opened his mouth to say No.

'Yes,' he said.

'You're sure?' The dark eyes were on him, searching his face.

'Of course.' He suddenly wanted to impress Ashman, wanted his respect, his trust . . . The man's presence affected him . . .

'It might be dangerous.'

Joseph shrugged. He didn't trust his voice in case it wobbled.

'Not that I'm expecting trouble – but there's always the possibility.'

Joseph nodded. His mouth had gone dry.

'Your main job'll be to rig up a block and tackle and a tarpaulin to work under.'

Joseph found his voice at last but it sounded strange to him. 'I see . . .' He cleared his throat. 'Anything else?'

'You'll get all the details at the briefing tomorrow night. We'll pick you up around eight.'

He gave a brief nod, said, 'See you.' And left. Joseph watched him cross the park. Big, strong, easy-moving, unafraid. Everything Joseph wasn't.

Ashman walked back to the Jews' Cemetery where Wally was waiting for him in the Rover.

'All right?'

'I'm not sure he's quite so keen as he was.'

'Something he said?'

Ashman shook his head. 'Just a feeling.'

'There's still time to get somebody else.'

'He'll do. Bad nerves, good heart – if you know what I mean.'

He looked for her first in the kitchen, then in the other downstairs rooms. Then he heard splashing and called up the stairs, 'You in the bath?'

'Just getting out. Come up.'

She was drying herself when he went in.

'Many happy returns,' he said, kissing her damp cheek. He held out the jeweller's box. 'Small present.'

'What is it?'

'Open it.'

'Let me dry my hands . . . Christ, it must've cost the bloody earth.' She sounded almost shocked.

'Do you have to swear?'

'You don't mind me swearing in bed.' She flung her arms round him. 'It's a *beautiful* present. But the money, Tom, the *money*.'

'What the hell, we'll all be dead soon enough.'

'Don't say that.'

'Today, tomorrow, in fifty years – who knows, who cares . . . ? You're making me wet.'

She laughed, went to the wall-cabinet, found a piece of blue ribbon, threaded it through the gold loop at the top of the pendant, then tied it round her neck.

'How does it look?'

'Sensational.'

'The *pendant*, Tommy.'

'That's OK, too.'

'Oh, come on. You've seen me naked often enough, haven't you?'

'No,' he said, after some thought.

They had dinner at home. Ashman wanted to take her out, but Beth wouldn't have it.

'It's my birthday and I want dinner here. In my beautiful kitchen.'

So they had roast saddle of lamb with wild rice and aubergines in her beautiful kitchen. They also had a bottle of Chianti Classico to go with it.

'We practically live in this bloody room.'

'I love it. All the yellowy wood everywhere. I love the feel of it, the smell of it. It's like being in a country cottage.'

'Till you look out of the window.'

'You're a pig,' she said. 'You spoil everything.' And went on about the kitchen and other trivia that Ashman pretended to listen to as he looked at her. She was wearing one of those off-the-shoulder frocks with a frill across the front. She'd put it on to set off the pendant, which it did beautifully. It also set off,

85

just as beautifully, the line of her neck and shoulders. And her hair, which shone in the shaded light of the wall-lamps. She had combed it out loose, the way he liked it, and it swung as she moved her head and sometimes fell across her face like a wing. He watched the movements of her hands as she talked and smiled, and the movement of her breasts under the frock as she reached for things. He watched all her movements. And that scent she wore – what was it? He leaned forward a little and breathed it in. Some kind of flower, he supposed. And that's what she reminded him of, really, because her presence brightened the whole place, like a bowl of fresh flowers.

'Tommy? *Tommy*.'

'What?'

'You're not listening.'

'Sorry, I was thinking.'

'Not about tomorrow – about the job?'

'All the thinking's been done for that.'

She shivered, as if touched by an icy draught.

'You will be all right?' She tried to keep the fear out of her voice.

'Listen', he said, 'it's a straightforward job and there's nothing much that can go wrong – and if it does we've got pretty good contingency plans. The risks are minimal.'

'It's just that . . . if anything happened . . .'

'Know what I was really thinking about? Something called pair-bonding.'

She smiled, feeling warm and reassured. The wind had taken its icy fingers away. She leaned across the table and hugged him.

'Careful,' he said. 'You'll upset the wine.'

7

AT ABOUT THE TIME Ashman and Joseph were sitting in the spring sunshine of Roundwood Park, Cunningham was slouching like a sleepy cat through the same sunshine in Battersea Park. He was hardly recognizable in grubby blue denim cap, blouse and trousers. His hair stuck out untidily from under the cap, the blouse was torn and covered a none too clean sweater, the trousers were stuffed into shabby chukka boots.

The funfair had recently reopened and was doing good business with the Saturday afternoon crowd. Cunningham made his way to the shooting-gallery and watched a man shooting at ping-pong balls balanced on a stream of water. He shot down ten out of ten, which wasn't too difficult – no prizes were offered so the guns weren't fixed. Cunningham took a gun next to him, paid for ten rounds and shot them off rapidly. He got nine out of ten and clicked his tongue in irritation.

'Hard luck,' the other man said, turning to face him. It was Frank Wilson. They strolled off together and joined the queue for the Big Wheel. Wilson paid for the tickets and they climbed into the open two-seat car. The attendant locked the safety-bar in place. Cunningham, though, felt anything but safe as they swung slowly up into space. Battersea Park spread out below them, a green oasis in a brick desert sliced by the slow brown waters of the Thames. A stream of cars crossing Albert Bridge looked like toys glinting prettily in the sun.

'Anything on Volcano?'

'Not really. But General Hudson and Joshua Murdoch are in town – and that's unusual.'

Cunningham nodded. It confirmed the reports of his informers. Hudson and Murdoch rarely left their secret headquarters, somewhere in the countryside around London, because they were too well known and too easily recognizable. When they did come into town it was usually for top-level policy meetings.

'So who are they meeting – and what for? Volcano?'

'Or that robbery I mentioned. Or both.'

'What about the robbery?'

'It's definitely on – and it's big.'

'Big enough for the Falcon?'

'He's the one who ordered the thermic lances. They say it's gold bullion he's after.'

'Any idea of the target?'

'A bank presumably – though there's a big bullion shipment due out of London Airport this weekend.'

'That wouldn't call for thermic lances.'

'Maybe they're for some other job.'

'A bank sounds the best bet. I'll put the word out to our informers.'

The turn of the wheel took the car down, then up again. Each time they went up Wilson noticed that Cunningham closed his eyes.

'Are you feeling all right, sir?'

'A touch of acrophobia.' As Wilson looked blank, 'Fear of heights.'

Wilson was surprised. He didn't think Cunningham was frightened of anything.

Cunningham dined at his Holland Park home with his wife and son. His relationship with both was uneasy. His son Hugo was silent and preoccupied and hardly raised his eyes from his plate. All three in fact were preoccupied and though present in one sense were absent in another.

His wife Evelyn had a long narrow body, narrow hands, narrow feet and, Cunningham suspected, a long narrow soul. Looking at her across the dinner table, cool, composed and well groomed as always, he wondered, as men before him had wondered, how he had ever come to marry her. He had loved her once, no doubt, and she him. What had happened – and where does love go when it dies? He couldn't remember and it embarrassed him to try. Like everything else, he supposed, it had turned to dust (and into bickering all his lust).

Conversation at the table was limited to polite banalities to which Cunningham contributed polite noises. Neither actually listened. She was busy planning her summer wardrobe; he was thinking about the usual problems, including Monday's meeting of the Inner Cabinet Committee to discuss some crisis or other caused, no doubt, by the resistance. Monday was invariably Crisis Day. After a good weekend the Prime Minister liked a good crisis. It gave him a buzz.

All governments have crises of course, and some fall by them. This government existed by them. And if, as sometimes happened, there was a nationwide shortage of crises one could always be manufactured. This allowed the Right Honourable Percy Smith to appeal to the Dunkirk spirit for whatever he wanted from the populace (blood, sweat, toil or tears) and, even more important, to retain the emergency powers he had assumed on taking office.

It was supposed to be a provisional government, but the provisional, as the French say, has a way of becoming the permanent. And after four years the Government were still in office and the Emergency Powers Act and all the other temporary acts still in force, and the promised general election as remote as ever.

Of course, Cunningham thought as he sipped a glass of Fleurie, our Percy was clever. He'd left the monarchy strictly alone, he allowed a token Opposition in Parliament to preserve a show of democracy and he hadn't yet destroyed private enterprise. He merely controlled it – because of the crisis – as rigidly as he controlled labour – because of the crisis. And of course he hadn't destroyed the unions (he was the Workers' Friend), merely replaced them by syndicates, which he also controlled. In effect, his powers were dictatorial.

There was some way still to go before the Corporate State was fully formed, but, Cunningham thought as he rolled the Fleurie round his tongue, in four short years Percy has taken us quite a way down the stony road to totalitarianism. And of course there were achievements. The Gross National Product had gone up, inflation had gone down. So had the standard of living – except for those the Russians call *Priviligentsia* – the Party members, bureaucrats and other so-called public servants (as well as black marketeers, who always get in under the wire anyway).

And unemployment had virtually disappeared. So had the workers' right to choose their employment. Labour went where directed and where required. The unemployed (those out of work for more than six weeks) and a new category, the unemployable (tramps, layabouts and general nuisances), were drafted to work camps where they were given pocket money and rations in proportion to the work norms they fulfilled. Selected political prisoners, after being suitably sanitized (the official word) in re-education camps, were allowed to serve out the rest of their sentences in the work camps where – as Cunningham put it in one of his little jokes that upset everyone – *Arbeit Macht Frei.**

---

*'*Work Means Freedom*.' The legend over the entrance to Nazi concentration camps.

This system not only cured unemployment, it also made those in employment extremely wary of losing or even trying to change their jobs. And it provided an excellent source of cheap labour for the State.

Finally, there was law and order. Tac Force saw to that.

So much for the achievements. But what about the people? Cunningham wondered about the people. They had their beer and their bingo – some even had their books and their Beethoven – but was that enough? Did they miss their freedom? Did they even notice it had gone? After all, they were conditioned to controls, especially after the collapse of the economy. All clever Percy had done was to extend those controls – and go on extending them.

So the crucial enigma was still the people. It was from the people that the resistance got their support. And it was the growth of that support that was behind most of the crises that the Inner Cabinet Committee endlessly discussed. Some of them, Cunningham thought, were real crises, what's more.

After the maid had cleared away, Cunningham took the bottle of Fleurie and went into his study, telling Hugo he would like a word with him. The boy followed him.

Cunningham sat down at a big leather-topped Victorian partners' desk. Hugo stood opposite him, hands clasped behind his back, blank-faced.

'For goodness' sake sit down, boy,' Cunningham said. 'You're not a soldier up on a charge.'

Hugo sat down. He was very thin, with a mane of dark hair that accentuated the pallor of his intelligent face. And, though he lacked his father's presence and force of personality, there was a seriousness, an intensity about him that suggested strengths of character not immediately apparent. He was in his first year at Oxford reading English, though now on vacation after Hilary.

Cunningham decanted the rest of the Fleurie and poured himself a glass.

'Going to have one?' he said.

'No, thank you.'

'You didn't have any at dinner.'

'I didn't want any at dinner.'

Apart from a ship decanter and two wine glasses on a tray, a calendar and a silver-plated paperweight from Israel with the ancient lion of Judah in high relief, the desk, in contrast to his office desk, was completely clear.

Cunningham sipped the Fleurie. 'One of the pleasantest wines of the Beaujolais, I think. The French describe it as plump. I wonder why?'

Hugo said nothing. But he knew his father hadn't asked him there to talk about the communes of the Beaujolais.

'I see you had another poem in *Isis* last month. I thought it was good – not that I'm any great judge. Very good.'

Cunningham paused for Hugo to comment. The boy still said nothing.

'I particularly liked the bleak imagery, the down-to-earth language and the non-poetic rhythms. Of course the whole thing had an internal rhythm of its own. Very impressive . . .' He smiled. 'Bit political in its implications though.'

'It was meant to be.'

'And why not? What the hell – if you can't have a bash at the Establishment when you're young, when can you? You sure you won't have a drop of the Fleurie? It really is most pleasant. A wine for all seasons.'

'No, thank you.'

'Of course, I've come in for a bit of leg-pulling about it – not that I care – and mostly from idiots anyway. You know the sort of thing . . . How's that brilliant boy, the Balliol Solzhenitsyn? Only they say bally old Solzhenitsyn, of course.'

'Very witty, your friends.'

'Not friends, colleagues. And you needn't exercise your irony on me. I know how stupid they are. The point is, I hold a politically sensitive job. I'm responsible, as you probably know, for the country's internal stability and security—'

'Are you telling me not to write any more political poems?'

'Good heavens, no. Write as many as you like. Revolutionary as you like. It's a free country. More or less.'

A thin small smile broke the blankness of Hugo's expression.

'The only advice I'd offer, and it *is* only advice, is to avoid getting mixed up in active politics.'

'You're mixed up in it.'

'I'm a different kind of man,' Cunningham said slowly. 'Remember that.'

'Anyway, I'm not mixed up in what you call active politics.'

'I'm glad to hear it.' He lit a cigarette, taking his time over it, tried to blow a smoke-ring and failed. 'Of course, there is that pub you go to sometimes – where a bunch of students meet in the back room—'

91

'How do you know? You having me followed?' Hugo's voice went thin with anger.

'My dear Hugo, don't be silly. We only have people followed who are a threat to national security. But if the Security Service or Special Branch happen to be watching a place because they've had a tip-off that a terrorist might turn up there and they see you there, of course they're going to report it to me. What can you expect?'

'If you must know, I go there to see the landlord's daughter.'

That was true, and Cunningham knew it. He also went there for other reasons, and Cunningham knew that too, but wasn't going to say so.

'Is she pretty?'

'I think so.'

'What's her name?'

'Sally.'

'Perhaps you should write her a poem.'

'I have.'

'What did you call it — "Down by the Salley Gardens"?'

The boy laughed. 'I might get away with a bit of plagiarism — but I can't pinch a whole damn poem.'

Cunningham finished the Fleurie and wondered whether to open another bottle. He decided not to. He had had three glasses and he wanted a clear head — he was seeing Amarantha later.

'Look,' he said, 'I don't want to lecture you or lay down rules or anything like that. I want you to enjoy yourself.' He smiled. 'That's the idea of being young . . . Of course, I know our political ideas differ — but why not? I think I'd be disappointed if they didn't. But, as I said, I do have a rather special position, and I would be grateful if you'd try not to embarrass me.' His smile broadened. 'Well, not too much anyway. You've no idea the kind of twits I have to deal with.'

The boy smiled, despite himself. There was no doubt about it — his father had a certain charm. No wonder the women liked him. True, he was handsome but it was more than that. The easy manner that was never condescending, the assurance that was never cocky, the hint of humour behind the slightly sleepy-looking eyes, the nicely modulated voice (which he knew how to use to full effect) and, he supposed, some indefinable quality of personality — charisma was the media word — which was so disarming. And so dangerous. Yes, his father

92

was charming, no doubt about it. He wondered why he hated him.

'I'll try not to embarrass you,' he said.

'Thanks. I appreciate that,' Cunningham said. 'More than you know . . . Seeing your girl tonight?'

'No. I have some reading to do. *Gorboduc*.'

'*Who?*'

'The first English tragedy – modelled on Seneca. Nobody ever reads it.'

'Except you.'

'And a few other students.'

'Well, shall I take Sally out for you? I'll explain you're having this mad passionate affair with Gorboduc.'

By now they were smiling at each other.

The phone rang. It was Hacker with nothing to report. He and his men were still searching for the underground press around the India and Albert docks.

'You'll find it in the end,' Cunningham said. And he would; he had the patience of an orb-weaving spider.

Cunningham and Amarantha lay in bed after love-making, staring out of the big northern light at the starless sky. The moment of perfect peace as pleasing in its different way as the love-making. A moment Cunningham always savoured, though distracting thoughts sometimes flawed the serenity (You want peace? You must be getting old).

'Those miners', she said, and the peace was gone, 'were never terrorists.'

'The local Tac Force commander over-reacted – and has been disciplined.'

'How a man of your supposed sensibilities can run that gang of hoods—'

'We've had this conversation before, my dove—'

'And we'll have it again.'

'And I've tried to explain: it's a world for winners – and I intend to be among them. I'm not interested in ideologies or the fate of the human race. Mankind is largely composed of shits. According to Nietzsche, man is the sick animal of the species. Actually, I prefer wild animals; they're nicer, cleaner and less savage. And they don't kill for the sheer hell of it. Finally, life being nasty, brutish and short, I try to protect myself and those I love. And if other people get hurt in the process . . .' He shrugged. 'That's the way it's always been and, from all the evidence, always will be.'

She changed her position, moving away from him, and lit a cigarette.

'All you're really saying is that goodness is dead. I don't believe that.'

'Long live goodness.'

'Your outlook is totally nihilist. You've backed down, given up, chickened out. Which is unlike you – I'd have thought.'

She was trying to goad him, hit the male ego in its pride. He didn't answer; there was no answer. He didn't even listen as she continued to attack him. It happened from time to time, and he had come to expect it. No doubt it was a relief valve for her liberal conscience, which must have been having a rough time (which was what it deserved).

'Since you hate everything connected with me and what I represent, every political thought and act, I can't help asking myself – with something close to suspicion at times – why you continue to put up with me.'

She put out her cigarette.

'Love,' she said.

There was no answer to that, either. After a while he said, 'Didn't look much like love the first time we met; you were bloody rude.'

'I apologized the second time, didn't I?'

'And charmed my heart off its hook. But why? Why the change?'

'Because I'd been bloody rude – and you'd given me no cause.'

'Is that all?'

'That's all.'

But it wasn't all. Not by any means all. After that first meeting, when she left shaking with anger, she had taken a taxi to Hampstead and walked on the heath for an hour to calm herself down. It was dark by the time she got home. She let herself in and went straight to the study. As she came into the room a voice said, 'Don't switch the light on.'

It was the voice of Yakov, her contact with the resistance, her cut-out. There was just enough moonlight to show the outline of him sitting behind the desk. Yakov was one of the few Jews who escaped from a concentration camp during the war and reached the Allied lines. He was a gentle man with a gentle voice, pale gentle eyes and a resolve that was unshakeable.

Amarantha once asked him how he had managed to survive the concentration camp.

'Luck,' he said simply. 'You cannot survive such conditions without great luck.' And great character, she thought.

The gentle voice spoke to her out of the darkness. 'The man you've just been rude to—'

'Colonel Cunningham?'

'DSO, MBE, MC, C-in-C Tac Force—'

'And shit, first-class, with diamonds and oak leaves.'

'Is one of the most powerful men in the country, though he keeps out of the public eye. His name is rarely given in the press, his picture never.'

'I sensed there was something dangerous about him,' she said. 'And not just to women.'

'He's a complex man,' Yakov said. 'And not always what he seems.'

She waited for him to go on, but he didn't. She looked out of the window at the moonlight silvering the trees in the garden which sloped down to the heath. She heard the chair creak as Yakov changed position.

'Did you find him attractive?'

'That bastard? That murderer, that hoodlum, that . . . ?' She let out a long breath. 'Yes.'

Another silence. Now it was Yakov who turned and looked out at the moon-silvered trees.

'It could be most useful', he said without taking his eyes off the trees, 'if we had someone . . . close to him.'

'Are you asking me to sleep with him?'

Yakov thought about this. 'Only if you want to.' He hesitated. 'And only if you don't fall in love with him.'

'Only a whore could guarantee that.'

'What can you guarantee?'

'To report everything he tells me.'

'That will do. Not that he's likely to give away anything important. But you never know – a hint here, a word there can sometimes fit into a pattern.'

He told her he would cut off all contact with her for at least three months because once Cunningham had shown interest in her she would be automatically screened to make sure she had what Tac Force called a negative (i.e. non-dangerous) background. Of course, she had right-wing friends, but they were regarded as negative, too. The milk-and-water opposition. The sort that would criticize the Government, but not too often and not too loud. The Government quite liked, in a way even encouraged, that sort of opposition. It retained the illusion of freedom of speech that the British are so proud of.

After three months the underground checked her phone to see if it was tapped, 'swept' her house for electronic bugs, even examined the window panes in case they had been painted with clear tin oxide which can turn a window into a transmitter and allow conversations in the room to be picked up by an outside receiver. The house was clean.

By this time Amarantha was in love with Cunningham and he with her. She reported everything he said that might be of interest to the underground. But Cunningham was not the kind of man who talks big in bed to impress his mistress. He did, of course, sometimes talk shop and even let slip minor details about Tac Force operations, but nothing (as Yakov had predicted) of importance.

Amarantha had long ago decided she would never consciously do him any harm. But what if she ever had to choose between betraying him or the resistance? It was a dilemma she turned her back on. I'll think about that when it happens, she told herself.

But there was another more central dilemma that she could never get away from. It came naturally out of the situation of loving the man while hating his work. Really, she should either give him up – or side with him completely. Both were impossible.

It was her own fault, she felt, as she lay beside him after making love and stared through the northern light at the starless sky. She was greedy and sensual and trying to have the best of both worlds. It could only end in disaster. The thought started tears in her eyes, and she turned her head so he shouldn't see. It was a hateful situation, and the most hateful part of all was the deception of someone she truly loved.

She needn't have worried.

Ashman and Beth slept after making love, but later in the night she woke up trembling from a bad dream.

'Tommy,' she said, 'Tommy.'

'Wha'?' he said sleepily.

96

'I dreamed we were dead in the forest. I saw us lying there in the forest, dead.'

'Go back to sleep, sweetheart.'

He tried to turn on his side, away from her, but she moved her nakedness against him.

'Ah, no,' he said.

Her hands searched him, softly insistent.

'I've got to sleep,' he said.

The silk-smooth female softness and dampness of her seemed to enfold him, the female smell of her filled his nostrils, her breath mixed with his.

'You know what tomorrow is?' he said.

'Love me, you bastard,' she said. 'Love me, *love* me.'

He loved her.

'I'd like to die like this,' she said.

'You know what tomorrow is?' he said again.

'Yes,' she said, 'the Day of the Dragon. Love me, Tommy. Love me for ever.'

Later they fell asleep in each other's arms, entwined like children. It only needed the leaves to cover them.

8

THE DAY OF THE DRAGON broke bright and clear, one of those smiling April days that fool everyone.

Wally and the spiky little Jock were already there, leaning against the skip-loader smoking cigarettes, when he arrived. The two watchmen from the resistance – the morning shift – were sitting in the driving cab listening to pop music on a transistor radio. Wally read out the items from a typed list of equipment while Ashman and Jock checked every piece down to the last bullet, even field-stripping and reassembling the guns. It took well over an hour. Then Ashman said, 'OK, Jock, you might as well shove off. See you at the meeting.'

Jock nodded and left.

'What next?' said Wally.

'The crane driver.'

Arthur Walby had been mutinous, saying he wanted the car before the job, not after. 'How do I know you haven't damaged it?'

'What does it matter? You're getting twenty grand, aren't you?'

Walby flapped his arms like an angry scarecrow. 'You don't understand these things,' he said, and refused to budge. Wally had tried everything from threats to cajolery. He still wouldn't budge. No car, no job.

'Give him the bloody car,' Ashman had said.

'Supposing he backs out?'

'He's not the type to break his word.'

Wally thought about this. 'Maybe you're right – but he's a cunning bastard. And once you're in all that skip, swinging on the end of the chain, he's got you, hasn't he? He could drop you right in the middle of a truck load of police – or Tac Force. He'll already have his car back, plus five grand – plus a bloody great reward to come. You think he hasn't thought of that?'

'Oh, he's thought of it all right,' Ashman said. 'But so have I.'

They found him in the garage polishing the ancient car as delicately as a jeweller with a gemstone.

'Don't come too near,' he said, 'if you don't mind.'

'Afraid we'll contaminate it?' Wally said.

Arthur Walby went on polishing with a concentration that excluded them totally. Wally opened his mouth to say something but Ashman shook his head. Wally sighed, took out a cigarette. Ashman shook his head again.

'Permission to bloody well breathe?' Wally said.

Ashman strolled over to the car and stared at the gleaming bodywork.

'What polish do you use on her?'

Arthur Walby gave him a ten-minute exposition of the make-up, qualities, defects, uses and several purposes of the polishes, waxes, powders and unguents he used, with special reference to a magical compound he made himself from certain secret constituents.

'Eye of newt and toe of frog, Wool of bat and tongue of dog,' Wally muttered in the background.

'She certainly looks good on it,' Ashman said.

Arthur Walby nodded happily, a dreamy half-smile on his face. Ashman turned away from the car, stared at him. The smile gradually went from his face.

'Well, we've kept our part of the bargain,' Ashman said.

'And I'll keep mine.'

'You know the programme?'

Walby nodded again.

'Repeat it.'

Walby repeated it.

'OK,' Ashman said, 'but remember the timing's crucial.'

'If your timing's right, mine's got to be. I don't move without your signal.'

'As long as you're there, ready and waiting.'

'I will be.'

'What about the nightwatchman's schedule – still the same?'

'Never changes. Goes on his round at eleven, then brews up and has his supper. Then listens to Sharon's Hour on his tranny. You know, the bird with the husky voice: "This is Sharon at the witching hour calling all you lonely folk in London but especially Harry Wilmot of Walthamstow East. Thank you, Harry, for your lovely, *lovely* letter. I know only too well, Harry, the heartbreak of having loved and lost . . ." And all that crap. And he sits there with tears in his eyes, silly old bugger. Still, there's nowt so queer as folk.'

'And *he* thinks he's normal, I suppose,' Wally said afterwards as they got into the Rover. 'Where now?'

'Ronnie Adams.'

'Don't tell me he's jittery again.'

'Nervous, Wally, that's all. A little nervous.'

It was a neat and pretty little Surbiton semi, three up and two down, in the kind of street that grows grass verges. Ronnie took them into the lounge.

'Everything OK?' Ashman said.

'Sure,' said Ronnie. 'Fine.' He gave a nervous laugh, walked up and down. 'I can't wait for the balloon to go up.' Another nervous laugh. 'Imagine robbing a bank. Or screwing a jug, as villains call it. Imagine.' He rubbed his damp palms down the side of his jeans.

'You seem a bit jumpy,' Wally said.

'Excited, that's all.'

'Not too excited, eh? You're going to need a clear head.'

'An hour on the bed with my wife will fix that.' He laughed again. 'I read somewhere it's the sovereign specific for clear thinking.'

Ashman turned to Wally. 'I'd better explain the set-up. There are always two men on duty in the control room. But if Ronnie's going to fix those cameras he's got to be alone there for two or three minutes. And that only happens when his partner goes to the loo. Problem: how to get him to go at the right time.'

'A firework up his jacksie?'

'There's a new fast-acting diuretic – works in about half an hour, sometimes less. Varies with the individual.' From his pocket he took two small paper sachets with 'Tate & Lyle' printed on them. 'It's in these – mixed with sugar.' He handed them to Ronnie and said, 'Right, take us from the tea-break.'

Ronnie started pacing again. 'Two a.m., girl comes round with tea. I take it from her . . .' He held up the paper sachets. 'I substitute these for the sugar packets. Two-thirty or thereabouts, Pete – that's my partner – goes for a pee. I go into the cubby-hole behind the control panel, put a duff fuse in the reception camera and loosen a wire to the strong-room camera.'

'Wait a minute,' said Wally. 'How will you know which wire to pick? There's a mass of them, isn't there?'

'I picked it a week ago and marked it with a ballpoint – looks like a speck of dirt. But I'll know it.'

'All right', said Ashman, 'so you've loosened the wire. What next?'

'Back to the control room, where I switch the lights off, then on again.'

'The signal that the cameras are down,' Ashman said to Wally. 'We won't see it, of course, because we'll be on the roof. But it'll be picked up by a look-out in the street below – and he'll flash his headlights a couple of times. And that's it – we go.'

On the drive back to Brook Green Wally said, 'Isn't there any way of making sure that bloody camera stays down?'

'Cut a wire or anything like that and they'll know it's sabotage – and make straight for the strong-room.'

'Your way still seems risky.'

'It's the only way, Wally.'

They drove in silence till the gilded turrets of Hammersmith Bridge came in sight, winking in the April sun.

Then Wally said, 'What will you do till the briefing?'

'Sleep.'

Wally looked at him. That was Tommy. Like a rock. Nothing shook him.

And sleep he did, lightly and dreamlessly, till four o'clock, when the bedside alarm woke him. He was meeting Jock at five to check the cutting equipment – and find out how it worked, since he was going to help Jock with part of the cutting.

After they'd checked the equipment he said, 'All I know about thermic boring is that it's fast, noiseless and vibration-free. Tell us a bit more – but keep it simple, eh?'

'It *is* simple,' Jock said. 'That's the nice thing. Start with the lance-holder.' He picked it up. 'It's just a handle really, with a hose connection and an oxygen valve – to control the gas flow – at this end. And an internal thread at the other end so you can screw in the packed lance.'

He put the holder down, picked up one of the ten-foot thermic lances.

'A piece of gas-barrel, that's all it is, tightly packed with steel rods throughout the whole length. You screw the lance into the holder, connect the holder by hose to your oxygen supply, pre-heat the point of the lance with an oxyacetylene blowlamp till it's bright red bloody hot – and you're ready to go. All you have to do is open the oxygen valve.'

'And then?'

'Combustion is promoted, as the instruction manual says, at the point of the lance, which generates so much heat it melts reinforced concrete like butter – in what's called an oxidation reaction.'

'And two hours is enough time?'

'The roof's fourteen inches thick, isn't it? A lance with a three-eighths bore can sink a hole a foot deep and two inches wide in reinforced concrete in less than a minute. And in hardened steel in two minutes. Now, you need an opening twenty inches square. So we mark it out in chalk, sink four holes along each side, then cut 'em together. Cutting takes longer – and we'll use lances with a three-quarter-inch bore for that. Plus time for screwing in new lances – they burn themselves up at the rate of six or seven feet for every foot bored.' He shrugged. 'But two hours should be enough.'

'What about all the melted steel and concrete—'

'The slag.'

'Won't it fall through into the strong-room?'

Jock shook his head. 'The pressure of the oxygen blows it up out of the hole in a stream of sparks. That's the only bit that's tricky – keeping the oxygen pressure right. A sudden rush of gas and the whole oxidation process will be blown cold.'

'What's that for?' Ashman pointed to something like a small metal table about a foot high with a hole in the centre.

'It's a shield to keep the sparks down – I've seen 'em shoot out thirty feet. Remember, it's about three thousand degrees Centigrade at the point of contact. Set your tarpaulin nicely alight, that would. You only get the real fireworks at the start, though – soon as the lance penetrates it all goes down to a quiet splutter and a steady stream of slag.'

'But what about when it goes through the last bit?'

'What do you mean?'

'When it cuts through the strong-room ceiling – the glare of the lance'll be picked up by the camera.'

Jock nodded. 'Then we don't cut the last bit till the bloody camera's out of action.'

'That means losing time.'

'Not more than about ten minutes if we only have a couple of inches to cut through.'

'Still won't leave us much time for the rest. We'll be working on a bloody knife-edge.' He stared at the cutting equipment for a moment, lost in thought. Then he shrugged. It was just another risk.

'Right,' he said, 'what will you want me to do?'

'Use the blowlamp to make the first cut – or kerf as we call it – between the holes. I'll follow close behind it with the lance.'

'Not too close,' said Ashman. 'I burn easily.'

That appealed to the little Jock. His face split into a sour grin. Or perhaps it was the gap in his teeth that turned it sour.

The dog stayed with her all the time – when she worked in the garden, when she came in for tea, when she went out into the garden again, when she sat down for dinner with Emily and her father. It sensed her worry, and put its head against her foot.

Emily chattered brightly through dinner, queening it like one of those suburban hostesses in the television ads. Beth and her father stayed silent apart from one or two polite responses, and neither listened. Beth hardly even noticed what she was eating. The only thing she noticed was the dog's head against her foot.

All her thoughts were with Ashman. She knew he'd be back at the house about this time, grabbing a bite to eat (if he remembered, there was a home-made quiche she'd made him) and preparing for the briefing. If only she could ring him. She was dying to ring him. Just to hear his voice, that's all. Just for a moment. But she knew she mustn't. She'd promised.

Emily's voice cut through her thoughts. 'You're not eating a *thing*, Elizabeth. I suppose that dumb-dumb's upset you.'

Dumb-dumb. The word they used as children.

Ashman was in the pinewood kitchen sipping a glass of wine and studying a large sketch-plan, about four feet by three, spread out on the table. He had drawn it himself for use at the briefing. Also on the table was an untouched hunk of bread and cheese, which he had forgotten about, as he had forgotten about the quiche.

He finished the wine, saw the carafe was empty and took it to the walk-in larder for a refill. That was when he saw the quiche – and remembered. But was he supposed to warm it up or eat it cold? What had she said? He'd forgotten. He took it back to the table and ate it cold. It went down very well with another glass of wine. The bread and cheese could go out for the birds. He wondered about another glass of wine, decided against it.

The phone rang. He picked up the receiver.

'Hallo?'

Silence.

'Hallo?'

Still silence. He said hallo twice more, then listened. All he could hear, faintly, as if far away, was the sound of uneven breathing.

He waited a little longer, then said softly, 'It's all right. I love you too.'

And put the phone down.

He always heard the things you never said. She went slowly back to the dining-room.

'Look at her,' Emily said. 'Tears in her eyes. *Now* what's the brute been saying?'

9

THE BRIEFING was to be held in the penthouse of a block of luxury flats in St John's Wood. The owners, a government junior minister and his monied wife, were taking a spring holiday in the Bahamas. They weren't connected with the resistance, but the caretaker was.

Ashman arrived first and set up a portable easel to display the sketch-plan, which he had pinned to a square of cardboard. The caretaker had already drawn the curtains and switched on the lights in the big sitting-room.

Then Jock, Paddy and Joseph arrived with Wally, who had picked them up in the Rover. This was the first time they had met one another.

A few minutes later the other handyman, Eddie, arrived. He lived in the area and had made his own way there. He was a big man, big as Ashman, who suspected that his mouth was even bigger. He spoke in a piping voice that seemed at odds with his big frame. Wally introduced him to the others.

Ashman watched them as they talked together. The little Jock was dour and silent. Spoke when he had something to say. But a hundred per cent reliable. Joseph was silent, too, and pale. Scared-looking. His imagination already getting ahead of him. Not so reliable. Maybe all right in a crisis, if he didn't have time to think. Anyway, Ashman liked him. The big Paddy was all right too. Flamboyant and full of Irish bull – but with the Irish guts to back it up. No problems there while he was off the drink. The only one he didn't care for was Eddie. Another talker, but a panic-merchant with it, he guessed. Still, that wasn't important. Any trouble and he'd get all the backing he wanted from Paddy and the hard little Jock.

He hadn't invited Arthur Walby or Ronnie Adams along since they'd already been briefed – and there was no need for them to meet the others. He was following the resistance rule of keeping the cell structure tight and separate.

After he'd given them what he thought was enough time to be easy with one another, he said, 'Right, gentlemen – business.'

He took the square of cardboard with the sketch-plan pinned to it and set it on the easel.

'Operation Dragon,' he said. 'Or the robbing of a burglar-proof bank.'

He pointed out the positions of the bank roof, the crane, the skip-loader, the skip – and the look-out in the street below. He got Jock to give a brief explanation of thermic cutting and boring, then himself explained about the security precautions and the closed-circuit camera scanning the strong-room. He said it would be put out of action – but he didn't say how.

'The critical bit's the timing, of course. We've got to get that hole cut in the roof by the time the camera goes down. And then we've got to clear fifty gold bars in less than half an hour – which'll be a sweat.'

He paused, looked around. He was going to add something about it all being for the cause, but he thought: Shit, if they don't believe in the cause by now a corny speech from me isn't going to turn anyone on. So all he said was, 'Any questions?'

Silence. Then the piping voice of Eddie. 'How can they fix a camera to go out of action for exactly half an hour?'

Ashman exchanged glances with Wally, who was beginning to smile. Someone had to ask it, but it would be Big Mouth.

'Not exactly half an hour, Eddie. At *least* half an hour. Probably nearer an hour. That's what our man on the inside says – and he's an expert. The camera's the least of our worries. Any other questions?'

Ashman's voice was casual and confident, like his manner. They might all be going on a picnic, Wally thought.

Joseph wanted to ask a question but was afraid he'd make a fool of himself. Paddy's soft Irish voice broke the silence. 'I take it once we've got the stuff aboard we'll be out of it like bloody hell – and no stoppin'.'

'Not even for the Pope.'

'Or an act of contrition?'

This brought a laugh from some of the others, and Ashman thought it a good note to end on, with the mood high and the tension relaxed.

They all piled into the big Rover and Wally drove them to the empty house that backed on to the house where the Leyland Clydesdale was parked. The mood was still high, maybe a little too high, a little too joky and excited. They were ready to laugh at anything – except for the Jock, who sat silent in the back, crushed between the big Paddy and the even bigger Eddie. Any moment now, Ashman though, they'll be chanting 'Easy, easy,' like those stupid bloody football fans. Well, let it ride. The mood'll change.

And it did, as soon as they got out of the car into the deserted street. There was a chill in the night air and the wind was playing with an old newspaper in the gutter, making a disproportionate amount of noise. The row of empty broken houses looked gloomy and forbidding.

'You take them in, Jock. You know the way. Tell the two men in the truck they can shove off. There'll be sandwiches and a couple of flasks of coffee in the driving cab, if anyone fancies something. I'll join you in ten minutes or so.'

Jock nodded and led the way into the house. Ashman got back into the car.

'Drop us at the corner of the next street, would you? There should be a Hillman Avenger there. Pull up behind it.'

The next street was the cul-de-sac with the building site on one side and the row of partly demolished houses on the other. As they pulled in behind the Avenger, Ashman said, 'Flash your lights once.' Then he said, 'Thanks. See you in a few hours, with a skipful of gold. Hopefully, as the jerks always say.'

He put out his hand and Wally shook it.

'Good luck, Tommy.'

Ashman got out and Wally drove off to report to a late meeting of OPSCOM. For him the Day of the Dragon was over. For Ashman it was just beginning.

A young man was sitting in the driving seat of the Avenger with the window down. He was the look-out. Beside him was a pretty girl. Ashman had never seen either of them before. He stopped by the driver's window and said, 'Hanger Lane around here, chum?'

'It's bloody miles away,' the young man said and handed him the car keys. Ashman went to the back of the car, unlocked the boot and took out what looked like a workman's tool-bag.

He gave the keys back to the young man and said, 'I'll be back in a few minutes. Why don't you give her a kiss?'

Then he walked down the street towards the entrance to the building site where he could see Arthur Walby waiting by the wicket let into the main gates. From now on everything was programmed. The key times were printed out in Ashman's mind as if by computer.

Walby was nervous and irritated. He could see no reason for another meeting, which had been sprung on him at the last moment.

'But we've *been* over everything – time and again,' he said when Ashman phoned him.

'Not quite.'

'What do you mean?'

'I'll tell you when I see you.'

'Can't you tell me now?'

'No.'

'But—'

'*Be* there, Walby,' he said and hung up. Walby had been shaken by the coldness in Ashman's voice. Walby was there.

'Well, what is it?' he said irritably.

Ashman looked up and down the street to make sure it was still deserted, then opened the tool-bag and took out a rifle with a folding metal stock.

'The Belgian FAL paratroop rifle,' he said extending the stock. 'Which, with modifications, is the same as the British SLR.'

'I'm not interested in guns,' Walby said.

'You will be in this one,' said Ashman. 'Especially if we shoot you with it.'

There was a short ugly silence. Walby could be heard swallowing.

'It'll go through a three-eighths steel plate from eighty yards – or a nine-inch brick wall. Go right through that little old cabin you sit in. And out the other side.'

Walby recovered his voice, though it sounded strange, as if partly strangled. 'What . . . are you talking about?'

'You,' said Ashman. 'I've been having bad thoughts about you.'

'About *me*?'

'Once we're back in the skip with all that loot, swinging up there halfway to heaven, we're in your hands. You could drop us anywhere. Straight into the arms of the police.'

'What do you mean? Why should I?'

'You tell me.'

'I've got the car – and twenty thousand to come.'

'What's that beside the reward? I reckon you'd be on at least a hundred grand. Which is known as a lot of money.'

Walby swallowed again, shook his head, almost wrung his hands. 'I wouldn't *do* it, I wouldn't do it – honest I wouldn't.'

'I don't believe you would, Walby – not even for a hundred gees.' The voice was warm and friendly, but Walby was beginning to think it sounded nicer cold. 'On the other hand, we don't want you being led into temptation. So on the return journey we'll be leaving a man on the roof with this.' Ashman patted the rifle, then put it back in the bag and took out something else. 'And this handy little attachment.'

He held up an image-intensifying night-sight and pointed up the street. 'See that car near the corner?'

Walby's weak eyes peered into the darkness. He nodded.

'Anybody in it?'

'I can only just see the bloody car.'

Ashman focused the night-sight. 'Now try.' He handed it to Walby.

'Christ,' Walby said excitedly, 'I can see . . . wait a minute – a fella. And a bird! And . . . yeah, he's *kissing* her!'

'Dirty bastard,' said Ashman.

'All right,' Ashman said when he got back to the car, 'you can leave her alone now.'

'I was beginning to like it,' said the young man.

Ashman got in the back and told the young man to drive him to the street where Wally had dropped the others.

'This'll do,' Ashman said when they were near the empty house. As he got out he handed the young man a miniature two-way radio.

'Don't use it unless you have to – if the police move you on or something like that. Then I'll tell you what to do. Otherwise keep radio silence. Your call sign's Fox. Mine's Dragon. OK?'

The young man nodded and drove off. He and the girl knew they were to watch a certain window in a certain building from 2 a.m. till the room lights went off, then on again. Then they were to flash the car's headlights twice. And that was all they knew. It was all they needed to know. They would be quite surprised when they read the morning papers.

Ashman set a small arc-light on the ground opposite each corner of the skip, switched them on and pointed them upwards. Almost immediately he saw the long boom of the tower crane swing out high above him, black and slender against the night sky.

Walby's crane was one of the latest with a closed-circuit television camera in the boom and a monitor in the cab – to give the driver a wide-angle view of the working area directly below the boom. From the window of the cab Walby saw the

109

sudden glow of light from one of the partly demolished houses below. He sent the boom swinging towards it, then watched till four lights appeared on his monitor. The rectangle they marked out was the dropping area. He lowered the crane's hawser straight into the middle of it.

Jock, Eddie and Joseph were already in the skip with the equipment. Ashman and Paddy were standing beside it, waiting for the hawser to come down. Then they grabbed it and fixed it to the skip chains.

Ashman climbed into the skip with the others and called to Paddy, 'Kill the lights.'

As the lights went out – the signal to Walby to start lifting – the chains tightened with a momentary screech. The four men grabbed the side of the skip. Then they were off the ground, swinging free, rocking gently as they rode up the sky and the night wind began to bite. No one spoke.

Above them and to one side Ashman could see the big black tower of the bank rising high and mighty, with the squat overhanging storey that contained the strong-room perched on top like a square hat. On the other side was the West End, a mass of glitter and lights – it was a wonder the sky didn't catch fire. He leaned over the side and saw the street lights below stretching away like a chain of stars upside down.

Suddenly they were level with the square black hat. Then they were over it. Then they stopped. Directly above them, almost within touching distance it seemed, was the steel lacework of the boom. And above that was the sky, thick with stars. Ashman reached into the tool-bag at his feet, took out a pair of night glasses and focused on the driver's cab. He could see Walby leaning forward to select a lever. He seemed to hesitate.

Just don't drop us is all I ask.

They were moving again, this time horizontally. Now they were right over the square hat – and starting to come down. Fast.

But not too fast, for Christ's sake, or we'll land with a bump that'll set off every vibration-alarm in the bloody building . . .

He needn't have worried. The gently swinging skip brushed the roof as lightly as a butterfly kiss from a girl's eyelashes, then settled. They'd landed.

He signalled the others to get out – he had devised a series of simple signals so that talk could be cut to a minimum. Another signal and they started unloading the equipment – he and Jock the oxygen cylinder, thermic lances and other gear, including the guns, Eddie and Joseph the tarpaulin, tubular scaffolding, and the block and tackle.

While Jock connected the oxygen cylinders together for a continuous supply, Eddie and Joseph helped Ashman put up a rectangular frame of tubular scaffolding with a central crossbar to take the block and tackle. It was placed, as nearly as could be judged, over the centre of the roof, which, according to plans of the building Ashman had studied, should correspond to the centre of the strong-room. It should also be clear of any pillars or steel bressummers.

A tarpaulin cover was thrown over the frame and lashed to it. Ashman marked out with chalk the twenty-inch square where the roof was to be cut, then went over to Jock, who was connecting the heavy-duty oxygen hose to one end of the lance-holder.

'OK?'

Jock nodded and screwed a lance into the other end of the holder. He put on a protective leather apron, goggles and breathing apparatus, picked up the lance and holder and went under the tarpaulin. Ashman moved to the parapet, signalling Eddie and Joseph to join him. He wanted them away from the working area. The fumes given off by thermic boring were poisonous – not that there was much danger in the open air. Still, why take chances that could be avoided? There were enough that couldn't – especially when it came to human beings.

He looked at the two men beside him. Big Eddie with the big mouth was apparently calm, except that he kept rubbing his chin like a man who's forgotten to shave. Trying to feel the bristles, feel his own masculinity. Bullshit. And Joseph, poor little old Joseph, was shivering like a bastard.

'Feeling cold?'

Joseph nodded, but it was nothing to do with cold, everything to do with fear. What the hell was he doing there anyway, standing on a roof in the middle of the night, robbing a bank? Him, the artist, the sensitive one. It was enough to make a cat laugh. It would've made *him* laugh if he hadn't been so shit scared. And that big dumb bastard asking if he was *cold*, for Christ's sake.

'Waiting makes everyone nervy,' the big man said.

He looked about as nervy as concrete. Still, maybe he wasn't so dumb. Joseph tried to stop shivering, but could not.

Then everyone's attention was focused on the crouching

figure of Jock as the blowlamp suddenly hissed and flamed. Jock adjusted the flame to a hard blue and held it to the point of the thermic lance. When it was glowing brilliant red he turned on the oxygen control valve – and the point of the lance burst into a white-hot glare as it lighted up at 3000 degrees Centigrade.

'Jesus,' Joseph breathed, and stopped shivering.

Jock pushed the lance down through a hole in the table-like shield till the brilliant white point touched the roof. A hurricane of sparks flew up against the underside of the shield, then subsided as the lance started to bite into the reinforced concrete, which melted like butter.

'Jesus,' Joseph breathed again.

For the first time he realized he was part of a process bigger than his own ego.

Two floors down, and almost directly below the point where Jock was turning concrete into a flow of liquid slag, Ronnie Adams sat in the control room playing chess with his partner, Pete, who was short and fat and suffered from high blood pressure. From time to time they flicked a glance at the bank of monitors on the wall opposite their desk.

Ronnie Adams was a much stronger player than Pete, but now, playing a line in the Modern Defence where White gives up his queen and two pawns for three minor pieces, he was losing.

'I thought that line was supposed to be good for White,' said Pete.

'Not the way I'm playing it.'

The trouble was he couldn't concentrate. Instead of weak squares and backward pawns all he saw when he looked at the board was the white-hot flare of a thermic lance liquefying all that steel and concrete over his head. Any moment he expected a lump of roof to come crashing down on to the ceiling of the control room. That was crazy, of course. The big one who looked like a fighter had explained the process, told him he wouldn't hear a thing: no vibration, no noise, no nothing. They'd cut through that roof like a wire through cheese – a neat square with a hole in the middle so they could haul it clear with a T-bar with folding arms and a block and tackle. As easy as that, the big man had said. He made everything sound easy. *Quod erat demonstrandum.*

'QED.'

'QE-what?' said Pete, thinking happily and incorrectly that Qe8 would win him another pawn.

Jock had bored the holes along the sides of the marked-out square. Then he signalled Ashman, who joined him under the tarpaulin. Ashman, who had already put on protective clothing, goggles and breathing apparatus, lit the blowlamp and started the first kerf between the holes. Once he had cut about three inches Jock followed with the thermic lance, moving the point slowly along the cut, just behind the incandescent spot made by the blowlamp. The concrete and steel started to liquefy, the slag flowed out in a molten stream.

Ronnie Adams was staring at the strong-room monitor. The camera, on its slow pan, showed the rows of deposit boxes lining the walls, broken at intervals by the massive steel doors to the vaults and walk-in safes. It also showed the central cage where the gold bullion was stored – under the camera's unsleeping eye.

The bars of the cage, which stretched from floor to ceiling, were made of a special carbon steel. The whole structure, including the steel entrance door, was electrified. The door had four separate locks, each with its built-in electronic alarm. And just outside the door, like an invisible mat, was an electro-magnetic field which, if stepped into, triggered off yet another alarm.

In the centre of the cage was a solid rectangle of 800 gold bars, laid out (at someone's whim, no doubt) like those expensive bricks at the Tate Gallery, but of course even more expensive – about thirty million pounds more.

And all the big man wanted, Ronnie Adams thought, was a mere fifty – about two million quid's worth. It seemed a modest enough portion of that lot. It was funny – it didn't seem real to him any more, all that gold. At first, when he joined the firm some months back, he couldn't take his eyes off it. The effect on him was almost sexual. But after a time, a surprisingly short time, he got used to it. And the more used to it he got the less real in some ways it became – or perhaps it simply lost its meaning . . . An inert yellow mass of . . . what? It seemed hard to think of it as gold – the magic metal that men schemed and sweated and died for.

He looked at the clock on the wall. It said one fifteen. Christ, would the time never go?

They had cut right round the marked-out square to a depth of twelve inches. 'Any more,' said Jock, 'and the bloody lot'll fall down.'

'That,' said Ashman, 'we can do without.'

Jock then bored a hole in the middle of the square to take the T-bar. Ashman had already folded back the arms of the T and tied a wire hawser to the iron loop at the other end of the bar. Now he passed the hawser through the pulley suspended from the overhead crossbar and lashed it to one of the uprights of the tubular frame.

'All we want now,' he said, 'is for the bloody camera to go down.'

'And we're laughing,' said the sour-faced Jock.

Ronnie Adams was the type that kept cool in a crisis but worried over little things. Now he was worrying because the tea-girl was late.

'Your move,' Pete said.

'I know.'

'What's the problem? Bishop takes bishop's practically forced.'

Ronnie Adams looked at the board, looked at the fat squat figure of Pete and played bishop takes bishop. Then he went back to his worries. But his lack of concentration was beginning to show.

'You all right?' Pete said.

'Think I've got a cold coming. Where's that bloody tea-girl? Cow's late.'

The clock on the wall said three minutes past two. Then the tea-girl put her head round the door and said, 'Tea up'.

'I'll get it,' said Ronnie Adams.

'No, it's my turn.'

'Toss you.'

Ronnie Adams spun a coin.

'Heads,' said Pete.

'Heads it is,' said Ronnie Adams, without showing him the coin. 'Lucky old Pete.'

He went out into the corridor where the tea-trolley was waiting.

The clock on the wall said five minutes past two.

*

On the roof all the preparatory work had been done. Now it was just a question of waiting. But waiting can be the hardest part. At least that was what Ronnie Adams was thinking as he sat in the control room staring at Pete, who was finishing his second cup of tea.

Why the hell didn't he *go*, the fat git?

'More tea, Pete?'

'Nah, I'll be peeing all night.'

Just once, just bloody once'll do, you fat slob.

The clock on the wall said 2.28.

At 2.31 Ashman was leaning out over the parapet looking down at the parked car in the street below and worrying in case the young man might be kissing the pretty girl. Not that he had anything in principle against young men kissing girls, but it had suddenly and unfortunately occurred to him that this young man might miss the signal from the control room if his mouth was enjoyably glued to the girl's. Ashman should have thought about that before. He had merely thought that a courting couple in a parked car were unlikely to arouse the suspicions of police or Tac Force patrols. He hadn't thought about sex raising its ugly head, and cocking the whole thing up. Till now. Till it was too bloody late.

At that moment the car's headlights flashed . . . Once. Twice. Ashman found himself sweating with relief. He turned to the others and gave the thumbs-up sign.

'For Operation Dragon,' Joseph muttered gloomily, 'Opportunity Knocks.'

Pete was urinating steadily and contentedly when the startling wail of the alarm came over the public address system (if a camera failed it automatically triggered an alarm). With a convulsive effort he cut himself off in mid-stream and ran back to the control room, zipping up his fly.

'Christ,' he shouted over the alarm, 'what's happened?'

Ronnie Adams, who was standing in the cubby-hole studying the wiring, shrugged and waited till Central Control switched the alarm off. Then he said, 'Couple of cameras gone down. Fuses probably. One blew last week, remember? I've rung Central Control. They're sending up a maintenance bod.'

'Christ,' said Pete, 'I nearly got a stricture or a rupture or something.'

*

Jock had already bored out the rest of the hole in the centre of the cut square. Eddie loosened the hawser holding the T-bar and Ashman pushed the bar down through the hole far enough to allow the folding arms to flip open. Then he pulled it up hard till he felt resistance. Then he nodded to Eddie, who tautened the hawser and made it fast again.

Jock started to cut the last two inches all round – which would leave the whole square hanging free. The others stood back and watched. It seemed to take for ever. Then Jock straightened up and switched off the oxygen supply. Ashman and the others joined him under the tarpaulin as he took off the goggles and breathing apparatus.

'Well, that's it,' he said.

Ashman leaned over and looked down at the cut square of ferro-concrete. Light was showing all round the edges. Light from the strong-room.

'Haul it clear.'

Jock, Eddie and Joseph undid the hawser and slowly pulled the square of concrete clear of the roof. Ashman grabbed it and pulled it to one side. Then they lowered it gently, an inch at a time, on to the roof. Then they gathered round the square hole and stared down.

Almost directly below them was a solid wall of gold.

No one spoke.

The maintenance engineer soon found and replaced the faulty fuse of the reception camera, and got it working again. But when he replaced the fuse of the strong-room camera nothing happened. It remained obdurately dead.

'Shit,' he said. 'I thought I was going to have it cushy for once.'

'What do think it is?' said Ronnie Adams.

'Dirty connection, loose wire, worn switchgear – you name it.'

'Here, I had a dirty connection last night,' said fat Pete, and nearly killed himself laughing.

Nobody else even smiled.

They had put a lightweight aluminium extension ladder down into the strong-room, where Ashman and Jock were lifting the gold bricks off the gold wall and putting them into a wire net slung from the block and tackle overhead. They worked fast, though fast is a relative term since a gold bar weighs about 27.5 pounds, and even a strong man needs two hands to shift it. Soon both men were sweating and breathing hard.

When they had loaded ten bars into the net Eddie and Joseph hauled it up and transferred the bars to the skip while Ashman and Jock started to load a second net.

Ashman checked his watch: ten minutes to the half-hour deadline – then they'd be living on borrowed time. Ten minutes to shift forty more bars of gold, haul them up to the roof and load them into the skip. It wasn't possible. He could feel the sweat from his armpits running down his flanks.

'Faster,' he said. 'We're running out of time.'

The little Jock grunted and tried to step up the pace, but he was working as fast as he could – deadline or no deadline.

Ronnie Adams looked at the clock on the wall. The half-hour was up. Were they clear? Or were they still in the strong-room? He had no way of knowing till the camera came alive – and then it'd be too late. All the big man said was that they *hoped* to be clear in half an hour – but the camera was to be kept out of action as long as possible.

Ronnie Adams leaned into the cubby-hole to watch the maintenance engineer – and saw he was now checking the central section of the wiring where the marked wire was located. Any minute now he'd find it. Test it. Tighten up the connection. And the camera would be alive.

'How's it going?'

The engineer sighed. 'A sweat – always is trying to trace a loose bloody wire. And that's what it is.'

'That one at the top – the yellow one looped round the green wire – the connection looks dirty.'

The engineer examined the wire, checked the connection and tightened it.

'Seems OK.'

'Bit warm in here, isn't it? Like a cup of tea?'

Six minutes past the deadline – and the last ten bars still to shift. Jock's face was the colour of lead, his breathing a wheezy gasp.

'I'll finish it,' Ashman said.

The little Jock shook his head. He couldn't speak; he didn't have the breath.

117

'That's an order. I've got another job for you.'

Jock just leaned against the gold wall, tried to get his breath back – and watched Ashman work even faster. It seemed incredible, but he picked up *two* bars together – half a hundredweight of solid gold – and took them to the net. Five times he did that. The last time, though, he was beginning to stagger – and his face was as livid as Jock's had been a few minutes earlier. Strength, Jock knew, came from will as much as muscle. Ashman seemed to have unending reserves of both.

At about the time that the last trawl of gold was being hauled on to the roof, the maintenance engineer was finishing the cup of tea and the cigarette thoughtfully provided by Ronnie Adams.

'Feel better for that,' he said. 'Much better.' And went back to work – on a different section of the wiring, Ronnie Adams was delighted to note.

Jock lined up the image-intensifying night-sight of the FAL paratroop rifle on the crane driver's cabin.

'Good view?'

'Practically see what he had for breakfast.'

'Remember, if he tries to drop us anywhere except between the four marking lights, shoot the bastard.'

'Dead,' said Jock.

Ashman went to the parapet and signalled with a torch into the darkness below. Almost immediately the four marking lights came on. He ran to the skip and climbed in. As he did so the chains were already tightening. There was a small scraping sound – and the skip was floating free. And all the tension that had built up over the past hours suddenly seemed to snap like a piano wire.

Joseph sat down on the gold. Eddie the Mouth started to laugh hysterically.

'We got lift-off,' he said. 'We got lift-off!'

'Shut up,' Ashman said savagely. He leaned over the side of the skip and looked down in the darkness as the four lights came up to meet them.

There was no doubt about Arthur Walby's skill, Ashman thought. The old maid put them down dead centre in the lights, near as dammit. Paddy only had to back the Leyland Clydesdale a few feet to pick up the skip.

As soon as the skip was hoist on to the loader Ashman

climbed out on to a specially built platform just behind the driving cab and said: 'OK, Paddy, let her go.'

Paddy, who already had the engine revving, let the clutch in with a jerk and floored the accelerator.

'Keep down,' Ashman shouted to Joseph and Eddie – and kept down himself as the big Leyland Clydesdale shot forward and smashed through the boarded-up front of the little house with a noise like a bomb. Bits of wood flew everywhere. The rest of the front wall crashed down behind them.

Paddy pulled the wheel over hard, and then they were racing up the street.

Ashman put his head close to the rear window opening – the glass had been taken out for better communication – and said, 'Give us a Magnum and an Uzi – and a couple of spare mags.'

Paddy handed the guns up one at a time, then the two staggered box-magazines for the Uzi. Ashman stuck the .44 Magnum in his belt and said to Joseph, who was still in the skip with Eddie, 'Can you handle a submachine-gun?'

Joseph recoiled as if he'd been bitten. 'I hate all violence,' he said.

'I can handle any gun,' said Eddie the Mouth.

Ashman leaned down and gave him the nine-millimetre Uzi and the two box-magazines. 'Just in case we run into trouble,' he said.

He straightened up and looked ahead over the roof of the driving cab. Though they weren't going fast, no more than forty-five, it felt fast in that echoing little street. The night wind blew hard in his face and hair, cold but exhilarating, and he felt good. For the first time that night he felt really good.

We've done it. Fifty bars of gold, two million quid. We've bloody done it.

Paddy took the corner with Irish exuberance, pulling the wheel hard over and putting his foot hard down. The sixteen-ton skip-loader leaned perilously into the bend, tyres squealing, engine revving, then straightened up as Paddy gave her an armful of opposite lock and backed off the accelerator.

That was when Ashman saw it: the Tac Force road-block at the junction ahead – two jeeps making a nose-to-nose chicane across the road; four troopers with Sterling submachine-guns in the jeeps; two more troopers, also carrying Sterlings, walking towards them and waving them down with torches. Behind the road-block, parked in a lay-by, was a radio jeep with an operator wearing a headset. Beside him was a young lieutenant.

As soon as Paddy saw the road-block and the advancing troopers he started to put his foot down again.

'No,' Ashman said quietly through the rear window. 'Slow right down as if you're going to stop – till I say go. Then bloody go.'

Paddy slowed down. The two troopers got nearer.

Had the alarm already gone out? Ashman wondered. Or was it just another snap check for stolen vehicles and false identity papers? Whichever it was there was only one answer.

The troopers were only a few yards away now.

'All right,' one of them called, 'that'll do.' And held up his hand.

'You didn't hear that,' Ashman breathed to Paddy, who drove slowly on, at little more than walking pace.

'Hey,' shouted the trooper, 'I said *stop*.'

The front of the skip-loader was almost level with them. Ashman leaned close to the rear window.

'Go, Paddy, go!'

The huge skip-loader leapt forward with a suddenness that almost jerked Ashman off his feet and a metallic snarl that rose to a scream as Paddy raced the engine to maximum revs.

Both troopers jumped back, but one was slow and the near-side wing caught him and flung him like a broken doll into the gutter.

The troopers in the road-block jeeps opened up with their Sterlings, but before they could concentrate their fire sixteen tons of screeching metal was on them, smashing their jeeps aside like Dinky toys and spinning their whole world into a blur of crazy angles.

They were through the road-block.

But the operator in the radio jeep parked in the lay-by was sending messages, and the young lieutenant was aiming coolly and carefully at Ashman with a long-barrelled Magnum .357.

'Get that bloody radio,' Ashman shouted to Eddie as the first bullet from the Magnum thumped into the driving cab a few inches from his shoulder.

But Eddie the Mouth was crouching on the floor of the skip blubbering with fear.

Ashman yanked out his own Magnum and took a pot shot at the jeep – but you'd be lucky to hit a house with a handgun at that range from the back of a swaying truck. And the darkness didn't help. He needed the Uzi, which was loaded with tracer shells.

'Give us that bloody gun,' he yelled to Joseph, who pulled the Uzi away from the still blubbering Eddie.

Then a strange thing happened. Instead of handing it to Ashman he leaned over the side of the skip, pushed the change lever forward to automatic – and squeezed the trigger.

A stream of tracers stitched the night with their golden thread – and poured into the jeep. Some must have hit the petrol tank because there was an explosion and the jeep disappeared in a sheet of flame.

The stream of bullets suddenly stopped. Joseph pulled at the trigger even harder.

'Bloody thing's jammed,' he shouted.

His eyes were shining, his pulse racing. Ashman knew the signs: he wanted more action – it had given him a real buzz. The timid ones were often like that, once they caught fire.

'Bloody thing's empty,' Ashman shouted back, 'not jammed.'

Joseph looked at the Uzi in surprise. He did not know its cyclic rate was 650 rounds a minute, which would empty even the big forty-round magazine in less than four seconds.

Ashman shouted to Paddy, 'First left and double back. We'll take the alternative route. And for Christ's sake slow up before we all go deaf or die of fright.'

He turned and grinned at Joseph, who grinned back.

'Come up here,' Ashman said, 'and bring the gun and those spare mags.'

Joseph climbed on to the platform beside him. Ashman took the Uzi, set the change lever to safety, pulled the empty box magazine out of the pistol grip and pushed home a new one. Then he gave the gun back to Joseph.

'Keep it on safety till you see trouble,' he said.

'Why are we doubling back?'

'Some of those radio messages will have got through and they'll be setting up more road-blocks the other way.'

'And this way?'

'Who knows? But at least we'll wrong-foot 'em for a bit.'

'Will there be . . . ?' Joseph hesitated. 'More fireworks?'

The rabbit had turned into a tiger. 'You *want* trouble?'

Joseph laughed. 'The mystery is, I'm not scared . . . Why?'

'It's in the nature of mysteries to be mysterious.'

And Joseph laughed again.

'Listen,' said Ashman, 'if we do run into another road-block, it won't be a couple of jeeps, it'll be Saracens and armoured trucks and Christ knows what.'

Joseph was silent a moment. The tiger had suddenly gone to sleep. Then he said, trying not to sound as shaky as he felt, 'What can we do against that sort of thing?'

The Dragon's glass-fibre container was lying on the platform up against the driving cab. Ashman touched it with his foot.

'This', he said, 'will stop anything from a light scout car to a main battle tank.'

'Jesus.' Joseph almost growled with excitement. Or maybe it was the old tiger waking up.

'What I'll want you to do is work the searchlight.'

He pointed to the light he had had fitted to the roof of the cab. 'It'll light up the target and help to blind the opposition.' He paused, looked at Joseph. 'And if I get clobbered you'll have to fire it.'

'Me? I've never even *seen* one before.'

'A kid could fire it.'

He picked up the sealed container.

'The Dragon,' he said. 'Or medium anti-tank missile. Made in the good old US of A. This container, by the way, is also the launch-tube. Very handy.'

He bent down and picked up a bulky-looking object which had been lying next to the container.

'This is the tracker. It's just a telescopic sight, a sensor device and some electronic gubbins we don't even need to understand.'

He fixed the tracker on top of the launch-tube, then fixed the front of the launch-tube to a tripod mounted on the cab roof. The other end of the tube rested on his shoulder.

'Now we're ready to go. All clear so far?'

Joseph nodded. 'What's the actual rocket like?'

'Bit like a cylinder in shape with a high-energy warhead with a rounded nose at one end and three curved tail-fins at the other. They flip open just after launch. Now – just in front of the fins are thirty pairs of little tiny rocket motors arranged in rows round the body. They not only propel the missile they guide it as well.'

'All by themselves?'

'With the help of electronic messages from the tracker. I'll show you the firing sequence and then you'll understand.'

'It sounds complicated.'

'It's dead simple. As soon as you see the target through the telescopic sight you launch the missile by pressing the firing button. And as long as you *keep* the sight on the target the tracker will do the rest.'

'And that's all there is to it?'

'Absolutely. The tracker will sense the position of the missile in relation to the line of flight, and send out signals to correct it if necessary. If it goes a bit off course, say, the sensor will pick out the right pair of rocket motors, fire them by electronic signal, and shove the old missile back on course. Clever, eh? And like I said, dead simple.'

Joseph drew in his breath sharply. 'Must be fantastic to see it actually *hit* something.'

From the skip came a moaning sound. Eddie. They'd forgotten about Eddie. He was huddled on the floor of the skip, shaking uncontrollably.

'I feel sick,' he called in his high-pitched voice. 'I feel sick. Let me off.'

'Be sick,' Ashman said. 'Puke your ring up.' He had a cold voice and at times, Joseph decided, a cold heart.

By now they had doubled back to one of the streets of derelict houses that were to be redeveloped into a brand-new estate around the brand-new burglar-proof bank they had just burgled. It was a long narrow street with no side-turnings, and seemed to go on for ever.

Joseph, who was looking ahead over the roof of the driving cab, froze. An armoured car had just turned into the street from the other end and was rumbling towards them. A bloody great Saracen.

'Look,' he said, 'a bloody great Saracen!'

Ashman looked. The Saracen was about 200 yards away. Perfect range. It put its headlights full on and sounded its siren. Its 7.62 mm machine-gun in the front turret fired a two-second warning burst into the air.

'Light her up,' Ashman said.

The searchlight came on, flooding the narrow street. Through the Dragon's telescopic sight the Saracen looked as big as a house. Ashman waited till she was about a hundred yards away, then pressed the firing button.

There was a sudden whoosh as the rocket left the launch-tube, then a brilliant white flash like sheet lightning that lit the whole street, then the reverberation of the explosion. The high-energy warhead had gone straight through into the driving compartment. The Saracen slewed off the road into one of the houses, bringing the whole front wall down. It was scheduled for demolition anyway.

'Go, Paddy,' said Ashman, and the big skip-loader accelerated away, skirting the wrecked Saracen.

Ashman looked at it carefully as they went by. It would be carrying a crew of two plus ten Tac Force troopers. It was difficult to know how many had been killed, but the blast and shock would have put everyone out of action for a time. Or so Ashman thought. But he was wrong. *Some* bugger wasn't out of action, because just as they were turning out of the street the ring-mounted rear gun started spraying them. The aim was wild, wild as hell – but at a rate of 700 to 900 rounds a minute you've always got chances.

Ashman was taking the tracker off the launch-tube when something hit him on the upper arm, just below the shoulder, and spun him round like a top. He swayed, then started to topple. He reached out with his good arm, grabbed at the tripod mounting and missed. His fingers clawed along the roof of the driving cab as he tried to stop himself falling.

Joseph saw him toppling at the edge of the platform – slowly, it seemed, like a great tree – and grabbed him. And tried to pull him back. For a long moment they swayed on the edge of the platform, locked together in a kind of suspended animation.

'Let go,' Ashman yelled. But Joseph held on – 130 pounds holding on to 200.

And together they fell.

Joseph remembered no more. His head hit the asphalt of the road and he was out cold.

Ashman didn't fall too badly. He fell like a thrown wrestler, rolling with the fall, rolling right into the gutter. He lay there a moment or two getting his breath back.

Then he saw three Tac Force troopers get out of a jeep and start running towards him. The street seemed suddenly full of troopers – or maybe it was just his dazed impression. He drew his Magnum .44 – probably the most powerful handgun in the world.

See how many of the bastards we can take with us.

He raised himself to one knee and took aim. Then something exploded inside his head and blackness came down like a blind. Somebody had hit him over the head from behind.

The next thing he remembered was waking up on a bunk in a cell in a Tac Force barracks. A sergeant and three troopers were staring down at him. They had taken his shoes off and put a rough bandage on the wound in his left arm, which was stiffening up and aching.

'Get up, scum,' the sergeant said softly.

Ashman moved slowly and uncertainly, as if still dazed.

'Don't hit me,' he said in a whining voice as he got off the bunk and cringed before them.

Then, suddenly, he straightened up in a blur of rapid movement and slashed the edge of his right hand across the sergeant's upper lip, at the base of the nose. The man's face split open like a ripe melon.

He managed to butt one of the others in the face and break someone's arm, but by then the cell was full of troopers and they beat him unconscious.

What the hell, he thought. They'd have done it anyway.

The next time he came round he was back on the bunk, and the place was still stiff with troopers. But there was one big change. It was no longer a sergeant staring down at him, but the top dog himself – Colonel bloody Cunningham.

'How are you?' Cunningham said politely, as if they were meeting over cocktails.

PART II
The Mousing Owl

10

The pain never stops. Even when the torturers stop the pain goes on. The world becomes pain. You live in it, you breathe it, you can never get away from it. It must have started when you were born; it won't end till you die – which will be soon, thank God. Because you cannot take any more pain. But you can, of course. There is no limit to it. And you won't die soon because pain changes everything – it even makes time stand still. Your screams become fixed in eternity, like flies in amber . . . You want to die. But you cannot. You cannot think, you cannot sleep, you cannot eat, you cannot die. You can only feel. Exquisitely. Excruciatingly. Through every tortured nerve-end.

Cunningham had warned him, had shown him the directive from the Home Secretary: 'You are to be handed over to our Special Interrogators.' He paused to give more weight to his next words: 'Special Interrogation is the official gloss for torture.'

Ashman's battered face remained expressionless. He said nothing. And would continue to say nothing, Cunningham thought. He had a distinct feeling that the Special Interrogators would fail for once, which gave him a perverse pleasure.

'You are the Falcon, aren't you?'

Ashman's black eyes continued to stare through him without expression.

'Well, it's obvious anyway – the whole planning and execution of the robbery. Brilliant. And successful – up to a point. The resistance got the gold; we got you. As well as the other one . . .' He glanced at a document. 'Lamont. Joseph Benedict Lamont. Small fry. We'll throw him back. Afterwards.'

Poor little Joseph, who'd tried to save him when he could have saved himself. The coward whose courage rose with his adrenalin. And fell with it. Who'd be terrified of torture, poor little sod.

'He knows nothing.'

Almost the first words Cunningham had heard him say.

'Well, well, so our prisoner has a tongue.'

Cunningham was sitting at his desk in the big office at Tac

Force headquarters. Ashman, manacled and still marked from the beating-up, was standing opposite him with an escort of four armed guards under the command of a Tac Force sergeant who looked more like a grossly obese gorilla in uniform and was known variously as Fat Charlie or Charles Arse'ole (his name was Charles Castle).

'Lamont', said Cunningham, 'is nothing. But you . . .'

He picked up the Home Secretary's directive. 'According to this order I should have handed you over to the Special Interrogators right away.' He smiled his crooked smile. 'I do not always obey orders – and if you answer one or two simple questions I shall not hand you over at all.' He paused again. He was a nice calculator of pauses. 'I shall simply tear this piece of paper up.'

He let it drop negligently to the desk, as if he regarded it as an irritating formality, a piece of red tape he wouldn't hesitate to cut.

The black eyes seemed to be staring through him again. No discernible reaction – always disappointing for an actor.

'I already know – from my own sources – quite a lot about the operation you've code-named Volcano.'

That should have surprised him, but there was still no re-action, not even a flicker from the black depths of his eyes.

'What I need to know is the exact date, the primary targets – most are obvious of course – and which army and air force groups have agreed to support you.'

Another calculated pause.

'I shall get this information anyway – again from my own sources. But I need it now. Time is of the essence.' A briefer pause. 'You've already had several hours. You now have five minutes.'

Ashman showed no sign of having heard. He didn't even look at the clock on the wall, just stared straight through Cunningham. He could have been carved from stone.

Finally Cunningham sighed and said, 'Take him away.'

After three weeks (or was it three years?) the torture was stopped on the orders of Cunningham (without reference to the Home Secretary). He feared Ashman might die. He needn't have worried. Within a week Ashman had recovered his strength sufficiently to kill a guard.

The automatic penalty for killing a guard was death. But

this was used merely as psychological torture: twice he was taken out to be shot, the entire ritual gone through with meticulous attention to detail; then, at the last moment, as the drum rolled and rifles came up to the ready, he was reprieved. In fact, these mock executions disturbed him in some ways more than physical torture. They entered his dreams, attacked his hopes.

He knew that two of the most important weapons in combating torture were hope and belief – religious, political or personal (as long as it was strong enough). Loyalty to a faith, a cause or friends and family gave a man something to cling to, something outside himself. Ashman had such a cause, and such friends. And he believed in them. Completely. He also had hope. Hope of rescue. It sustained him as strongly as his belief.

For he knew, as surely as he knew electric shocks to the genitals made you scream, that the resistance would try to rescue him. It would take a major operation, of course, which they couldn't afford now, with Volcano so close. But the rescue could easily be combined with Volcano – since Tac Force headquarters was one of the first targets.

This hope of rescue never left him; it obsessed him, occupied his waking thoughts, his dreams. Especially his dreams, which were really one dream with different details – variations on a dream.

Each time it started with him being taken out to be executed. And each time he was about to be rescued when something went wrong and he woke up in the cell. As long as he didn't wake up dead.

11

IT WAS THE THIRD TIME they'd come for him and taken him out into the execution yard and stood him against the wall. Another mock execution? The officer gave the command, raised his sword. The drum rolled, the carbines came up . . . He knew the scenario; it never changed.

Then he saw the grenade come curling over the wall, spinning in the air, twinkling in the sun, hitting the ground halfway between him and the firing squad. He dropped. The earth lifted, trembled, settled. There was a dim roar like the sound of the sea when you hold a shell to your ear, and he wondered if he'd been concussed.

There was dust all over him and he was coughing. There was dust everywhere. It was across the courtyard in a rising curtain that bellied out over everything and changed the dawn to dirty brown. From somewhere above came the hollow rap of automatic fire. The smoke and dust were terrible. He kept down, tense and flat against the earth. He could see two of the firing squad stretched out in grotesque attitudes. One had only half a head.

The chapel bell was still tolling, as it always did for executions, and above the firing, above all the noise, right up above the hanging plume of smoke from the grenade, it boomed madly on.

Then he saw men astride the wall above him, men he recognized, and he stood up and shouted to them. One of them jumped down and cut the cords binding him. Then they threw a rope down and he grabbed it and started clambering up – in slow motion, it seemed. Up to freedom. Up to heaven and the face of Christ. A voice (his own?) was shouting, 'Save me, save me,' as the face leaned out over him.

Not the face of Christ but the face of Charlie Arse'ole, who was shaking him awake and smiling at him with teeth that were black and decayed at the top, white and immaculate (and false) at the bottom.

If he closed his eyes, perhaps it would all go away and he'd be back in the dream . . . But nothing went away and he was back in the same old cell with two bunks, wooden table, wooden stools, plastic washbowl and latrine bucket.

And Fat Charlie was leaning over him and saying, 'What was it this time, girls or freedom? All we ever dream about in this place, eh?'

And behind Fat Charlie thin Joseph, and behind thin Joseph the usual armed guard lolling in the doorway with a Sterling submachine-gun slung from his shoulder.

Yes, the same cell he'd occupied for four weeks. It seemed a lifetime. It was a different world, a different regime with different values (a cigarette was above rubies and Charlie Arse-'ole was king). A different time-scale even, where minutes were hours and there was no night because the cell was always lit – and anyway, night was the time for interrogation under lights that were brighter than the morning sun now spreading across the floor like a slow stain.

'I said what was it this time, girls or freedom?'

'Girls,' he said and yawned.

Fat Charlie cocked his head like a puzzled dog. 'Girls? Didn't sound like girls. Sounded very strange.'

'She was a strange girl.'

'What do you mean?' Fat Charlie's eyes started to glisten with private dreams.

'You know – strange.'

But Fat Charlie didn't know. All men's dreams were strange. 'What was she like?'

Ashman suddenly tired of the game. 'Usual equipment – two arms, two legs, two tits.'

'Witty bastard.'

Fat Charlie was annoyed – his monkey face flushed with anger – and he turned to Joseph, looking for an excuse to pick on him since he hadn't the nerve to pick on Ashman. But Joseph lowered his eyes and turned away. He knew how dangerous it was to annoy the all-powerful, the princes and the prelates.

Fat Charlie grunted with frustration – then took out a cigarette. He couldn't have had a greater effect if he'd taken out a gun. But the powerful have many ways of punishing the powerless.

Ashman stared. Joseph stared. Neither had tasted tobacco for a fortnight, when they had shared half a cigarette. Tobacco was the only thing to stifle the almost constant hunger pains. It was a food in itself, and more than a food.

Fat Charlie lit the cigarette and breathed out a stream of smoke that gradually filled the cell with its tantalizing scent. Ashman's nostrils quivered like a dog's, saliva came up into his mouth.

'Got one for us?' He wondered if his voice was quivering too.

'For you? For *you*?' Fat Charlie turned to the guard in the doorway. 'The bastards'll be wanting nuts and brandy next.'

He sat at the table. Ashman sat himself on the opposite side, drawn by that short white magnet with the glowing end.

'Cigarettes for prisoners is strickly agin the rules,' Fat Charlie said, leaning forward and breathing beautiful cigarette-tainted breath over him. 'However, as is well known, to every rule there's an exception. Right?' He leaned forward again, breathing out more smoke. 'For them as co-operates. Right?'

'Right,' Ashman said, dizzy with the smoke. 'Right, right, *right*.' He could have killed the bastard. 'But you wouldn't believe it if I told you.'

'Wouldn't I?' said Fat Charlie, his eyes beginning to glisten again. He got up abruptly, crossed to the window and tossed the cigarette through the bars.

'Never smoke more'n half. Otherwise me mouth gets dry.'

'Poor bastard,' Ashman said.

Fat Charlie sat down, took out another cigarette and stood it carefully on end on the table top. It looked slim and white and beautiful against his short thick fingers. Ashman tried not to look at it.

'She was like the Prime Minister,' he said suddenly, and added, because he didn't know what else to say, 'In boots and braces.'

Fat Charlie stared at him, his cunning little eyes narrowing to slits. 'Here, you're having me on.'

Ashman shrugged. 'I said you'd never believe it.'

Fat Charlie thought about this but got nowhere. 'What else was she wearing?'

'Nothing.'

'Then what was the braces holding up?'

'Nothing.'

'Impossible,' Fat Charlie said. 'Braces has to hold something up. It's in the nature of braces.'

'It was a dream,' Ashman said as if to a child. 'All dreams are mad.'

'No, they ain't, they're very instructive.' He tapped the table with his fingers. 'I've made a deep study of dreams. And them braces stand for something, mark my words. But what? That's the point.'

He thumped the table in triumph. 'They're a symbol,' he said. 'The whip. They stand for the whip. She wanted you to beat her, right?'

'Wrong,' Ashman said gently.

Fat Charlie's face crumpled with disappointment, giving him the look of an elderly and obscene child. 'She *was* naked, though?'

'Naked as the moon.'

Fat Charlie described a woman's breasts with his hands. 'Nice, er . . . you know?'

There were words he thought indelicate in a sexual context that he would use freely as expletives.

'Like Kentish cooking apples,' said Ashman.

'Ah, I know what you mean,' said Fat Charlie. 'Firm. And smooth.' He drew his breath in sharply. 'I can just see 'em.' But all he could see in his mind's eye, however hard he tried, were cooking apples.

'Did you, er . . . ?' He hesitated before another indelicacy. 'Have relations with her?'

'Six times.'

'Good heavens.' Fat Charlie whistled under his breath.

'But she wanted more.'

'Get away!'

'She was . . .'

Ashman stopped. He didn't know what to say. He wasn't an imaginative man and it had been a tremendous effort to make up any kind of story as he went along. And this one was getting sillier and sillier . . . But all the time he was inching a hand towards that beautiful cigarette.

'She was – I don't know how to put it.'

'Like a fiend incarnate?'

'That's it. You've got it.' Ashman made another inch towards the cigarette, then had a sudden inspiration. 'The kind that used to appear to men in their dreams – and draw the vital juices out of their loins.'

'My Gawd,' Fat Charlie said in an awed whisper.

'They had a special name for them in the olden days . . .' His hand was almost touching the cigarette. 'Joseph's the educated one, he'll know it.'

Joseph said nothing. He wanted to stay out of it, uninvolved and if possible unnoticed – a fly on the wall. Fat Charlie turned to him.

'Come on, then, out with it.'

Joseph hesitated, still reluctant. 'I think he means a succubus.'

'That's it,' Ashman said, picking up the cigarette. 'She was a succubus.'

134

'Here,' said Fat Charlie, 'that sounds dirty.'

Ashman got up and went and lay on his bunk. Joseph moved as far away from him as he could. He wanted no part of what was coming.

'And then what happened?' Fat Charlie said, niggled by a vague feeling he'd been cheated.

Ashman was staring at the cigarette. He had concentrated his whole mind on getting it. And now he didn't want it – not with the same hunger anyway. It was the achievement that mattered. He wasn't given to self-analysis but he knew it was vital in his present situation to win any kind of victory, by any means.

'Then what happened?'

'What?' He was miles away.

'In the dream. What happened in the dream?'

'Oh, that,' said Ashman. 'Well, I remember yelling out.'

' "Save me." That's what you was yelling out. "Save me." '

Ashman grinned. 'And you did, Charlie, didn't you? You woke me up. Otherwise Christ knows what would've happened.'

There was a long silence while Fat Charlie tried to work out all the implications. Then his face went a dirty shade of red. 'You bastard,' he shouted, 'you bin having me on.' He jumped up. 'Gimme that cigarette.'

He started forward, then stopped as Ashman rolled off the bunk and on to his feet in a fluid movement unexpected in a big man.

Fat Charlie turned to the guard. 'Take it away from him.'

The guard brought up the muzzle of the Sterling and made a production of pulling back the cocking handle and moving the change lever to semi-automatic. Then he cleared his throat and took a couple of steps towards Ashman, who stayed by his bunk, shoulders hunched and very still, like a big cat about to spring.

Joseph shrank back against the wall, as if trying to bury himself in it.

'Come on,' said the guard, 'hand it over.'

'And if I don't – you going to shoot me?'

The guard, who was young, looked at him, at the ridges of scar-tissue above the eyes, the flattened nose, the big hands and big shoulders – and hesitated. Ashman would have made a lot of men hesitate. He had the confidence of a man who could handle himself in any company.

'Clobber the bastard,' Fat Charlie said. 'With the butt end.'

The young guard slipped the change lever to safety and stepped back. 'We're not allowed to. Colonel Cunningham's orders. I just remembered.'

He had also just remembered that Ashman had already killed a guard.

'Orders, my arse,' said Fat Charlie. 'You're scared, that's what you are.'

'I am not,' the guard said with the dignity of youth. 'Well, no more'n anyone else.'

The mounting tension and the incongruity of two men trying to frighten a man they were frightened of themselves was too much for Joseph. He made a strangled sound between a giggle and a cough. Fat Charlie, glad of the excuse, turned on him.

'What are *you* laughing at?'

'Nothing. It's my nerves. All artists are nervous.' Joseph started to shake with fright. He shook easily.

'Where's that bloody guitar?'

He knew where the guitar was: in its case under Joseph's bunk. And he knew what it meant to Joseph. Without it part of him would die.

'Suppose it got broke?'

'No, please . . . C-C-Colonel Cunningham said – he said if I p-played at the concert, he said—'

'I know what he said.' Fat Charlie showed all his bad teeth in a smile. 'But supposing it got broke accidental?'

'No, please . . . p-p-please.'

'Or your hands – suppose they got broke?'

He took a step towards the cowering Joseph, but Ashman was between them before he could take another. The big man could certainly move. Fat Charlie grinned and backed off. Honour had been satisfied – he knew that frightening Joseph was one way of getting at Ashman. The trouble was though, Ashman had a nasty habit of getting back.

Fat Charlie crossed to the door of the cell, hesitated on the threshold, then made a mistake – unable to resist one last dig.

'If you'd played square with me,' he said, 'I'd have played square with you.'

He took some postcards from his breast-pocket, held them up. 'Naked birds,' he said. 'In colour. Doing strange things. Very sexual in colour. How about that?'

'How about dropping dead?' said Ashman.

'In the fullness of time, my friend. But not in approximately twenty-four hours – when *you* are due for the chop.'

'How do you know? Maybe you'll choke on a fishbone or get knifed over a whore.'

'I don't eat fish—'

'And you don't go with whores, only postcards. What about a natural death, though? Being eaten alive by some disease. What's natural about that?'

Fat Charlie revealed his bad teeth again. 'Then you're lucky, aren't you? Think of all the aggro we'll be saving you, when we take you out and stand you up against the wall.'

Ashman got up and stared at Fat Charlie, frowning slightly.

'What are you staring at?'

'You always that colour?'

'What colour?' He turned to the guard. 'I got a funny colour?'

'No,' said the guard. 'Well, no more'n usual.'

'I remember a man up in the Peak District when I was a kid, travelling with the circus. He came into our tent – my mother read hands, she was a gypsy – and he had that colour. Big handsome laughing fella, full of life. And he had that colour. And my mother wouldn't read his hand. She just looked at him and said: "Go away." And when we came back to that place about a year later we passed a funeral on its way to the graveyard. And it was his, the big laughing fella's. A whole year dying, he was. Nobody knew what of. They said cancer but they didn't really know. That's a thing to have, isn't it? Growing in your guts, creeping through your blood—'

'Shut up!' Fat Charlie yelled. 'Shut your dirty rotten mouth.'

He swung away like a shying horse and went quickly out of the cell, followed by the guard and a metallic crash as the door slammed shut.

Ashman laughed. Joseph was still shaking. He tried to control his limbs but it was no good. They felt like leaves in the wind.

Ashman tossed the cigarette up in the air and caught it. 'Shall we smoke it now – or later?'

Then he saw Joseph was shaking, and said, 'Now.' And took a match from his shoe, struck it on the wall and lit the cigarette. Then he passed it to Joseph, who took a deep drag and felt his nerves calming, the wind dying. He almost hated Ashman for his generosity. No one likes to be obliged. He took another drag and handed the cigarette back.

They shared it in silence, each taking a drag, then passing it to the other in a ritual that was almost religious in its solemnity and discipline. After half the cigarette had been smoked it was carefully doused and hidden behind one of the bunk supports where the wood had warped and come away from the wall.

'Was that story about the circus true?'

Ashman nodded.

'And your mother really was a gypsy? Yes, you've got that dark look. What about your father?'

'He was with the circus, too. Trapeze artist. Till he fell and broke his back.'

'Did it kill him?'

'After a couple of years in a wheelchair he got a gun and blew his brains out. What's the weather doing?'

Joseph climbed up one of the bunk supports and leaned out to peer through the barred window. 'Blue sky. Going to be a nice day.' He dropped to the floor. 'What the hell,' he said. 'What difference would it make to us if it snowed?'

He got out the guitar and picked a melancholy chord or two, then related them to a melodic line, filling the cell with liquid sounds that soothed him and drew him into a gentler world. Then the door was flung open and Fat Charlie came in with four of the biggest guards, used to escort prisoners to interrogation. Joseph shrank back and clutched the guitar as a woman might clutch a child.

Ashman was on his feet, shoulders hunched, ready to fight. He always fought when they came to take him for interrogation. He never went quietly.

Fat Charlie looked at him and laughed.

'Your lucky day,' he said. 'The date of your execution's been made *sine die*. Which means there's no set date. So any day could be your last.'

If he was hoping for a reaction he was disappointed. Ashman merely stretched out on the bunk and ignored him.

'Course, some people couldn't stand not knowin' – the suspense'd kill 'em.'

He must have thought this funny because he grinned hugely, showing all his enormous teeth, the beautiful white lower set and the black stumps above them.

Ashman looked at him, shook his head. 'When are you going to get the upper set?'

This got Fat Charlie on the raw. 'How the hell do I know?' he said angrily. 'They promised 'em months ago. Bloody months.'

'I expect', Ashman said sympathetically, 'they're waiting for the second gorilla to die.'

12

THE WOUND STILL WEPT. Not very much. In fact, very little. But it never actually stopped. And it would go on, she knew, deep inside her, till he was free again and back with her again. Only then would it stop weeping.

After the first paralysing shock she thought she was going to die, bleed to death from grief. Then a sort of numbness set in, damping down the pain, driving it inwards, and cutting her off from reality. The world went on around her but she felt separated from it, rocking in her cradle of distress.

She was young, though, and young nerves recover. She recovered: began to take part in life again, listen again, speak again, even smile again, on the outside, though the wound still wept on the inside.

She knew something had happened when she woke up that morning and found he wasn't there beside her. He said he'd be back between four and five.

The night before she'd got back late from Epsom, after midnight, and sat in the warm yellow kitchen, drinking Chianti and trying to find music on the radio and not think about him. But she couldn't find any music she liked or could even put up with, and she couldn't stop thinking about him. The whole place felt empty of life like a tomb, and everything reminded her of him.

Wherever she looked she saw something he'd made with his own hands. She remembered the hours of work, and the loving patience that had gone into the work. He liked the smell of wood, the feel of wood. He said it was warm to the touch. He said different woods felt different. He said the wide-grained woods were softer and rougher. He said coniferous trees were soft and if you sawed through one you could tell if there'd been a hot summer from the thickness of the sapwood rings. He said . . .

She sat there in the yellow kitchen, her head and her heart full of him.

It was nearly two o'clock when she got to bed, and she had drunk too much Chianti. She lay on her back in the dark, staring up at the ceiling and listening to the sound of traffic in Shepherd's Bush Road. It never stopped – half the world drove down the Shepherd's Bush Road at night. The whiteness of the ceiling glimmered through the darkness and advanced on her, then retreated. A car door slammed in the street outside. A girl laughed. Her high heels tapped the pavement.

Only another couple of hours. She might as well stay awake. She fell asleep, fitfully, and woke at daybreak, startled by a wild knocking – then realized it was the beating of her heart. The place beside her was empty. And cold.

She got up, dressed in jeans and a sweater, went down to the kitchen and made tea and waited for the seven o'clock news. It was just after half-past six, a grey morning, chilly and overcast with rain in the air. You could smell the rain.

She didn't want to switch on for the news. She didn't want to know. She suddenly hated the little radio standing on the dresser – as if it were somehow to blame. In the old days didn't they kill a messenger who brought bad news?

She couldn't bear to switch on, and she couldn't bear not to. It was the first item, of course, and the biggest. The Falcon, the Falcon, the Falcon . . . Every time the newsreader said the name it went through her like a knife.

The news had hardly finished when there was a knock at the door. It was Wally. He had Hannah, the Jewish girl, with him; they were living together now.

He stared at her a moment, then said, 'We'll get him out.' Then he took her in his arms, held her close and said again, 'We'll get him out.'

'That's all I wanted to hear,' she said and led them through to the kitchen.

'Let's have some coffee.'

'Shall I make it?' Hannah said, smiling. She had a sweet voice and a warm dark Jewish handsomeness. Beth liked her.

Wally sat at the table and took out a cigarette. 'May I?' She noticed his hand shook when he lit it.

'You know about the forty-eight-hour rule,' he said.

The rule was the same as the wartime resistance rule: if an agent were captured, all his field contacts would change their addresses immediately. The agent would try to give nothing away for at least forty-eight hours to give them a chance to get clear. The Gestapo knew about this rule, and the worst torture often came in those first forty-eight hours.

'I'm not moving,' Beth said.

'Look,' Wally said, 'it's the rule, and it's my job to see it's carried out.'

'Are *you* moving?'

'We're not discussing me.'

'Are you, though?'

'Never mind what the other bloody fools are doing,' Wally shouted in sudden anger. 'I want to know what you're doing.'

'I'm staying.'

'Of course she is,' Hannah said, serving the coffee. 'It's their home. It has memories. Besides, staying's an act of faith.'

'Will you please keep out of this?' Wally said.

'No,' Hannah said sweetly.

'Beth,' said Wally, 'we ask people if they get caught to try and give us forty-eight hours. It's like a bargain. We should keep our side. It's not fair to expect them—'

'He'll never talk, and you know it,' said Beth. 'They'll kill him before he'll talk.'

She felt tears springing in her eyes but blinked them away. She wasn't going to cry like some soppy girl, not in front of other people anyway.

'Beth,' he said, almost sighing, 'if we make rules we've got to stick to them.'

'Are *you* moving?' she said.

'Of course I am.'

'He keeps telling himself,' said Hannah. 'Keeps telling me too. Neither of us believes him.'

'You realize I'll have to report your refusal to OPSCOM,' he said, though he knew he'd do no such thing.

'I want to see OPSCOM – or Hudson. Yes, Hudson would be better. I want him to put me on the active service list – and I want to know what he's doing about Tommy.'

On the way home in the car Wally said, 'There are times when I hate bloody women.'

'I wish you wouldn't drive so fast when you're in a temper,' Hannah said.

'I am not in a temper,' he said, putting his foot down to catch the lights as they went from amber to red.

'You went through a red light,' she said.

'It wasn't red,' he said. 'Well, maybe a bit on the pink side.'

After a while she said in her sweet voice, 'Do you hate me, too?'

'You more than anyone,' he said.

*

General Hudson agreed immediately to see Beth.

'Do anything I can to help,' he told Wally. 'Nice girl. Met her a couple of times with Tommy. Very nice.'

'And very beautiful,' Wally said coldly. Hudson had something of a reputation as a womanizer.

They met at a hotel on Seaford Head a few days later. It was cold and grey, with a blustery on-shore wind that blew her hair about and brought white horses out on the sullen sea.

As she got out of the Mini she saw there were already two cars parked in the forecourt of the hotel, a big Jaguar and just behind it a fuel-injected Ford Granada. Two men looking remarkably like bodyguards were sitting in the Jaguar. Two other hard-looking men got out of the Granada and came towards her. They didn't say anything but escorted her into the hotel lounge, then left.

Hudson was there alone, staring out of the window at the grey sky and the white-topped waves. He turned as she came in, stepped forward and took both her hands in his. His movements were precise, military. Though she had met him before, it was some time ago and she hardly remembered him. He looked slim and fit for a man in his late fifties, with grey hair and grey, rather cold-looking eyes, though they were smiling at her now. He was wearing an expensively tailored lightweight grey suit, a white shirt, a dark blue knitted tie and hand-lasted suede shoes.

Piss-elegant, Tommy would have said.

She felt windblown and scruffy in her old denims with her hair all over the place. A perfect sight. Hudson thought so too, but literally.

'I realize how you must feel,' he said as they sat at a table by the window, 'and I can assure you we will do everything we can.'

'What does that mean?'

'I cannot discuss our plans in detail, but action will be taken in the near future.'

'How near is the future?'

He turned and stared out of the window. There was a heavy swell, making the sea even more sullen-looking.

'Again I cannot give precise information. All I can say is that we are planning a major operation – and the rescue would be part of that operation.'

143

He had this careful yet opaque way of speaking, like a politician phrasing a promise he knows he cannot keep.

He'll promise you everything, give you nothing and take that away before you get it, Tommy once said.

'I want to go back on active service.'

'At the moment we're keeping a low profile, as they say.' He smiled coldly at the sea. 'The lull before the storm.'

'What about all the preparations? There must be something I can do.'

He contemplated the sullen sea and the sky, then turned and looked at her.

'How would you like to be my personal assistant?' he said.

'What would that involve?'

'It would mean living in with the rest of my personal staff and travelling with me wherever I go. I travel a great deal.'

He paused, but went on staring at her. 'You would at least be party to much of our planning – and actually be involved in some of it.'

He paused again. 'I need someone. I would like it very much if you accepted.'

He smiled at her.

My God, he fancies me, the old stoat . . . Well, he can have me – any way he wants – if it'll get my Tommy out of that place.

13

ASHMAN lay on his back in the lower bunk, eyes closed, hands clasped across his chest – like one of those carved figures on a tomb, Joseph thought, feeling the guilt rise in him like bile in his throat.

'I can't help it,' he said suddenly.

'Can't help what?'

'Being a coward.'

Ashman didn't answer at once, and Joseph thought he was asleep. Then he said, 'You shot that jeep up when Big Eddie was paralysed with fright. And you got caught trying to save me. Some coward.'

'Reflex actions – no time to think. But *these* bastards didn't even have to *touch* me and I talked. Coughed the lot.'

'Coughed nothing. The code-name of a cut-out, the phone number of an answering service, maybe the address of that flat in St John's Wood – which belongs to a government minister anyway. And a few other bits of useless information.'

'You don't understand. Even if I'd had information that *wasn't* useless I'd have talked.'

He picked up the guitar, struck a flourish of chords. 'Introducing Joseph Benedict Lamont, gutless wonder of the western world . . . They thought their livers were white till they looked at mine.'

He put the guitar down on the table, pushed it away from him like a disconsolate child and looked across at Ashman – to find Ashman looking across at him. He was propped up on one elbow, his face pale from prison and cratered like the moon, his deep-set eyes almost hidden by the scar-tissue of his brows. A disconcerting sight. Even more disconcerting was his stillness, which was like the stillness of an animal about to spring.

'Why do you watch me?' he said.

'Watch you?' said Joseph, suddenly frightened. 'I don't watch you, I observe you – as an artist. Observation, someone said, is the basis of all art.'

He waited for a response but Ashman went on looking at him without expression or movement.

'Tomorrow you die. Or the next day. Or whenever the bastards take you out and shoot you. And me, I'm just . . . observing your reactions.'

'To what?' Ashman lay back and closed his eyes again.

'To death, man, death – one of the facts of life. And don't tell me you don't feel anything because you must – deep down you must. In that place where it's always three o'clock in the morning and the truth stares at you with eyes of stone. You must feel something there.'

Ashman opened his eyes, sat up. 'I feel afraid.'

'Of death?'

'I don't know.'

'Anyway, it's preferable to torture surely.'

Ashman shook his head. 'While you're being tortured you're alive.'

Now it was Joseph who shook his head. 'I don't understand you . . . And I don't believe you're afraid. You're not really afraid.'

Ashman got up and went over to the window. Looking up through it he could see a patch of blue sky and the top of a chestnut-tree heavy with white candles. Sometimes, when he was weak after torture, his mind hazy and wandering, he imagined he was one of those white candles, high above the ground, blowing in the wind, living and dying with the seasons, detached from mankind.

'No,' he said, 'I'm not afraid. I know I'm not afraid . . . I just feel afraid. If you know what I mean.'

Joseph grunted. 'Not so simple, is it? Not that I ever thought it was. That's what I can't stand about that formula. You know, the right amount of adrenalin in the bloodstream equals courage, too much equals cowardice. The fight or flight reaction. What price courage if it all boils down to a bloody formula and a bit of adrenalin? I don't believe it. There's more to it than that.'

'Who cares? The whole world doesn't depend on it.'

'Whose world are you talking about? I remember in Mexico City once, when I was giving some concerts, I was dragged to the bullfight to see some boy-wonder. I hate boy-wonders and I don't go much on bullfights, either, but this girl I had—'

'He loves them,' Ashman said, looking up at the ceiling, as if trying to see into Cunningham's office.

'I know. Even got a pair of banderillas hanging on the wall. Made in Birmingham, no doubt.'

'No,' said Ashman, 'they're real.'

'Anyway, I'm suspicious of foreigners who are dotty on the

bullfight. I mean, it's all right for the Spanish and the Mexicans, but other people – especially the English . . .' He shook his head. 'There's something wrong with them. Where was I?'

'This girl you had,' said Ashman.

'She was mad on it. But, then, she was Mexican. Or part Mexican, part Indian. Murderous bloody mixture. And she murdered me all right . . . Wish she was here now, though . . . Just to see a woman again . . . I bet if one passed by, below that window, even though I couldn't see her, I'd pick up her scent. Like those dogs that smell out explosives.' He stopped, took a deep breath. 'When did you last have a woman?'

'What happened to the boy-wonder?'

'Oh, he turned out to be a smash-flop. Couldn't keep his feet still when the bull charged. He'd try to stand there like a statue, but at the last moment his feet would jitter away. The crowd laughed. So he tried again. And again. Same thing. And the crowd went on laughing . . . That's me, you know, me all over. My heart wants to stay in one place but my feet run away . . . Every time. The trouble is—'

'Finish the story, amigo. What did he do?'

'Oh, in the end he tried a kneeling pass – so his rotten feet *couldn't* run away. But you could see he was thinking more about the crowd than about the bull, and he misjudged the line of the charge and it got him. And there he was riding round the ring with a horn in his chest . . . Finito.'

'He stopped them laughing though,' Ashman said and stretched out on the bunk again.

'Yeah, but what a price.' Joseph shook his head. 'Know what Scott Fitzgerald said? Show me a hero and I'll write you a tragedy.'

14

COLONEL CUNNINGHAM stood at the window of his second-floor office watching the helicopter come in. The control tower had identified it, cleared it and given it permission to land. It sailed prettily over the fifteen-foot wall with its sinister-looking watch towers, and made for the landing pad almost directly below him. Apart from the pilot it contained the Home Secretary and his personal bodyguard.

If it crashed it would kill two skilled and useful men and one who was largely useless. It seemed immoral to hope that it would crash.

'I am immoral,' Cunningham said.

'I beg your pardon?' said Bishop, who was collating a file of agents' and informers' reports.

The helicopter landed without incident.

'Caramba,' said Cunningham. 'Foiled again.'

The Home Secretary was dismounting from the helicopter. Three tufts of grey hair standing up on his dome-like head made him look vaguely like Mr Pecksniff.

'The Home Secretary is here. Go down and meet him, Peter.'

Bishop crossed to the double doors, hesitated and turned. 'I hear on the grapevine that he's angry with us.'

'Then use your undoubted influence to smooth him down.'

'Yes, sir,' he said, wondering what Cunningham meant. It was often difficult to know whether he was speaking literally or freely. It was one of the more disturbing things about him. Bishop closed the double doors gently – Cunningham hated noise – and gave Miss Skinner a rictus grin as he hurried through the outer office. Her long sad empty face came alive, and for a moment she blossomed.

Cunningham picked up the file of reports from Bishop's desk and took it to his own desk. He studied it till he heard quick heavy footsteps crossing the outer office. The double doors were pushed open and the Home Secretary came in like a galleon in full sail, head thrown haughtily back, his topcoat, which he wore over his shoulders like a cloak, flowing out behind him. He was a big man and tried to give an impression of dignity and power, but the Pecksniffian hair, pear-shaped figure and feminine hips were against him. Usually he had the bogus bonhomie of an unfrocked priest. Now he was angry.

Cunningham indicated a chair, but he remained standing.

'I take it you know why I'm here?'

'No, Minister,' Cunningham said, knowing quite well.

'Information has come to me that the prisoner Ashman, known as the Falcon, has been taken off Special Interrogation.' He paused. 'Without my permission.'

'Your information, wherever it came from, is correct.'

'You have an explanation, I take it?' His plump pale face was flushed with anger.

'I didn't want him to die, Minister, I wanted him to talk.'

'Prisoners who die under interrogation instead of talking have only themselves to blame.'

'This prisoner is too important to kill by torture.'

'Special Interrogation. Please keep to the official phraseology.' The Home Secretary felt he had put Cunningham in his place, and sat down.

'All right,' said Cunningham in a grating voice. 'He's too important to kill by official phraseology.'

He shouldn't have said it, of course, it would put the Minister's back up even more, but he had never suffered fools gladly – he'd sooner deal with villains. At least you could guess what a villain was likely to do.

He controlled his irritation and smiled, trying to take the heat out of the situation and wondering where the hell the girl with the coffee and cakes was. The Minister had a passion for cake; it had a calming effect.

As if in answer to a prayer there was a knock on the door and Miss Skinner came in with coffee and sticky buns.

'No buns for me,' said the Home Secretary, 'I'm on a diet.' He was always on a diet.

'One can't hurt,' Cunningham said soothingly. 'Cream and sugar for the Minister. Black for me.'

Miss Skinner handed him a memo. He read it, screwed it up and threw it in the wastepaper basket. The Home Secretary bit into a sticky bun and felt immediately better.

'Tell Peter to take the prisoner's statement and bring it to me when it's typed,' Cunningham said.

Miss Skinner nodded and went out. Cunningham waited till the Home Secretary had finished his bun.

'The trouble is, Minister, we need specific information from Ashman – and we need it quickly.'

'What information?' The Minister bit into another bun, telling himself this was definitely the last.

Cunningham hesitated. He had to be careful how he gave the Minister facts he had so far kept from him. He didn't want to offend or frighten him too much. His behaviour, like most people's, was founded on vanity and fear. At that moment, well into his second bun, he was relatively calm.

Cunningham sketched in the background to Operation Volcano. 'The objective, of course, is a coup d'état.'

'The resistance are always planning a coup d'état.' The Minister's tone was contemptuous.

'This time we have evidence they'll go through with it. Or try to.'

'When?'

'I don't know. But soon. Very soon. The one who does know of course is Ashman.'

'Then he must be made to talk – if we have to tear the flesh off his bones.' The Home Secretary carefully licked the sugar off his fingers.

'That might kill him; it wouldn't make him talk. Anyway, there's no time.' He paused to make sure the next words went home. 'We might only have a few days left.'

The Home Secretary stopped licking his fingers. 'Good God, man, you talk as if the bloody coup might succeed.'

Cunningham shrugged. 'That depends how much support they have in the services.'

'Are you serious?'

'Never more so.'

The Home Secretary thought for what was for him a long time. 'What would happen to people like . . . you and me?'

Cunningham shrugged again. 'Who knows? But coups are usually accompanied, or even preceded by assassination.'

The Home Secretary jumped up out of his chair as if he'd been bitten.

'Relax, Minister. Six of my best men have followed you everywhere for the past month.'

'*I* haven't seen them.'

'You weren't meant to. But you may have noticed the men repairing the road outside your house, the council workers pruning the trees, the telephone engineers . . . All crack shots with orders to shoot first and apologize afterwards.'

'Ah, well, that's more like it,' the Home Secretary said, and sat down again. 'Not that I've ever doubted your efficiency. I said to Percy only the other day – I call him Percy, you know, except in front of inferiors – "That Cunningham's a first-class man," I said. "First class." '

He felt definitely better. Another bun and he'd feel better still.

'With me,' he explained as he took the bun, 'a crisis goes straight to the balls or straight to the belly. I have to have food or a woman.'

Bishop came in with a typed statement which he gave to Cunningham, who started reading it.

'When do you want to see the prisoner, sir?'

'When I've looked through this. I'll buzz.'

Bishop left and there was another brief silence while Cunningham read and the Minister ate.

'You know, Colonel,' the Minister said between mouthfuls, 'I still think the only way to deal with Ashman—'

'He dreams of rescue; he wants to live,' Cunningham said, buried in the report.

'Is to put him back on Special Interrogation.'

' "While you're being tortured you're alive . . ." Remarkable. Excrucior ergo sum. "I suffer therefore I exist." Almost a motto for the Party – or perhaps the people . . . "I know I'm not afraid. I just feel afraid." And you think you can break him down with nothing but brutality?' He grunted. 'You're fighting out of your class.'

'But what's the alternative?'

'Excuse me,' Cunningham said, flicking down the desk intercom switch. 'I'll see him now, Peter.' He switched off and turned to the Home Secretary. 'This might be the alternative.'

Bishop came in followed by Fat Charlie and two armed guards.

Between them was Joseph.

His hands were manacled in front of him; he kept his eyes on the ground.

Fat Charlie barked orders at prisoner and escort till they were drawn up in front of Cunningham's desk.

Cunningham signalled to the guards to leave, then studied Joseph, who kept his eyes lowered. Bishop drew up a chair behind him, sat down and opened a shorthand notebook. The Home Secretary also stared at Joseph, curiously and with distaste. He could almost smell the man's fear, and it disturbed him. He took another sticky bun.

'Is there anything you can add to this report?' Cunningham's voice was like dry ice; its coldness seemed to burn.

'No, sir,' Joseph said without looking up.

'Look at me when you speak.'

Joseph raised his eyes. 'I've . . . put down everything I can remember.'

'Good. I want to see you walk out of here a free man. And a healthy one.'

There was a silence broken only by the occasional scratch of Bishop's pen as he took notes. Then Cunningham spoke, slowly and deliberately, his eyes holding Joseph's eyes.

'You've never experienced Special Interrogation.'

'I'm doing all I can,' Joseph said, starting to shake. 'I swear. On my life.'

'On your life is right.'

'I listen to every word he says, every beat of his heart. I can't do more, I can't. Not if you kill me I can't.'

'I'm merely reminding you of the situation.'

'I can't question him direct, can I? It'll make him suspicious – you said so yourself. Be clever, you said, be subtle. Subtle. How can you be subtle with a rock? And if he suspected he'd kill me. Like he killed that guard.' By now he was shaking all over. 'Remember how he killed that guard? I saw it. Broke his neck like a stick. Only louder – you've no idea how loud it was—'

Cunningham pushed a glass of brandy into his hands. 'Drink this and calm down . . . Besides, he wouldn't hurt you; he likes you.'

'Oh yes, he likes me. Oh no, he wouldn't hurt me. Just kill me. Like he'd kill anyone on your side. No hard feelings, just kill them—'

'Drink it,' Cunningham said sharply.

Joseph drank the brandy down. It took his breath away. His throat seemed to burn, then the burning turned to a warmth that spread down to his belly, then right through him. The shaking subsided. Cunningham handed him a cigarette and lit it.

'Does he ever talk of relatives or friends?'

Joseph dragged deeply on the cigarette and felt slightly giddy.

'He mentions his mother and father sometimes. But they're dead. And there's a cousin in the States he hasn't heard from for a long time . . . Oh yes, and a younger brother – Jack. He

152

was very fond of Jack and often talks of him. But he's dead too, I think.'

Cunningham nodded. 'We executed him eighteen months ago. Anyone else?'

Joseph frowned in thought. 'No-o, I don't think so ...'

'All right,' Cunningham said, and nodded to Bishop, who tapped Joseph on the shoulder. They crossed to the door, then Joseph stopped and turned.

'He did mention some girl – just a passing reference though. Didn't seem important.'

'I knew he had a girl once but I thought ... m'm ... I wonder ...' He paused, lost in thought. Then he said, 'Sit down.' Joseph sat down. Cunningham stared at him till he began to feel uncomfortable.

'Ever had a woman?'

'What?'

'A woman.'

'Of course.'

'One never knows with artists. Do you ever talk about women with him?'

'Well, yes. You know how it is in prison.'

'Then start a conversation about women – and draw him out. Gradually, almost by accident.'

'Draw him out? How?'

'That's up to you; you're the artist. But make a job of it. Find out anything you can about this girl. Anything. Who she is, where she is, what she looks like – anything. But find out.'

He dismissed him with a wave of his hand.

Joseph got up. 'I'll do my best.'

'Lamont,' Cunningham said softly, 'I don't want your best, I want results. And if you value yourself you'll get them.'

Joseph nodded and swallowed. Cunningham turned to Bishop. 'Tell the escort to take him away.'

When they were alone again the Home Secretary said, 'Don't tell me Ashman trusts that little stool-pigeon.'

'That little stool-pigeon', said Cunningham, 'was only captured because he tried to save Ashman – and nearly succeeded, what's more. Ashman trusts him all right.'

'I take it the cell's bugged?'

'If you bug cells the prisoners always find out – then nobody talks.'

That sounded too simple an explanation, but the Home

Secretary didn't think it worth an argument. 'So you've got a stool-pigeon working for you. What else?'

Cunningham didn't answer immediately. He had no intention of revealing his plans, especially as they were not yet complete. 'There's an old army saying that the difference between rape and seduction is salesmanship.' He smiled a brief crooked smile. 'Well, we've tried the rape. Now let's try the salesmanship.'

'You mean you're going to make him an offer he can't refuse?' His voice was dry and sarcastic.

'Something like that.'

The Home Secretary glanced at his watch, got up. 'Well, it's your responsibility. I hope you know what you're doing.'

He waited for a comment, but Cunningham had nothing to say.

'We hear things, you know, Colonel. You'd be surprised what we hear from loyal members of the Party – about your anti-government jokes and remarks, your flouting of regulations, your dislike of our methods. Oh, we hear things all right.'

'What big ears you have.'

'Not that it bothers us – as long as you continue to be successful. But one bad mistake, Colonel, one slip-up . . .'

He shook his head.

There was a knock on the door and Bishop came in.

'The Prime Minister's on the line for the Home Secretary. Will you take it here, sir, or in the other office?'

'In here.'

'He sounds rather angry, sir,' Bishop said as he went out.

'I wonder what's wrong?' the Home Secretary said worriedly. 'He's supposed to be having his massage at this time in the morning.'

'Perhaps they rubbed him up the wrong way.'

The phone rang and the Home Secretary picked it up.

'Morning, Percy . . . What?' He put a hand over the mouthpiece. 'He knows about Volcano.'

'He should,' said Cunningham. 'I sent him a memo this morning.'

'And what the bloody hell are we doing about it?'

'Tell him all service chiefs have been warned . . .'

'All service chiefs have been warned, Percy,' the Minister said into the phone.

'And troops and Tac Force units are guarding public utilities, key ports and airports, radio and television stations.'

The Home Secretary repeated Cunningham's words like a worried parrot.

'Tell him there are full details of the precautions in the four-page appendix to the original memo – if he'd only taken the trouble to read it.'

'You'll find full details of the precautions in the appendix, Percy, if only you'd—' He caught himself in time. 'If only you can find the time to read it ... Yes, Percy – yes, of course – I'll tell him ...'

He put the phone down with a relieved sigh. 'He wants you at Thursday's meeting of the Inner Cabinet Committee – and he wants to see me now.'

He started to cross to the double doors, then stopped. 'Oh yes – and he wonders why it's taking so long to break Ashman down. If I were you, I'd get a move on.' He smiled. 'Percy won't care if you use rape, seduction, salesmanship or magic spells – but you'd better get a result. And soon.'

He went out quickly through the double doors, leaving them open.

Cunningham lit a cigarette and stared at the over-large portrait of Jeremy Percival Twistington-Smith as was ... But he didn't see it; he was thinking. He had a lot to think about.

One of the outside phones rang and he picked it up. It was Reg Hacker. He had located the underground press – in a disused warehouse on the Isle of Dogs, near the India and Millwall docks.

'Do you want us to raid the place?'

'No. Just keep it under observation, and set up a camera somewhere discreet—'

'To take pix of anyone who goes in or out. That's already in hand, Colonel.'

'Good. I'll be down later for a look round. Meet me in the Feathers about six. And Reg – well done.'

As he hung up he saw Bishop standing in the doorway. He wondered how much he had heard.

'Would you like the doors shut, Colonel?'

'No, it doesn't matter now. Leave them.'

Bishop turned to go.

'Peter.'

'Sir?'

'Are you a loyal member of the Party?'

155

Bishop, taken aback for a moment, said, 'Why, yes – of course.'

'I thought you were,' Cunningham said and rode back on his chair and blew a long stream of smoke at the ceiling.

If only he could hate Ashman, maybe he wouldn't hate himself so much. Oh yes he would, of course he would. You bet he would . . . It had all started with the girl (everything starts with girls). If only he hadn't wanted to impress that dummy of a girl who didn't care for him anyway . . . He wished he'd never met her. He wished he'd never heard of the resistance. He wished he were dead.

'What's the matter?'

'Nothing,' he said. 'I'm hungry.'

'Low-calorie diet. It takes the fight out of you. One of the things they copied from the Russians.'

'Hasn't taken any fight out of you. Only out of me.' He shook his head. 'Not that they have to starve me . . . Just threaten me – and I'll tell 'em all I know.'

'You've told 'em what you know. They won't bother you any more.'

'Is that a fact? Well, let me tell you—'

But whatever he was going to say was cut short by the clatter of a helicopter overhead. He looked up through the barred window.

'Looks like Cunningham's personal helicopter,' he said. 'Let's hope the bastard crashes.'

'Amen.'

Cunningham looked down at the countryside flowing away beneath him. Wood and heathland. Then over Farnham . . . Guildford . . . Chertsey on the left with the brown Thames looking silver . . . More or less following the A3 with the strips of ribbon development getting longer and uglier as they neared London. Soon he was looking down at the great huddle of Wandsworth with Battersea heliport jutting out into the Thames like a matchbox. It grew bigger as you approached, he thought. But not much. He hated flying.

A waiting car took him through Kennington to Bermondsey, then across Tower Bridge. He left the car near Cable Street and walked to the pub off the West India Dock Road where he was to meet Reg Hacker. He was wearing the clothes he wore

156

the last time they met: jeans and an old army battledress blouse.

Hacker was waiting for him and said there was little to report. They had taken pictures of people entering and leaving the warehouse, but none seemed important. He pointed out the location of the warehouse on a street map.

'Hell of a great rambling place. I've done a reccy but I didn't go too close in case I was spotted. Trouble is, it's connected to other warehouses – a whole complex, like a rabbit warren. Must be a dozen ways of coming and going. And you couldn't surround it – it's got a sixty-foot river frontage.'

Cunningham nodded. 'Let's take a look while it's still light.'

The disused warehouse stood in a street of disused warehouses pierced by narrow alleys and backed by a wharf and the river. The whole place had a derelict air. Most of the London docks, apart from Tilbury, had been closed down years before because they lost money.

The street was empty. Their footsteps echoed as they strolled past the warehouse. Cunningham stopped near the entrance to light a cigarette. He could see a tarnished and damaged brass plate, but the only part of the legend he could make out was: '. . . Pachman Ltd . . . Importers & . . .' Below it was a much smaller and newer plate with the legend: 'H. Dobson & Son, General Printers.'

'Where's your OP?' he said as they moved on.

'We're coming to it,' Hacker said.

The observation post was on the first floor of some empty commercial offices on the other side of the street, about forty yards away. They went up rickety stairs to the office where Special Branch men worked round the clock in shifts of three which changed every four hours. One man operated the tripod-mounted camera, which could take infra-red lenses for night shots, another kept watch with field glasses, the third manned a newly installed telephone and radio-telephone. From the big sash window, which was partly screened by ragged net curtains, there was a good oblique view of the warehouse entrance.

Cunningham watched through the field glasses for a few minutes and saw a man go in. He didn't recognize him.

'Is there a back way out of here?' he said.

'Follow me,' said Hacker.

They came out into an alleyway and went down one of the narrow streets that led to the wharf, which was deserted and silent except for the slap of water against its sides, the creak of crane cables swinging in the wind and the crying of a gull. The cranes reminded Cunningham of gibbets. A couple of malefactors ought to be hanging from them in chains.

They stood in the lee of a rotting barge, out of the wind, studying the back of the warehouse that held the underground press. It looked like all the other warehouses.

'See what you mean. Impossible to cordon off without being spotted,' Cunningham said.

'When are we going to raid it?'

'I don't know,' Cunningham said slowly. 'When something happens.'

'Like what?'

'Like a big fish swimming into the net.'

'And how long are you prepared to wait?'

'That's another thing I don't know.' Cunningham smiled wryly. 'There's quite a lot I don't know.'

By now the docks were blued over with dusk and the wind backed to the north-east and freshened. Cunningham shivered. 'Let's go.'

15

CUNNINGHAM was more preoccupied than usual during dinner, wondering whether the Home Secretary had found out, from his own sources, about the underground press. If he had, he would almost certainly blow the gaff at the meeting of the Inner Cabinet Committee.

After dinner he went into the study to ring him, but the phone rang as he was reaching for it. It was Amarantha.

'You *are* coming to my party, aren't you?'

'Your party?'

'Don't say you've forgotten my birthday again.'

'Of course not, flower.'

'Lying sod.'

'I've just bought you a beautiful etching by a new young artist.'

'Ah, you're too sweet.'

'I might be late though. There's a meeting of the Politburo this evening.'

'My parties go on for ever.'

'I know. How old are you, flower?'

'Twenty-nine. Same as I've been for the last three years – and will go on being till it sounds ridiculous . . . It doesn't sound ridiculous, does it?'

'Of course not, flower. Especially in the dark.'

'*Don't* come to my party. I won't *have* you at my party. I won't let you *in*.'

'See you later, flower.'

'But don't bring that etching.'

'No?'

'It's probably the same one you gave me last year when you forgot my birthday. Then you took it back a couple of weeks later, saying it wasn't suitable, and gave me a bottle of perfume instead. The wrong perfume.'

Cunningham sighed and made placatory noises. He wasn't very good at birthdays. He put the phone down, waited a moment and reached for it again. And again it rang before he could pick it up.

The caller asked for a number that didn't exist. The number was also an identifying code for Frank Wilson. Cunningham was surprised. Their next meeting wasn't due for a week.

'What is it?'

'Can I see you?'

'When?'

'Now.'

'I have a meeting with the PM in an hour.'

'This won't take five minutes.'

'Where are you?'

'In a phone box near Pelham Street.'

'I'll pick you up by South Ken station in twenty minutes. I'll be in a red Alfa GTV.'

Nice and convenient – only a few minutes away from where the Home Secretary lived in Egerton Gardens. He rang him and offered him a lift to the Prime Minister's London home. 'There's something important I want to tell you.'

'Can't it wait till the meeting?'

'It's for your ears alone, Harry.'

He thought that would do the trick, and it did.

Then he rang the chief of his bodyguard. 'Take the Jag and meet me at the Home Secretary's place in half an hour. I'll be taking the Alfa.'

He wasn't supposed to travel anywhere alone, but the bodyguard had long ago given up arguing.

Frank Wilson was leaning against the wall outside the station, hunched in an old raincoat, as Cunningham pulled into the kerb. He got in quickly and they drove to an empty meter bay in a side-street.

'I've been co-opted to the executive council. Just heard. Going to my first meeting in the morning.'

'Where?'

'Don't know. They'll ring me tonight to give me the time and place where a car will pick me up.'

He paused and lit a cigarette – to calm his nerves, Cunningham presumed. He could sense the man's suppressed excitement.

'It's a very special meeting. All the regional commanders of the resistance will be there.'

He blew a stream of smoke against the windscreen, then turned and looked at Cunningham.

'We're going to be briefed about Volcano,' he said. 'Date, main targets, everything.'

When he picked the Home Secretary up his mind was still racing with what Frank Wilson had told him, and he kept silent apart from a brief greeting.

As the Alfa pulled into Brompton Road traffic and the big Jag with the four bodyguards eased in behind it, the Home Secretary said, 'Well?'

Cunningham looked at him blankly. 'I beg your pardon?'

'I thought you had something important to tell me.'

'Ah yes – yes, of course.' Cunningham's mind was momentarily as blank as his expression.

'For my ears alone, you said.'

Then Cunningham remembered. 'We've found the underground press.'

'Really? Splendid. Splendid.' The Home Secretary tried to look surprised, but it was plain to Cunningham that he already knew.

'I don't want it mentioned at the meeting, though.'

'Why not?' The Home Secretary would have loved to boast about it, and make it sound as if he'd had a hand in it – as supervising genius.

'You know what some of the others are like,' Cunningham said. 'They might go off at half-cock – and insist on raiding the place right away. Whereas if we wait a while we might catch a really big fish. Anyway, we can't *lose* anything by waiting.'

'I suppose you're right,' the Home Secretary said, disappointed.

'They haven't all got your judgement, you know, Harry.'

Outside office hours they were on first-name terms, and Cunningham believed in flattery. The more blatant the better with most people. The flush of pleasure on the Home Secretary's plump cheeks confirmed his belief.

The Prime Minister's London home, where the meeting was to be held, was in the shabbiest part of North Kensington. He used 10 Downing Street only for full cabinet meetings and other official business. He liked to keep his image as the friend of the working class. He also wanted to stay in touch with what he called the grass roots.

He had chosen, or rather Cunningham had chosen for him, a cul-de-sac of sixteen crumbling terraced cottages, once occupied by railway workers.

The middle four on one side had been converted into a single residence for the Prime Minister and his wife. The two cottages on either side were occupied by his chauffeur, personal secretary, masseuse, doctor and servants.

The eight cottages opposite had been converted into a Tac Force barracks with a flat roof constructed as a helicopter pad. They housed what Cunningham called the Praetorian Guard. The street was constantly patrolled by police and was said to be more difficult to get into than the Kremlin.

The Prime Minister had not called a meeting of the full committee but only of the two ministers concerned with internal security – the Home Secretary and the Minister of Defence – plus the exofficio members, Field Marshal Sir Arthur Rawley, Chief of Defence Staff, and Cunningham.

They met in the first-floor sitting-room, which was large and comfortable. The Prime Minister (or perhaps his wife) had a chintzy taste reflected in soft furnishings more suited (Cunningham thought) to a country cottage.

The meeting opened with Cunningham being questioned by Rawley and the Defence Minister about Operation Volcano. Cunningham dealt with the questions easily, answering some, parrying others, but always with an air of candour and charm.

Smooth bastard, thought the Home Secretary.

The Prime Minister, looking calm and boyish, puffed at his pipe in silence. Then he said, 'Your memo mentioned the possibility of assassination. Are there any grounds for that?'

'We had a report, admittedly hearsay, that General Hudson said after a recent meeting of OPSCOM that if the bomb that went off in Hitler's headquarters had actually killed him the rest of the so-called July Plot would have succeeded—'

'Are those bloody terrorists comparing the Prime Minister to Hitler?' said the Home Secretary.

'Do be quiet, Harry,' the Prime Minister said mildly. 'Go on, Colonel.'

'The July Plot, or Operation Valkyrie as the Germans called it, would have succeeded because, with Hitler dead, a number of army commanders would have joined the plotters – and taken over the country. Of course, I'm over-simplifying. Valkyrie could still have succeeded if certain generals hadn't lost their nerve. But that's another story. As it turned out, the success of the coup d'état depended on the assassination of the head of state.'

'And you assume that's what the resistance have in mind?'

'I'm sure it's what Hudson has in mind.'

The Prime Minister puffed at his pipe again. 'Then you must also assume that certain of our army commanders have already been approached by the resistance.'

'I know they have. But Field Marshal Rawley can give you more details about that.'

Rawley, slim, trim, hard-faced and cold-eyed, looking younger than his sixty-odd years, said: 'One of my bright young staff officers, a lieutenant-colonel, was approached at various social functions over a period of some months.'

'By whom?'

'A number of people – men and women. It all started very lightly, I gather – veiled in jokey references to the resistance and so on.'

'Call them terrorists,' said the Home Secretary. 'Terrorists.'

'Please,' said the Prime Minister, still mild, 'save it for the newspapers. No propaganda here.'

'But gradually', Rawley went on, 'the references got more open and less jokey. He was a bright lad and went along with them. Eventually it was put to him that he might like to join the resistance. He agreed – and went straight to his commanding officer, who immediately contacted me. That was his mistake.'

'I beg your pardon?' the Prime Minister said, taking the pipe out of his mouth.

'Two days later he fell down a lift shaft – from the ninth floor – and was killed.'

'You think he was pushed?'

Rawley shrugged.

'That would mean the resistance have infiltrated the Ministry of Defence?'

'I'm quite sure they have,' said Rawley. 'Not more than one or two perhaps – but that could be enough.'

'I find this hard to believe,' said the Home Secretary. 'Very hard.'

'So do I, I must say,' said the Defence Minister.

'Three other senior officers', said Rawley, 'who reported being approached by the resistance also met with fatal accidents. I have the details here if you'd like to study them some time.'

He took a file from a briefcase and handed it to the Prime Minister, who opened it, glanced at it for a minute or two, then put it on an occasional table.

'And you've not been able to trace any of the people who approached these officers?'

'No,' Cunningham broke in. 'And it wasn't for lack of trying. I've had Special Branch and Tac Force Intelligence working on it for months. They all gave false names – and no doubt carried false identity cards.'

'But presumably they did win over a number of other senior officers?'

'Presumably. In fact, almost certainly.'

Rawley nodded his agreement.

'No doubt', said Cunningham, 'they picked their prospective candidates very carefully and, as far as we know, made only three mistakes. So they didn't win 'em all. But how many *did* they win? That's the question.'

'You're just guessing,' said the Defence Minister.

'That's right,' said Cunningham. 'I'm guessing.'

'M'm . . .' The Prime Minister was puffing at his pipe again. 'I wish I'd known about this before.'

'Prime Minister,' said Cunningham, 'I assure you there's not much point in reporting things till a pattern begins to emerge. You get so many false leads it becomes confusing – and can sound like scare-mongering.'

The Prime Minister nodded. 'I suppose you're right.' He had great faith in Cunningham. 'And at least you've taken precautions.' He smiled. 'I have at last found time to read your appendix. Most impressive. Especially the extra bodyguards – I hadn't even noticed them. *Very* discreet.'

'That was the idea, Prime Minister – to increase their effectiveness.'

The Prime Minister nodded again, discovered his pipe had gone out, turned up the flame of his gas lighter and relit it. 'Tell me,' he said, disappearing in a cloud of fire and smoke like God on Sinai, 'has the resistance much support among the community at large?'

'Of course not,' said the Home Secretary.

'I'm afraid it has,' said Cunningham.

'A few fascists maybe,' said the Home Secretary. 'A bunch of misfits and malcontents. And some of those Mensa cranks, no doubt.' He had applied for membership of Mensa as a young man but failed the intelligence tests.

'No underground group can exist without support from the local population,' said Cunningham.

'I agree,' said the Prime Minister. 'But what can we do about it?'

'In general,' said Cunningham, 'the key to anti-terrorism is intelligence. But you need an overall central security department with a computerised information and records centre.'

'Then set it up,' the Prime Minister said to the Home Secretary. 'Money no object.'

'What shall we call it?' said the Home Secretary, who always had an irrelevant question to ask.

'Why not the State Central Security Department?' said the Defence Minister.

'Or even the Reichssicherheitshauptamt, as the Nazis called it,' said Cunningham with a faint cold smile.

'I thought you'd get the point,' said the Defence Minister with a smile equally faint and cold.

'What are you talking about?' said the Home Secretary.

'A joke,' said Cunningham. 'Forget it.'

'Anything else we can do?' said the Prime Minister.

'Try to get the population on our side,' said Cunningham.

'Are you saying they aren't?' The wide boyish eyes had the cold gleam of steel.

'A section of them obviously aren't.'

He was suddenly aware that the Defence Minister was staring at him.

'And what should we do about them?'

Be nice to them for a change, Cunningham nearly said. But he knew he must be careful (and resist the temptation to provoke the hostility he could feel around him).

'The long-term solution, I suppose, is to persuade them.'

'I agree,' the Defence Minister said – to Cunningham's surprise. 'Persuade them.'

'Or weed them out – and stamp them out,' said the Prime Minister. Now the voice was cold and steely too.

'That, of course,' said Cunningham smoothly, 'would be the final solution.'

He heard the soft laugh of the Defence Minister. He was a handsome man, thin-faced with grey streaks in a head of dark hair and brilliant black eyes. Perhaps he was of foreign or of Jewish extraction, as his name, Leo Pachman, suggested. For a reason Cunningham couldn't explain he felt uneasy about him. He was something of an enigma, with a mind that was far more subtle and complex than might be supposed from the rigid conventionality of his left-wing views.

'You know what I think?' said the Home Secretary. But his thoughts were to be lost to the waiting world – a maid had entered with a refreshment trolley. On it were two bottles of

Pol Roger in ice-buckets and two platters of smoked salmon sandwiches. The Home Secretary looked at the food and drink and forgot what he was going to say. He was too busy calculating more important things.

It wasn't long after dinner and the others weren't big eaters. None was likely to have more than one or two of the sandwiches – unless Cunningham, whose eating habits were irregular, hadn't had dinner. In which case the bastard might scoff the lot. He sighed with relief when he saw Cunningham wave the sandwiches away. It momentarily mollified his dislike of him.

Cunningham was irritated by the interruption – he wanted to get to Amarantha's party and later, he hoped, to her bed. While the maid was in the room, pouring the champagne and handing round the sandwiches, there was the usual rhubarb of small talk, which Cunningham took no part in. He was not interested in small talk except with certain women, when it acquired sexual overtones and even at its silliest acted like a soothing verbal massage.

After the first round of drinks and sandwiches the Prime Minister signalled the maid to leave. For a minute or two there was silence as the company ate and drank. Then the Prime Minister, who had put his glass of champagne aside after a token sip – food and drink meant little to him – said in his cold voice, 'The crucial points about Volcano are, of course, one – the date. Two – the targets.'

He paused, looked around the company. 'If we had this information we could crush it out of hand.'

'We also need to know', said Cunningham, 'which service chiefs have pledged their support.'

The Prime Minister didn't like the interruption but nodded in acknowledgement.

'One person who has the information, I understand, is the prisoner Ashman.' He turned and stared directly at Cunningham. 'Why has he been taken off Special Interrogation?'

Cunningham had been expecting something like this. He knew the Home Secretary, who kept his eyes firmly on his sandwiches, would have been stirring things up.

'I stopped the torture because I didn't want to kill him.'

In the electric silence he watched the Prime Minister's eyes grow cold again.

'I understand he is now fully recovered. Why wasn't he put back on interrogation?'

'We have very little time, Prime Minister – perhaps no more than a few days. If he's kept silent for four weeks he's not likely to break now.' He should have left it there, but he added, 'Torture for the sake of torture seems pointless.'

He knew they'd hold it against him in the future, but he didn't care. For a man whose philosophy was supposed to be founded on survival he had curiously little regard for the future.

The Home Secretary looked up from his sandwiches. 'The official phraseology—'

'Never mind, Harry,' the Prime Minister said in the patient voice he reserved for his brother-in-law and children.

'Anyway,' Cunningham said casually, 'by tomorrow I'll have all the information we need.'

The air was suddenly charged with a different kind of electricity. He picked up his champagne. 'Cheers,' he said, drank it down and poured himself another glass. Still no one spoke.

Then the Prime Minister said, his voice still cold and level, 'You didn't mention this in any of your reports.'

'I didn't know till this evening.'

'You didn't tell *me* when I met you this evening,' said the Home Secretary.

'I didn't tell anyone.'

'Then you'd better tell *us*,' the Prime Minister said in his cold level voice. 'And tell us everything.'

'Well,' Cunningham said, 'we've known for some time that the resistance have been trying to recruit bright young army officers – we've got four dead men to prove it. And it seemed obvious they'd also be trying to recruit Tac Force officers.'

He lit a cigarette, blew out a stream of smoke. 'So I decided to give them one. I picked the best young officer I'd got, sent him to the sort of parties and social gatherings those other chaps went to . . .' He shrugged. 'The rest was easy. They recruited him – and very soon promoted him. Which was the whole idea. That's why I gave them the best man I'd got – so they'd have to promote him. And go on promoting him.'

He paused to blow out another stream of smoke – and to keep them waiting a little longer. 'That was eight months ago. Now he's on their executive council.'

He felt surprise go round the room like a shock wave.

'Tomorrow morning, at a special meeting, the council will be fully briefed on Volcano. And by the afternoon I'll have the date, the targets, the battle order, the lot.'

Leo Pachman gasped, the Home Secretary burst into an

excited babble of questions, Rawley seemed stunned – and the Prime Minister let his pipe go out.

Then everyone started to congratulate Cunningham at once. The Prime Minister called the meeting to order and relit his pipe, disappearing once again in smoke and flame.

'And who', he said, 'is this Wunderkind who has so brilliantly penetrated the resistance?'

Cunningham hesitated. 'I decided no one should know about his mission except me. I would be his only contact – so there would be no leaks. And I told him I didn't want information about local cells or operations. I wanted something big – however long we had to wait.'

'And by God you got it,' said the Home Secretary.

'No,' Cunningham said. 'I didn't get it. He got it. Let's never forget that.'

'And you still haven't told us his name,' said the Prime Minister.

Cunningham hesitated again. 'This is the time there could be a slip-up. The time he's starting to take chances. I didn't want to add to those chances. And it's not just *his* life that's involved – but *our* survival.'

'My dear Colonel,' said the Prime Minister, 'the information is safe with *us* surely?'

'Of course, Prime Minister, of course. It's just . . . Well, a careless remark, a moment's thoughtlessness . . .' He was thinking of the Home Secretary, who was as discreet as a loud-hailer.

He smiled. 'Perhaps I'm being superstitious having kept his name to myself for so long, I feel it would be bad luck to part with it – especially at this critical point.'

'I don't want to press you,' said the Prime Minister – which meant that he did. 'But I have a reason for wanting his name.'

Cunningham sighed. He felt, irrationally, it would somehow be a betrayal of Frank Wilson.

'I *am* head of Tac Force as well as head of state,' the Prime Minister added gently.

Cunningham sighed again. All his instincts were against it. 'His name', he said, 'is Lieutenant-Colonel Frank Wilson.'

The Prime Minister got up and served everyone with champagne.

'Without his name', he said, 'I couldn't propose a toast, could I?'

What a bloody reason, Cunningham thought.

The Prime Minister raised his glass. Everyone stood.

'To Colonels Cunningham and Wilson.'

'Please,' said Cunningham quickly, 'just Wilson.'

'Very well,' said the Prime Minister. 'To Lieutenant-Colonel Wilson.'

Glasses were raised, Wilson's name was murmured by the others, the toast was drunk.

'I suppose,' said the Prime Minister, 'to add the historic touch, we should smash the glasses in the fireplace. But since it's Murano cristallo and quite valuable, even if only a nineteenth-century copy, as I suspect – and this *is* a socialist economy – perhaps we'd better settle for some more champagne instead.'

There were dutiful smiles and laughs all round except from Cunningham, who felt sick.

16

IT WAS AFTER MIDNIGHT when he got to the party but it was still swinging, as he expected. And as he feared (he was in no mood for parties). He had changed into a black velvet jacket and black silk cravat, and looked elegant and refreshed. In fact he was tired and worried.

But as soon as he saw Amarantha the tiredness and most of the underlying tension seemed to disappear. Looking at her as she came towards him, her big red mouth smiling, her eyes half-closed in that short-sighted sexy look, he supposed he was in love with her – though she wasn't even beautiful. She was more than beautiful, she was real – in a way that few people were – and that in itself was a kind of beauty. You're getting sentimental, he thought.

'Good evening, Amarantha,' he said. 'I'm getting sentimental.'

'You're getting old, that's all. What would you like to drink?'

'I've been drinking champagne.'

'So have we – so there. Want to try the Widow? It's all we've got.'

'Then I think I'll . . . try the Widow.'

They were standing in the hall. From one of the two reception rooms leading off it came the sound of a piano and a young man singing a satirical and anti-government song.

A curious, or perhaps not so curious, change had come over Hampstead – or the intellectual part that considers itself Hampstead. There was a time when a Hampstead intellectual was automatically left-wing, and Hampstead was the heartland of radical chic. Now it was radical chic to be right-wing. It was not that their mostly moderate politics had changed, merely the name. The trendies were now on the right, the fascists on the left. Fascist, of course, was simply a term of political abuse for the other side.

'You're not listening to that song, are you, sweetheart?'

'Intently.'

'Not officially, I mean.'

'In five minutes I shall ring the nearest Tac Force barracks – if the champagne hasn't arrived.'

'Freddie,' she called. 'Freddie.'

Amarantha had boutiques in Chelsea, South Kensington

and Hampstead and an *haute couture* dress shop within spitting distance of Harrods. She was in the springtime of her reputation and making money while it lasted, which she was sure wouldn't be long – 'In another five years, dear, I'll be the wrong image – like yesterday's pop star. Then I'll sell up and become an asset stripper. If it means what I think it means.'

Freddie was her head cutter, adviser and personal friend. He was homosexual and lived in a flat in Hammersmith with a boy who was something in television. He came in from the other reception room with a bottle of Veuve Cliquot and two glasses on a tray.

'Freddie,' said Cunningham, 'you must be psychic.'

'No, dear, observant. As soon as I saw the car draw up I thought, it'll be champers for the master. Where d'you want it served?'

Amarantha looked at Cunningham's face. 'In the study, I think, Freddie.'

They went into the study, which was at the back of the house. It was a quiet book-lined room with a picture window overlooking a sloping garden that led down to the heath.

'Going to join us, Freddie?' Cunningham said.

'Good heavens, no,' said Freddie. 'I have someone in a pink shirt waiting for me in the other room.'

Cunningham sat in an armchair behind the big leather-topped desk. Amarantha perched on the edge and poured the champagne. He raised his glass.

'Cheers.'

'Cheers.'

Neither touched the champagne. They looked at each other over the glasses.

'Do we have a date tonight?'

'It's a bit early to leave my guests,' she said, 'and I do have to be up at five. I'm on the first flight to Paris.'

'Forget it,' he said.

'Don't sulk,' she said. 'It's out of character.'

The phone rang and she answered it.

'Hello? Speaking.' She listened, then said, 'Christ, I've got to be up at five—' But whoever was at the other end interrupted her, and again she listened. 'All right,' she sighed, 'I'll do what I can.' And put the phone down.

'What was all that about?'

171

'Business,' she said. 'Boring bloody business with boring bloody people who expect bloody miracles.'

She was really upset, not just irritated. It surprised him.

'I wasn't sulking,' he said. 'I meant it when I said forget it—'

'I'm not *going* to forget it,' she said. 'I just want time to think about it. And rearrange what is known as a tight schedule. Drink your champagne.'

The switch of mood also surprised him.

He sipped the champagne and watched her sip hers. She was frowning. Her mouth was too big, her jaw too wide, her cheekbones too prominent and her eyes too often half-closed as she tried to focus them. He wondered that the whole world wasn't in love with her.

'All right,' she said. 'As long as you leave by about half-past three so I can get an hour's kip.'

'No,' he said, 'that's ridiculous. You need—'

'I can sleep on the plane.'

'Yes, but—'

'And you're better than sleep.'

'I'm pretty short of sleep myself—'

'Oh, do shut up,' she said. 'You're becoming a painus.'

'A what?'

'A pain in the anus. But first we must circulate a little. It's only polite.'

They emptied their glasses and went into the reception room where most of the guests were. The other reception room had been turned into a buffet and bar. The young man was still playing the piano, no longer singing but syncopating a sad little melody which drifted over the conversation like a tinkling lament.

Cunningham entered behind Amarantha – and the conversation died. Even the tinkling piano, sounding louder in the sudden silence, faltered before picking up its plaintive rhythms. Then the talk started up again, but it was subdued and there was a chill in the air.

Cunningham rarely went to parties because politically conformist parties bored him, and the only nonconformist parties he was invited to were Amarantha's. And he put a blight on them – not because they wanted to talk politics all the time; they didn't. The main topics, as at most parties, were sex and gossip – or shop if people were in the same business. But his appearance was like the appearance of a KGB colonel at a dissidents' party – you could almost pluck the tension like a string.

Most of the guests knew him by sight, a few even knew him as Julian, but none had the nerve to ignore him as he moved elegantly around at Amarantha's elbow.

Two bankers were talking about poetry, some writers were talking about money, and one of those men who tell Irish jokes was telling Irish jokes ('What's dead, black, shrivelled and hangs from the ceiling rose? An Irish electrician'). A plump poet with a slim volume of verse was seated in a coil of pretty girls, discussing sex ('Prevention is better than curettage, my dear'), and two fat women were discussing slimming as if it were religion. There were other groups, too, mostly nondescript. The saddest-looking were the trendy middle-aged, with their air of quiet desperation.

Amarantha seemed able to have a word with everyone without getting drawn into conversation.

'You'd make a marvellous diplomat,' Cunningham murmured.

'I am a marvellous diplomat,' she murmured back as she swept out into the hall and made for the other reception room.

'Do we have to?' said Cunningham.

'Yes,' she said, 'it's my farewell performance. For tonight.'

There was still food on the tables and drink at the improvised bar set up in a corner. Those sitting down balancing plates of food on their knees were the serious eaters. The serious drinkers were leaning on the bar. Among them was Freddie, talking to two young men in tight jeans, one blond with blue chiffon at his throat, the other dark in a pink shirt.

Another quick whisk round, a word here, a smile there – from Amarantha, sweet and fair . . . And Cunningham always at her elbow like a lean and half-tamed panther. She left Freddie and his two boys till last.

'Freddie, darling,' she said, 'would you look after things for me? I have a date with Julian.'

'Leave it all to me, dear heart. I'll say goodnight, lock up, put the cat out and see no one's sick on the carpet. And', he said to the two boys, 'please don't tell me she hasn't got a cat.'

'Who needs one with you around?' said the blond boy.

'Oh my God, a *wit*,' said Freddie. 'I bet you tell Irish stories too.'

Cunningham and Amarantha lay in bed sipping the last of the champagne and watching the stars through the northern light.

'Luxury,' she said, and sighed with happiness. 'Didn't it once mean licentiousness?'

'In Shakespeare's time. From the Latin *luxus*.'

'So this is luxury in both senses,' she said, laying her head on his chest.

The warmth of the bed, her naked body against him, the relaxation induced by the champagne gave him a drowsy drifting feeling as if part of him had broken loose and was drifting among the stars. It wasn't a dream; he was still awake. Hallucination.

'I'm hallucinated,' he said. 'Or in love. Why don't we live together?'

'You've got a wife.'

'And I'm in love with you.'

'Think of the trouble it would cause.'

'Cause who – whom?'

'You. I've got too many right-wing friends. Your masters wouldn't like it.'

'They don't like it now. They think you're bad company.'

'They're right. I hate this regime.'

'So do a lot of people. That doesn't make them dangerous.'

'How do you know I'm not?'

'I've had you screened.'

'Nice bastard.'

'Sensible bastard. Anyway, it was soon after I met you – as soon as I realized I wanted you. A mistress in the resistance for the C-in-C Tac Force? Dear me . . .'

'So you were sure I was going to be your mistress?'

'I'm a conceited bastard, too.'

'You've cost me a lot of friends. It's practically like sleeping with the head of the Gestapo to them. They can't understand it. I'm not sure I can either.'

'Love is a matter of feeling, not understanding.'

'Oh, balls. Don't play word-games with me. And don't do that, it excites me.'

'Not even love-games? What am I allowed to play? We are in bed, aren't we? Or is that another hallucination?'

She pulled away from him and he knew she was upset.

'Solzhenitsyn says there are no Shakespearian villains any more – the ones who realize their villainy – only the ones—'

'I love Solzhenitsyn too, flower, but not in bed.'

'Only the ones who justify their villainy: who rationalize it

174

into some kind of ideology or religion or other belief. Otherwise they couldn't put little children into gas ovens or throw them out of third-floor windows at Ma'alot – they're not all psychopaths.'

He could hear the shake in her voice and wondered who had been getting at her. Her right-wing friends or resistance friends, presumably. Any moment now she'd cry.

'Listen,' he said gently, 'I'm not even going to try to justify myself. And Solzhenitsyn's wrong – *I'm* the last of the Shakespearian villains.'

She turned her back to him. 'Go away. I don't want to see you again.'

'You're crying.'

'I'm not.'

'What's the matter?'

'Women cry sometimes. The pull of the moon or the tides or something.' She turned to him abruptly. 'Make love to me.'

He kissed her wet face and made love to her, urgently at first because her need was urgent. Then it became less urgent, like the love-making of old friends, easy and caressing. They felt, as other lovers have felt, that there was something special in their love-making. And there was, Cunningham thought, because the joy of the flesh implies the joy of the presence in the flesh, which is individual.

'You're the best lover a woman could have.'

'How do you know what all the other women have had?'

'Because I've had all the other men.'

He laughed and kissed her ear, and she rubbed her face against his neck. It was nice making love like old friends, comforting and sensual. And it suited their mood, as loving should.

Afterwards, as he was dressing by the northern window, he looked out at the sky and said it was a nice night, and she yawned and stretched like a cat and said it would be nice anyway.

When he left she went into the tiny kitchen that led off the studio. Its window overlooked the front of the house. She watched him drive away, then went back to the studio, picked up the phone and dialled.

'He's left,' she said when a man's voice answered.

Then she went back to bed, and lay there watching the stars through the northern light. Then she started crying again.

Cunningham got home just before the dawn chorus. As he

approached the drive he could hear the mellow fluting of a blackbird. He pressed a rocker switch on the dashboard to transmit a signal that would de-activate the electronic beam that covered the entrance. If broken it set off an alarm in the semi-basement where his Tac Force bodyguards were permanently quartered. There were also portable devices, about the size of a matchbox, for de-activating the beam. These were carried by members of the family and staff when they went out.

Cunningham pulled up in front of the garage without bothering to drive in. The big Jag, with more bodyguards, pulled in immediately behind him.

He had driven with the window down and felt refreshed by night air, alive and vigorous and at peace with the world. He ran up the steps to the front porch, pausing only to press a hidden button to de-activate another alarm – the front door mat.

Then he stopped cold. In the darkness he could make out what looked like a body lying by the front door. Behind the door he could hear his wife's springer spaniel whimpering. The hair came up on the back of his neck. Was it a body? And whose? And dead bodies could be booby-trapped.

He could hear the bodyguards chatting as they crossed to the area steps leading down to the semi-basement. He should have called them but now his eyes were adapted to the darkness of the porch and it was obviously a body. He decided to chance the risk of a booby trap. He bent down, turned the body over on to its back.

It was Frank Wilson with his throat cut.

The phone rang by Amarantha's bed. She was wide awake, waiting for it.

'Well done,' a man's voice said. 'It went like a wedding.'

'I'm so glad,' she said. 'Whose throat are you going to cut next – Julian's?'

'If we ever get the chance,' the man said.

'Not with my bloody help,' Amarantha said and banged the phone down.

17

THE AFTERNOON SUN threw a barred pattern on the floor and for some reason, perhaps the warmth, it reminded Joseph of the summer he toured South America, giving recitals. If he fancied a place he'd stay there. He was welcome everywhere. Life was a dream.

Ashman himself, stretched out on the lower bunk, was half dreaming, half listening to Joseph, who was sitting by the table, idly picking the guitar as he talked about that summer long ago.

'And what a summer. Like the one we had in England once. No rain, no wind. And everyone praying for the wind to blow and bring the cool cool rain . . .

He picked some tinkling raindrop chords.

'But what's the use of praying? You pray for the wind to blow one way, there's always someone praying for it to blow the other way . . .'

He tried a wailing effect to suggest the soughing of the wind.

'So the crops were no good, food prices sky-high, the rich farmers getting richer, the poor getting poorer and everyone cursing. Except me. I was happy. So was she. At least, I think she was. Some idiot said happiness and unhappiness are states that cannot be defined except in relation to each other. If one is absent, the other must be present – *ipso facto* and how's-your-father. Those logic-chopping sods, I'd shoot 'em. Up the arse. Where they deserve to be shot. They'd be able to define unhappiness then all right . . .'

He paused to tighten a string.

'And happiness, let me tell you, is when you *know* you're happy. And you know how I knew? The mornings. I didn't hate the mornings any more. You've heard of manic depressives, there are also morning depressives. I'm a morning depressive. The best thing to do with the mornings is to avoid them. Sleep till noon. But that's not easy; the city's too noisy and the country's too quiet. You wouldn't think you could hear silence, would you? But you can. It has a faint ringing sound.'

He tried to reproduce the sound on the guitar.

'But all that summer I was up at sunrise every morning. Ah, the city at sunrise. The streets still damp with dew and the air still sweet to smell . . . You feel like you're on the wings of the morning. Actually, I was on a concrete balcony. But happiness was humming inside me – like music. And I'd lean over and pluck a leaf from the lemon-tree by the window. Then I'd go in and hold the leaf under her nose and slowly crush the scent out of it. Till the whole room was heavy with the scent of lemon. Then the tip of her nose would quiver, her eyes begin to open. She'd look at me . . . Sleepy. Warm. Naked. And with a tendency to smile . . .

'I picked her up in the hills. In a travelling show. Ragged, filthy, frightened – and hungry. She looked after the animals. But there was something about her . . . Anyway, I took her out and bought her a meal. Christ, could she eat. I think she got less than the animals she looked after . . .

'I had to leave next morning. I was on tour, halfway to an engagement. But I didn't get far. Her face haunted me – and I nearly ran into a tree. In the end I turned round and went back, picked her up, bought her some clothes, took her to the hotel, made her bath, burned her old clothes in the grate . . . All on the spur of the moment. Hadn't the faintest idea what I was going to do with her. Then the boss of the travelling circus showed up, a giant of a man, blowing like a whale and threatening me with a knife. But I wasn't worried. In those days I had the charm that works all miracles – money. I shoved a roll of notes into the giant's hand and he became a dwarf, bowing and scraping and backing out of the door . . .

'So – there I was, stuck with her. So – I took her with me. Venezuela, Brazil, Mexico, Paraguay – all over. She had a special quality. She made me feel I was a man. It's funny – you can sleep with dozens of them without feeling that. Then a particular one comes along – and suddenly you're a man. Not just because you happen to have a couple of whatsits, but because you *feel* it. Like happiness . . . Or maybe it's because you're in love . . .'

He fell silent, with an air of sadness, as if the juxtaposition of happiness and love reminded him that one didn't necessarily go with the other.

'Anyway, I brought her back to this place I had in the city, with the garden and the balcony. In one of the quiet squares in the classy quarter . . . She was getting to be quite a madam by then – and I was getting to feel not quite such a man. I wanted to take her back to England but she threw such a tantrum I thought: What the hell, you can play the guitar anywhere – and I was getting plenty of engagements.'

He fell silent again as images of her filled his mind.

'Anyway, we were happy. All summer we were happy. Ah, that summer . . . the silence of those long days . . . the stillness of the afternoons – when we'd pull the blind down and lie on the bed . . . I can see her now, with the sunlight coming in through the blind, falling across her body like tiger-stripes . . .'

He sighed. 'Yes, all summer we were happy. And all summer she had a lover. No wonder she didn't want to go to England. A lieutenant in the army . . . I was a fool, I suppose. But you know how it is when you love them. Anyway, when the revolution came – it was the sort of place that has one every month – and all the theatres shut down and I couldn't get any more engagements, she left me flat and went and lived with him.'

Joseph sighed again. 'Big fella, looked like a pig. I saw them in the street together once. I was going to go up and hit him in that pig face. But as usual, my heart wanted to go one way, my feet went the other . . . That was the last time I saw her. Now even the memory doesn't hurt. All it brings back is a taste of dead love. Sometimes sweet, usually bitter.

'Ah well, there's always music. The last consolation. Wasn't it Shaw who called it the brandy of the damned? And I never knew what he meant. But I do now. He meant you can get blind drunk on it.'

He went into a wild *rasqueando*, which he suddenly cut. Then he looked across at Ashman, who had closed his eyes.

'Didn't you tell me you had a girl once?' Ashman didn't answer. 'Hey, you, sleepy. Dreaming again?'

'No,' Ashman said, opening his eyes.

'Then why don't you answer me?'

'I am answering you.'

'You didn't answer me about the girl.'

'What girl?'

'You see? What girl? The one—'

'With two arms, two legs—'

'The one that was in the resistance with you.'

Ashman opened his eyes, sat up and looked at Joseph.

'Why do you want to know?'

Joseph shrugged. 'Only asking.' But he felt his belly tighten with fear. Ashman was still watching him – black eyes in a cratered face.

'If you don't want to talk about her . . .' He shrugged again. 'Don't.'

He started to play a flamenco piece, harsh and rapid. He had to bury himself in music to forget his fear, forget the world, forget everything. He filled the cell with music.

Cunningham sat at his chaotic desk, smoking and staring out of the window at the top of the chestnut-tree. But he didn't see it. He didn't see anything except the face of Frank Wilson with his throat cut.

It was too much of a coincidence that it happened after his name had been revealed at the meeting. Yet it was unthinkable that he'd been betrayed.

So let's think it, Cunningham thought. But by whom? The Home Secretary might do it through stupidity – but he'd hardly had time to tell anyone except his wife . . .

The only other possibility was the enigmatic Pachman – until you considered his impeccable background.

He had been appointed Minister of Defence when the former minister died of a heart attack. His rise from a backbench MP to be one of the Parliamentary Under-Secretaries of State for Defence was swift enough to be surprising. Or perhaps not so surprising when it was remembered that he was a personal friend of the Prime Minister's – and had always, as far as was known, held similarly extreme left-wing views.

Within a very short time, after a cabinet reshuffle, he became Minister of State for Defence. The papers talked of a rising new political star. After the Defence Minister's death there was a good deal of newspaper speculation, but Leo Pachman's name wasn't even mentioned. He was considered too young and inexperienced, despite his intelligence and talents.

It caused a minor sensation when the Prime Minister appointed him. Now he was considered in line for the leadership, if ever Percy Smith stepped down.

So, Cunningham thought, unless all those radical left-wing views are a front he's kept up for a very long time, you can cross him off the list too. Which left no one.

The only other explanation was that Frank Wilson had taken a chance too many. And no doubt that was the explanation. It was only the coincidence that bothered Cunningham. He didn't believe in coincidences. He knew they happened. He just didn't believe in them. Facts he believed in. And one of the facts was that Frank Wilson was dead.

So where are we now? Cunningham said to himself. Back to that famous Square One.

Back to the problem of Ashman too – and how to make him talk.

'Her name was Elizabeth,' Ashman said out of the silence that followed the music.

'Who?' said Joseph, still lost in sounds that only he could hear.

'The one you asked about.'

Joseph came out of his private world and picked up the guitar. 'What was she like? Pretty?'

He picked out a run of light rapid chords.

'No.'

'Handsome, then?'

'I don't remember.'

'You don't remember the face of the woman you loved?'

'Every time I remember it,' Ashman said, 'I remember it differently. And sometimes, when I want to remember it most, I can't remember it at all.'

'Memory and desire, they wax and wane like the bloody moon.'

He played a run of chords that rose to a crescendo, then faded in a diminuendo to final silence. But music was still in the air.

'Dark or fair?'

'Dark.'

'Dark. Of course. Dark.'

He started another run of chords, stopped, tried some thirds and changed to a different key.

'I'm getting warm, man, I'm getting warm.' The music got faster. He laughed excitedly. 'Eyes? They must be dark, too.'

'Sometimes.'

'And a mouth that's full – maybe heavy . . .' His fingers moved in a blur across the strings. 'And gay – I feel gaiety. Or is she wild, man, wild?'

He went into a crazy *rasqueando*.

'But sad underneath – like us all, eh, man? Like us all.'

He dragged the tempo and brushed the sounds with melancholy. 'And gentle . . . gentle as a girl can be.'

Then he laughed again, changed the tempo and went into a one-movement sonata with a wild rising melodic line and sudden cadenzas.

The music possessed him. Nothing else existed. The whole world vibrated in a crescendo of sound and colour.

Suddenly he started shouting over the music, 'I see her, I see her . . . Her heavy mouth and her changing eyes . . .' The crescendo reached its peak. 'And jasmine – do I smell the scent of jasmine?'

He cut the crescendo, and the cell, which had been throbbing like a discothèque, was now silent – except for Joseph's gasping breath.

'I'm a madman,' he said, still gasping. 'I know it, I admit it.' Then he laughed with excitement and pleasure. 'Well, where is she, this woman we've created? Over the hills and far away?'

Ashman hesitated, then said, 'In an unmarked grave with half a dozen others.'

Joseph stared at him in shocked silence, then seemed to crumple. 'Why did you let me go on?'

His voice was shaking with emotion. It made Ashman uneasy.

'It's all right,' he said. 'It's not important.'

'How can you say that?'

Ashman shrugged. He wished Joseph would shut up about it.

'Is that why you . . . hate them?'

'I've always hated them. And for better reasons.'

'You should've stopped me,' Joseph said, the emotion coming back into his voice. 'I didn't know – I got carried away – I forgot . . .' He trailed off miserably as he remembered his orders. 'I mean I . . . forgot what I was doing.'

Then he jumped up, angry. 'Why didn't you stop me?'

His anger went as quickly as it came. He sat at the table, put his head in his arms and started to sob.

'For Christ's sake,' Ashman said, 'it doesn't matter.'

'You should've *stopped* me.'

'I tell you it doesn't matter.'

Joseph went on sobbing. Ashman pulled him to his feet, shook him.

'Cut it out.'

Joseph broke away, but Ashman grabbed him and swung him round with a violence that startled him – and stopped the sobbing. Ashman's deep-set eyes seemed to go deeper under the scarred brows and his voice was low, like a rasping whisper.

'She's here,' he said. 'In London – with the resistance – but *they* think she's dead.'

Joseph's eyes widened. He shook his head and started to back away as if from a kind of horror.

18

CUNNINGHAM was on the phone. Bishop, at his desk at the other end of the office, was pretending to work and trying to listen.

'Of course it's vague,' Cunningham was saying, 'bloody vague. But we're lucky to have that much. I must say the police artist you sent was very patient with him. Trouble was he kept having to play bits on the guitar to recall the picture the music suggested . . . Yes, Reg, the music's probably all wrong . . . And artists are notoriously unreliable, possibly even a little mad – which was no doubt why Plato wanted to do away with them . . . No, forget it, Reg, that was all long ago and far away. But at least we've got *something* – even if it's only an artist's impression – and I've had it circulated to the Met police stations and Tac Force barracks and interrogation centres. All we can do now is hope. Or pray, if that's the way it takes you . . . But I have a hunch – about the warehouse. If Hudson's in town, he might well go there. And he'll have Murdoch with him. Murdoch's even more important in a way – the political brain behind the military muscle. The next PM if they ever get to power. Anyway, keep that warehouse under watch. Who knows? Maybe even the girl will show up there. I'll have a chopper standing by if you want me. All right?'

He was about to hang up, then changed his mind. 'And, Reg, listen. If you get close enough, you might even catch the scent of jasmine . . . Yes, Reg, that's what I said.'

He hung up, laughed briefly and lit a cigarette. Then he stared at Bishop, who was still pretending to work. But Bishop sensed that Cunningham's eyes were on him, and it made him uncomfortable. For all his charm – and Bishop could see that he had charm – Cunningham was an uncomfortable man.

Cunningham got up from his desk and wandered over to the bullfight poster on the wall. It showed Manolete executing a left-handed *pase natural*, called by Hemingway the most difficult, the most dangerous and the most beautiful pass in bullfighting.

Manolete, tall, thin, lugubrious, the shadow of death already on him, was leaning in close to the black bulk of the bull, bringing it past him in a slow tight circle controlled by the magic of his left wrist.

'The great Manolete,' Cunningham said. He turned to

Bishop. 'Ever been to the bullfight?'

'No, sir,' said Bishop. The phone rang and he answered it. 'Yes . . . Just a moment.' He turned to Cunningham. 'Do you want him in now?'

'I saw him once in Alicante,' Cunningham said dreamily. 'I couldn't have been more than fifteen or sixteen. My first trip abroad . . . But I'll never forget the way he dominated a big black Miura with the cape.'

'Just keep him there,' Bishop said into the phone wearily. 'Yes, I'll let you know.' He hung up and said to Cunningham, 'Wasn't he killed though, the great Manolete?'

'At Linares, in 1947.'

'And by a big black Miura?'

Bishop was actually having a dig at him. Cunningham smiled.

'They say he made a mistake when he went in for the kill, the so-called Moment of Truth . . .' Cunningham paused. 'I wonder though . . . I think the real moment of truth is when the bull first comes out into the ring. Out of darkness into sunlight. You watch his reactions. Try to access his speed, his strength, his temper. What the Spanish call his caste . . . That's when you plan your campaign. And that's when the big mistakes, the fatal ones, are often made . . .'

He stopped, then said abruptly, 'All right, bring him in.'

Bishop picked up the phone and said: 'We're ready now.'

The double doors were pushed, almost flung open, and Fat Charlie entered, stamped to attention and saluted. Then he turned towards the doorway and bellowed, 'Prisoner and escort at the double quick MARCH! Leff-ri, leff-ri, leff-ri, leff-ri!'

Nothing happened. Cunningham smiled.

All prisoners, except informers, were brought in at the double between an escort of two guards.

This prisoner was dragged in by an escort of four guards. And nobody was at the double. They were all over the place, trying to get him into the room at all.

The prisoner, of course, was Ashman. The guards were partly hampered by the machine-pistols slung over their shoulders: they kept slipping. But they were hampered mostly by the strength, savagery and professional fighting skills of Ashman.

At last they managed to get a sufficient grip on him and he quietened down. Or so they thought. One of them relaxed his grip and Ashman, with a sudden twist and heave of his shoulders, sent him reeling. One of the other guards raised his rifle butt to smash him in the face.

'No.' Cunningham's voice cracked like a whip.

Ashman said casually to the guard, 'I'll kill you for that. You'll get careless some time and I'll kill you.' Then he said to Cunningham, 'I enjoy killing your guards.'

'There are times', Cunningham said, 'when I'd enjoy killing them myself.' To Fat Charlie he said, 'Unshackle him. Then get out.'

Fat Charlie's small eyes went glassy with shock.

'But he's not safe, sir.'

'What man is? Do as I say.'

Fat Charlie looked at the guards, shrugged, then took off Ashman's shackles.

The guards formed up and Fat Charlie led them out. 'Leff-ri, leff-ri, leff-ri . . .'

'How's the dirty postcard business?' Ashman said to him.

After they had gone, Cunningham said, 'You too, Peter.'

'But you must have a witness, Colonel. "During interrogations a third party and/or shorthand-writer must be present" – Home Office Rules of Procedure for Interrogation of Prisoners, section three, paragraph one.'

'I make my own rules.'

'But Colonel, if the Minister hears—'

'He will, Peter, he will. Now get out.'

Bishop left, carefully closing the double doors behind him. Cunningham was still sitting at his desk. Ashman was standing, rubbing his wrists. Each stared at the other hard-faced, without attempting to speak. If it was to be a war of nerves nobody was going to win.

After a time Cunningham pointed to an easy chair and said, 'Make yourself comfortable.'

Ashman sat down without taking his eyes off Cunningham, who cleared a space on his desk by the simple act of sweeping a filing tray and a pile of documents on to the floor. He pushed a cigarette box towards Ashman, who looked at it, then at Cunningham.

'You think they're doped?'

Ashman took one and lit it from a lighter on the desk. Cunningham also took one and lit it, then went to the drinks cupboard.

'Gin, whisky, brandy, vodka?'

Ashman didn't answer. Cunningham turned and looked at him. 'Well?'

'Are you trying to sell me something?'

'Yes,' Cunningham said. 'But have a drink anyway.'

'Any beer?'

'No.'

Cunningham looked down at a wine rack in the lower part of the cupboard.

'What about a Chénas? That's nice and light.'

'A what?'

'It's a Beaujolais.'

'Oh, plonk. Yes, that'll do.'

'Chénas', Cunningham said patiently, 'is one of the communes of Beaujolais—'

'That's what it said on this bottle I bought once. Beaujolais, it said. The taste was plonk.'

'Wine-labels, like politicians, do not always tell the truth. Especially in England.' He held up the bottle of Chénas. 'This is genuine enough. And very pleasant. Try it.'

'You really must want to sell me something.'

'I really do.'

Cunningham opened the bottle, sniffed the cork, poured a little, tasted it, then poured a glass for Ashman and some more for himself.

Ashman took a sip. It tasted good. 'So what's the proposition?'

Cunningham took what looked like an old sock from a drawer in his desk.

'What's that?'

'Exactly what it looks like,' Cunningham said. He went to the Prime Minister's picture and lifted it down with great care. Behind it was the same kind of squared panelling that panelled the rest of the room. In the centre of each panel was a patera and rosette. The centre of one rosette contained a tiny microphone. Cunningham stood on a chair, folded the sock and fixed it over the microphone with Scotch tape. He then replaced the picture of the Prime Minister, and went back to his desk.

'Interesting, eh? The cells aren't bugged, as I'm sure you know. But my office is. There must be a moral there. But I'm not very good at morals. How's the wine?'

'Pretty good.'

Cunningham took a sip and nodded his agreement. 'And now at least we can talk freely . . .' He smiled one of his slanting smiles. 'When taking over a new office always search for the hidden microphone – Colonel Cunningham's Rules of Procedure, section three, paragraph one . . . I suppose they didn't think even I'd be profane enough to look behind the Prime Minister's picture. But it was the first place I looked . . . Of course, they have no imagination.'

'They?' said Ashman. 'Aren't you one of them?'

'Of them, no. With them, yes.'

'Of them, with them – what's the difference?'

'The difference between men like you and men like me. You see, you're not just with the resistance, you're an intrinsic part of it. Committed – which is another word for blind. The mark of the emotional as distinct from the intellectual man. You're emotional, I'm intellectual – in a specific sense of course.'

'I see. You're a clever bastard, I'm dumb.'

'You don't see, and you're not dumb. Or I wouldn't waste time on you. I said intellectual in a specific sense – a man who can largely dissociate his intellect from his emotions. A realist.'

He paused to take a sip of wine. 'Remember what Walpole said – the world's a comedy to those who think, a tragedy to those who feel . . . You, I'm afraid, are one of those who feel.'

Ashman shrugged. 'So what?'

'I was hoping to persuade you of the advantages of the . . . realist attitude.'

Ashman looked at him and grinned. 'All right then, where's the carrot?'

'The what?'

'The carrot. You've tried the stick, where's the carrot? That realist enough for you?'

Cunningham sipped a little more wine, relishing its lightness and fruit – and giving himself time to think.

'Well now,' he said, 'it's a question of co-operation, of mutual assistance—'

'Give it to me straight, Colonel, nice and straight.'

Cunningham held up his glass of wine and pretended to study it. He should have known better, he supposed, than to try to fence with a brick wall.

'All right,' he said. 'Help us – and we'll help you. Give us the information we want, and the Government will get you out of the country with enough money to take care of your future.

Now, before you reject it out of hand, think about it. With your brains, not your emotions.'

Ashman grinned again. 'My brains, such as they are, wonder if the Government would keep their word.'

'The Government always keep their word.'

Ashman nodded gravely. 'Like they did to the unions and all the other fools who helped to put them in power.'

'That', said Cunningham, 'was politics – the art of the possible.'

'And what's this?'

'A choice – between freedom and death.'

'Freedom to do what? Betray my friends? In order to live – belly to earth like a frightened fox? That what you call freedom?'

Cunningham shook his head. 'Always the emotional answer. Everything seen through a haze of emotion – darkly. It's your character, of course. And a man's character is his fate, according to Heraclitus.'

'You're a quoter, aren't you? Always quoting other men's words.'

'Ashman, I'm trying to help you. I know you won't believe it, but it's a fact.'

'Oh, I believe it. The day I was captured, the first time I saw you – just after the first beating-up – I said to myself, Tommy, I said, that man has your interests at heart. I was going to thank you, only it would have been rude to speak with my mouth full – of blood and broken teeth.'

Cunningham smiled his crooked smile. 'I walked into that one, didn't I? However, I did stop the torture – and against orders, too.'

'Why?'

'Time. I knew from intelligence reports that the resistance were planning a major operation. And soon. Perhaps next week. Or the week after. Perhaps tomorrow. And if the torturers couldn't break you down in three weeks, it was going to take a long time . . . Time we couldn't afford.'

'An interesting assessment,' said Ashman. 'But how do you know I've got the information you want? And how do the resistance know I haven't already talked? In which case they'd change their plans.'

'You're obviously a leader – it's written all over you. Whether you're the Falcon is immaterial – though I believe you are. I

188

believe you not only know the plans, I believe you helped to draw them up.' He smiled. 'Your second question's easier still. Both sides are riddled with informers. There are even some here – in my headquarters. If you talked under torture, the resistance would know within hours. Maybe minutes.'

Cunningham walked over to the window, stared down at a Tac Force squad drilling on a parade ground. The stiffly moving figures looked like puppets.

'That's why', he said, 'I took such precautions to keep this meeting strictly between ourselves. No witnesses. And if we do a deal the only other person who'll be told is the Prime Minister.'

'If we do a deal,' said Ashman.

'I said if,' said Cunningham.

'And how do you rate your chances, Colonel?' There was no irony in his voice or eyes, only in the question.

'Not very high, I'm afraid,' said Cunningham. 'Because, as I said before, your character is your fate. Which is why you're doomed.'

'Crap. I'm doomed because you bastards are going to shoot me.'

'That's merely the specific situation – which I can alter at a moment's notice. You're doomed because you can't adapt. You're out of date, like a knight in armour. And the age of heroes, like the age of chivalry, is dead.'

'So now I'm a hero, am I?' Ashman grinned widely, puckering a scar high up on his cheek. It had been put there by one of his torturers.

'With vine-leaves in your hair. And society doesn't need heroes any more – it doesn't take a hero to press a button. They're dying out, like the aborigines and the white rhino. Not needed and not adaptable. "Cometh the hour, cometh the man." Now cometh the hour of the adaptable man.'

'The creep,' said Ashman.

'Oh, he's not particularly nice or admirable. He's not even new. He's always existed, somewhere in the shadows. The only difference now is that he's in fashion. His kingdom's come. His will be done. They don't even call him rude names any more. They call him the anti-hero. And even if the title's old hat the type isn't.'

Both glasses were nearly empty and Cunningham refilled them.

'Why do you keep sniping at your own side?' Ashman said.

'I'm not sniping at them,' Cunningham said drily. 'Just looking at them with detachment, because I'm with them, not of them. Not committed. That's why I can face the facts without emotion.'

'What facts? And don't give me any more propaganda, it makes me sleepy.'

'Facts. Very well. Let's look at the general situation first.'

Ashman sipped his wine. 'This really isn't bad,' he said.

Cunningham went to the window again, stared out, then turned abruptly to Ashman.

'Once you lose what we call democracy it seems that you never get it back. Look around you. Russia, Eastern Europe, most of Asia, all under extremist regimes. Can you see democracy coming back to them?'

He paused to light a cigarette, then paced the room.

'Look at Western Europe – at the size of the communist parties in France and Italy. How long will their governments be able to hold back the rising tide? Look at Spain and Portugal. Trouble. Look at South America. Chile goes communist and brutal, then fascist and brutal. Uruguay kills off more political prisoners than Russia. Or is it Nicaragua? So many totalitarian regimes killing so many people it's easy to get them muddled . . . And finally Africa, where virtually every regime, black or white, is corrupt and repressive. And sitting on top of the muck-heap there's good old Colonel Gaddafi, fuelling every extremist movement from Black September to the Provisional IRA with money and guns. A sweet picture.' He stopped to light another cigarette. 'Out of a hundred and forty-five countries in the world, only thirty are democracies. Correction: twenty-nine, now that Britain's gone down . . . So what price democracy? I'll tell you. In the words of my favourite TV character: Nutt'n, baby. Zilch. Big fat zero.'

He raised his glass. 'Cheers,' he said, and drained it.

Ashman raised his glass, took a sip of wine and rolled it round his mouth, then let it slide over his palate. He could still taste it after it had gone. He liked it.

'Well?' said Cunningham.

There was a long silence. Ashman sat motionless in his chair, his deep-set eyes appearing hooded. Cunningham wondered if he was asleep till he realized Ashman was watching him through narrowed lids.

'What you say', Ashman said, 'may be the truth. But it's only part of the truth. You leave things out. And one of the things you leave out is the common people, who just want to live in peace and lead an ordinary sort of life. The common people. Common as dirt – and almost as indestructible. And we're everywhere – an army without banners. And people like you won't keep us down for ever with your bullets and your beatings. For a long time maybe, but not for ever.'

'Perhaps you're right,' said Cunningham. 'But the evidence is against you. The history of the world, the present state of the world and its foreseeable future all point to the fact that it always has been and always will be a world for winners.'

'And you're one of the winners?'

'It looks like it.'

'For ever?'

Cunningham stopped pacing and went back to his desk. 'Now we're getting down to what politicians call the specifics. Let's look at the coming coup. Let's even assume it's successful. The present regime is overthrown and a new government led by Murdoch, Hudson & Co. take over. What's the first thing they'll do?'

Ashman grinned till the scar puckered his cheek again. 'That's easy,' he said. 'Shoot men like you.'

'On the contrary,' Cunningham smiled back, 'the first thing they'd do is to shoot men like you.'

Ashman half-rose in his chair, then dropped back. His first real reaction. Cunningham felt he had drawn blood.

'The ones who've done the dirty work, who know too much . . . And, of course, the idealists, the ones who insist that all those bright shining promises must be kept. They're the ones who always get shot.'

Ashman didn't appear to react and his eyes had that hooded look again. But Cunningham still had the scent of blood in his nostrils.

'The first thing to do when you seize power is to trump up charges against your more ambitious supporters – and kill them off. Know who said that? Machiavelli.'

He smiled again. 'After any revolution the wrong man always gets into power. And those who help him never realize it till it's too late. Then the light dawns – he's a bastard. And they wag their fat heads and cry, "Of course, he's changed. Power corrupts." Wrong again. It doesn't corrupt. But any man who's ready to ride to power over a pile of corpses is already corrupt. He doesn't change – his opportunities change. Think about that when you think about men like Murdoch and Hudson.'

'And you? You think you'd get away scot-free?'

Cunningham shrugged. 'I'd have a good chance. Of course, when guns go off anyone can stop a stray one – bullets have no brains. But if I survive the initial shoot-out I'll survive the rest.'

'Such confidence.'

'Why not? I'm an able soldier and administrator with considerable experience of police and security work – and I know where the bodies are buried. Besides, men like me are the salt of this kind of earth. The job-holders, the politicians, the little lawyers and policemen, the mainspring of the Establishment. We run the state. We *are* the state. Governments may come and governments may go, but we go on for ever. Leaders may get liquidated – like the Nazi leaders. People need scapegoats. But where are the job-holders, the administrators, the middlemen? Why, back in their old jobs, most of them, basking in the Western sun. It happens everywhere. The power-seeking psychopaths can't do without us. So to hell with coups and revolutions and counter-revolutions. They start the same and they end the same. And men like me step in afterwards to clear up the mess. And you, my sea-green incorruptible, would be part of that mess. An embarrassment to our new masters.' He drew a finger lightly across his throat. 'Finito.'

Another silence. I've scored, Cunningham thought. I've scored. He got up and started pacing again. Then Ashman gave a short laugh.

'Remember Bert Lutterworth?'

'Who?' Cunningham was literally taken out of his stride.

'Big fat Bertie. Photographer with a studio in the Fulham Road and six kids. Always broke, always smiling. Executed last February . . . No?'

'No,' said Cunningham, his voice cold with suspicion.

'He hid me in his studio once. Amazing what he could do with a few lights. A low-angle flood here, a fill-in there, a reflector, a spotlight on the background and a bit of butter-muslin – and he'd turn a fat cow into a beauty. All by a trick of light. And you don't remember him?'

'No. And I fail to see—'

'You had something in common. He played with lights, you play with words. A half-truth here, a lie or two there and you'd turn black into white. All by a trick of words.'

'Wouldn't it be simpler to call me a liar?'

'You're more than a liar – much more. I get high on booze, Lamont gets high on music, and you – you get high on words. But facts . . .' He shook his head. 'To you they're like pipe-cleaners – for bending into fancy shapes to amuse the kids.'

Cunningham stopped in front of him, stared down at him. 'Here's a fact for you. That wound in your arm you got when you were captured wasn't made by a 7.62 mm bullet from the Saracen's rear machine-gun. You weren't even in its field of fire after it crashed into the house. It was firing over your head. And your wound had a downward trajectory. You were hit from above. And in an upper room in one of the empty houses in that street we found an abandoned .222 Parker-Hale high-velocity rifle with telescopic sight. The ideal sniper's rifle to my mind. Now, as you know, the Army and Tac Force use the SLR and the sniper's version of it, the L39A1. The police also sometimes use the L39A1. Nobody uses the Parker-Hale.'

He added a little more wine to each glass, held up the bottle to make sure it was empty, then dropped it into the waste-bin.

'Except your side. We've captured several. Interesting, eh?' He raised his glass. 'Cheers.'

Ashman sat like a statue, not touching his drink, watching him with hooded eyes.

'Of course,' Cunningham went on, 'you lot also use the SLR and the L39A1, and anything else you can get hold of. But you prefer the Parker-Hale because the SLR and the L39A1 suffer from the defect of over-penetration – they'll go right through a building and kill innocent people, as you well know. But the Parker-Hale won't. And you're a lot more worried about killing innocent bystanders than we are – because we can always blame it on to you anyway.'

Ashman shrugged. 'What are you trying to prove?'

'That you were shot by one of your own side. Or do you think I'm making all this up?'

'You're clever enough. And dirty enough.'

'And note the timing. *After* the operation, when the gold is safe. The only thing that went wrong was that the sniper missed a vital spot. Perhaps the truck swerved or hit a bump as he squeezed the trigger . . . Well, what do you say to that?'

'Two things,' said Ashman, after a reflective pause. 'And they both bounce.'

Cunningham smiled. 'We've also heard through the usual

sources that there's friction in the resistance. Between the extremists, led by Murdoch and Hudson, and the moderates – led by the Falcon . . .'

He wandered towards the double doors.

'Well, you've enough problems. Perhaps I've added to them – if you've believed any of what I've said. But I've also suggested a solution. The rest is up to you.'

He turned to pull the double doors open, stopped and turned to Ashman again.

'One more thing: I *am* a liar, of course. I have to be. Truth is a luxury no government can afford – least of all this kind of government. But to me it's more than a luxury; it's a constant temptation. Truth draws me like a woman. Now it has become my secret vice – punishable by death. And therefore never indulged, except in the presence of the enemy. Which is ironic. So, in everything I've said there's been an element of truth. An element. And it's that element I want you to think about in the coming hours.'

He turned abruptly and pulled the double doors open.

'All right, take him away.'

Fat Charlie and the four armed guards came in and approached Ashman warily, who sat motionless in his chair. He ignored them and allowed them to manacle him and take him away. It was the only time he had ever gone quietly.

19

CUNNINGHAM rang for Bishop and was surprised to hear he had already left. It was after six, but Bishop was no clock-watcher – and would have been anxious to hear about the interrogation of Ashman. Miss Skinner explained that he had an appointment with the doctor. She always spoke rapidly, almost breathlessly on the phone, as if afraid of boring the person at the other end.

'He has an incipient ulcer, you see. The doctor says it's only indigestion and keeps giving him these pills, but Peter *knows* it's an ulcer. I mean, just because it doesn't show on the X-rays doesn't mean a thing, does it? Of course, he *will* eat this Chinese take-away – you know, deep-fried prawns and sweet-and-sour balls that's all batter and no balls, I mean no meat. Of course I do try to watch his diet and that but—'

'I'm sure you do, Miss Skinner, and thank you,' Cunningham said firmly, and put the phone down.

The rays of the late evening sun slanted almost horizontally across the poster of the sad-faced Manolete and silvered the barbs of the banderillas just below.

Cunningham was thinking of Amarantha when one of the outside phones rang. Perhaps it was her . . . It was Reg Hacker.

'Listen,' he said, 'about an hour ago a little yellow Volkswagen Golf pulls up in the alleyway by the side of the warehouse. The chap who's driving doesn't get out – just waits. I put the glasses on him, but you know how difficult it is to see through a windscreen because of the reflections. But he looked sort of familiar.'

'Was he alone?'

'Far as I could make out. Anyway, a few minutes later some geezer comes out of the warehouse with a bundle of galley proofs, slips round the corner and hands 'em to the bloke in the car – who leans out to take them. Now by this time I got a film camera with a zoom lens pointing at the car.'

'You didn't recognize him when he leaned out?'

'Maybe we will when we get the film blown up.'

'What about the other chap.'

'One of the editorial or printing staff, I think.'

'And the car?'

'We're checking the registration with the Swansea computer. I told 'em it was urgent, so it shouldn't take more than three years. And the film's being processed now. I'll ring you as soon as we get anything.'

'Well done, Reg.'

Cunningham went to the window and stared out. Dusk was beginning to blue the camp, softening the outlines of the barracks and parade ground, the exercise quadrangle, the execution yard, the wall and its watchtowers ... In the hazy countryside in the distance lights were beginning to come on. Soon the perimeter floodlights and the revolving ones on the watchtowers would be switched on. The white candles of the chestnut-tree stood out beautifully in the blue windless air.

A slight noise made Cunningham swing round. One of the double doors was opening. The figure of a man slipped quietly in and started to cross to Cunningham's desk. Then he saw Cunningham by the window, and stopped cold.

'Colonel – what are you doing here?'

'The question I was about to ask you, Peter. I thought you were at the doctor's.'

'I was but – well, I came back to ... tidy the place up a bit. I didn't expect to find you still here, sir.'

'That I can believe.'

'How did it go with Ashman? Successful?'

Cunningham stared at the bullfight poster. 'I think so.'

'Don't you know, Colonel?' Bishop said. His nerve was recovering.

'I know I'm not satisfied.'

'Then you could hardly have been successful.'

'You should listen more carefully, Peter. I said I wasn't satisfied.'

'But if you'd been successful you'd be satisfied. It follows surely?'

'As the night the day? Success equals satisfaction. If you seduce a woman, that is success. But is it satisfaction?'

'I'm sorry, Colonel, these ... distinctions are lost on me. They might be lost on the Minister too. He might not think you've accomplished very much.'

'But he won't know, Peter. So he won't be able to jump to one of his famous conclusions – and ruin everything. Will he?'

'Well, he's ... bound to find out in the end.'

'Everything's found out in the end, Peter. As long as he doesn't find out now.'

196

'But look how he found out about the printing press – and your stopping the Special Interrogation.'

Cunningham moved towards him, stared down at him. Bishop, who was slighter and smaller than Cunningham, instinctively stepped back.

'Yes, how *did* he find out, Peter?' In the half-dark Bishop could just make out the crooked smile. 'Well, perhaps it was luck the first time, coincidence the second time . . .' He took another step closer. 'But if there's a third time, Peter, that'll be enemy action.'

Again he moved closer, forcing Bishop towards the wall.

'But supposing he rings up when you're not here?' Bishop said. 'I mean, he knows you were going to interrogate Ashman. Supposing he wants to know how you got on? What am I to say?'

'I see your dilemma, Peter,' said Cunningham thoughtfully.

They were close to the bullfight poster. The barbs of the banderillas (or sticks, as the Spanish say) had no silver lights on them now. Cunningham reached out, took them down, weighing them like a man who has to do something with his hands while thinking.

'Say this: that the fight isn't over. That we've managed to confuse him with the cape a little . . . and to draw blood with the sticks.'

He raised the banderillas and thrust them down at Bishop's shoulders. Bishop jumped back, stumbling against the wall, yelping with fear.

'It's a joke, Peter,' said Cunningham, the banderillas poised for another thrust. 'That's all.'

'Please, Colonel. *Please.*'

'Don't be frightened, Peter. It's only a joke.'

'Colonel Cunningham,' Bishop said, trying to bluster, 'you've no right, absolutely no right' – as Cunningham made a threatening movement. 'Please, Colonel, let me *go.*'

'But, Peter,' Cunningham said softly, 'you're free to go any time. Why didn't you go last month, when the Ministry of Information offered you a better job? Why didn't you go then?'

Bishop started to shake. A sudden feeling of doom turned his belly to ice. 'I should've . . . hated to – leave your service.'

'I'm touched, Peter, I really am,' Cunningham said in the same soft voice. 'And I would have hated to lose you. After all, a good man's worth his weight in gold . . .' He thrust the banderillas into the panelling on either side of Bishop's neck. 'Or should it be in pieces of silver?'

He turned away with a laugh. Bishop leaned against the wall, shaking. He thought he was going to faint.

An outside phone rang and Cunningham answered it. It was Hacker again. Cunningham listened, then said, 'So *he* could be our mystery man. Well, well . . . Hold on a moment, will you?'

He put a hand over the mouthpiece and said to Bishop, who was still leaning against the wall, and still shaking, 'Go home. Take my car and chauffeur – you're not fit to drive.'

'Thank you, sir,' Bishop said, trying to steady his voice.

'And remember the old saying: if you're afraid of wolves, don't go into the forest.'

Bishop went to the door.

'Shall I turn the light on, sir?'

'No,' said Cunningham. 'I can see in the dark.'

Bishop shut the door behind him. Cunningham spoke into the phone again. 'Did the Swansea computer come up with anything?'

'It's his brother-in-law's car.'

'And the film – what did the blow-ups show of the driver?'

'Everything except his face. He was partly masked by the other man. And wearing dark glasses.'

'And if he's clever – and he is,' Cunningham said, 'that car'll be reported missing in the next hour or so.'

'It already has.'

'Well, we could always guess his identity – if we wanted to.'

'Guesses can be bloody dangerous when you're dealing with that class of trade, Guv'. I mean, if they backfire on you . . .'

'Exactly,' said Cunningham. 'So let's have no guesses. In fact, let's have no reports, no inquiries, no nothing. It never happened.'

'What about the films and the blow-ups of the stills?'

'Deliver them to me yourself in the morning. Negatives as well.'

'Right, Guv'.'

'And don't talk. Even in your sleep.'

He sat there for half an hour wondering what to do. Nothing, he told himself as the darkness deepened in the room and the big lights came on outside. Nothing. Let it swim away. But he was not a man to whom doing nothing came easily, especially if there was a hint of danger in it.

He picked up an outside phone and dialled an unlisted number.

'Hello?' said a voice. 'Leo Pachman here.'

'Good evening, Minister, sorry to disturb you but I just heard about your brother-in-law's car being stolen.'

'You're out of date, Colonel, the police have already found it – somewhere around Epping Forest, I believe.'

'Good, good. Not too much damage, I trust?'

'None at all.'

'That's unusual. These joyriders – and no doubt that's who took it – usually bend it a bit or vandalize it in some way.'

'My dear Colonel,' Pachman's voice was cold, 'I really don't see why you should trouble yourself over something as trivial as this.'

'Ah, but with the imminence of an attempted coup nothing is trivial, Minister. And I wondered if I ought to increase the bodyguard on your sister's family.'

'No, no, they're quite adequately guarded, thank you.'

'I'm glad to hear you say so.'

'Yes,' Pachman said after a fractional pause, 'you've done an excellent job.'

'Thank you, Minister. Well, I won't detain you . . . Oh, just one thing. After the car had been reported stolen, a patrol car pulled up at traffic lights in Queen Victoria Street and the chap in the passenger seat – a young constable – noticed a yellow Volkswagen next to him. And he thought the driver, who had dark hair brushed back and was wearing dark glasses, looked a bit like you in profile.'

'I expect there are quite a number of middle-aged men with dark hair brushed back and a Jewish profile. Some of them may even drive yellow Volkswagens – and wear dark glasses on a sunny day. I suspect that your young officer may be the suggestible type – especially after the event. Association of ideas.'

'Exactly what I told him, Minister. Only not in so many words. "Don't be a cunt," I said. "The Minister was at a cabinet meeting all afternoon." '

There was a brief silence, partly because Leo Pachman was surprised to hear Cunningham swear, partly because he was thinking what to say.

'I had one of my headaches, as it happened, and the PM told me to go home. Which I did – and lay on the bed for a couple of hours.'

'But you're recovered now?'

'Completely, thank you.'

'I sympathize, Minister. My wife suffers from headaches, too.' He gave a thin laugh. 'Usually when she wants to get out of social or sexual intercourse.'

Afterwards he was glad he had telephoned the Minister instead of going to see him. The telephone distorted not only the voice but the meaning. It left words in isolation without the context of the face to give them body and nuance. You could hide behind the telephone. He wanted the Minister to be able to hide, wanted to give him a hint and no more – not even a warning.

Was Pachman a highly placed informer for the underground? It would explain a lot, including the death of Frank Wilson. It would also be very difficult and dangerous to prove. Pachman was a personal friend of the Prime Minister . . . And supposing the coming coup was successful? Cunningham would need all the friends he could get. And one good turn . . . It was a tenuous sort of insurance – but you never know.

And what about Pachman Ltd, who had once owned the warehouse? Were they related, however distantly, to Leo Pachman? Or was it simply another one of those coincidences Cunningham didn't believe in? What's in a name?

Cunningham shrugged in the dark, reached for the phone and rang Amarantha.

'Can I see you tonight?'

'Well, I was going round to see Freddie about some new patterns . . . Is it important?'

'Yes.'

There was something in his voice. 'OK,' she said. 'When?'

'About nine.'

'Will you have eaten?'

'No.'

'I've got a couple of escallops of veal I can melt some cheese over – and some aubergines and green salad. Will that be enough or would you rather go out?'

'That'll be fine.'

'Oh, and I've got some of that Moulin-à-Vent.'

'You've also got me. Did you know that?'

They had dinner in the big chaotic studio at the top of the house, and talked trivialities as people sometimes do under tension. The tension was in Cunningham, but Amarantha could feel it too. And see it in his eyes, hear it in his voice – in all the nuances that lovers pick up.

'Is anything wrong?' she said.

'A great deal,' he said. 'But there always is. Nice piece of veal.'

'Between us, I mean.'

'We love each other. What can go wrong between lovers?'

'Anything. Everything.'

He smiled. His dark eyes seemed even more enigmatic than usual. 'I can never make up my mind which is my favourite vegetable – aubergines, fried courgettes or artichokes. Or a certain kind of very large mushroom. I go from one to the other. I'm fickle.'

'What *is* wrong?'

'The resistance are planning a big operation. Probably a coup d'état.'

'It's not likely to succeed, is it?'

'Depends how many army and police units they have on their side – plus the ones who'd join them if they looked like being successful. It's surprising, or not surprising, how many people like to be on the winning side.'

Amarantha was about to take a sip of wine. She put the glass down. 'If they did win, you'd be one of the losers.'

'Exactly.' He smiled. 'At the moment I'm one of the most powerful men in the country. I could arrest almost anyone below ministerial rank just by lifting the phone.' His dark eyes fixed on her, no longer smiling. 'I could even arrest you.'

'Well, that's very nice of you,' she said lightly. 'Perhaps I should've put a little arsenic in the aubergines.'

'If I was one of the losers, I could be hunted down like a criminal.' His eyes were still unsmiling. 'Would you take me in? Hide me?'

'I've got to say yes, haven't I? Otherwise you might arrest me now. Though I suppose I could lie to you.'

'Not very successfully. Anyway, I'd make you promise. And you know what you are about promises.' His own voice had a touch of lightness now – or was it irony? She could never really tell.

'First you're about to arrest me, next you want me to promise to hide you.' Her tone was still light.

'I know your hatred for this regime.'

'You also know my love for you.'

201

'But if I were the enemy—'

'There are no buts, Julian. You love or you don't love. At least, that's how it is with me.'

'And love is all, as the song says?'

'Don't make fun of me . . .' She stopped. 'If you don't know how I feel . . .' She stopped again, suddenly close to tears without knowing why.

'You know, these aubergines really are delectable.' His eyes were smiling again. 'It must be the arsenic.'

In bed later his love-making, or so it seemed to her, was especially tender and lingering, as if he wanted it to last for ever.

'How could you ever think I could bear to lose you?' she whispered as he bulked over her in the darkness.

Afterwards as they lay sharing a cigarette, still carelessly entwined, staring at the stars through the northern light, he said, 'Supposing I were to find out, while I'm still in power, that you were a member of the resistance. What do you think I'd do?'

She went cold with fright and nearly pulled away from him. He must have felt some slight *frisson* because he said, 'Not getting cold, are you?'

'No,' she said, 'no.' Now, irrationally, she wanted to get as close to him as possible, hoping perhaps to influence him by sheer physical contact. Or perhaps she just wanted the feeling of male nearness and protection. She didn't know what she wanted. She only knew she was miserable.

'Well, what *do* you think I'd do?'

'I don't know,' she said unhappily. 'Have me arrested, I expect.'

'Why would I do that? Don't *I* love *you*?'

'Men love differently from women.'

'How?'

'I don't know. But they do . . . Besides, you'd think I only slept with you to get information.'

'Remarkable. You know what I'd think and you know what I'd do.'

He had that funny way of saying things at times so that you didn't know whether he was joking or serious.

They finished the cigarette and he kissed her and caressed her with great warmth and tenderness and she didn't feel miserable any more.

'I must go,' he said and got up and started to dress.

'Shall I put the light on?'

'No, the moonlight's enough,' he said. 'And I like the dark.'

As he dressed, standing in a patch of moonlight, she thought how handsome he looked and how she loved him.

'Returning to the hypothetical supposition of having a mistress in the resistance—'

'Really, Julian, that's a very tiresome and pointless supposition. You know very well I've been screened.'

'Ah, but would a clever bastard like me *trust* anyone else's screening – when my own safety was at stake?'

'What do you mean?'

'Wouldn't I do a bit of screening for myself?'

'How?' She hoped her voice sounded steady.

'Well, one simple way would be to feed you the odd bit of information – and see if the resistance acted on it.'

She felt the coldness in her belly again. He knew. The bastard knew – and was playing cat-and-mouse.

'After all, a man in my position has to take precautions. Supposing you had a couple of armed men hidden in that big wardrobe . . . I mean, fancy Colonel Julian Giles Cunningham, C-in-C Tac Force, getting kidnapped in bed with a bird . . . I'd never live it down, would I? If I lived at all.'

'What are you trying to say?' She knew her voice was unsteady, but it hardly mattered now.

'Only that if I *had* found out you were in the resistance, and had done nothing about it, it would show, would it not, that though my love might be different from yours it was just as real? I know it's all supposition, but what would you say to that?'

'Ah'd say,' she said in a Southern drawl, hoping it would disguise her wobbling voice, though it was now wobbling for an entirely different reason, 'Ah'd say you were the lovingest sonofabitch ah ever did see.'

She leaned forward because she didn't want him to see the emotion in her face.

When she looked up again he'd gone. So had the patch of moonlight, cut off by a drifting cloud.

20

CUNNINGHAM was late at the office next morning, but Bishop must have seen or heard the helicopter coming in because there was a cup of coffee waiting for him on his desk.

He said good morning pleasantly to Bishop, who was at his own desk, head bent over his work. Bishop replied with equal politeness without looking up. The banderillas had been replaced on the wall below the Manolete poster. The only signs of what had happened the evening before were two small gashes in the panelling, which would no doubt be made good and stained to match the rest – and soon there would be nothing to show for it but two fading scars. The scars on Bishop's mind would take longer to fade.

Cunningham put his feet on the desk, drank his coffee and wondered about Ashman and his girl. As if in answer to his thoughts an outside phone rang. He answered it.

'Hello? Speaking . . . You have? Both of them? Did you get a good look? . . . Never mind, get in touch with the local Tac Force commander and tell him I want the area cordoned off . . . Yes, I know the river makes it awkward. Troopers and vehicles are to keep out of sight. The object is to make sure we've got all the escape routes covered and can set up road-blocks at key points. We'll discuss the actual dispositions when I get there. And tell the river police I want two boats up- and downstream of the warehouse. Any questions? . . . No, nothing special – Tac Force'll carry whatever we need in the way of tear-gas and so on. Your OP's big enough to use as operational HQ, isn't it? I don't want to foul up the cameramen and all their gear . . . Good, see you in an hour.'

He hung up, turned to Bishop. 'Reg Hacker's seen a girl go into the warehouse who more or less answers our description. She was with a man – and, though he didn't get a good look, he thinks it could be Hudson.'

'General Hudson?' Bishop sounded incredulous.

'He wasn't sure. But five men went in ahead of him. And five behind him. All big and hard-looking and wearing bulky rally jackets – over Uzi submachine-guns, no doubt. Anyway, it sounds like Hudson.'

He smiled in reminiscence. 'I was his adjutant once – years ago . . . Real bastard, he was.'

Two of a kind, thought Bishop.

'But clever. Good soldier too. Would've been a field marshal by now – if he hadn't led that abortive coup.'

'And the girl? The description we circulated could fit a hundred girls.'

'It also happens to fit the one who went into the warehouse with Hudson – if it was Hudson . . . Right, let's go.'

'Me too?' Now he was terrified. Was this another macabre joke?

'You too.'

'But I'm a civilian, Colonel. I've – I've never seen action.'

'Then it's time you did. Don't worry, you can sit in the OP and watch from a safe distance.'

'The what?'

'Observation post.'

'But – but who's going to look after the office?'

'Miss Skinner can take messages, can't she?'

'But what if the Home Secretary rings?'

Cunningham smiled more crookedly than ever. 'That, Peter, will be too bloody bad.'

So that's it, Bishop thought. That's why the cunning bastard wants me with him.

'Very well, Colonel,' he said, almost sighing. 'But the very *thought* of violence makes my ulcer ache.'

'Then don't think of it,' said Cunningham. 'Relax and enjoy it, as someone said of rape.'

He started for the door. Bishop followed, reluctantly.

Operational headquarters were two rooms behind the first-floor observation post. One, fitted with a switchboard and radio-telephone, was the communications room, the other was the operations room, whose main furniture was a table and chairs. On the table was a large hand-drawn map showing the warehouse and the network of streets round it. On the wall was a much bigger conventional street map of Greater London.

In the room were Cunningham, Captain Kemp, his adjutant and second-in-command of the assault group Cunningham would lead himself, Reg Hacker, Major Lomax, the local Tac Force commander, and Captain Adams, the communications officer. And, of course, Bishop, the interested observer.

Cunningham, Kemp, Lomax and Adams were in uniform – dark blue battledress with matching flak jackets and black jackboots. They carried .357 Magnums (with the four-inch barrel) in belt-holsters and Sterling submachine-guns slung from their shoulders. In action they would wear the specially designed Tac Force riot helmet, which was like the German army helmet in general shape. It came down at the back to protect the neck. It also had a rounded vizor made of a special laminated perspex formed into small air-filled bubbles. These vizors slightly distorted the wearer's vision but helped to deflect bullets.

Cunningham pointed to the map on the table and said, 'Major Lomax, with a captain and troopers, will be stationed in this yard, where there's a Saracen parked. He should be able to reach the back entrance of the warehouse within twenty to twenty-five seconds. The Saracen will follow him out and block the back entrance. It will be carrying its full complement of sergeant and nine troopers – not counting the crew of two. But they will only come to his assistance if he radios them. Their main job will be to stop escapes. Any questions so far, Major?'

'No, sir.'

'Other Saracens will set up road-blocks at the junctions and crossroads marked by red triangles.' He indicated them on the map. 'The only vehicles allowed through while the operation's in progress will be police cars, Tac Force vehicles and, if necessary, ambulances.'

'Excuse me,' said Lomax, 'but who's leading the assault on the front entrance?'

'I am.'

There was a short silence, then Lomax said: 'Is that wise, sir – to jeopardise yourself? Wouldn't it be better if you stayed here?'

'Issuing radioed orders based on radioed information? I think not, Major. I want to see what's going on. And make my decisions accordingly.'

As Lomax opened his mouth to speak, Cunningham smiled and put a hand on his shoulder.

'And no arguments, Major, please.'

He turned to Captain Adams.

'You will give the radio signal for the operation to start. We'll call it "Animal" – Hudson's an animal all right, and a very wily one. At thirteen hundred hours precisely Captain Adams will announce over the RT: "Animal. Repeat, Animal." And Major Lomax will go into action. I will give him ten seconds, then start the frontal assault – the point being that my men will only have to cross the street. We'll be stationed on the ground floor below the OP. I'll also want back-up from a Saracen.' He pointed to the map. 'This one looks the nearest.'

He looked around. 'I think that's about all, apart from checking equipment, synchronizing watches and arranging radio signals for the Saracen commanders and for ourselves if anything goes wrong.'

He looked round again. 'Any comment or questions?'

'We seem to be carrying a lot of fire-power for a small operation,' Lomax said.

'If it is Hudson in the warehouse, the ten men with him will be ex-paratroopers or ex-SAS men. They'll have guns and they'll know how to use them. And they won't panic. Hudson will have told them exactly what to do in the event of an attack.'

'But he won't be expecting an attack.'

'He's always expecting an attack. That's why he's stayed alive so long. And free so long.'

Cunningham frowned, started to pace the room, then stopped. 'And he'll have an escape route worked out. He always does – wherever he goes.'

He went to the map again, stared down at it.

'The river or the roof,' he said. 'That's the way he'll go.' To Adams he said, 'Tell the river police to station two more boats . . . let's see, here and . . . here.' He put two thick black crosses on the map with a felt pen. 'And I want extra Saracens at either end of the wharf. Here and here.' Two more thick black crosses. 'I know the map's not to scale, but this alleyway – how wide is it?'

'About six feet,' said Hacker. 'You couldn't get a car down it.'

'So a fit man could jump across from one roof to the other . . . But if I know Hudson, he'll have a couple of planks lashed together and ready to shove across. I want a man with a two-way radio watching that alleyway to see if anyone tries to make it to the other roof. But I don't want them shot at. I just want to know what's happening. I'll take the decisions.'

He started pacing again. 'And I don't want any of the top men – Hudson or Murdoch or whoever – killed or wounded in any circumstances. *Any* circumstances. Even if they're armed and firing back. I want them overpowered. I don't care if they're roughed up. But bring 'em back alive. And fit for questioning. Clear?'

There was a silence. Then Lomax said, 'That's going to cost lives.'

'Then it's going to cost lives,' Cunningham said. 'By the way, the results of this operation, successful or not, will be reported by me. And me alone. Nobody else talks. I trust that is also clear.'

Lomax, Kemp and Adams nodded, wondering what he was talking about. But Bishop knew.

Cunningham produced the picture of the girl drawn from Joseph's description and laid it on the table.

'Above all, this girl, or anyone who looks like her, must be taken alive – and unharmed. And don't think that'll be easy. If she's a trained resistance girl she'll be a tiger-cat. Right, let's move.'

He started for the door, then stopped.

'I wonder if I've missed something,' he said. 'Some trick the wily bastard's thought of and I haven't.'

'You make him sound like a magician,' said Lomax.

'He is,' said Cunningham. 'He even makes himself disappear.'

One minute before 1300 hours Captain Adams switched on the radio-telephone, then watched the seconds change on the liquid crystal display of his chronograph till 59 appeared. Then he leaned forward and said into the RT, 'Animal, repeat, Animal.'

Lomax and his twenty men broke cover and made for the back entrance of the target warehouse. Behind them the six-wheeled Saracen rumbled out on its big run-flat tyres.

Ten seconds later, from a boarded-up office below the observation post, Cunningham led the dash across the street with Kemp, Sergeant Quinn and two of the toughest troopers in close support.

Kemp and Quinn kicked open the swing doors of the warehouse entrance, and the two troopers flung themselves through, opening fire with their Sterlings as they landed on the floor. Cunningham, Kemp and Quinn did the same. Within seconds their fire was being returned. More troopers dived in and rolled across the floor, firing as soon as they were stationary.

They were in a large reception hall with a corridor leading off it. Across the corridor were couple of big packing-cases. Four men crouched behind them were firing rapid controlled bursts with automatic weapons. Quinn lobbed a stick-grenade over the packing-cases, there was a deafening explosion – and the firing stopped.

Two Tac Force troopers had been shot dead and five wounded.

Behind the packing-case were two dead and two badly wounded men, all armed with Uzi submachine-guns. Quinn called up a stretcher party and ambulance on his radio, left a trooper in charge of the wounded, then followed Cunningham, Kemp and the rest along the corridor.

At the back entrance Lomax had run into similar but tougher resistance from four other men, also with submachine-guns. The fight took place in an enormous loading-bay and storage area where there were large brick pillars from floor to ceiling as well as piles of crates and a couple of builder's skips full of debris from some work that had been abandoned.

The four resistance men split up, used the cover cleverly and shot accurately and coolly. All four were killed – but it took twenty minutes of hard fighting and the lives of five Tac Force troopers.

Cunningham and the others had meanwhile broken into the printing works by shooting the lock off the door to the print shop – a small place mostly taken up by a linotype and a mono-type machine, galleys of movable type and other equipment.

Three men were crouching down by one of the machines, obviously terrified.

'Arrest them,' Cunningham said and kicked open the door to the editorial office. There, sitting at his desk and trying not to look frightened, was the editor. He was a thin middle-aged man with glasses and bushy greying hair. At another desk was an editorial assistant who looked like a younger version of the other. He was shaking with fear.

'What is all this?' the editor said in a voice that was meant to be strong and indignant.

'A raid on an illegal press,' said Cunningham, 'and a search for General Hudson and his companions. Where are they?'

'I don't know what you're talking about,' the editor said.

Cunningham looked at the boy at the other desk. 'Your son?'

'Yes,' said the editor.

'Take him outside,' Cunningham said to Sergeant Quinn, 'and shoot him.'

He turned and started for another door, which looked as if it led to a corridor, perhaps the same corridor (the print shop was simply the first door they came to).

'Wait,' said the editor. 'Please.'

'Don't tell them,' said the boy, still shaking. 'Don't tell them a bloody thing.'

Cunningham stopped and looked at him. Everything about the boy was shaking but his heart. Quinn looked at Cunningham.

'You've got your orders,' Cunningham said.

Quinn and a trooper grabbed the boy and started to drag him from the office.

'I'll tell you . . .' The editor gulped. 'I'll tell you where they are.'

'Don't—' the boy started to say, but Quinn gave him a backhander that knocked him down and dazed him. Then he yanked him to his feet again.

Cunningham signalled Quinn to release him.

The editor pointed to the second door. 'The corridor. At the end are some stairs that lead to the roof.'

'Who was with General Hudson?'

The editor swallowed again. 'Mr Murdoch and a girl. And two bodyguards.'

Cunningham detailed four men to guard the prisoners and search the office and print shop. Then he hurried out into the corridor, followed by Kemp, Quinn and the remaining troopers.

There were six flights of stairs to the roof exit. Trouble was waiting on the fifth and sixth landings. On the fifth landing were the last two of Hudson's bodyguard. On the fourth landing Cunningham heard on his radio that an observer on the ground had just seen two men crossing the narrow alleyway on planks pushed across from one roof to the other.

On the fifth flight of stairs they were met by a burst of automatic fire and the two leading troopers went down (one died in hospital later). Kemp threw a canister of tear-gas on to the landing. Quinn threw a smoke-discharger. The Tac Force men slipped on their quick-action gas-masks and rushed the landing, shooting blind into the smoke. Both the resistance men were wounded and out of action.

As they started up the sixth flight they ran into more fire, from a pistol this time. Quinn was hit and knocked down, but the bullet came in at an angle, glanced off his flak jacket and went into the wall. Cunningham caught sight of a girl's dark hair and told everyone to get back.

'Smoke and tear-gas, then rush her?' said Kemp.

'No,' said Cunningham, 'I don't want any accidents. To her, that is. Might be our only worthwhile capture at this rate. Anyone see the gun? Looked like a German Army Walther P38 to me.'

'It was,' said Quinn, 'firing the nine-millimetre Parabellum. And it bloody felt like it, too. I'll have sore ribs for a month.'

Cunningham pointed to a window ledge on the landing. 'Keep firing just to the right of that ledge,' he said. 'That'll stop her poking her head out to get an accurate shot.'

'But even if she did we'd miss her.'

'That, Captain Kemp,' Cunningham said, 'is the whole idea. But she won't know we're aiming to miss. I'll creep up, as close as I can get, and try to talk her into surrendering. And if she won't – I'll try to grab the gun.'

'No,' said Kemp. 'Far too risky. I'll do it.'

'Kemp,' said Cunningham, 'you're a much better shot and I'm a much better talker. You and Quinn give me covering fire. And make sure you aim high enough. Otherwise you might not only hit the girl, you might even hit me – which I should take very unkindly.'

He started to crawl up the stairs, keeping close to the banisters, on the same side of the stairs as the girl. Kemp and Quinn gave him covering fire. The moment her head appeared they fired just above it – and she had to duck back before she had time to take aim. As Cunningham inched his way up, he spoke to her softly, easily.

'You might as well give up, you know. If you kill me, the next man will get you. Or the one after him . . . There really isn't any point in this rearguard action. The two men who crossed to the other roof will soon be caught – if they haven't been already. You see, we were watching for them, waiting for them. All the rest of your friends have either been captured or killed . . .'

Her head appeared again, and this time she managed to get in a snap shot, despite the covering fire, but it went wide. Snap shooting was the best she could do against that kind of covering fire – with bullets crunching into the wall behind her every time she showed her head.

'So there really isn't any point in holding out—'

She took another snap shot, missed again.

'Unless of course, you want to commit suicide.'

By now Cunningham was only a few feet from her. One leap and he'd be on her.

'Listen,' he said, gathering himself, 'all I want to do is *talk* to you.'

As he started his spring she took another snap shot – and hit him. It was a coincidence. It was also bad luck (especially for a man who didn't believe in coincidences). The bullet caught him on the side of the head just behind the temple. He went over backwards like an inexperienced gymnast attempting a somersault and not quite making it. Kemp rushed the girl and grappled with her. Cunningham was lying on the landing below, unconscious and bleeding from the head.

Quinn was the first to reach him. 'Better call up an ambulance. I don't know how bad the head wound is, but he fell badly and I think he's got a broken arm or wrist as well.'

Kemp called for an ambulance and stretcher party on his radio, then turned to the girl, who was being held by two troopers.

'If you've killed him,' he said, 'you'll die young and in pain.'

At that moment an RT message from Captain Adams announced that the two men escaping over the roofs had been captured. It turned out they were two of the printing workers.

'Then where the hell are Murdoch and Hudson? Over,' said Kemp.

'Good question,' said Adams. 'Over and out.'

General Hudson and Joshua Murdoch had taken an escape route discovered and prepared nearly eighteen months before – soon after the underground press had taken the premises and Hudson started making regular visits. An architect had discovered it when studying old drainage plans of the area. A disused sewer ran under the cellar of the next warehouse. It had been a simple matter to knock an access hole in the wall. Another hole was cut in the floor of the cellar to give entry to the sewer and covered by a carefully concealed trap-door.

Nobody except the editor knew about this arrangement – and even he didn't know about the trap-door and the sewer. He merely thought Hudson and Murdoch were hoping to escape by way of the next warehouse while this one was being searched. He thought their chances of success were nil.

In fact, they came up three streets away through a manhole just short of the spot where the sewer had been blocked off when a new one was laid. They were still, however, within the main Tac Force cordon.

The next part of the plan was also simple. Hudson's face was not well known to the police and public. And he had dyed his hair, changed the parting and grown a beard. Murdoch's face, however, was far too well known for simple disguises. He had been a prominent and controversial political figure for years, appearing frequently on television, where his calm but messianic manner and lucid arguments did not quite hide the maniacal obsessions just below the surface. It all made for good viewing, though.

Hudson produced the Smith & Wesson .38 known as the Chief's Special (a favourite with plain-clothes men), and marched Murdoch along as if under arrest – a couple of paces ahead of him and with arms raised.

After turning into another street Hudson saw a patrolling police car and flagged it down. He produced a forged warrant card and said, 'DI Richards, Special Branch.' He waved the gun at Murdoch. 'I don't have to tell you who this is. Take us to the local Tac Force HQ, will you?'

The constable riding passenger was already out of the car and opening the near-side back door.

'Don't s'pose you're carrying these?' he said, and took out a pair of handcuffs.

Hudson smiled and held out his left wrist. 'Perhaps you'd like to marry us.'

The constable handcuffed the two men together and gave Hudson the key.

'Your prisoner,' he said, and got in the front seat. Murdoch and Hudson, who had put the gun away, got in the back. They went through the road-block with no trouble. Hudson unobtrusively unlocked the handcuffs while chatting to the constable and driver, then took out the Smith & Wesson. Murdoch took out a Webley .455 automatic.

'Constable,' Hudson said softly. 'Turn round a moment.'

The constable turned round, saw the Smith & Wesson pointing at the back of the driver's neck, turned a little more and found himself looking down the barrel of the Webley.

'Tell your friend', Hudson said, softly as ever, 'that we're not going to Tac Force HQ.'

21

CUNNINGHAM was still unconscious when he was brought into the hospital's casualty department. The wound in his head was cleaned up and he was examined by the senior consultant surgeon and a senior surgical registrar.

'The head wound doesn't look too bad,' said the consultant. 'But he's bound to be concussed – could even have a haematoma. Let's get him X-rayed.'

'Looks as if he might also have a Colles' fracture of the left wrist,' said the registrar.

The consultant nodded and said to a staff nurse, 'Staff, I want the wet plates as soon as they're ready.'

The wet plates confirmed the Colles' fracture but were inconclusive about the head wound. That the wound was superficial could be seen; its effects could not. Concussion doesn't show on X-ray plates. Nor does intracranial bleeding. The only thing to do, they decided, was to keep the patient in overnight and see how he was in the morning.

Cunningham came round to find himself in bed, propped up on pillows, his head heavily bandaged, his left arm in plaster. Both ached. He felt muzzy and weak.

The first thing he saw was a vase of garnet roses on the mobile bed-table at the foot of the bed. Then he saw the nurse sitting by his side. She was young and pretty in an open-faced way and high-breasted. She was reading a magazine. He was in a private room and high up presumably. All he could see through the window was sky, most of it blue with one or two fat white clouds. He began to feel less muzzy.

'What happened?' he said.

The nurse looked up. 'You've been shot.'

'I know that. What happened to the girl?'

'What girl?' The nurse looked blank.

'Get me an outside phone.'

The nurse picked up the bedside phone and dialled the switchboard. 'Find Mr Soutar, will you? And tell him Colonel Cunningham has regained consciousness. He sounds weak and a little confused.'

'I'm not confused,' Cunningham said. 'Where the hell's Kemp?'

'I'm about to take his temperature,' the nurse said. She put the phone down and stuck a thermometer in his mouth. By the time she had taken his temperature and entered it on the chart at the foot of the bed, Soutar, the consultant surgeon, had arrived.

'Well, how are we?' he said in that slightly hearty voice common to surgeons.

'Aching like a bastard,' said Cunningham.

'Where?'

'Mostly in the head and arm. Where's Kemp? I want to know what happened to the girl. Phone Tac Force headquarters . . .'

He stopped. He had lost concentration. The muzziness was back.

'I feel funny,' he said.

'We'll give you something for all that. Soon have you as right as rain, won't we, nurse?' Soutar said. Then he said something to the nurse that Cunningham didn't catch, partly because the bandages covered one of his ears, partly because Soutar normally lowered his voice when not being professionally cheerful.

'Now,' Soutar said, back to the cheerful voice, 'let's take a peep at the peepers, eh?' He chuckled and took out an ophthalmoscope.

If only he wasn't so bloody hearty, Cunningham thought. Like a mock-auctioneer with a crowd of hicks.

The nurse came back with a glass of water and four tablets, two red, two white.

'What, no blue?' said Cunningham. 'And me so patriotic?'

'I beg your pardon?' said Soutar, who thought Cunningham's mind was wandering again.

'Forget it,' Cunningham said. Within a few minutes of taking the tablets he fell into an exhausted sleep.

The hi-jacked police car was found on Ashstead Common, near the Epsom Gap, which is off the main road to Kingston – and London if you turn right at the Hook roundabout and go down the access road to the A3. Both constable and driver were still in the car. One had been shot through the back of the head with a Webley .455, the other with a Smith & Wesson .38, the model known as the Chief's Special.

The captured girl had been flown by helicopter to Tac Force headquarters, stripped and body-searched, none too gently, by

215

two women warders with probing fingers. She was allowed to dress again (in her black sweater and black jeans) and taken, hands handcuffed behind her back, to Cunningham's office. Her only accessory, a shoulder-bag, was given to Bishop. The contents were mostly feminine paraphernalia apart from an identity card and some letters.

The identity card gave her name as Elizabeth Fitzsimmons. But in the letters, which he glanced at, she was called Beth. He put the letters and identity card back in the bag, put the bag on Cunningham's desk and studied the girl. It was amazing – with a little hindsight, of course – how close Joseph's musical description had come: the dark hair, almost shoulder-length, the dark eyes, high cheekbones and heavy mouth . . . Handsome rather than beautiful. And proud, you could tell. Well, Bishop thought, we'll soon take care of that – and anything else that gets in the way. But there certainly was something about her. She took your eye. And Bishop wasn't a man whose eye was easily taken by a woman.

Miss Skinner came in and stared at her, walked right round her, staring all the time. Beth ignored her.

'Is it true she killed at least one of our men and wounded Colonel Cunningham?'

'You should've seen her,' Bishop said. 'Fought like a wild-cat, took three men to hold her down and handcuff her.'

He spoke as if he had actually been present instead of safely tucked away in the observation post.

'The big fish got away though, didn't they?'

Bishop nodded. 'Still, this one's big enough.'

'How bad is Colonel Cunningham?'

He told her about the head wound and broken wrist.

'The hospital didn't think it was too serious – though he was still unconscious when I went there. They weren't sure about the head wound though. Let's ring them now and find out.'

Miss Skinner rang the hospital and got the usual as-well-as-can-be-expected answer. The only positive fact she learned was that they were keeping him in overnight.

'M'm,' said Bishop. He indicated Beth. 'I suppose we'd better put her in the cells . . .' He paused, thinking. Then he took her aside and spoke in a low voice.

'I wondered . . . if I should tell the Home Secretary we've got her here.'

'Why not?'

'Well, you know how funny Cunningham is about prisoners.

216

And this one's very important to him – after all, he practically got killed capturing her.'

'The Minister's bound to want to see her. Perhaps even bring the Prime Minister to see her. I mean, she *is* quite a prize, isn't she?'

'But if Cunningham were to find out—'

'Why should he?'

'He already suspects me. I had a quite terrifying experience with him yesterday. Quite terrifying.'

'Anyone could've reported the capture to the Home Secretary – Lomax, Kemp, Hacker, anyone.'

Bishop shook his head. 'No. They're his men. They won't say a word. They think the bloody world of him. Besides, he gave all of us the strictest orders about keeping the whole thing secret.'

'Peter, you have a clear duty to the Minister – and to yourself. He was the one who appointed you, remember. He thinks highly of you. And he has the ear of the Prime Minister. People like that don't forget favours.'

'Perhaps you're right.' Bishop was still reluctant.

'Of course I am. Go on, ring him.' He looked at her, still doubtful. '*Now*, Peter.'

Bishop picked up the phone on his desk.

'No, not through the switchboard. Those giggling bitches are all sweet on Cunningham. I've heard them talking – Isn't he charming? And so handsome and somehow sad-looking – you know what girls are. I bet they check every call for him.'

'You could be right. I've often wondered why he's so nice to them. I'll use one of the outside phones.'

He started to cross to Cunningham's desk, then stopped.

'No,' he said. 'They're connected to a tape-recorder that automatically switches on when the receiver's lifted, and switches off when you put it down again. I know there's a secret button somewhere to switch it off manually . . . I suppose if we had a good look—'

'Why bother? Take a car into the village and phone from there – then nothing can go wrong. You can be there and back in ten minutes.'

'You're right.' He indicated Beth. 'Keep an eye on her. There are a couple of guards outside if she gets troublesome.' He turned to the door. 'Oh, and make an inventory of the things in her bag.'

'Have you got change – for the phone?'

'Yes, yes,' he said, and went out quickly.

Miss Skinner went to Beth, who was standing with her head lowered, apparently staring at the floor.

'You can sit down now.'

Beth ignored her. Miss Skinner shoved her roughly into the chair facing Cunningham's desk. It was awkward sitting with your hands handcuffed behind you; it forced you to sit upright. It had been more comfortable standing.

Miss Skinner sat at Cunningham's desk and stared at her.

'So you're his girl. Well, well . . . You look as if you could do with a good wash. But I don't suppose you bother with details like that in the resistance. Or do they like it a bit gamey?'

She made a snorting sound that was meant to be laughter. Beth still stared at the floor. Miss Skinner got up, went round the desk and stood in front of her.

'I'm talking to you.'

At last Beth raised her head and Miss Skinner found herself facing a black unyielding stare.

'Do you love him?'

Beth went on staring at her.

'I said, do you love him?'

'What would you know about love?'

Miss Skinner slapped her across the face, leaving a red mark. The black unyielding stare was still on her, the only sign of anger a slight narrowing of the eyes.

'God, you even look like him when you look like that . . . Women always pick up something from the men they live with, don't they? And you lived with him all right.' She wrinkled her nose and gave an exclamation of disgust. 'You reek of him. *Reek* of him . . . Or perhaps it's only the sweat.'

She went back to the desk, cleared a space and emptied out the shoulder-bag. She took a sheet of paper and started making an inventory.

'One packet containing eight cigarettes.' She wrote it down. 'One lighter, one powder compact, one lipstick. What colour do you use?'

She opened the lipstick, examined it. 'M'm. Dark red. Thought you'd've tried something more *femme fatale*. Orange or something . . . Purse containing, let's see, seven pounds and . . . forty-four pence. And a booklet of postage stamps. One bottle of scent . . . And by God you need it.'

She opened it, put a little on the back of her hand, rubbed it in and sniffed it.

218

'Not bad,' she said in a surprised voice. 'Not bad at all. Delicate. Subtle. Faintly – what? Flowery, I suppose . . . Five letters – from some man by the writing.' She took one out of the envelope, started to read it. 'Oh yes, that's from a man all right – only one thing *they* ever think about.'

Beth raised her head. Again that black stare. And a low angry voice.

'Don't read my letters, you bitch.'

Two red spots of anger showed on Miss Skinner's cheeks.

'I'll read what I like. You've no rights any more, none at all.' A note of pleasure came into her voice. 'We can do what we like with you.'

She picked up another letter. 'Ah, an unopened one – from you no doubt.' She slit it open. 'Yes, that's it: "Love, Beth" . . . She started to read it. 'Love? *Love?* It's nothing but sex to you.' The anger spots were showing on her cheeks again. 'That's all it is – sex. Oh yes, I've heard about you bitches. On heat all the time – coupling in the fields like animals. That's why half the men join the resistance – because you're easy.'

The anger spots spread till her whole face was flushed. Even her grey, usually unexpressive eyes darkened and seemed to sparkle with anger. She got up, went round the desk and stood in front of Beth, hands on hips.

'Whores,' she said, shaking with anger. 'The lot of you. Strumpets, harlots, whores.'

Beth looked at her, one side of her mouth beginning to lift in a smile of contempt.

'Why don't you piss off, you dried-up virgin?'

Miss Skinner snatched a metal ruler off the desk and raised it to slash Beth across the face. Then, with a visible effort of control, she put it down again.

'No,' she said, still shaky, 'I mustn't mark you till you've been . . . interrogated.'

She went back to the desk, fighting her anger. A pulse began to throb in her temple like an old familiar pain.

'You're right,' she said. 'I am a virgin. And proud of it. For five years I've been waiting. Keeping myself pure for the man I love. For five years we've been friends – and we've never even . . . touched. Only our minds have . . . touched.' She seemed to be trying to distance herself from a word whose sensual implications might trigger off some strange and dangerous emotion. A note of hysteria came into her voice.

'Only our minds, our spirits . . . touched. And embraced.

With a love you wouldn't understand. All you understand is done in the dark – the deed of darkness, the lust of the flesh . . . And you think that's everything. But you're wrong, you're wrong. There's something else.'

She got up, started to wander, distracted.

'A something more exquisite still, it says in the Bible. And there is. And we have it, Peter and I . . . A something more exquisite still.'

The double doors opened and Bishop came in.

'Don't we, Peter?' Miss Skinner said, turning to him. 'We have it.'

'Any word from Colonel Cunningham?'

'No.'

'Good. Done the inventory?'

'Yes. We have it, don't we, Peter?'

'Have what, Lorraine?'

She blushed, suddenly confused and sad, not knowing what to say.

'Look,' said Bishop, 'the Home Secretary's on his way in one of those executive jets. Tell the senior officer of the guard to meet him with two or three troopers – make up a little reception party. Tell the control tower to give him clearance – well, you know the drill.'

Miss Skinner crossed blindly to the doors. 'Five years,' she said as she went out. 'Five years.'

Bishop studied Beth with asexual curiosity. The Home Secretary had seemed excited by the news of her capture and said something about striking while the iron was hot. Bishop wondered what he had in mind.

Cunningham woke up to find Kemp sitting at his bedside. The young nurse was on the other side.

'Hello, Kemp.'

'How are you, sir?'

'Better.' And he was, or felt he was. 'Now, tell me what happened.'

Kemp told him about the capture of the girl, the escape of Hudson and Murdoch, the casualties on both sides.

'Hudson. The bastard's always got a trick you haven't thought of.'

'How could you have known about the cellars and that dis-used sewer?'

'How did he know about them? He found out. Where's the girl?'

'You said fly her to HQ. We did.'

'And no one's been told? The Home Secretary's not been told?'

'You said no one.'

'Where's Bishop?'

'He flew back with her.'

Cunningham sat up. 'Nurse, my clothes.'

'Your clothes? You can't possibly get up.'

'Nurse,' Cunningham said slowly and distinctly. '*I* give orders, even here. Get my clothes.'

The nurse picked up the phone and dialled the switchboard. 'Put out a call for Mr Soutar and tell him Colonel Cunningham wants to discharge himself.'

Then she crossed to a wall cupboard, took out Cunningham's uniform clothes and hung them over a chair near the bed.

Soutar, who was middle-aged and running to fat, came in hurriedly and out of breath.

'What is this nonsense I hear about your wanting to discharge yourself?'

'I take it I'll need a sling for this,' Cunningham said, indicating his left arm, which was still in plaster. To Kemp he said, 'Hand me my shirt.'

'Colonel Cunningham,' said Soutar, 'there is no question of your leaving this hospital tonight.'

'If you try to obstruct me you'll leave it, too – under arrest.'

'You realize there may be intra cranial bleeding that doesn't show on the X-ray plates.'

'What does that mean?'

'You may be suffering from brain damage. We must keep you under observation for at least twenty-four hours. Otherwise your life could be at risk.'

'If I stay in this bed the whole country could be at risk.'

He pushed the bedclothes aside, put his feet on the floor and tried to stand up. He collapsed and fell partly on the bed. The nurse quickly picked up his legs, swung them back on to the bed and pulled the bedclothes over him. It was very neat and professional.

'There,' said Soutar, 'you see? It's impossible. Quite impossible.'

'Balls,' Cunningham said weakly.

*

The Home Secretary was met on the tarmac by the senior officer of the guard and four troopers and taken straight to Cunningham's office. Miss Skinner was waiting for him in the outer office. She was holding a file which she offered him.

'Do you want to see her file, sir?'

'File? She can hardly have a file yet, surely?'

'We start a file on each new prisoner immediately. So far it only contains details taken from her identity card and Polaroid pictures of her when she was stripped and body-searched.'

The Home Secretary, who was crossing to Cunningham's office, stopped and turned to her.

'Yes,' he said. 'Perhaps I'd better see it.'

There were four photographs of her. Two close-ups, one of her face, one of her profile and two full-length pictures showing her naked from the front and from the back. The Home Secretary studied them intently.

'M'm,' he said, 'good-looking, isn't she? Good figure, too. Very good.'

Those little red spots began to appear on Miss Skinner's cheeks. 'She's nothing but a whore,' she said. 'A strumpet. In the old days she'd have been tied naked to the tail of a cart and whipped through the streets.'

She hadn't meant to say so much or in such a vehement tone, but it was out before she could stop it. The Home Secretary looked at her sideways.

'So you think she's, er, in need of a . . . good whipping?'

There was something in his voice, an inflection, a hint of vibrato, something odd – and sexual. A signal perhaps. Miss Skinner was very good at picking up sex signals, however faint and fleeting, partly because she was always on the look-out for them, partly because she got so few.

She dropped her eyes modestly. 'Yes, sir,' she said. 'Since you ask me, I think she needs a good whipping.'

'Very interesting,' the Home Secretary said. 'Very interesting.'

He would have liked to prolong the conversation with its sado-masochistic overtones, but didn't know how to. Anyway, a minister of the Crown could hardly indulge in that sort of thing with a typist.

They looked at each other for a long moment, then the Home Secretary turned away with some reluctance and went through the double doors into Cunningham's office.

Miss Skinner sat down. She felt weak and a little trembly, and put her head in her hands.

'Five bloody years,' she said.

The Home Secretary shook Bishop by the hand, a signal recognition of his gratitude; he never shook hands with inferiors.

'Well done, Peter. I shan't forget.'

'You do understand I'm going against Colonel Cunningham's strict orders.'

'And quite rightly.'

'But if he should find out—'

'He won't, he won't,' the Home Secretary said airily. 'Who's going to tell him?'

'But your very presence here—'

'Why shouldn't I drop in? These are critical times, Peter, and it's natural for me to keep in touch with my subordinates.' He paused to wag a finger. 'And let's not forget that Colonel Cunningham is a subordinate – even if he doesn't act like one.'

All the time he was taking sidelong glances at Beth, still sitting unnaturally upright in the chair in front of Cunningham's desk.

'You see, sir, he already suspects I give you information and I'd be the first—'

'Don't worry, Peter. You run along. I'd like a word with Miss Fitzsimmons . . . alone.'

'Excuse me, sir, but you know it's against regulations to interrogate—'

'I *make* the regulations, Peter. And who said anything about interrogation? I just want a word. You organize some coffee and cakes.'

'Yes, sir,' Bishop said. He sounded tired and worried.

As soon as they were alone the Home Secretary turned to Beth.

'Get up,' he said. The feeling of power was as heady as wine.

Beth was glad to get up. It was more comfortable than sitting bolt upright with her hands fastened behind her. She kept her eyes on the ground. The Home Secretary put a hand under her chin and lifted it till he got the full benefit of her black uncompromising stare.

'Yes,' he said, 'you are good-looking. Better than your pictures. You strip well, too. Our special interrogators appreciate a good figure. Tell me, my dear, what do you know about

Operation Volcano?'

She didn't answer.

'I'll repeat the question. What do you know about Operation Volcano?'

'Nothing. And if I did I wouldn't tell you.'

The Home Secretary smiled. 'Brave words, my dear, brave words. How often I've heard them before.'

There was a knock on the door and Miss Skinner came in with a tray of coffee and cakes.

'Ah, thank you, Miss Skinner.' The Home Secretary rubbed his hands. 'I'm quite peckish.'

But he found he wasn't hungry at all. Hunger for food had been replaced by hunger for power – a far more satisfying compensation for inadequacy. And he actually *had* someone in his power. He waited till Miss Skinner left, then stepped closer to Beth.

'So you know nothing about Volcano?' he said, and smiled. 'Never mind. Your friend Ashman does.'

Despite herself she reacted to the name. The hardness went out of her eyes and she looked away.

'Oh, yes, he's here. But I expect you knew that.' He pointed to the floor. 'Down below. Almost under your feet, I should think.'

She stared down at the floor as if trying to see through it.

'Obstinate fellow. One of our few failures – well, so far. We simply can't get him to talk. Still, you'll change all that, won't you, dear?'

'*You* won't change anything, you fat poof.'

The Home Secretary's face and eyes darkened with anger. His voice was as soft as ever.

'Not me, dear. Oh, no. But our special interrogators will. They're very ingenious – especially with a pretty girl. It seems to turn them on.'

'What turns you on? Little boys? Or something freakier?'

'One trick they've found particularly successful with girls consists of two wires ending in electrodes. No, that's not quite accurate. They end in two plastic . . . well, how shall I describe them without being indelicate?'

'Try calling them plastic pricks.'

'All they do is insert them – you can guess where, can't you? Then pull a switch. The more they pull the switch the stronger the current. You should see the contortions the girl go through.

Almost comic if it weren't for the shrieking—'

Beth spat in his face. The Home Secretary took out a handkerchief and carefully wiped the spittle off. Then he jabbed his fingers as hard as he could into her solar plexus. She collapsed and lay writhing on the floor, fighting for breath.

'We'll tame you, dear. We tame lions in this place.'

Bishop, who heard the noise of the fall, came running in.

'Minister,' he said, 'what have you done? You shouldn't touch her, sir, you really shouldn't. You should wait—'

'You know, Peter, I've had rather a bright idea,' the Home Secretary said, picking up a cake and starting to eat it, slowly and enjoyably, as he watched Beth writhing on the floor.

22

THE LIGHTING WAS DIM: one twenty-five-watt bulb in a wire cage in the middle of the ceiling. It stayed on all night, bathing the cell in a kind of yellowish twilight.

Ashman was lying on his bunk, Joseph was sitting on the edge of the table, picking out a love-song on the guitar, when the door was flung open and Fat Charlie came in with two armed guards. Ashman was already on his feet, but Fat Charlie ignored him, pointed at Joseph.

'You – out.'

'Me?' said Joseph, terrified.

'You,' said Fat Charlie. Then to the guards: 'Put him in twenty-four.'

'What's wrong?' said Joseph. 'I haven't done anything.'

'Get moving and shut up.'

Joseph grabbed the guitar. 'Can I take this?'

'Take what you want – but move.'

Joseph went out, escorted by the two guards. Fat Charlie looked at Ashman and laughed.

'You got a visitor,' he said and signalled to someone outside that Ashman couldn't see. 'And this one's no dream.'

Beth came in between two other armed guards. She was no longer handcuffed. Fat Charlie threw a packet of cigarettes on the table.

'Compliments of the house,' he said, gave another bark of laughter and went out with the two guards. The door slammed shut with its usual metallic crash.

Ashman and Beth stood staring at each other. Then, as if he didn't quite believe his eyes, Ashman took a step towards her. Then another step. Then he stopped. Then they were in each other's arms. They had been apart little more than a month. It felt like for ever. She clung to him, murmuring unintelligibly. Then she leaned back.

'Tommy, listen—'

'I never thought I'd see you again,' he said.

'Listen, I must tell you something—'

'Your face again.'

'Tommy, please—'

'Your eyes and mouth again.'

'Please listen to me, I must tell you what happened.'

'You saved Hudson and Murdoch, shot a couple of Tac Force thugs and wounded Colonel Cunningham – may the bastard snuff it. You and some of the press people were taken alive.'

'But how did you—?'

'Jungle drums. No place gets that kind of news quicker than this place. The details aren't always accurate but the guts of it are.'

'You mean we've got . . . men here?'

'Two of the guards. One will be on duty soon. I'll point him out . . . Christ, it's wonderful to see you.' He hugged her again, then let her go.

'Here, I'm forgetting my manners. Sit down.' She sat at the table. He sat opposite. 'And have a cigarette. We've got a whole packet.'

He gave her a cigarette and lit it. Then he leaned forward, lowering his voice.

'It's still on, isn't it?'

She didn't need to ask what he was talking about.

'It's on.'

His voice went even lower. 'The date?'

'I don't know,' she said.

Ashman didn't know either. He knew Volcano was planned for the month of June, but the exact date was to have been fixed by a special meeting of OPSCOM towards the end of May – by which time he was already in jail. But it won't be long now, he thought. Two or three weeks at the most. Maybe sooner.

And the clever Colonel Cunningham had been wrong in thinking that he, Ashman, knew the date – though he knew everything else about Volcano.

'What are you smiling at?'

He slid his hand across the table and took hers. 'I can't get over it. Seeing you, I mean.'

The Home Secretary had finished the coffee but left the cakes. Bishop was wandering restlessly about the office. From time to time he glanced at his watch.

The Home Secretary said, 'I feel like a drink, Peter. Give me a brandy, will you, with a splash of soda?'

Bishop went to the drinks cupboard, poured brandy, added soda. He was glad to do something; it quietened his nerves.

'Have one yourself.'

'I'll have a mineral water, if I may.' He opened a small bottle of Perrier, then glanced at his watch again.

'They've been together half an hour now, sir. Isn't that enough?'

'No, Peter, it is not enough. I said an hour and I meant an hour. Time is precious to lovers. To cut it even by a minute would be . . .' He gestured. 'Cruel.'

'It's just that if Colonel Cunningham finds out—'

'Stop worrying about Colonel Cunningham. I'll take the responsibility. You won't be involved at all.'

'I'm already involved. He is my superior, and he did give me certain orders.'

'And I'm his superior, and I gave you other orders. Anyway, whatever else he is, Cunningham's no fool. He'll be the first to appreciate what I've done.'

Bishop wasn't so sure. 'I hope you're right.'

'He'll appreciate the psychology of it.' He looked at Bishop's doubtful nervous face. 'You appreciate it, don't you?'

'Oh yes, of course,' Bishop said quickly. 'It was a most . . . astute move.'

'Well, then.' The Home Secretary made one of his airy gestures and drank some brandy and soda.

'It's just that he's . . . such a strange man. You never know how he's going to react.'

'The only thing he can react to at the moment is hospital treatment. And for once he'll have to do as he's told. I'd love to see him being pushed around by those bossy little nurses.'

'What sort of dream?' Beth said.

'Oh, you know, crazy. But at the last moment somehow I was saved.' He frowned. 'At least I think I was.' He shrugged. 'Prisoners are always dreaming of freedom.'

'Dreams can come true,' she said.

'Yeah, you can win the pools, too.'

'They'd set you free if you talked.'

'If I *talked*?' He gave a grunt of laughter. 'After what you've done? The whole country'll be full of it – despite their bloody press censorship. What a story. What a girl.' He smiled at her, held her chin in his hand. 'My little Beth, the gentle one. The lamb who held the lion at bay. By all the rules, you know, you should've been terrified.'

She smiled back. 'There wasn't time. It was all so quick and . . . exciting. All of a sudden I was crouching on the landing,

228

firing. Shooting down the stairs, the gun jumping in my hand. It felt marvellous. The noise, the stink of cordite, the way the men went down. I always thought they'd crumple when a bullet hit them – like on the telly. But they don't, do they? Crash, bang! They go down like ninepins.'

'That depends on the type of gun.'

'And I loved it. Me . . .' Her voice went quiet, unbelieving. 'The killer.'

'Don't worry about that. That's what they call the heat of battle – or getting a buzz.'

'And now all the heat's gone. It's cold . . . Or is it this place?' She looked around. 'I don't know how you stand it.'

'I'm thinking of putting in for a transfer,' he said, trying to be jokey. 'To the Ritz. I don't like the staff here. The bastards lack refinement.'

'I know,' she said. 'They're going to torture me.'

'Unless I talk.'

'Or I talk.'

He studied her face but it gave nothing away. She threw her half-smoked cigarette on the floor and trod it out. He was about to explain that you don't waste cigarettes in prison but changed his mind. This wasn't the time.

'How much do you know?' he said.

'Not the operational details – but enough. I've been working with Hudson, remember.'

'And everything's on schedule?'

She nodded.

'You realize what that means?'

She could hear the excitement in his voice. She nodded again.

'It means we're ready. It means it could happen any time . . . Tonight, tomorrow, next week. Any time.'

He got up. He had to move. The movements were abrupt, impatient, as he tried to hold down his excitement and the feeling of violence that went with it.

He looked up through the barred window into the falling darkness. The white candles on the chestnut-tree stood out clearly.

Maybe even now somewhere out there in the half-light men were moving into position, checking equipment, making phone calls, arranging transport. Certain army, police and air force officers standing by for the code-word, certain runways and approach roads already mined . . . The fuses already laid . . .

Maybe Operation Volcano was already rolling.

He laughed again from excitement. He could feel the adrenalin rising; he couldn't keep still; the cell had shrunk; it felt smaller than ever, cramping and confining him like a lion in a travelling cage. Only an old circus lion maybe, but now he'd smelt blood. The image amused him and he smiled.

'Will they torture me in front of you?' Her voice sounded small and far away but it was like cold water in his face. It stopped him short, stopped his pacing. He turned and looked at her. She looked small and defenceless, fragile almost. He wanted to take her in his arms and protect her for ever. What do you do in an impossible situation?

'Listen,' he said, 'they always threaten you with torture – to try and frighten you.'

'They succeeded,' she said. 'I am frightened.'

'Beth,' he said, 'all we have to do is hold out for a little while. A day or two. A week or two. That's all.'

'We?' she said. '*We* have to hold out? Oh, I see. You mean, if you have to watch it'll be pretty bad for you, too.'

Christ, he thought, what do you say?

'Let me explain something,' he said. 'Their biggest trick is imagination. That's what they play on. Like an exposed nerve . . . I've known them tie a man up so he can watch while they heat an iron in the fire. Then they blindfold him. He hears the iron being pulled out of the fire. Feels the heat of it as they bring it close to his face. He holds his breath, goes rigid – every muscle in his body rigid, screwed up tight. Sweat breaking out on him like dew. Then they shove a lump of ice in his face. And he screams. He thinks he's been burned . . . A trick. All done by imagination. It can break a man down quicker than anything. Break his spirit and you don't have to break his body.'

That sounded good, he thought. That ought to impress her.

'The scar on your left cheek,' she said. 'Was that done by imagination?'

'That', he said gently, 'was done by a guard. But, you see, he had an excuse. He was trying to stop me killing another guard. And he didn't succeed. Which put him out. He also got a busted arm. That put him out, too.'

'You make it sound like a rather jolly romp,' she said. 'But I don't suppose it was.'

Christ, he thought, you can't win. He sat at the table and smiled.

'Have another burn,' he said, taking a cigarette from the packet and giving it to her. He struck a match on the pitch-pine table, lit the cigarette. Something about his actions that had been bothering her ever since she came into the cell suddenly became clear.

'Why do you do everything with your right hand?' she said.

'Because I'm right-handed.'

'Apart from when you had your arms round me you've kept your left hand in your pocket.'

'I always scratch my balls with my left hand. Didn't you know?'

'No,' she said, 'I didn't know.'

'For Christ's sake, Beth, it's a joke. Or meant to be.'

'Next time I'll laugh.'

There was a silence. Then he said, 'If you really want to see my left hand—'

'No,' she said, 'I don't. Unless all the fingernails are there.'

Shit, he thought. 'And the next clever guess?' he said.

'I don't know how people can even *do* it,' she said. 'Never mind put up with it. I couldn't do it – to *anyone*. I'd be sick. Physically sick.'

Her big eyes looked at him with their unanswerable questions, and that protective feeling ached through him again. He wanted to get her off the subject of torture, but she was trying to exorcise it like an evil spirit, make it go away by talking about it. But nothing would make it go away. Talking would only bring it nearer.

'How do *you* put up with it?'

'There are what we call counter-techniques.'

'So that it doesn't hurt any more?'

He ignored the sarcasm and said patiently, 'The idea is to try and . . . strengthen yourself as much as possible.'

'Teach me,' she said. 'Strengthen me.'

'It takes time. You have to go through a course.'

'You mean learn a discipline – like medicine or music? I think I'd sooner learn the violin.'

'I mean there are methods against sensory deprivation,' he said in the same patient voice, 'methods for lessening the effects of loss of sleep, lack of food—'

'Got anything for those electrodes they shove up a woman?'

She was suddenly on her feet, shouting at him, shaking with anger and fear. He grabbed her by the shoulders and shook her.

'You think you're the only poor cow that's ever been tortured?'

His anger against her was the last straw. She started to sob uncontrollably. He pulled her into his arms. Held her, stroked her. The ache to protect her turned in him like a knife. He went on holding her and stroking her. The warmth and feel of his body against hers must have had an effect. The sobbing quieted down, then stopped.

'If I'd died in that warehouse,' she said in a voice that was almost steady, 'it would've been all right. If they put me in front of a firing squad even . . . If it was quick. If it was clean.' She looked up at him. 'Help me,' she said.

He hugged her, rocked her in his arms like a child.

'Tell me what to do. What do *you* do – when it gets bad?'

'All kinds of things,' he said, still trying to keep off the subject.

'Tell me one,' she said. 'Just one.'

Let the sphincters go, darling. That always upsets them. And gives you a break while they hose you down and change interrogation rooms. Of course, you can't do it often on a prison diet . . .

Was that the kind of thing she wanted to hear?

'You can try praying,' he said. 'I do.'

'I thought you didn't believe in God.'

'I get a sort of ache for him sometimes.'

'Even though he doesn't exist.'

'Because he doesn't exist.'

'I don't believe in him, I don't ache for him.' She said it as if she almost wished she did.

'There's an old joke about the chap who spilt some salt and did the usual thing – picked up a few grains and threw them over his left shoulder. And someone said, "Hey, I thought you didn't believe in that rubbish." And the chap said, "They tell me it works whether you believe in it or not." And that's the point about prayer. It doesn't matter whether you believe in it or not. The idea is to . . . focus on something outside yourself.'

'And that helps?'

'It helps.'

There was a long silence, then she said, 'The real trouble is, I don't believe in anything – even the resistance movement. Not the way you do.'

She rubbed herself against him like a cat, then pulled away and sat at the table.

232

'I can't think straight if you're holding me,' she said. 'And I want to.'

She took a cigarette from the packet. 'May I?'

He nodded. How polite she always was. 'Give me one, too, will you?'

She gave him a cigarette. He lit both, no longer bothering to hide his left hand. She could have seen the puckered skin where three fingernails were missing, if she'd looked. But she didn't want to look. After a while he casually put his left hand back in his pocket.

'If you didn't believe in the movement,' he said gently, 'why did you join?'

'You,' she said. 'To be with you. That's why I joined.' Her mouth curved in a wry smile. 'At the time – if you remember – you hardly noticed me. I was little more than a kid to you, I suppose . . . A nice middle-class girl in a gingham frock—'

'Who nursed me for two weeks when I was wounded and on the run. I remember.'

Her smile widened. 'I think those two weeks were the happiest of my life. In two days I was in love . . . In two days I went from a girl to a woman . . . I couldn't think, I couldn't sleep, I couldn't breathe. I'd lie in bed at night, holding my breath – with my heart knock knock knocking against my chest. Like a hammer. It's a wonder you didn't hear it through the wall . . .'

His mind was racing. There were two possibilities, both impossible . . . She was still talking. Let her talk. It gave him time to think – though he was beginning to think in circles, as if his brain was anchored to one central idea that there was no getting away from . . . And that was impossible too.

'One night I heard you walking in the garden. I got up and watched you from behind the curtain. I wondered why you couldn't sleep . . . if you were thinking about a woman. I know now what you were thinking about – bombs and guns and bank raids. The movement – your own true love. Well, I was thinking about love too. A love I couldn't contain. I could feel it stretching down to touch you like the moonlight . . . For a moment I thought it had touched you – you stopped and looked up at my window. I caught my breath – and waited. But you turned away. And I wanted to fling the curtain aside and lean out, naked, and call your name. But I was frightened. Not out of modesty – a woman in love doesn't know the meaning of the word. But in case you were shocked. It's funny how easily men are shocked . . . And when you left I followed – within a week.

233

Like a whore. And when I took the oath of allegiance it was to you. In my heart it was to you. Thomas William Henry Ashman – my own true love.'

She got up, moved round the table, sat on his knee, put her arms round him.

'Funny,' she said. 'I feel cold all of a sudden. Not frightened – cold.'

'It's probably shock,' he said, stroking her hair. 'You've had quite a day for a nice middle-class girl.'

'Nothing to report really,' Fat Charlie said. 'Except they had a bit of a barney at one point. By the time I got there and had a butcher's through the grating, though, they was all quiet again. Well, she was crying a bit, but that's to be expected, I s'pose.'

'What were they quarrelling about – do you know?'

'Not really, sir. You see, we kept well away, like you said, but when they was yellin' at each other I did hear him say, "You're not the on'y poor cow what's ever bin tortured." '

'I see. Thank you, sergeant.'

The Home Secretary gave a small wave of dismissal. Fat Charlie stamped to attention, saluted, about-turned and marched out. Bishop, who had been hovering near the double doors, closed them behind him. He was quick and nervous in his movement, like a scared cat.

'Really, sir, the hour's up. I do think—'

'Relax, Peter. Everything's going splendidly. He's shouting, she's crying, they're pulling each other apart – beginning to crack.'

'Yes, sir, but—'

'As planned, Peter, as planned. Soon they'll be like putty in our hands.'

'Yes, sir, but . . .' He stopped, listened. 'Wasn't that a helicopter landing?'

'No, Peter,' said the Home Secretary. 'It was a helicopter taking off.'

Bishop looked unhappy. He felt unhappy. He also felt that the Home Secretary, though quite a good administrator and a cunning committee-man (he hadn't got the job entirely by nepotism), was totally out of his depth dealing with men like Ashman and Cunningham. So was Bishop, but at least he knew it. He lacked the kind of male vanity that armoured other men against such insights.

234

Another reason for his unhappiness was that he was beginning to wonder whether he had backed the wrong horse. He had noticed that Colonel Cunningham, though paying lip service to the Home Secretary as his immediate superior, often dealt with the Prime Minister direct. Could it be that the Home Secretary would be promoted sideways to some nice tax-free job at the United Nations once the regime had been stabilized, and Colonel Cunningham would take over his job?

As for the present situation, it was all very well Cunningham being in hospital, but unless he was dead, unconscious or too ill to use the phone he'd be up to something. Bet your sweet life on that.

Beth had started shivering again.

'This time it's not the cold,' she said, 'it's fear.' She clung to him. 'I can't help it.'

'It's shock, I tell you,' he said, holding her, trying once more to soothe her.

'It's no good,' she said, 'is it?' She closed her eyes and shook her head. 'No good.'

'Listen,' he said. 'Listen carefully.' His voice was low and confident. 'One thing you've got to do in a place like this is to think about escaping. That means watching and waiting, especially watching. After a while you'd be surprised what you notice – details you'd never notice in a million years outside. And no place is impossible to break out of – whatever they say.'

'You mean you've *found* a way?'

'I didn't say that. But in a corridor near one of the interrogation rooms there's a ventilation shaft. Now if we could hide you in there – with the help of them two guards – get you out of the way for a few days – who knows? Might be all over by then.'

She stared up at him. His eyes were as dark as hers. She couldn't read anything in them.

'You're making this up, aren't you?' she said. 'Trying to give me a boost.'

'Have I ever lied to you?'

'I don't know. Maybe I never found out. Anyway, there's no need to lie to me.'

'What do you mean?' He felt himself going cold inside.

'I'm not stupid, you know.' She said it quietly, almost gently.

He looked into her eyes and said, 'There's something I want you to know. You remember the night you saw me in the garden?'

'What about it?'

'You said I was thinking about guns and bombs and things. I wasn't. I was thinking about you.'

'You don't have to bullshit me, either.'

'You remember how hot it was? It had been hot all day, but the night was even hotter. You remember that?'

'I remember it was hot,' she said.

'Hot and still. The air was so dry it seemed parched. Then a wind sprang up.'

'I don't remember that.'

'You wouldn't notice it inside. It was only a light wind, blowing off the Downs, I suppose. But cool. I could feel it cool on my face. That's when I looked up at your window and saw it was open. And I thought . . . You know what I thought? I thought the same wind touching my face is touching hers. And I kept taking great big deep breaths of it – because it was touching you.'

There was one of those long silences, then she said, 'It's all right, Tommy, you don't have to make speeches.'

'It wasn't a speech. I was trying to tell you something.'

'I know that,' she said. 'I'm reading you pretty well.'

He didn't know what to say, so he put his arms round her. Physical solutions always came easier to him.

'Do you want to hear my next clever guess?' she said.

'No,' he said. 'No, I don't.'

Her head was on his chest. She reached up and touched his face.

'Christ, Tommy,' she said gently, 'soldiers don't cry.'

Across the prison corridor Joseph started playing a passage from Albeniz's *Leyenda*.

'Hold me close and ask him to play it louder,' she said.

23

IN THE HOUSE that backed on to Epsom Downs the Alsatian bitch raised her head and howled.

Bishop looked anxiously towards the window.

'Yes,' said the Home Secretary, 'that's another helicopter landing. One of the troop-carrying sort. Not the little two-seater job that Cunningham uses. And even if it was it wouldn't matter. 'Let us not forget who outranks whom.'

'It's not that, sir,' Bishop said in his unhappy voice. 'It's just that I have to work with him.' He looked at his watch. 'It's past the hour, sir.'

The Home Secretary, who was sitting at Cunningham's desk, looked at his own watch. 'You're fast. There's nearly forty seconds to go.'

There wasn't, but Bishop knew better than to argue.

'Yes, sir,' he said. 'But perhaps we'd better ring the hospital again and find out if Colonel Cunningham—'

'Find out what?'

Cunningham was standing in the doorway, leaning on a stick, left arm in a sling, a bloodstained bandage round his head. If he'd had a black patch over one eye and a knife in his teeth, the pirate-picture would have been complete. His face was taut and hollow-looking, his eyes like two burnt holes in a blanket.

Flanking him were Lomax and Kemp, carrying bundles of newspapers and galley proofs.

'Good God,' the Home Secretary said, as if he'd seen a ghost, which he thought he probably had. 'What are you doing here?'

'I might ask you the same question, Minister.'

'I was just passing.'

'In your executive jet? And decided to drop in? How nice. May I have my desk back?'

The Home Secretary got up guiltily (though why the hell he should feel guilty he was damned if he knew). Cunningham turned to Lomax and Kemp.

'Leave me the galley proofs and you two sort the newspapers out in there.' He indicated the outer office. 'Send Miss Skinner to the officers' mess for whatever food you want and – yes, half a dozen bottles of champagne – the best they've got. Take a 'couple of bottles for yourselves and send the rest in here.'

Kemp put the galley proofs on Cunningham's desk and went out with Lomax. Cunningham turned to Bishop.

'I take it you've told the Minister?'

'Well, yes, sir. I mean, I had to.'

'Of course, Peter,' Cunningham said mildly. 'You acted quite properly. My instructions didn't allow for getting shot.' He gave them a crooked smile. 'No one thinks he's going to get shot. Bullets are for other people.'

He was clearly in a good humour. The Home Secretary was still having difficulty getting over his surprise.

'But how did you get out of hospital?'

'Broke out,' Cunningham said. 'Killed three nurses and a doctor.' He sat at his desk. 'Are these the girl's things?'

'Yes, sir,' Bishop said. 'I asked Miss Skinner to make an inventory.'

'I must congratulate you,' the Home Secretary said. 'Pity about Murdoch and Hudson. Still, you got the girl. You know, I had rather a bright idea about her—'

'Love-letters,' Cunningham said. 'Why do they keep them? Tied up with ribbon, too.'

He undid the ribbon, started to read the letters.

'I said I had—'

Cunningham held up his hand. 'Please, Minister, I have a lot to do. And I have to' – a tight little smile – 'husband my strength. I'll be with you in a minute. Here . . .' He handed him one of the galley proofs. 'Ashman's obituary. They had to have it ready, of course. It's quite interesting – if you remove the adjectives and read between the lines.'

The Home Secretary, who was wondering whether to insist on saying his piece, get into a rage, or maintain a dignified silence, was mollified by Cunningham's attention and even more by the arrival of the champagne and a tray of sandwiches. He realized he was hungry. It was a realization that came upon him frequently.

'What are they?' he said.

'Chicken, turkey and tongue,' Miss Skinner said, pointing to three separate dishes. She put the tray on a table well within his reach. She asked Cunningham what sort of sandwich he wanted, but he didn't even look up from the letters.

'Just a glass of champagne.'

She was about to withdraw when he suddenly looked at her

238

and said, 'Thank you for the trouble you've taken, Miss Skinner – and for staying late.' He smiled at her and she blushed even though she disliked him. She found it hard to deny his charm.

'Peter,' he said, 'order a car for Miss Skinner, will you?'

She felt a glow of pleasure. Well, a little diplomacy couldn't hurt. He had enough enemies, he thought, as he went back to the letters.

'I say,' said the Home Secretary, munching happily, 'they *have* given him a send-off, haven't they? Cold-blooded bastards . . . Listen to this. "Our gallant comrade-in-arms who died a martyr's death before a firing squad at the notorious Tac Force headquarters blah-blah-blah . . . And we, his friends, refuse to mourn. We rejoice in the name of Thomas Ashman, whose death brings ever closer the day of Nemesis when the clouds of tyranny will be swept away blah-blah-blah." And what about *this*: "The supply of heroes must be maintained"? Oh my God, what bullshit. Worse than the House of Commons . . . I see what you mean about reading between the lines. It sounds as if they're glad to be rid of him.'

Then he drank some champagne and said, 'I say, this is good stuff. What is it?' He turned the bottle to see the label. 'Krug seventy-one . . . Don't know anything about champers, except that I like it.'

He drained the glass, belched lightly, poured himself some more.

Cunningham, who had read through the letters carefully, as if trying to commit them to memory, said, 'I think we've got something here.'

'Isn't anyone going to say cheers?' the Home Secretary said.

Cunningham, who suddenly seemed more relaxed, smiled and lifted his glass, which had remained untouched.

'Cheers,' he said. 'To success.'

The Home Secretary and Bishop murmured their responses.

'Well, now, let's have the girl in.' He reached for the phone and said to Bishop, 'Is she in the women's section – or did you put her in an isolation cell?'

Bishop nearly choked on his champagne.

'Well, Colonel,' he said, 'the fact is—'

'It's all right, Peter,' said the Home Secretary airily. 'Leave this to me.' To Cunningham: 'I tried to tell you I had this bright idea about her.'

Cunningham was on his feet, his pale face even paler, his dark eyes darker still with anger.

'About the girl? The key to the whole situation? The one I nearly got killed trying to take alive?'

'Please don't adopt that tone with me, Colonel Cunningham—'

'What did you *do*?' The words were ground out.

'Well, nothing really. Call it psychology. I mean, I just . . . put her in the cell with Ashman.'

'Christ.'

Cunningham was already making for the double doors – and he didn't need a stick for support – when the alarm phone rang with its peculiar stridency. The red light above flashed on and off.

The three men were momentarily frozen. Cunningham was the first to break the tableau. In a few strides he reached the phone. For a split second, with his hand on the receiver, he hesitated. Then he jerked it off its cradle.

'What is it?' He listened without expression and in silence, except for an occasional grunt. Then he said, 'Yes, yes,' in a tired voice. 'No, nobody's blaming you.'

He hung up and went back to his desk, moving slowly and with effort, as if suddenly feeling the effects of his injuries. He sat down and took a sip of champagne. It tasted flat.

'What is it?' the Home Secretary said.

Cunningham put his head in his hands. He had to think . . . Think, he told himself, *think*.

'Colonel Cunningham, I demand to know—'

'She's dead.'

'Dead?' Bishop said, and sat down.

'Dead?' The Home Secretary echoed him, and also sat down, but slowly, like a bladder losing air. 'But . . . how did it happen?'

'He killed her.' Cunningham's voice was flat and dry.

'No,' said the Home Secretary. 'No.'

'It seems the guards had been told to keep away from the cell. And they did – except when they heard them having a row. And when there was silence. They didn't notice it at first because Lamont, who was in a cell across the corridor, was playing the guitar. It was when he stopped they noticed it. The silence. No murmur of conversation, nothing. Just silence. After a time the sergeant of the guard got worried and had a look through the grating. Ashman was sitting on his bunk with the girl in his arms. The lighting was dim and the sergeant thought she was asleep. Then he thought there was something funny about the way she was holding her head. Then he realized – and called for help. It took eight men to get her away from him. And two of those are in the hospital. They had to beat him unconscious with rifle butts.'

In the silence that followed, Cunningham raised his glass. 'To psychology,' he said.

'But he was supposed to love her,' the Home Secretary said in a bemused voice. 'What is he? A psychopath?'

'A hero.'

'A what?'

'A kind of throwback,' Cunningham said in his flat voice. 'They've made trouble since the time of Achilles and before. They ought to be drowned at birth, only there are no distinguishing marks.'

Another silence. Then the Home Secretary, separating each word carefully, said, 'What are we going to do?'

'I don't know, Minister,' said Cunningham. 'Unless you have any more bright ideas.'

He put his elbows on the desk, his chin in his hands, and stared unseeingly at the chaos of papers in front of him. He let his mind wander, hoping for an intuitive answer to an equation composed entirely of unknowns.

The Home Secretary let his feet wander. In fact he could hardly stop them. He had to be on the move or something inside him, something that felt like a rising scream, might actually come out. He stopped for a moment by the window, but the light of the sodium lamps which turned your lips blue and spread a ghostly light everywhere, depressed him. He moved on, still distracted, till he caught sight of the Prime Minister's portrait. He stopped again, stared at it, then whirled round on Cunningham.

'Jesus!' he said. 'What's Percy going to say? It'll be the finish of me – and you. Don't forget that. It's your responsibility, it was in your hands. I left everything in your hands. And he knows it – I told him. So don't think you can get out of it.' Then he whirled on Bishop. 'Or you, either. You're in it, too – up to the bloody neck.'

'Me?' said Bishop. 'I didn't do anything.'

'Oh yes you did,' said the Home Secretary, his voice loud

241

with panic. 'It was your idea really. Well, in a way it was. I mean, if you hadn't told me—'

'Minister, this is absolutely monstrous. I protest—'

'Protest all you like, you scheming little bastard. I had you weighed up from the start. If you'd betray one man you'd betray another—'

'Quiet!' Cunningham roared over them. Then he said softly, 'I'm trying to think, gentlemen.'

The Home Secretary sat down, his panic-bred rage changing to hope as he watched Cunningham. Bishop went to his desk at the other end of the room, trying to get as far away as possible.

'I'm sorry, Colonel,' the Home Secretary said, adding, as if Cunningham had said something, 'No, really, I apologize. The circumstances, the strain. Apart from the burdens of office . . . And my health's not good – I'm on a cholesterol-free diet, you know . . .' His voice faded away. Then he cleared his throat and said, 'Do you, er, think there's any . . . hope?'

'Depends on his condition.'

'He's badly hurt?'

'He's made of cement. A bucket of water and they had him on his feet spitting blood and blinding at them. No, it's his mental condition. His spirit. When a man's driven to extremes something gives . . . He's been damaged. To what extent and in what way I don't know. But I can find out.' He turned to Bishop. 'Get me the sergeant of the guard.'

Bishop picked up the phone and said, 'Sergeant of the guard, A Block – and hurry . . . Just a moment, Colonel Cunningham wants you.'

Cunningham picked up his own phone and said, 'Has he quietened down? . . . Good . . . He is? . . . M'm, not so good. Put Lamont in with him. I don't want him left alone. Then bring him to my office – no hurry. And don't try to force him or handcuff him. In fact don't touch him at all. And cut the escort to one armed guard. Nothing formal, no marching, no bullshit. Let him come at his own pace . . . That's right. Oh, and don't provoke him.' A tight smile. 'No, I didn't think you would.'

He put the receiver down and stared at it, again lost in thought.

'How is he?'

'Quiet. Too quiet. They're afraid he's going to explode. But they don't know when.'

'Then you'll need to go easy on him. And take your time.'

'On the contrary, I intend to be brief and brutal. The time to hit a man is when he's down. Well, he's down.'

The Home Secretary was shocked, despite himself. 'Really, Colonel, that might be a mistake.' He was going to say psychological mistake but changed his mind. 'And I'm not exactly soft in these matters, am I?'

'No,' said Cunningham, 'just illogical. You could still be right, of course – the illogical often is. And I may be wrong.'

'And if you are?'

'Then he'll explode. Right in my face. Anyway, we'll soon see. He'll be here in a few minutes.'

The Home Secretary got up as if he'd just remembered an appointment. 'Then you, er, won't need me, will you?'

'No.'

'Then I'll – ah – be getting along.'

Cunningham nodded in Bishop's direction. 'And take your little friend with you.'

Bishop needed no encouragement and quickly opened the double doors for the Home Secretary, who hesitated in the doorway, then said, 'One thing puzzles me. You seemed to guess what had happened—'

'Call it psychology, Minister.'

The Home Secretary opened his mouth to say something, changed his mind and went out, followed by Bishop. Cunningham waited till the doors closed behind them, then picked up the phone.

'Who's the Duty Officer? Get him for me, will you? Yes, I'll hang on . . . Captain Grant? Colonel Cunningham here. I'm expecting the prisoner Ashman in my office in a few minutes. As soon as he leaves his cell I want it cleaned up and any broken furniture replaced – I believe there's been some damage. And make sure there are plenty of cigarettes there and some bottles of wine. Yes, that's right, wine. From the officers' mess . . . Anything as long as it's red and not less than twelve degrees – prison doesn't exactly refine the palate. All right? . . . Good.'

He hung up and went into the outer office where Lomax and Kemp were finishing their champagne and sandwiches. Lomax pointed to a pile of newspapers on one of the desks.

'We've marked everything we think might be of interest,' he said.

'Nothing sensational, I take it?'

Lomax shook his head. 'Mostly propaganda. One or two

references to Ashman – in the past tense – what a great chap he was, an inspiration to all, etc. And hints that the Great Day may soon be upon us.'

Cunningham thanked them and told them to arrange with Captain Grant for a helicopter to take them back to town. Then he went back to his office, phoned Amarantha and asked if he could see her later.

'What's later?'

'Eleven. Maybe twelve. Depends.'

'Oh great. I'm supposed to be available any old time, day or night. I have a business to run, you know that?'

'I know that.'

'Are you all right?'

'I'm fine.'

'You sound kind of funny.'

'I'm tired.'

'Then what's the point – I mean, are you going to stay the night?'

'No. An hour. Maybe two. Then I must get back.'

'You want to see me for an hour or two in the middle of the night? You must be crazy.'

'That's possible.'

'And you think I'm crazy too?'

He didn't answer.

'You still there?'

'Yes.'

'Something *is* wrong. I can feel it.'

'I just want to see you.'

'In the middle of the night? Oh fuck you, oh all right.'

She hung up.

Cunningham lit a cigarette and took a sip of champagne. After a couple of drags he put the cigarette out. His head was throbbing. He should have had something to eat. He looked at the empty plates where the sandwiches had been, and felt hungry. He thought about ringing the mess and having some more sent over, but knew he wouldn't eat anything.

He drank some more champagne and felt better. His head still throbbed, but he felt better. Or imagined he did, which was the same thing. He wondered why his left arm wasn't aching – then realized that it was.

There was a knock on the door and Fat Charlie came in, followed by Ashman and an armed guard. Ashman still showed

244

signs of a savage beating. His face was bruised and streaked with blood, his eyes puffed, his hair matted and not yet dry from the water thrown over him. Nor were his shirt and trousers. The shirt had been nearly ripped off his back, revealing more bruises on his arms and chest. With his head lowered, his thick neck and big shoulders and the streaks of blood on him he looked like a fighting bull at the end of the *faena* – dangerous and full of fight, though deceptively quiet. Well, let's not push the analogy too far, Cunningham thought. Analogies are always false.

'Sit down,' he said, pointing to the chair the Home Secretary had sat in.

Ashman sat down. Cunningham thought he also looked dazed but decided it was more from emotional than physical shock. He waved Fat Charlie and the guard away.

'I'll call you if I want you.'

Fat Charlie and the guard went out. Cunningham lit a cigarette, leaned on the edge of the desk and studied Ashman. His head was still lowered.

'Did you know she was having it off with Hudson?' Cunningham's voice was cool and hard.

Ashman half-rose, pulling his lips back in a frozen snarl – though he made no sound. Then his lower jaw started to shake. So did his hands. Then he lowered his head again and sank back into the chair.

'The bitch deceived you. Like Hudson deceived you. It's getting to be a habit among your friends. Who'll be the next, I wonder?'

He took the letters from the desk, offered them to Ashman.

'See for yourself. You must know Hudson's writing. Take them.' Ashman showed no reaction, kept his head lowered. '*Take* them.'

Ashman took them and let them drop to the floor. Cunningham shrugged.

'Very well. But if you want the evidence there it is. Five letters from Hudson, one from her – which she apparently didn't have time to deliver. Study them, they're enlightening. You're mentioned in every one. She asks him about trying to rescue you. Hudson, of course, is full of excuses. He tries to shift the blame on to OPSCOM – with which you had some differences of opinion, it seems. Perhaps your ideals were beginning to show . . . It also seems she felt guilty about sleeping with Hud-

son – a vestige of that old middle-class morality, I suppose –
but he cheerfully assures her you won't be coming back. Of
course, he wraps it up a bit more elegantly than that. But that's
what he means. He also devotes most of one letter to a denial
that he ever said it was time the movement had another martyr
. . . M'm. Well, who knows what he said? But it's suspicious
that he should deny it so strenuously and at such length. He
doth protest too much, methinks. Of course, my interpretation
may be wrong.'

He paused, pointed to the letters. 'There's the evidence,
though. Take them, read them, judge for yourself.'

He took one of the galley proofs from his desk, dropped it on
top of the letters. 'Read this too. Your obituary. No comment.
It speaks for itself. Loud and clear. And remember this: my
original offer is still open – till sunrise tomorrow.'

He crossed to the double doors as if about to open them,
then swung round.

'I almost forgot. I never told you I once knew Hudson. I
was with him in that tough little war in Korea. I was a lieutenant; he was a major. Both very young, very ambitious. He
was the perfect example of the power-seeker, even then. He'd
tread on anyone's face to get to the top. He used people, ruth-
lessly and continually. It seems he hasn't changed. He used
you – and betrayed you. Used your mistress for a whore – and
betrayed her. Correction: sacrificed her. Sacrificed her – to
save his own skin. That's typical of Hudson – the real Hudson.
That's the man you're going to die for. The man you murdered
your mistress for.'

Ashman bent over his chair as if in pain, a pain he was trying
to hold in. Then an ugly choking animal-like sound tore itself
from him.

Cunningham pulled open the double doors.

'All right,' he said. 'Take him away.'

24

AMARANTHA was shocked by his appearance. He cut short questions and explanations. 'A shoot-out' was all he said.

'You should be in hospital.'

'So everyone says. Any coffee?'

She tried to persuade him to go to bed. He refused.

'I had enough trouble getting dressed. I'm not getting undressed.'

'I'll undress you.'

'Not even that prospect tempts me. A cup of coffee would though.'

In the end she persuaded him to lie on the bed. She pulled his boots off, propped him up with extra pillows, and made a pot of coffee. Lying there, relaxed and at ease, he suddenly realized how tired he was. He looked it too.

'Why don't you have a sleep for an hour or so?'

'I'd sleep the clock round.'

'Why not?'

'Because I might wake up dead. Or as good as. Coffee's nice.'

'Why did you want to come here?'

'To get away from things. Get a breath of sanity.'

'Is something wrong?'

'Practically everything's wrong. And my seismograph's recording tremors – from underground, naturally. Where all the best tremors come from.'

'Stop being so goddam smart.'

'I fear I'm not being goddam smart enough. Any more coffee?'

She poured him another cup, then lay on the bed beside him.

'Would you like a cigarette?'

'You'll have to light it for me – it's awkward with this arm.'

She lit a cigarette and gave it to him. As he took it she noticed his hand was shaking.

'Can't you tell me about it – whatever it is?'

He drew deeply on the cigarette, blew a stream of smoke at the ceiling and watched it dissipate into vagueness.

'We've got very good wild-life laws in England,' he said. 'Did you know that? Every rare and endangered species is protected.'

She looked at him – the pallor of his face made his eyes seem even darker – and said quietly, 'What are you talking about?'

'A falcon, towering in her pride of place, Was by a mousing owl hawked at and killed.'

He took another deep nervous drag on the cigarette.

'I'm the mousing owl,' he said.

Ashman was drunk, or appeared to be. He was sprawled on one side of the pitch-pine table. Opposite him Joseph was sitting, tense and sober. Each had a glass of red wine. Joseph sipped his occasionally; Ashman drank steadily. Three empty bottles were lying on their sides on the floor near a case of wine. Their smoking was in reverse: Joseph smoked continually, Ashman occasionally. Lying near them on the table were the letters and the galley proof of the obituary.

After a time Joseph said, 'You're not really going to do it, are you?'

Ashman finished his drink, poured another, held the bottle out to Joseph.

'No. It goes to my head.'

'Let it go to your head. Good for your head . . . "Oh man of morals tell me why, Should every creature drink but I?" I can quote, too, see? That's from . . .' He frowned. 'Something.'

'You're not really going to do it,' Joseph said again.

'Do what, my friend?'

'Talk.'

'I'm talking now. My tongue', he said slowly, 'has been loosened by the demon drink.' He stood up. 'In answer to your question, I am not going to talk. I am going to sing. Get out the guitar and let us sing.' He thumped the table so hard it shook. 'Everybody sing!'

'For tomorrow we die.'

Ashman looked at him, then sat down. 'Oh no. Tomorrow we don't die. Or the next day. Or even in the foreseeable future.'

'If you don't, others will.'

'Why should I do their dying for them?'

'You said once, when I was trying to explain my own cowardice, you said, however frightened you are, however far you retreat, there must be some ground on which you'll turn and fight. Well, I never found that ground . . . But you – you stood firm all the time. Like a rock. Like a colossus. What *happened*?'

Ashman took another drink of wine. 'They cut the ground

from under my feet. That's what happened.' He smiled. 'My friends did. Or my enemies. What's the difference? I'm rich in enemies like you're rich in nerves.'

Joseph finished his drink, picked up the bottle but found it empty. He opened another, poured a drink and drank it quickly. He began to feel heady, and less afraid.

'So you're going to talk. Pity you didn't think of that before you killed that girl.'

Ashman was suddenly on his feet. 'I can kill you too,' he said. 'One more won't make any difference.'

Joseph was also on his feet, shaking with fear and anger.

'Do it then – *do* it!'

Ashman's big shoulders hunched, then relaxed.

'Ah, shut up and have a drink,' he said and sat down. 'You're too emotional.' He laughed. 'Emotional man and intellectual man. You're emotional, I'm intellectual.'

He laughed again, poured himself some more wine and drank it.

Joseph was still shaking. 'You don't want to talk about it, you don't want to think about it. But you can't avoid it for ever. And you can't drink for ever.'

'I can drink now though,' Ashman said – and did. 'But I can't get drunk. Not what I call drunk.'

Joseph, who had remained standing, sat down and turned his back on Ashman.

Ashman went on drinking. Then he said, 'She betrayed me.'

Joseph swung round to face him. 'You'd like to think so, wouldn't you?'

Ashman pointed to the letters. 'You read them.'

'Sure. And every line says she was sleeping with Hudson because he'd promised to try and rescue you. Christ, man, it shouts at you. Every letter he writes mentions you and excuses himself. And when *she* writes it begins with Ashman, ends with Ashman, and it's Ashman all the bloody way through.'

'That's how you read them.'

'And how you read them too. Only you won't admit it.'

' "Facta non verbum," ' said Ashman. 'That's Latin, and it means deeds not words. Motto of the Royal Navy.'

He belched and poured himself some more wine. 'You talk too much.'

'What happened to those great beliefs you were ready to die for?'

Ashman emptied the glass in two gulps. 'What beliefs have you ever been ready to die for?'

'I'm a coward. I can't help it.'

'Sure, that's always the excuse.'

'But it's true. I *couldn't* help it, they made me—'

He stopped short as he realized what he was about to say. The realization hit him as it had never hit him before. He felt he ought to die of self-disgust. But that was something he was inured to. He'd taken it in increasing doses for so long he'd developed an immunity to it. Like you can to snake poison, he thought bitterly.

Ashman, who had gone on drinking steadily, said, 'I'm getting drunk at last. I can feel it. I can actually feel it. Nice feeling . . . Nice.

He sprawled even more across the table and put his head in his arms. Joseph wandered towards the window and looked up at the night sky. He didn't want to look at Ashman. Better to look at the stars.

'They can't do it, I thought. For once the big battalions can't do it. And they couldn't. They tried every brutal bloody trick in the book – and you just got braver. Lighting yourself at the irons, as that Mexican bitch would say. Did you know that? When a brave bull feels the iron biting into his shoulders he just gets braver. And that's when they say he's lighting himself at the irons.'

He waved his arms in an excited gesture. 'But it doesn't mean just courage, it means something else too . . . I don't know what, but you had it – whatever it was . . . And now you've lost it.'

'The same wind touching you,' Ashman said sleepily. 'Touching me.'

'Maybe Colonel bloody Cunningham took it when he murdered your mind. Or maybe, like God, it doesn't exist except in the minds of men. But I thought it did. I was sure it did. And you know what? It sounds crazy but . . .'

He stopped and looked at Ashman, whose head was still buried in his arms.

'Sometimes when I couldn't sleep I'd get down quietly in the middle of the night to look at your face while you were asleep. I thought I might be able to see it there. You know, like a sort of light. The light of the world . . .'

He shook his head, gave a half-laugh. 'And all I was looking at was a beaten-up face. But by Christ how I admired it. And

250

the strength and courage and this – mysterious whatever it was that lay behind it. Or that I thought lay behind it.' He let out a long sigh. 'Or were you fooling me? Or was I fooling myself? Eh? What's the answer, I wonder?'

The only answer from Ashman was a light snore. Joseph went to him, took him gently by the hair and lifted his head up to look at the face he had been talking about. It was just a battered face.

Cunningham was swaying with tiredness when he left Amarantha and was driven to London Heliport in the V-12 Jaguar. His specially equipped command helicopter was waiting for him, and lifted him into a sky already pale with fading stars. Within five minutes he was asleep.

The pilot called up Tac Force One Control and said briefly, 'Command Chopper Alpha Charlie airborne London Heliport. ETA twenty-five minutes.'

He settled down to read his map but within a few minutes the radio suddenly crackled into life.

'Tac Force One Control calling Chopper Alpha Charlie.'

'Alpha Charlie reading Tac Force One Control,' the pilot said.

'This is Lieutenant-Colonel Henderson for Colonel Cunningham.'

'The Colonel's asleep in one of the rear seats, sir. And he hasn't got his earphones on.'

'Then wake him up, sergeant. This is an emergency.'

'Yes, sir, I'll try, sir.'

The pilot put a hand over the microphone, turned and yelled Cunningham's name several times. But there was no response.

The pilot uncovered the microphone and said, 'I been shouting me head off, sir, but he's flaked out – and I can't leave the controls.'

'Right, sergeant, but if he does wake up tell him Operation Volcano has started.'

So Amarantha had managed to undress him, after all – without even waking him. Which was very clever of her, especially with his arm in a sling. But she was a clever girl. They were lying naked together and she was whispering to him, but he couldn't hear her, though she was so close the smell of her skin was in his nostrils. If only he could hear what she was saying. Speak

251

up, he said. I can't hear. Colonel Cunningham, she said, Colonel Cunningham. You don't have to call me Colonel Cunningham, he said, especially in bed. Her voice grew louder – then it broke (he thought that only happened to boys – something to do with descending testicles).

'We're coming in to land,' she said in a loud man's voice, and he woke up.

The pilot landed the helicopter on the pad and cut the engine. Cunningham leaned forward and tapped him on the shoulder, which made him jump.

'Colonel, you're awake.'

'Evidently.'

Before the pilot could say any more Lieutenant-Colonel Henderson, Cunningham's second-in-command, was on board.

'You've heard?' he said to Cunningham.

'Heard what? I've only just woken up.'

'Operation Volcano's started.'

Cunningham, already refreshed from his short sleep, felt the adrenalin rising in him like a spring tide.

Henderson's report was brief because there was nothing much to report. A couple of bridges on roads leading to army camps had been blown up, certain airfields sabotaged (the runways mined), two commercial radio stations in the London area taken over, and he had flown five hundred Tac Force men to Chequers at the request of the Ministry of Defence.

'What the hell do they want five hundred of our men for?'

'The Prime Minister's spending the weekend there.'

'So what? They've got plenty of protection. I've seen to that. So has General Rawley.'

'The request came from him, sir.'

They were walking towards A Block, the administration block which housed both Cunningham's office and the interrogation centre below. Cunningham stopped and looked at him.

'General Rawley is at a secret meeting of military chiefs in Warsaw.'

'Well, it came from his aide at the Ministry, Major Gilchrist. Anyway, we're getting a replacement battalion from Swindon.'

'At a rough guess the distance by air must be about the same. So why not send the Swindon lot straight to Chequers?'

Henderson shrugged. 'I suppose it was thought they needed crack combat troops.'

252

'And what the hell do you think we need at Tac Force HQ, Jack? Boy Scouts? We're likely to be one of the first targets. There's something rotten in the State of Denmark, Jack – and I can smell it all the way from here. Anything else?'

'Not unless Communications Room have anything new. According to their last report the situation was – well, confused.'

Cunningham nodded. 'That I can believe. Snafu.' And disappeared into A Block with Henderson at his heels.

By now the eastern sky was red with the rising sun.

25

SUNLIGHT shining through the barred window woke Joseph up. He rubbed his eyes, then turned and propped himself up on one elbow.

Ashman was still sitting at the table, his head supported by a hand. He was awake, staring at a patch of bare wall. Joseph felt constrained and did not know what to say. He cleared his throat to attract Ashman's attention, but it failed.

'Going to be a fine day,' he said at last.

'Red sky in the morning, shepherd's warning,' Ashman said in a flat voice without looking at him.

Joseph got down from his bunk and splashed some water in his face from the plastic bowl.

'You all right?' He tried again. 'I mean, no hangover or anything?'

'No.'

'You must be made of iron.'

Ashman looked at him at last. 'No,' he said, 'flesh and blood.'

Joseph started one of his nervous walkabouts.

'Look, I'm sorry about last night.' He waited for an answer, got none. 'I mean, you're quite right – deeds not words. And I'm all words . . . Anyway, I'm sorry – for everything.'

'Nothing to be sorry about,' Ashman said slowly.

Oh yes there is, Joseph thought. Christ, there is. To see Ashman broken – to know he'd helped the bastards break him . . . There was plenty to be sorry about all right. But sorrow was useless. Anger was the only thing.

'Christ, how I hate them,' he said in a low voice.

'I heard the birds sing,' Ashman said.

'You what?'

'The dawn chorus. But it wasn't dawn. It was still dark when they started singing.'

There was something odd about him, Joseph thought. Was his mind going? It would hardly be surprising.

His wondering was cut short by the crash of the door flung open. Cunningham came in followed by the captain of the guard (in dress uniform, including sword), Fat Charlie, four armed guards and two powerfully built guards with ropes to secure the condemned man. Bringing up the rear was a despondent priest. The execution squad.

Joseph was already on his feet. So was Ashman, but not in his usual aggressive crouch. He simply stood up. His shoulders drooped, his eyes, hooded by his scarred brows, looked dead.

'I gave you till sunrise,' Cunningham said briskly. 'And sunrise it is. Have you made up your mind?'

'I've no choice,' Ashman said in a voice as dead as his eyes.

Cunningham studied him. 'What do you mean?' He waited a moment, then said, 'Your decision, man, your decision.'

Then his pocket radio came alive. He took it out, extended the aerial.

'Henderson calling Colonel Cunningham,' it was saying. He pressed the button on the side and said into the microphone head, 'Cunningham reading you. What is it?'

'The replacement battalion from Swindon are coming in by chopper. ETA twenty minutes. They've just called up for clearance, and I've given it to them. Over.'

'Yes, yes, all right,' Cunningham said impatiently. 'I'll be with you in a minute. Over and out.'

He slipped the radio into his pocket, turned to Ashman. 'Well?'

'No choice,' Ashman said in his dead voice. 'Never was.'

A burst of laughter, nervous and mocking, came from Joseph.

'Listen,' Cunningham said, 'they betrayed you. Everybody betrayed you : Hudson, the girl – and him, he betrayed you too.' He pointed at Joseph. 'Did you know that?'

'You bastard,' Joseph said, and sprang and hit him in the face before a guard could drag him away. Another guard raised a rifle butt to smash Joseph in the face, but before he could bring it down Ashman had him by the throat and they were both rolling on the floor.

The two powerfully built guards threw themselves on Ashman while the other three clubbed him with rifle butts. Fat Charlie shouted encouragement. After a short savage struggle they managed to pull him off and rope his hands behind his back. Blood ran down his face from a gash on his forehead, one eye was closed, his lips were puffed and bleeding and he was gasping for breath.

Cunningham went close to him. 'Your life,' he said. 'I'm offering you your life.'

The dark dead-looking eyes stared at him out of the bruised and bleeding face.

'I don't sell myself for small mercies,' Ashman said.

Cunningham swung round to the captain of the guard. 'Let the execution be carried out.'

He dabbed his mouth with a handkerchief – there was a trickle of blood where Joseph had hit him – and went quickly out of the cell, his mind already concentrating on other problems.

The prisoner and escort formed up under the orders of the captain and left the cell in single file, the captain first, Fat Charlie last.

In the corridor they re-formed so that Ashman was surrounded by the guards. The captain was still in front and Fat Charlie at the back. The priest, who was supposed to walk beside the prisoner, stayed as far in front of him as he could. He did not even want to look at him. He was from a local village and hated the whole business. He also tried to put a psychological distance between himself and the prisoner by praying in Latin. He walked just behind the captain, his hands clutching a bible, his eyes fixed on the ground.

'In manus tuas, Domine, commendo spiritum meum. Redemisti, Domine, Deus veritatis.'

As soon as he was alone in the cell Joseph picked up a tin mug and started banging on the door with it. This was a recognized signal, and all the other prisoners picked up mugs or tin plates or anything else that would make a noise, and banged on their cell doors. The din drowned the priest's prayers and nobody could hear them. But he kept on with them just the same. God could hear them.

'Adjutorium nostrum in nomine Domini, qui fecit coelum et terram.'

'Wrap it up, you sacrilegious bastards,' Fat Charlie shrieked above the din. The prisoners ignored him. They always banged on their doors at executions. It was part of the ritual.

'Pater noster qui es in caelis, sanctificetur nomen tuum . . .'

Cunningham was in his office with Henderson, studying a map showing the disposition of all Tac Force and armed services' units and all military airfields and installations. It also showed other obvious targets, including power stations, main telephone exchanges, TV and radio transmitters.

'If only we knew what the initial targets were,' said Henderson.

'We'll know soon enough,' Cunningham said. 'And you can bet we'll be one of them.'

'I'll be glad when those choppers arrive. We need the extra men.'

Cunningham grunted and moved to the side window overlooking the execution yard.

'Oughtn't we to be getting down to the command bunker, sir?'

'I want to see the execution,' Cunningham said. 'I don't know why,' he added with a sour smile. 'Perhaps I just want to make sure he's dead.'

He turned to Henderson. 'I've always had a feeling that he's a hard man to kill.'

He turned to the window again. 'Pity in a way we weren't on the same side.'

'A nice combination,' Henderson said drily.

For a moment he wondered if he was in the dream again. No, this time it was for real. But he kept remembering the dream. And he was walking like a man in a dream, slowly, as if stepping in and out of reality. Or maybe the condemned always walk slowly. What's the hurry after all?

The dim-lit corridor seemed endless. The door to the execution yard was at the far end, past the exercise yard. The noise seemed endless too. It would only stop when he passed the last cell, and stepped out into the harsh light of the yard (daylight always seemed harsh after the dimness of the corridor and cells).

The chapel bell started tolling, and the banging on the doors stopped abruptly, as if cut off by a knife. One noise succeeding another. But it didn't bother him. It all seemed faraway, like the drowned-out prayers of the priest, which he wouldn't have understood anyway.

The bell went on tolling, but that seemed faraway, too – like reality. Perhaps he was back in the dream after all. Not that it mattered. Nothing mattered . . . Cunningham had offered him life . . . But what could life offer now anyway? It almost made him smile.

Cunningham, sure that the first strike would be against Tac Force headquarters, had made his dispositions with great care. His main difficulty was his ignorance of the quantity and quality of the opposition, both in manpower and firepower. He had to assume they would have army leadership and help – without it Operation Volcano would become Operation Fiasco. He could easily hold and crush a small-scale attack. But a big attack . . . Well, it depended how big – and how much clout it carried.

Another difficulty was that Tac Force headquarters hadn't been built to withstand a major attack. It was an old army prison. Of course, it had been extended, partly rebuilt, new buildings added, including a huge barracks, but there were not enough defensible strongpoints. He had tried to remedy this by building bunkers at strategic points covering the entrance gates and approaches to the two main buildings, A Block, where his office was, and the barracks about a hundred yards away.

Between the two buildings was an underground command bunker which could be reached by underground passages from both buildings. It was, in fact, a command complex whose main feature was an operations rooms with maps, a bank of closed-circuit television monitors and a panel for firing SLAM (surface-launched air missile), which is simply a cluster of Blowpipe missiles mounted on a pylon with an electronic package for remote-control firing and radio-command guidance.

A single Blowpipe missile, which is less than 4 feet 6 inches long, can be shoulder-fired by an infantryman. It has a high-explosive warhead with an infra-red proximity fuse (it blows up when it's close enough to hurt) and is highly effective against low-flying aircraft, whether they're coming in at you or going away from you. It can also be fitted with a fully integrated identification (IFF) system which stops you shooting your own planes down by mistake, which is very easy to do when things are going bang and you're getting excited.

Among other weapons fired from the command bunker were eight Swingfire anti-tank missiles in two emplacements in front of the bunker and aimed at the main entrance gates – though in fact the emplacements were behind brick-built stores which blocked a direct line of sight to the gates. But that didn't matter, because Swingfire has what the military call a ninety-degree firing arc. In other words it can shoot round corners. Very clever, but rather un-British.

Some of the television monitors were part of weapon-guidance systems, the rest were for surveillance. These were linked to miniature TV cameras stuck on roofs and concrete pylons disguised as arc lights. Since they were carefully built into and just below the light mountings they were very difficult to detect unless you were up close and knew what to look for.

The rest of the command complex consisted of a communications room, dining-room, dormitory, kitchen and lavatories. The whole complex was covered at ground level by a series of flower beds filled with roses and flowering shrubs, which concealed ventilator shafts.

Apart from senior officers the only people who knew the whereabouts of the command bunker, the concealed TV cameras and ventilator shafts were a maintenance electrician and Fat Charlie, who tended the flower beds with loving care. He had green fingers, even if they were thick and clumsy.

About twenty yards in from the heavy main gates (now shut and barred, except for the small postern) were two concrete blockhouses that had been there since the Second World War. They were positioned at an angle so that fire from their gun-slits would enfilade anything coming through the gates. Though they were now used as stores, Cunningham had put a couple of .50 Browning M2 heavy machine-guns in them.

In between the blockhouses, which were about forty feet apart, was a Striker combat vehicle with its launcher-box of five Swingfire missiles in what is called the elevated position (which means ready to fire). The Swingfire has a hollow-charge high-explosive warhead capable of destroying any known tank. In front of the launcher-box was a 7.62 mm machine-gun in a cupola mounting.

Flanking the Striker were a couple of Fox combat vehicles with 30 mm Rarden cannons, which can fire 90 rounds a minute.

Backing these up were some APCs (armoured personnel carriers) and Saracens. Then there were two more SLAMs and three mobile Rapiers on tracked M548 vehicles to complete the air defences. The Rapier is a seven-foot missile (guided by radio command) with a high-explosive warhead. It travels at more than twice the speed of sound and has what the military call a 'high kill probability' against helicopters, subsonic and supersonic fixed-wing aircraft at any height from ground level to over ten thousand feet.

Finally there were the PBI, the Tac Force troopers, some in slit trenches and machine-gun bunkers, some in the barracks in reserve. All combat ready.

One way and another, Colonel Cunningham thought, as he stood at the window overlooking the execution yard, Tac Force headquarters, all ninety acres of it, was pretty well covered – though he'd be glad when the reinforcements arrived.

He could see Fat Charlie offering Ashman the bandage and Ashman shaking his head.

'Well then,' Fat Charlie was saying, 'would you like to be tied to the post? For support, you understand. In case your legs give way at the last minute. Be surprised how their legs give way at the last minute.'

'Would you mind?' the priest said diffidently. 'I have to administer the last rites.'

Ashman looked at him. He was young and timid with a pale face that was almost featureless apart from large sensitive eyes.

'You don't have to administer anything,' Ashman said.

'Oh, but I do,' the young priest said. Ashman knew, of course, that he'd been picked (probably with a pin) by Tac Force and ordered to do the job.

'I don't understand Latin anyway.'

'I could pray in English,' the priest said hopefully.

Ashman didn't think any kind of prayer would help, but it hardly mattered.

He looked up at the window where Cunningham was watching, and saw he was smiling.

Ashman looked at him, turned his head and spat. In fact, it was only a gesture. He had no spit left.

The sun wasn't high enough to clear A Block, but he was facing north-east and it had crept round the side a little and was coming over the end of the wall on his right, catching his eyes. It wasn't strong because of the early morning haze, but he narrowed his eyes, as in the dream, making everything seem smaller and farther away. The firing squad looked like chocolate soldiers . . .

Then he heard a big chopper coming in to land. Then he saw it. It flew right over the execution yard and landed (he imagined) somewhere behind the wall he was standing against.

Cunningham saw it too, and wondered if it had overshot the landing pad through a technical fault or (more likely) pilot error. But it was only a passing thought. His attention was on the execution.

Ashman saw, over the wall to his left, more helicopters approaching, but they seemed some way off, more than a mile maybe.

The sword came up, its back edge rim-lit by the rising sun, and the drum began to roll. Ashman felt every muscle in his body tighten – an instinctive if pathetic shield against the shock of high-velocity metal – and his heart began to thump.

The drum was still rolling and he raised his head for a last look at the summer sky and was in time to see the grenade come curling over the wall.

26

FROM A RANGE of more than half a mile the leading echelon of six helicopters started loosing off their eight-foot Maverick missiles. In the Maverick's nose-cone is a small TV camera which is focused on the chosen target by means of a monitor screen in the cockpit. The missile can then be locked on to its target – and the pilot can forget about it and turn away to pick out his next target. Also very clever and un-British (which is not surprising since it's made in America).

The missiles, launched at two-second intervals, destroyed the Striker combat vehicle facing the main gates and wrecked both the flanking Fox combat vehicles. The second hit a SLAM surface-to-air missile cluster and destroyed two other SLAMs on either side.

The third blew the main gates to bits and killed the men in the gate area bunkers. The blast probably also killed the machine-gun teams in the concrete blockhouses. Or they might have been killed by blast from the missile that destroyed the Striker and caused collateral damage to the blockhouses.

Two other missiles, each with the maximum 250-pound warhead, tore half the barracks down, with many casualties and much panic. The sixth missile destroyed an M548 – but not before it had loosed off its four Rapier guided missiles and blown four of the leading choppers out of the sky.

As soon as the incoming helicopters started firing their rockets Cunningham, who had moved to the front window, was radioing instructions to Henderson in the command bunker.

'Keep the three remaining SLAMs in their silos. They can't home in on them if they can't see 'em. If any of the big personnel choppers tries to land, bring up the SLAMs and let 'em have it. Over.'

'Won't they be picking up your commands, Colonel, unless we keep radio silence?'

'I don't suppose they'll understand them any better than I understand theirs. See if you can get reinforcements, including guns and ammunition to slit trenches D1 and D5 – I think most of their present complement have been killed or wounded. I want all main approaches enfiladed. Keep the Ferret Mark fives with their Swingfires out of sight for the moment. The same applies to the other Ferrets, especially the ones carrying Vigilants. I'm expecting tanks and APCs to come through the main gates any time – and I want to have something to clout them with. Also keep our two remaining Strikers and M548s out of sight – you know where – unless, of course, you see choppers trying to land. Then they can be brought out to support the SLAMs. The main attack's still to come, but this'll do for starters. And get some stretcher parties moving, if you haven't already done so. Any questions?'

'Shouldn't you be in the command bunker, sir?'

'I'll join you there in a minute. Oh, and get some men over to strengthen A Block at ground level. I doubt if they'll try to hit it with anything but small arms fire because of the danger to their own men – I mean the prisoners of course.'

He knew he should be in the command bunker but he wanted to make sure of something first. He went to the side window overlooking the execution yard.

The place was a shambles. Smoke and dust and bodies everywhere. Men astride the rear wall were firing smoke-dischargers and 40 mm grenades into the yard. From below him the return fire was sporadic. He couldn't see much of the rear wall because of the smoke, and couldn't see Ashman at all. Had he been killed? He'd believe that when he saw it.

He tried to call up the captain of the guard but could only raise Fat Charlie, whose voice quavered like a ghost's.

'Cap'n Stratton's dead, sir. Sergeant Castle in c-c-command, sir. Over.'

'Then organize your fire, sergeant. You've got some Sterlings, haven't you?'

'Only two, sir.'

'That's enough to spray the back wall from top to bottom. Ashman must be somewhere there in all that dust and smoke. And I want him dead. Over and out.'

There was a sudden rift in the smoke and he saw someone cutting Ashman's bonds. He pulled the .357 Magnum Special out of his belt-holster, took a snap shot and missed. He held the gun in both hands, sighted carefully, squeezed the trigger – and missed again.

The range was about forty yards – too difficult with a short-barrelled Magnum and a moving target obscured by swirling smoke. By then a rope had been thrown down to Ashman and he was clambering up the sandbagged wall.

If only he had something longer barrelled . . . Then he remembered his Smith & Wesson M41 with the seven-and-a-half-inch barrel and micrometer-adjustable rear sight. Only .22 calibre, but it held ten rounds and was precision built for target shooting at ranges up to fifty yards. He kept it in his desk, and it was loaded.

The radio in his pocket was crackling and chattering away and had been for some time, but he ignored it. He had only one thing in mind.

By the time he got the pistol and returned to the window he could see nothing but smoke. Someone had fired more smoke-dischargers into the yard and the wall was completely hidden. Then the smoke cleared a little where the breeze caught it – and Cunningham saw him, near the top of the wall.

Two men reached down and grabbed his hands and pulled him up on to the wall. He had his back to Cunningham, who took careful aim. For some reason Ashman turned and seemed to look straight at him as he fired.

Then he started to topple slowly off the wall, very slowly, Cunningham thought – like a slow motion film. It had that air of unreality. Then suddenly he was gone.

'Got him,' Cunningham said to the empty room. 'Got him.'

The command bunker was reached by an underground passage from the officers' mess on the ground floor of A Block. Cunningham made it in less than a minute, out of breath and with his head and arm starting to throb again. But he soon forgot about them when he looked at the bank of surveillance monitors.

Tac Force headquarters looked like the surface of the moon with buildings – mostly wrecked. There were craters everywhere and bodies in the strange attitudes that death by bullets, blast and high-fragmentation shells had thrown them. There was a constant stutter of machine-gun and small arms fire from the bunkers and slit trenches still in action, and the occasional earth-shaking thump of mortars.

The resistance had got two APCs behind the concrete block-houses, one armed with Swingfire missiles, the other with 81 mm mortars. They had also taken over some of the bunkers and slit trenches to the south of the gate area and were machine-gunning the ground floor of A Block, which was returning the fire.

A Chieftain main battle tank, which had driven in through the shattered front gates, was hit by two Swingfire missiles as it turned towards the barracks – and blew up spectacularly. Another Chieftain following behind it loosed off its 120 mm shell at the remaining wing of the barracks and flattened it in a cloud of dust. It then fired one of its six-barrelled smoke-dischargers, blotting out most of the area between the block-houses and the barracks with black smoke.

One of the APCs behind the blockhouses hit a main ammunition store with a Swingfire, causing an explosion that rocked even the command bunker and put three of their monitor screens out of action. It also killed a stretcher party carrying a wounded man to the hospital in the north-east corner next to the armoury.

A state-of-battle report from Henderson was depressing: heavy casualties and reduced firepower – most of their surface-to-air and anti-tank guided-missile launchers were out of action. And judging by the enemy radio traffic they had both air and armour reserves, including main battle tanks, to call up.

Of course, Tac Force had had their successes too: knocking out some APCs, missile- and troop-carrying helicopters and at least one MBT (a Chieftain). Perhaps the brightest bit of the report was that the enemy had asked for a half-hour cease fire to allow both sides to attend to their wounded.

'Tell them we agree to a cease fire as soon as they like – say somewhere around 0600 hours.'

Henderson went to the door of the Communications Room, called out instructions, then came back to Cunningham. He picked up a folder on the map table and handed it to him. 'Reports of attacks in other parts of the country,' he said.

'What's the overall picture?'

Henderson hesitated. 'Bad,' he said.

Cunningham nodded. 'Anything else?'

'Assassination of three cabinet ministers – including the Home Secretary. And the Prime Minister, it appears, has been kidnapped.'

'From *Chequers*?'

'He wasn't at Chequers.' Henderson almost sighed. 'That was a bluff. He was weekending with the Minister of Defence – who took him prisoner. And disappeared with him.'

'I thought Pachman would be involved. No wonder the bluff worked.'

And no wonder, thinking back, Frank Wilson got his throat cut that night.

'Go and make sure our side of the cease fire arrangements is properly carried out,' he said.

'Yes, sir,' Henderson said and went into the Communications Room. A good soldier, Henderson, not too much imagination. Perhaps that was why.

Cunningham felt suddenly tired and sat in one of the armchairs facing the TV monitors. A bleak prospect.

Orders for the cease fire went out by radio and loudhailer – and there was a sudden silence. It seemed to make the wrecked and cratered compound even more like the surface of the moon. It needed silence. The only thing that spoiled the effect was the sight of dead and dying bodies.

Henderson came back into the Operations Room. 'General Hudson would like to speak to you, sir.'

'So Hudson's here himself? It doesn't surprise me.'

He went into the Communications Room and called up Hudson.

'Colonel Cunningham calling General Hudson. Over.'

'General Hudson reading you. I'd like to arrange a meeting with you as soon as possible, if you're agreeable.'

'Are you about to make me an offer?'

'We worked together once very satisfactorily in the past. Why not in the future?'

A meeting was arranged in the ruins of the main gateway. Each would be accompanied by a two-man escort armed only with submachine-guns. All other forces and armour were to be kept back a minimum of fifty yards. The instructions again went out by radio and loudhailer.

Cunningham's dominating thought was survival. He knew they were losing. And Ashman, dead or alive, was winning. But that was a subsidiary and ironical thought.

Ashman, in fact, was alive. The .22 bullet that had knocked him off the wall was lodged in his left shoulder. The fall, though broken by some bushes, did more immediate damage because his head hit the trunk of a tree growing by the side of the chapel. It knocked him out for several minutes. He came to just before the cease fire. All around him were the dead bodies of his rescuers. They had been caught by machine-gun fire when the smoke had cleared from the top of the wall. In a way he had been lucky to be hit by the .22.

He tried to get to his feet but couldn't. He left shoulder ached like hell. So did his head. Any attempt to get up made him dizzy. He started crawling towards a slit trench where he could see a dead Tac Force sergeant draped over his machine-gun. Progress was slow and painful.

One thing that bothered him was that now and then he got double vision. Something to do with that crack on the head, no doubt.

The trench was full of dead men, including an officer with a Sterling submachine-gun and a pocket radio – still crackling out instructions to its dead owner. He took the Sterling and the radio and started crawling towards the main gate by a round-about route that would give him cover from wrecked bunkers and buildings.

He stopped crawling when he heard the cease fire announced. He was glad of the rest, took out the little radio, extended the aerial and listened.

We worked together once very satisfactorily in the past. Why not in the future?

The words hit him like a kick under the heart. A kick so hard that he felt no pain. Only numbness, as if his heart had suddenly been frozen. He couldn't even feel it beating. Perhaps it had stopped. Perhaps that was why he had difficulty breathing.

So the bastards were going to do a deal. A sell-out. A Hudson–Cunningham carve-up.

'Over my dead body,' he said aloud in the silence of the cease fire. He started crawling again, slowly and painfully, like a three-legged animal, because he couldn't put weight on his wounded shoulder. His face was caked with dirt and streaked with blood from the gash on his head, and he still had occasional double vision. Otherwise I'm fine, he thought.

Cunningham and Hudson, who was in full general's uniform, met in the main gateway, saluted each other and shook hands. Neither was carrying arms. The escorts were left about twenty yards behind – far enough to be out of earshot.

Hudson's terms were obvious: if Cunningham surrendered Tac Force headquarters and telexed or radioed all local head-quarters to lay down arms . . . Pachman had spoken well of him . . . He, Hudson, had always thought highly of him . . . Avoid more pointless bloodshed . . . the success of the *coup* was assured . . .

Suddenly Hudson said, 'What the hell's that?'

He pointed over Cunningham's shoulder. Cunningham swung round.

An almost unrecognizable figure was crawling round the

267

side of one of the concrete blockhouses. But Cunningham recognized it.

'It's Ashman,' he said.

Ashman lifted himself almost to his knees and gave them a two-second burst. It cut down both of Cunningham's escorts. Hudson's escorts ran to his side, dropped to one knee and opened fire in timed bursts at the still crawling figure.

Hudson threw himself flat on the ground.

'Get down,' he said to Cunningham. But Cunningham remained standing, staring fascinated at Ashman's blood-streaked face. He was still crawling, though he had been hit several times and his left arm shattered. He managed to raise himself for another burst, tucking the stock of the Sterling into his right shoulder and firing one-handed. He was still coming forward.

Hudson snatched the gun from one of his escorts and, as Ashman raised himself once more, gave him a burst full in the chest.

Ashman fell forward, pulling the trigger perhaps by reflex action. The shots went harmlessly wide. Ashman lay face down in the dust, unmoving.

Hudson and his escort got slowly to their feet.

'Better give him another burst,' Hudson said. 'Just to make sure.'

'No,' said Cunningham sharply. 'He's dead.'

He went over to Ashman and stared down at him. Hudson followed slowly, warily, as if half-expecting Ashman to come alive again.

'What I don't understand', Hudson said, 'is how he took all those bullets and still kept coming.'

'There was a Japanese in the last war', said Cunningham, 'who kept going for fifty yards – with thirteen rounds in him.'

He looked down at Ashman. 'I said he'd be a hard man to kill.'

AFTERWORD

THE COUP WAS SUCCESSFUL. The Prime Minister, the Home Secretary and several other cabinet ministers, according to official press reports, were killed in the fighting. In fact, they were either assassinated when the coup began or secretly executed just after. But then history, according to Marx, is made behind men's backs. It's certainly written behind their backs. A number of other leading politicians were also secretly executed.

A new government was formed under Joshua Murdoch and most but not all political prisoners were released. They were soon replaced by others. The Emergency Powers Act was still in force. So was the Prevention of Terrorism Act – and the all-embracing Protection of the State Act, under which anybody could be arrested for anything.

All these would be repealed, of course, when the country was stable and secure once more . . . When the remaining pockets of resistance had been stamped out . . . And when pigs could fly . . . Then free elections would be held and everyone's ship could come home.

Colonel Cunningham had his old job back as C-in-C Tac Force, except that it was now called the Home Security Force. The new government liked the new title, especially the word Home. It was, as someone pointed out, so homely.

The bodies of leading members of the resistance killed in the fighting lay in state in Westminster Abbey for a week. Chief among them was the body of Ashman.

Joseph filed by it in the slow-moving queue, but the dead face had no meaning. The light of the world had gone.

He went out into the rain and said to a complete stranger, 'I saw it, though. I saw it.' And walked on.

Wally Le Gras was on the run. If he survived, he would join the next resistance movement – with Leo Pachman.

Ashman was buried with full military honours. His coffin was draped with a Union Jack and at each corner was a bronze replica of a falcon.

The two leading men carrying the coffin were General Hudson and Colonel Cunningham, in full dress uniform.

Everyone agreed it was a funeral fit for a hero.

APPENDIX

Extract from the official history of the National Democratic Party (2nd revised edition © State Publishing Corporation)

The dominant feature of the seventies was inflation. It crippled industry, cut living standards, sent unemployment soaring and led to deep social unrest. Palliative measures by a weak and spiritless Labour administration were ineffective in the short term, disastrous in the long. They were neither radical nor far-reaching enough, and by the early eighties inflation had spiralled to catastrophic heights – and put the economy in a permanent state of crisis.

The final disintegration was brought about, naturally enough, by the free-booting capitalism and neo-fascist policies of the two Tory administrations that followed the downfall of the Callaghan government. The pound and the economy collapsed, unemployment hit the six million mark, there were hunger marches, strikes, looting and, finally, violence in the streets.

Three more frightened governments came and went in as many months, while the situation deteriorated into anarchy.

With the breakdown of law and order virtually complete, Britain turned at last to the only remaining political figure with any credibility – Percy Smith, strong man of the Left, scourge of the fascist Right. At that time he was a political outcast, branded as a revolutionary, a wild man, a demagogue and a danger. But the unions, the workers, the whole proletariat of our great country were solidly behind him. He swept to power on a tidal wave of popular support. As Prime Minister with emergency powers he embarked on a series of radical and far-reaching reforms which marked the beginning of what was to become known as the Social Revolution.

Within six months he had restored law and order, cut unemployment to less than half a million and raised the pound very nearly to parity with the dollar.

Then came what might to any other man have been a setback – a military uprising that threatened to plunge the country back into anarchy. It was led by the despicable Sir Henry Hudson, then Chief of the General Staff, backed by reactionary and subversive elements in the armed forces, plus the usual mob of fascist politicians and sympathizers. It was quickly and brilliantly crushed by loyalist forces under the inspired direction of the Prime Minister himself – with some technical aid and advice from our new Warsaw Pact allies (soon after assuming power the Prime Minister took Britain out of the imperialist NATO alliance – *vide* EUROPE : THE NEW POLICY).

General Hudson went underground and has since formed what he calls the resistance movement. It is in fact no more than a rag-bag of failed revolutionaries, subversives, drop-outs, amateur terrorists and other rebels without a cause. It has no significant support among the population at large and exists, where it exists at all, in tiny scattered groups – hunted, harried and doomed.